BLOOD
ON THE
VERDE
RIVER

DUSTY RICHARDS

BLOOD ON THE VERDE RIVER

PINNACLE BOOKS
Kensington Publishing Corp.
www.kensingtonbooks.com

PINNACLE BOOKS are published by

Kensington Publishing Corp.
119 West 40th Street
New York, NY 10018

All Kensington titles, imprints, and distributed lines are available at special quantity discounts for bulk purchases for sales promotions, premiums, fund-raising, educational, or institutional use.

Special book excerpts or customized printings can also be created to fit specific needs. For details, write or phone the office of the Kensington special sales manager: Kensington Publishing Corp., 119 West 40th Street, New York, NY 10018, attn: Special Sales Department; phone 1-800-221-2647.

PINNACLE BOOKS and the Pinnacle logo are Reg. U.S. Pat. & TM Off.

ISBN-13: 978-0-7860-3193-1
ISBN-10: 0-7860-3193-X

First printing: August 2013

10 9 8 7 6 5 4 3 2 1

Printed in the United States of America

First electronic edition: August 2013

ISBN-13: 978-0-7860-3194-1
ISBN-10: 0-7860-3194-8

CHAPTER 1

Dust boiled up from the cloven hooves of the herd of three hundred head of cattle. An arrow struck his saddle fork hard, only inches from his chap-covered leg and Chet Byrnes put spurs to the big horse's sides, shouting, "Indians. Indians."

The bare-chested Indian took off on foot for some juniper cover.

Chet's gloved hand filled with the .45 Colt from his holster as he drove the bay horse through the sagebrush to his right, racing after the Apache archer. A shot from his gun might stampede the cattle, but the arrow shooter had meant business. That turkey feather–fletched arrow quivering in his saddle fork could have been his death.

A young cowboy, Cole Emerson, fired the first shot. His bullet took a war-painted, pistol-shooting buck who had came charging at them.

Chet realized the result of the shot as he tried to overtake the breechcloth-clad arrow shooter leaping to clear the knee-high sagebrush and escape. The cattle behind him were already on the run. Chet could hear the drum of hooves and their bawling. The screaming sound of their panic—familiar from past cattle drives—forced a feeling of dread that came from deep in his belly. The boys would have their hands full getting them under control again. He considered turning back and helping them, but wanted that arrow slinger more, to teach him a lesson.

Coming from the left, Cole was trying to cut off the Indian, as well. The buck finally stopped and threw his hands up in the air.

Chet reined in his horse knowing full well there had to be others. They must have disappeared quickly into the juniper brush to strike again. Since his youth, he'd fought them. In Texas, he'd fought Comanche/Kiowa. Three of his siblings had been taken by them years before and were never heard from again. In the Arizona Territory, he was fighting Apaches, but all were alike in their vicious ways of making war.

"What should we do with him?" Cole asked, nodding at the buck.

"Tie his hands behind his back and put a rope around his neck. Then bring him to camp. I need to help the crew with that stampede."

"You bet I can handle that. Where did the other red devils go?"

"Damned if I know. But keep your eyes open. They may be back." Obviously the boy could handle the buck, so Chet charged off after the plume of dust in the northeast sky. Damn worthless bunch of Injuns, anyway.

The cattle were part of his contract to deliver beef to feed the Navajos. A task he had to make work for the financial welfare of his ranch and many of his neighbors', too. Beef markets without a railroad to ship on were a serious source of income. The Tucson Ring and Old Man Clanton held all the Army beef contracts and those for the tribes in southern Arizona, plus the ring supplied Tombstone, which had the largest population of any city between St. Louis and San Francisco.

Chet's racing horse took a cow path through the sagebrush. Chet never saw any more attackers, and soon he was on the ruts of the road. The cattle were milling when he drew near.

One of his main men, Hampt Tate, rode back to see him. "What in the hell went on back there?" the thick-chested big man asked.

"Cole and I had war on our side with some Apache bucks. He shot one and then we captured the shooter who gave me this arrow in my saddle. Cole's bringing him in with a rope around his neck."

Hampt stood in the stirrups, looking over the sagebrushy world of the northern Arizona Territory. "When the cattle have settled down a little more, we'll go on to that watering hole."

"It will be hard to slip them in on it," Chet said recalling the site. "Not like a river in the Indian Territory or Kansas, where you can feed them in sideways and not push the first ones in the water from the ones in back."

The big man agreed. "You already promised this job of getting them there would be hell."

"I also said we had to make it work. Selling beef to the reservation will be a great shot in the arm for the Quarter Circle Z and all the rest of the ranchers in the region."

"I ain't complaining, but it's damn easy to get mad about Injuns causing stampedes. I see Emerson coming. He sure ain't got no Apache on his rope."

Chet turned half around. "No, he don't. Well, that boy's got himself two bucks today."

When the freckle faced boy in his late teens reined up, he shook his head. "When I got down to tie his hands, he drew a knife on me and I shot him."

"Fine," Hampt said. "You see any more?"

Cole shook his head, obviously shaken by the way things turned out.

Chet wanted to reassure him of his action with the Apache. "Sorry. I'd have stayed if I thought he'd try that on you."

"No sir. I just handled it."

"Did you reload your pistol?" Hampt asked.

"No sir."

"You know you could have been jumped again?"

"Yes sir. It won't happen again."

Hampt rode in closer and clapped him on the shoulder. "You did good, son. Lots of things we all have to learn to stay alive out here."

"I won't forget what you told me. I like living." Cole rode on to join the others.

"He'll make a good hand one day," Chet said as

he and Hampt rode stirrup to stirrup down the wagon tracks. Hampt had recently married Chet's brother's widow May and the arrangement had satisfied the whole family. The newly acquired Hartley ranch with a fair dwelling would be Hampt's place to run.

Chet's wife Marge was two months pregnant with their firstborn and she'd never carried a baby to term in her two previous marriages. At twenty-nine, she had high hopes and had stopped riding her hunters, just in case. But Chet wasn't too sure it made her any easier to live with, though they both were excited about the prospect of a child of their own.

He looked over his shoulder, wondering why those damn Indians attacked a cattle drive. Maybe to cut out a cow to eat, though Apaches preferred mules first, horse second, and cattle last as a meal of choice after deer and elk meat.

He shook his head and looked back at the cattle. The biggest spoilers in the Verde County range had sold out after a big shoot-out that left the two Hartley brothers dead. Some of their sale cattle were being moved to the recently obtained Joseph McQuire Windmill Ranch, now simply called the Windmill. With its two windmills and tanks to water stock, it was the in between place where Chet could park cattle, and had lots of grass to fatten them while they waited to be shipped to the Navajos. There, they were also closer to the reservation for the next month's drive.

The agency people had been pleased with his first delivery to the five places from where the cattle was dispersed. They'd told him it was the best stock they'd ever received. But Chet needed to cut down on help and the big expenses to make it work. He could see how the Windmill, as the shipping point, would make it smoother than driving cattle out of the Verde River valley up on the rim and then across the northern plateau to the four corners country.

Sarge and his bunch had already cut and stacked hay at the Windmill for when snowstorms swept that country in winter. The former Army NCO had been on the Quarter Circle Z payroll almost two years and had proved his ability to get things done.

It was dull, rolling land compared to the range under the rim, but it had lots of strong grass. The power of the forage was obvious in the cattle delivered up there earlier. He hoped the range being developed at Hackberry Ranch proved that good. His nephew Reg and his new wife Lacy were stocking the ranch with maverick cattle they gathered up in the region. The hay crew had hauled mowers, a beaver board stacker, and rakes from the Windmill to Hackberry to gather some forage before winter set in. The carpenters and crew were building a house, bunkhouse, and corrals for Reg and Lacy on that ranch as well.

All of McQuire's good cows and calves had already been moved down to the Verde Ranch, so the upper one held only sale cattle getting ready each month for the Navajo contracts. It made the sorting system simple and was the best plan. The operations were evening out, but the damn Apache raid earlier made Chet mad. He'd done nothing to those people, but they still were on the uproar. With his jackknife he sawed off the arrow's shaft and tossed it aside. He left the deep-set arrowhead in the saddle fork. Damn them, anyway.

"This about the end of the Hartley dispersal cattle?" Sarge asked Chet while he was unsaddling. The straight-backed former Army man was about the same age and the same height as Hampt, but thinner. One of the original employees Chet had hired to take back the Quarter Circle Z, Sarge was a level-headed tough veteran.

A guy named Ryan had been running the ranch to suit himself. The former owner had feared him so much, he would not fire the man, despite his stealing and misdeeds, and Chet had stepped in.

The Hartleys had been two greedy brothers who'd filled the range with cows, complained when folks ate them, and ended up dead after trying to boss everyone.

"Yes, this is all we have of that stock besides the rebranded stock that Tom needed to replace the culls he sold off the River Ranch," Chet answered Sarge's question.

"The men and I'll have six hundred ready to ship in two weeks."

"It will be colder then. Better get the men equipped for some hard cold after you make this October run. They tell me the snow's going to fly any time before that November delivery. Folks who've been up here say the years vary in temperature and snowfall, but it can be damn tough. We'll face that, getting over there with our cattle."

"We can figure it out. How's Susie?" Sarge asked.

"Fine."

"Word's out she ain't going to marry Tom Hannagan."

"I don't think so. Leif Times has been around a lot."

"A good young man. He ride with you and a posse a couple times?"

"Yes, he did. I like him. His dad has the Rafter Eight Ranch. He's a polite young guy."

"That's my luck. I guess I should have tried harder. I always really liked her and felt if there was a way, I'd have proposed. But I never felt there was much chance of her agreeing to marry me."

Chet shook his head. "You should never let things like that hold you back."

"Well"—Sarge turned his hands up—"I guess I've been a bachelor too long, anyway."

Chet laughed and clapped him on his shoulder. "You know I count on a whole bunch of you guys. You, Tom, Hampt, and even Hoot."

"Speaking of a guy . . . I promised Victor I'd take you right over to the cook tent when you got here. Man, he's a helluva great cook. We sure like him."

"Victor took Marge and I on our honeymoon to buy the Hackberry Ranch. Never had a bad meal with him."

"What's your nephew JD doing?"

"Helping Tom. He ain't been like himself ever since he and Kay Kent broke up."

"He's young enough to come out of it."

Victor, the smiling, handsome Mexican, came out of the cook tent and shook Chet's hand. "Good to see you boss man."

"They say you been poisoning these men." Chet grinned.

"Oh, they gripe all the time. If it ain't my food, it's my music."

"I doubt that."

"How is Marge?" Victor asked.

"Fine. She sent her love to you."

"Tell her I miss her. The hands that just came in from the drive say some Apaches attacked you today."

"Put an arrow in my saddle."

Victor frowned. "What did they want?"

"Maybe some beef to eat."

He shook his head. "Spooky isn't it?"

"At times, damn spooky."

Victor frowned again. "I thought all them renegade Apaches were in Mexico."

"Some were left behind, I guess. But two of them are dead now."

"Will the Army find the others?"

"I hope so."

Victor nodded. "I am getting some food ready. Are you hungry?

"Yes, thanks."

"Come inside and drink my coffee."

"Sure."

As soon as coffee was poured, Chet launched into his plan for Sarge and his men to take the cattle to the agencies for the October delivery. With all he had to do back home, Chet needed this business handled by one of his men. Sarge could handle it. That taken care of, he closed out the rest of his business and thanked the two men for their good work.

After the meal and anxious to be back with his wife again, Chet resaddled his horse and headed back for the Verde outfit. It would be a long ride through the night, but he wanted to be back with Marge and handle more necessary business. He thanked Hampt and told him to take his time coming back with the rest of the men.

"I'd sure like to ride with you back through that Injun country." Hampt looked awfully concerned about Chet's safety.

"Naw. Apaches don't attack at night. I'll be close to home by sunup."

Hampt still frowned. "You just be damned careful. We're all counting on you."

Chet rode out, short loping the tough bay horse the crew called Sam Brown—a stout six-year-old gelding. With lots of ground to cover, he pushed the horse to make as much progress as he could before sundown. Nighttime would slow him, but the moon should come up early. His mind raced over all the business things that involved him. The Hartley Ranch dispersal was about complete. He'd paid a fair price for the place and the cattle. The sale to the Navajos would save him. Plus he would have all the cattle sold after this month, except for the hundred and fifty mother cows Tom had chosen to replace the Quarter Circle Z aged ones. The rest of the culls Tom sold to the Indians at Fort McDowell. Things were taking shape, but the cool nights told him he'd not make great progress in the winter. Best he got it all done by the time snow flew on his northern range.

Tired and stiff, he arrived at the main headquarters of the Quarter Circle Z at dawn. Tom and the men were saddling up and looked shocked to see him back so soon.

Chet waved off their concern. "Aside from an Apache raid on the herd, it was uneventful."

"What happened?"

"Oh, one shot an arrow in my saddle. Cole shot the other one off his horse. I ran down the arrow shooter and he surrendered then tried to kill Cole, so he shot him, too."

"That boy got him two Apaches?" one of the hands asked.

"Yeah. We had a small stampede because of it and finally got them all up there."

"Cole's going to get a reward?"

"I don't know. Who'd award him one?"

"Damned if I know, but we'll sure award him when he gets back." Everyone laughed.

Chet grinned. "Be a good deal. He's a tough enough guy." Then he waved Tom away from the men and spoke to him about his plans.

"We're riding up to Perkins to check on the Herefords. Routine head count is all."

"JD around?" Chet asked.

Tom shook his head and never said a word.

That was enough for Chet. He thanked him and went to the house. He could see his sister standing on the porch with her hands shading her eyes against the sun's glare.

"Saddle a roan for me," he said to the young man who took his horse.

"You back already?" Susie asked. "Come in. I'll have coffee and breakfast in a few minutes."

"How are you doing without May?"

"Boy, I really miss her. But she brought the boys over to fish yesterday, since Hampt was gone. She says the house on the Hartley place is nice now that they have it cleaned up. Ray and Ty fish some below the house on that part of the Verde, but they like the river better over here."

"She's happy?"

"Oh, yes. She's really happy to have a man who treats her nice and loves her."

"Good. I sure like Hampt, but I don't have to live with him."

Susie laughed. "I like Leif, but I wonder if I could stand to be married. I have become so independent since I don't feed the crew meals. Now May has married Hampt and moved over to the Hartley place and . . . well, I wonder what my role is. Aunt Louise lives with Harold Parker most of the time. I suspect they will get married some day, which is fine, but I don't know what I should do."

"Don't do anything unless your gut tells you that's what you want."

She nodded. "Leif is serious and would take me if I was a raving witch. Will being married to him make me feel more his wife than I do today?"

"Hell, you know how wild my life has been. I really worried about how marrying Marge would work out. But I love her ten times more as my wife than I did when we were going together. We have a wonderful private world that I miss every time I step out of it."

"I know that. I really misjudged her. You two are like a gentle stream flowing together when you are in each other's company. In fact, I am jealous of the ease in your marriage. Everyone doesn't have that or get that way after the honeymoon."

"Sis, I can't tell you what it is, but we have it all. I hope for Marge's sake, and my own, she can carry our child. I think she wants it for me even more than herself. But win or lose, I'll still love her."

"She confided to me it was her main goal in life to have a son."

Chet nodded and cupped the warm coffee cup in both hands. "What have you decided?"

She looked at him hard. "I guess I'll jump in the water, if he still wants me."

"Good. Don't make plans about everything. Let the plans come to the both of you. Where you will live? What you will do with your lives? Be dedicated and that will find you a better path to float down. I am going to go see my wife. God bless you two."

"Big brother, will you pray for Leif and me?"

He reached over and grasped her wrists. "I used to pray more out loud."

She agreed.

"Let's pray." He dropped his face and swiped off his hat "Our heavenly father I want to thank you for all our blessings in this new land. We are grateful. Be with all the family members and their families. Lord help JD to find his way. He is lost at sea, but show him the way back, sir. I want to ask you to bless the coming wedding of Susie and her fine young man Leif. Lead them into an inspiring life of love that will carry them to higher places in life together as man and wife. And Lord protect the unborn we await. Amen."

Susie sniffed. A tear ran down her cheek before she could capture it and when she tried to stop it with her finger, it only spread more.

"Thanks, that really helped me, Chet."

He swallowed and stood up. "I better go tend to my own wife."

"Yes, you should."

Susie hugged him and whispered, "Thanks. You made me feel so good."

"I meant it. Go rent a cabin in Oak Creek for your honeymoon. Have him show you how to fish."

"Can he fish?"

"Damned if I know. But do it. Fall in the creek, let loose."

She shook her head, hanging on his arm as he went out the front door.

"I'll see you." He saw his saddled roan at the rack.

Three hours later, his wife exploded out of the big house when he rode up and dismounted. She flew into his arms from the porch. "You're home a day early. Gods, it is good to have you back."

"I need a bath and a shave." Chet nodded at the stable hand Jesus, who'd come on the run to welcome him and take the gelding and roan away.

"You came to the right place. I have a nightshirt for you to wear back from the shower. Have any problems?"

"Apaches tried to attack us, stampeded the cattle, and two of the Apaches got shot."

"Oh, my heavens. I thought they were all on the reservations."

"Not all of them stay there."

Turning to the housekeeper who also cooked, Marge said, "Monica, look who got home early."

"Ah, señor. Always so good to see you."

Chet used his thumb to point to his wife. "Cause she's asked you a thousand times, I hope he hurries back?"

"Oh, *sí*. But that is a wife's duty, no?"

"I guess so. It is good to be home."

"I have some lunch ready when you two are ready to eat it,"

"Fine. I'll be clean and get shaved then. Has she been minding me when I was away?" he asked Monica quietly.

"Oh, *sí*. She is well behaved."

Marge gave him a shove. "I am the perfect minder."

They laughed and the two of them went on to the sheepherder's shower tank atop the shop building that the sun heated. Undressed and standing on the wooden grates, he soaped and showered it away by pulling on a chain. The water wasn't hot but warm enough he didn't shiver too much. Then she personally dried him off and brushed his hair.

"You can't tell anyone, but Susie is going to say yes to Leif this Saturday night. Act surprised."

"Oh, how wonderful. They will make a neat couple."

"I thought so myself. But now I'm not certain.

She might have fretted a lot about it. He's younger than she is."

"So what about that?"

"I don't mean anything. But she's had some kinda reservations about him."

After Marge shaved him, they ate lunch and he told Monica about the Apaches and their raid.

"They are blood thirsty devils. They will never settle down and live on those reservations. They are too free-spirited."

"Then they may all be dead. It is that simple."

Monica agreed.

CHAPTER 2

That evening, Jenn drove out from town all red-eyed and obviously distraught. The big blond-headed woman ran the café in Preskitt—what the locals called Prescott. She had fed Chet and his nephew Heck when they first came to Yavapai County three years earlier looking for the ranch. She'd found him most of his help for the ranch, too.

Later, on their way home one night his brother's son was killed by road agents. Chet hunted them down and put them away.

Hearing the rig pull into the yard, he and Marge met Jenn at the door.

"What's wrong?" Chet asked as the two of them led her to the couch.

Marge went for a towel, pausing in the doorway to hear her say, "It's my daughter in Tombstone. She's disappeared. No one knows where she went or what happened to her. Here, read this letter from Mr. White, the town marshal."

Marge turned back and sat next to Chet as he read the letter.

Dear Jenn,

I have checked where she was working and no one there knows where your daughter Bonnie Allen went. She's been gone for over a week and took most of her things. Strange, but in many similar cases the girls run off with men they have become attached to and leave their scarlet life to start a new one as a wife. If I learn anything about her I will contact you.

> *Sincerely yours,*
> *B. White*
> *Tombstone's chief marshal*

"What can we do?" Marge asked.

Jenn raised her chin. "Only man I know who could find her if she's alive is your husband. I won't be mad or upset if you throw me out. I know I'm not family nor kin. My respectability ain't too shiny, but I am her mother and God bless her soul I begged her not to get in that business. I knew the day she told me what she aimed to do something like this would happen to her—but I still wasn't ready for it. Chet's got a million irons in the fire, but let's face it. He can do what no lawman can do—get results."

"I won't stand in your way," Marge said to both of them. "You have some good men to handle the ranches. I can do the books or your sister can. Jenn's been a big help to you getting started here. Damn it, Chet you have not said a word to either of us."

"I really don't know where to start. I have never

been to Tombstone. They say it's a tough town. Finding your daughter will be like looking for a small gold nugget on the floor in the dark." He held up his hands to both women when they started to protest. "I will go and look hard for her, but when all the roads end, I'll simply come home, Jenn. I don't want you to hate me if I fail." He closed his eyes. They were burning and no tears flowed to wash the flame away.

"Take someone with you," his wife said softly.

"Only one who isn't tied up is JD. I lost one of those boys already." He dropped his chin. "I can't lose another of Louise's sons."

"It might change his life," Marge said. "He's rudderless now."

"I'll go wake Jesus and have him ask JD if he wants to go with me."

"I can—"

Chet stopped her. "Not everyone on the ranch needs to know our mission."

"Will you go by stage from here?"

"No, we'll go as cowboys. As far as folks in Preskitt are concerned, we will have gone bull buying. To the people who see us, we'll be drifters and look like we're out of work. Make less of a scene that way. We'll stay in the shadows. Jenn, make me a list of the girls Bonnie worked with. I want to talk to them privately. Do you have a photo of her? That might help."

He took the tintype in the metal case that she'd fetched from her purse. An oval pocket-size picture of a pretty girl in her late teens. "Reddish hair?"

"Yes. Green eyes, too."

"You two make the list of those other girls' names. I'll go talk to Jesus."

Marge nodded and Jenn agreed, thanking him for accepting the job.

In answer, he looked at her hard. "We will go look is all I can promise you."

She nodded. "I understand."

He left the women in the house and found the young man in his room in the stables.

The youth bolted up in his bed. "What is wrong, señor?"

"Shush. I need you to do a special job for me. Ride to the Verde Ranch and find JD. Tell him I need to go look for a lost woman. No more. Ask if he wants to help me. I will leave in the morning to go find her."

"What if he says no?"

"Thank him and ride back here."

"If he won't, may I go with you?" The boy was quickly dressing in the dark room with starlight streaming in a couple small panes.

"I would have to ask my wife."

"I can ride and shoot. And I can speak Spanish to people who would not understand you."

His words amused Chet. "I don't doubt that, Jesus. I will consider your offer."

"*Gracias.* I will be back by dawn." In minutes, Jesus was gone in the starlight to saddle a horse to ride.

Chet went back to the house. Marge opened the door. "Did he understand?"

"Yes." Chet smiled at her. "He wants to go along

with us. Says he could talk to people that would not understand my Spanish."

She laughed. "I guess your Spanish is shy of being all right."

"I guess."

"What is that?" Jenn asked, coming in from the kitchen.

"Aw, my stable man thinks he should go along," Marge said. "He insulted Chet, saying his Spanish was not too clear."

Chet shook his head at her words. "I wasn't insulted. I was amused."

"Will JD come and go with you?" Jenn asked.

Chet shrugged his shoulders.

"If JD's brother Reg was here, he'd go too, but he's at Hackberry," Marge said to her. "They're Chet's boys."

"They are my boys until the new one gets here." He hugged Marge.

She escaped. "You go sleep, Chet Byrnes. Jenn and I will put the things you will need in a pannier or two and have them ready. Raphael can pick you out some good horses and have them saddled in the morning. If Jesus wants to go, take him along. He needs to know these things, too." She stomped her heel on the floor. "Go sleep."

"Yes ma'am."

Marge woke him. "JD came back with Jesus last night. Jenn told both boys the story of her daughter."

"Neither of you women slept?"

"No. Raphael has the packhorses loaded and ready. I could not think of one more thing some unemployed ranch hands might need. I think he'd like to go this time. He still regrets that deputy telling him he could not follow and help you go after those horse rustlers and murderers."

"He has no need to fuss over that. Consider the source."

"What do you really think happened to Bonnie?"

Chet shook his head. "A whore is a simple commodity. Some people kill them out of meanness. They sell them into slavery. For no reason, they torture them and slap them around like they were jackasses."

"I'd simply never thought about that being the case."

"It is not peaches and sex. The dark side is so close to them every day they work. The people who manipulate them don't care. Abuse is a tough game they must play."

She hugged him and wept on his shoulder. "Be careful, my love. Don't take any chances. Our baby is resting good. I never had one kick me before. I can't wait for it to do that to me."

"God bless it and you. I will be back. I promise."

She kissed him hard. "I'll pray for your return. If you need anything, send a telegram. I'll send the men to help you."

"Word travels fast. That is all they need to know."

"Yes. Jenn has to go back and run her business. I'll help her get through this some way."

"That's great. I bet those two guys are worn out riding all night."

Marge shook her head. "They're as anxious as you are to ride on this morning."

In the backyard, Chet met up with JD and Jesus and shook Raphael's calloused hand. "Thank you for packing the horses."

The short foreman hugged him. "Be very careful. Those men in that business will cut your throat for a quarter. I hope you find her, *mi amigo.* I can help you, wire me. I know that country well."

"Take care of my wife. I will return as soon as I can."

The three swung in the saddle. Chet waved goodbye and then led the way down the lane to the road. JD fell in behind him. Leading the two packhorses, Jesus rode last, and they left at a long trot in the first rays of sunlight.

After crossing the Prescott Valley, they turned left on the Black Canyon stage route headed south. He planned to get past Hassayampa City, where they knew him, before dark and stay at a ranch near there. The day grew hotter as they rode south, passing by north and south bound stages in clouds of dust that obscured them from being recognized by anyone.

When they passed the cutoff where the stage robbers took Heck as a hostage, Chet felt a knot in his throat that he could not swallow. He spent the saddest days of his life on that road to the mountains trailing the kidnappers and then still hadn't found that boy alive.

The three pushed on south and found a rancher willing to put them up for the night. He wouldn't take any money for the hay and grain they requested to buy.

"I know you, Chet Byrnes. I know it was you hung them killers over at Rye. You ever need a dollar or even fifty cents, you come see Jimmy Dicks. That's me. I'll find some money for you. And you got them stage robbers murdered your boy, too. Oh, and if you ever want to be sheriff up here, I'll campaign my heart out for you."

"I hope I never have to be the sheriff, Jim Dicks."

"We could damn sure use you as one. You boys be all right out here, tonight? Mrs. said to tell you all could sleep on her floor inside the house."

"Tell her we're obliged. Out here is fine. We may ride off early," Chet told the man.

"I can tell you right now, you won't beat her getting up. She'll have you three breakfast fixed before daylight. Eat with her. She's a fine woman and don't get much company down here."

"We will. Thanks," Chet said.

The light was on in the house the next morning as they saddled and loaded the packhorses.

"You boys get ready," she shouted to them from the back door. "I've got hot water in the bowls out here to wash your hands and face. Towels on the nails. Food gets cold fast."

Chet told them they could finish up later. They followed him to the porch, taking off their hats, putting them on the hat holders, and washing up.

Hands dried, they filed in to look at the huge meal she had spread on the table.

"I knowed you had hard jerky last night, so I made it up for you in this breakfast."

"You did swell, ma'am."

"*Sí, señora*, this is wonderful."

"Sure looks great," JD added, shocked by all the food they had to eat.

She served them coffee, so Chet knew they weren't Mormons. The woman, in her thirties, was willowy-shaped and attractive. Nearly bashful, she quietly asked about his wife.

"Oh, Marge is at home running things. We are going south to look for bulls. This is my nephew JD Byrnes and Jesus is my wife's horse trainer."

"Nice to have you men here with us this morning."

"Well, this is sure lots of good food. Thank you, ma'am," JD said.

"Very good, gracias," Jesus added and went back to eating.

They finished in due time and returned to the task of loading the packhorses.

When they rode out, Jim Dicks was still trying to get Chet to reconsider running for sheriff. Chet gave a wave and headed away from the ranch.

He noticed the frequency of large saguaro cactus studding the mountainsides around the ranch. "How old are those tall cactus, Jesus?"

"I was told that they watched the first Spaniard Conquistadors centuries ago when they first came here."

"I see." The spiny desert flourished and Jesus pointed out the century plant stalks. "It will only bloom once and die. Apaches consider them a marker of where they live."

"I'll recall that someday. What is the light colored cactus?"

"Cholla. Jumping cactus. You brush close to it and it will stick many thin, barbed needles in you."

"We have prickly pear beds in Texas like these here."

"Later, I will show you the barrel cactus. If you are out of water, you can use it for water. It tastes like an alkali water melon, but you can live on it." Jesus talked on. "The Indian women use long sticks to harvest those saguaro fruit and the prickly pears. There is a small wild pig here called a javelina who eats the prickly pear pads. They run in packs and sometimes charge men on foot. They also eat the pods from the mesquite trees."

"We have some of those kind of pigs in west Texas. JD, you listening?"

"I just want to stay out of those damn spines." JD laughed. "It is sure a tough country. I've been seeing a few cows out there. How the hell do you round them up?"

Jesus laughed. "Being a vaquero is a tough job."

"Damn tough. I'll stick to the high country or Texas to cowboy in."

Chet wondered if asking his nephew to come along was his best move. JD was not the same youth who rode with him and Reg after those horse thieves stole the entire ranch remuda in Texas that started the feud with the Reynolds. Chet hoped he was wrong. Somewhere ahead he might need a steady gun hand.

"What's our next town?" JD asked as they rode on.

"A place on the Salt River with a water mill that they call Hayden's Mill."

Jesus nodded as the packhorses followed him.

They stabled the horses late at night, located an open café, ate spicy Mexican food, and found a rooming house to sleep in for a few hours. By sunup, they were on the road.

Chet was pleased with their progress when they reached the wide-street town of Mesa at midday.

JD frowned at the design. "Why, these streets are wide enough to turn a wagon around anywhere."

"The Mormons designed it that way," Jesus said as they rode on through.

That night, they stayed in the small village of Chandler where the stage changed teams. Spitting all over, a tobacco-chewing man let them stable their horses and store their panniers. After another poor meal in a café, they slept the night in the stable's haystack.

In the morning, a Mexican woman street vendor made them tasty burritos before they rode on.

They stopped in Casa Grande and looked at the adobe ruins of an ancient civilization.

"What happened here?" Chet asked Jesus.

"It may have been a drought caused them to go back south. No one knows."

"Like the big cactus, those ruins aren't talking," Chet said.

"Maybe it was so bad they didn't want to," JD added, sounding bored.

Chet shook his head and they rode on, stopping only for meals and sleep.

Two days later, they reached the walled city of Tucson. A dead hog, half rotten and feasted on by bold vultures, lay in the street at the curb. The birds barely hopped around at their passage. A block later, a dead burro with his eye sockets empty was prone on the side of the street.

"Do they bury dead people here?" JD asked.

Chet pointed out a file of Sunday dressed people and a priest coming down the street. Several men carried a coffin. The riders halted, removed their hats, and let them to pass.

"I guess you better belong to the church or you will be feed for the buzzards," JD said as they moved out again.

"This is the town that competes with Preskitt for the capitol every time the state legislature meets," Chet said.

"Who in hell's name would vote for being down here?" JD frowned.

"Jesus, doesn't a powerful ring run the business down here?" Chet asked.

The young man lowered his voice. "Oh, *sí*. A strong secret organization runs the services to the army and Indian reservations. So they make sure the large number of soldiers stay here and protect them from the Apaches."

JD looked around with another frown. "I damn sure see why the command for the Army is up there at Preskitt and I don't blame them."

Jesus took them to a relative who owned a small farm on the Santa Cruz. Ronaldo Vargas was a man in his thirties. His small irrigated farm had alfalfa, a milk cow, and several acres of corn that was made in the shuck. His wife, a smiling woman named Rio, welcomed them to get down and she would cook them some food.

Road weary, they dropped off their saddles and undid the girths. Vargas talked to his kinsman and told them to put the animals in a pen and the panniers inside the tack room so the dogs didn't get into them. The horses soon rolled in the pen's dust, grunting and appreciating their escape from saddles and packs. Then they rose and shook off dust like a whirlwind.

The Vargas's young children took pieces of hard candy from Chet and thanked him politely.

Rio sat them at her long table and served them flour tortillas, fried beef strips, sweet peppers, onions and spicy salsa, and brown beans.

"Best damn food we've had all this trip." JD

shook his head, looking amazed between bites. "Ronaldo your wife is a wonderful cook."

The other two agreed. Rio beamed, and they ate their fill of her rich food.

"What brings you hombres to Tucson?"

Chet spoke up. "A secret business to look for a woman's daughter who was in Tombstone and disappeared a while ago."

The man frowned hard at them. "You have no idea where she went?"

"None. Her mother wrote Marshal White down there and he found out nothing."

"What is the daughter's name?"

"Bonnie Allen. If you can find out anything do not expose us," Chet warned, "but please tell us all you know. I can pay you a reward."

Vargas nodded. "I will check around Tucson. If I find out anything, how will I contact you?"

"Send a letter to me, Chet Byrnes, General delivery, Tombstone. I'll check the post office daily or so."

"Rio, get him an envelope and he can put that address on one," Vargas requested.

"Sure," Chet agreed between bites of food.

Taking the envelope from her, he used her pencil to address the envelope, handed it back, and thanked her. "Bonnie has red hair. I have a picture." He dug it out of his vest.

The man and his wife examined it and then nodded. "She is a very pretty lady," Rio said.

"Yes. Her mother is a good friend and we want to find her."

"Oh, yes, I would, too, if I knew anything about her."

"We will ride on this morning. If I can pay you—"

"No senor. Jesus is our favorite cousin. We are so glad to see him and learn about his life and meet you two as well," Vargas insisted.

"This is a nice farm. I wonder how two young people like you could afford it."

"This was Rio's grandfather's farm. We worked very hard for him for seven years and when he died, he left this farm to us because he knew we could make good, farming it."

Chet nodded. "I understand that. My grandfather left me our ranch in Texas. But we had to leave because of a feud. My brother was murdered in Kansas, taking cattle to market for the ranch."

"It must have been hard to leave your home. If I lost this place, I know I would cry. I am so glad to meet you, señor." Vargas frowned. "You said this woman who lost the girl is a friend of yours?"

"She helped me find a ranch in Arizona Territory for my family and she found most of my help."

Vargas shook his head, confused by the search business. "Where will you look for her?"

"Under every rock we can turn over."

Vargas laughed. "Lots of rocks in Tombstone."

"No. Everyone leaves a trail, even a thin one. There is a trail. We must find hers."

"I bet you do that."

"That is why we came here."

"You are a busy man. Why would you do this?"

"I owe her mother," Chet answered. "I know the girl may already be in a shallow grave, but her mother needs to know if that's the case, too."

"I believe you will solve this mystery about her disappearance."

"See, you are more confident than I am." He clapped Vargas on the shoulder. "Pray for us to find her—alive."

"We will, señor. We will."

The next day, the three travelers left early and headed for Benson—another forty-mile hitch in their travels across the hard desert.

When they rode into the town on the San Pedro River about sundown, Chet noticed several *putas* in scanty clothing standing by the doors of the narrow adobe cribs. As the men passed, the women offered their services loudly.

Coming to Wheeler Livery Stable, the men put up their horses and planned to sleep in the bunkroom. When Chet and Jesus headed out for supper, JD parted their company, telling them he'd see them later.

Chet recalled the ladies of the night they'd seen earlier. He had no interest and neither did Jesus so they went on without JD to a café the stable man said served decent food.

After dinner, Chet and Jesus returned to the bunkhouse and turned in.

Chet didn't hear JD came in, but he was asleep in the hay the next morning. Chet woke up the two young men. "Better get some breakfast. That gal at the café said she'd have food ready at daybreak."

The men grumbled a bit, then rose and made their way to the stable.

"Damn I'm sore. Are you two?" Chet asked them, busy slapping on saddles and packs.

"Just my back," JD said, holding his hips and drawing a laugh from Chet and Jesus.

"You can't complain about that," Chet said. "All this riding is the real work."

They led their horses to the café and hitched them out front. The lamps were on when they went inside. Each one took off this hat for the woman in her thirties named Lizzy. She sat them down at a large table in the back and took their orders.

The town law sauntered in. He strolled to the back and told them good morning. Chet told him to take a seat and introduced his men and himself to the man.

"Earl's my name. Earl Stover. I'm the law here and want to welcome you three to Benson. You chose a good place to eat breakfast. Lizzy is a great woman and if she ever shuts down, I'd find a new town to be the marshal in. Nice to meet 'cha." He nodded to each one and took his place at the table.

"You fellers look prepared to do some serious traveling."

"We're looking over the country," Chet said.

"Lots to see around here. Down the road is Tombstone. Hell on wheels, I call it. Here, things are pretty quiet. It's not a bad place to settle down and make a home."

"Well, we'll be looking. Thanks."

"Just wanted you to know that."

"You've been the law here for a long time?" Chet asked to make conversation.

"Three years. Pretty quiet. Oh, I get a few drunks and some petty stealing of chickens, but most times it's quiet. I did some boomtowns back a few years ago in Colorado. Got enough of that in a big hurry."

"I bet you did."

"Lizzy," Stover called to the woman. "Bring me some hot sauce with my eggs."

"I will. I'm fixing the usual for you."

"Good girl. Thanks. That's why I'm here. She sure takes good care of me."

Chet nodded. Something about the man struck him. He looked capable of exploding if things stressed him. Chet figured the marshal could get angry fast if things didn't go his way.

When they finished eating, Chet and the others said good-bye to the marshal, then JD and Jesus left the café. Chet paid the woman, giving her a tip that she thanked him for.

"Did he think we were outlaws?" JD asked, looking back at the diner before he mounted up

"I don't know. He is the law here. Maybe checking us out." In the saddle, Chet smiled at Jesus. "You think we look like outlaws?"

"No. But he was a tough acting man. I was glad to get out of there, but her food was good."

"It was fine food. Let's find Tombstone, guys."

"I'm ready," JD said, and they swung out from the livery and trailed down the empty street.

Chet saw Stover standing behind the glass window of the café, giving them what he called the hard eye. They'd done nothing in his town but sleep and eat. JD had no doubt sampled some local dove the night before, but that wasn't law breaking. Perhaps the man was overprotective. Maybe it was nothing.

They rode through St. David an hour or so later. A Mormon town with small acreage farms, the LDS Church was clustered in the middle. The plots were alfalfa, corn, beans, and gardens. The irrigation was extensive. Water from the river and some artesian wells poured out at the wellhead into the ditches.

"That kind of a well would be nice up our way," Chet said, impressed by the fact that the liquid came free from the ground to the top of the well's large faucet that could be shut off until one needed it again.

"These people are neat farmers, too," JD added. He stood up in the stirrups and looked around. "Have these folks got several wives that live here?"

"I don't know. They say some of them do." Chet saw no signs of polygamy but he didn't doubt there could be some.

"There are Mormons with more than one wife up by us," Jesus said.

"I never knew that." JD frowned. "You know of any, Chet?"

"A woman who lives beyond the western boundary of the Quarter Circle Z has a ranch there. She runs some cows for her husband and grows most of her own food." He'd sent Hampt there to check on her and learn if there were any rustlers working the area. Hampt had come back smiling, but Chet had never asked him anything about it.

"I'll be damned. Was she good looking?" JD asked.

"She's not ugly. Heck and I met her when I was trailing Ryan after he shot my good horse."

"She ever get lonely?"

"Hell, JD, I don't know. She sure don't see many faces in a year's time."

"I just wondered. I'll be damned."

Chet frowned. "You planning on becoming a Mormon?"

"No. What would a man do with five wives?"

"Feed them, I guess."

"Well, I didn't see any back there, but you find one, make sure you show her to me."

Chet laughed. "I will."

A few hours later, they rode up Boot Hill to look at the entire town of Tombstone spread across a mesa at the foot of some bare hills. The sounds of large mine machinery running full steam filled the air with a whine that one heard in industrial places. Clanging and banging, steam whistles, and sharp peeps. Huge ore wagons piled high with the loads pulled by six draft mules headed for a stamper mill south of town. Freight wagons with many yokes of oxen laying down, resting, and chewing their cuds, clogged the street. The railroad had not arrived in Arizona yet so there were no trains or tracks, but it would some day pass through Benson, thirty miles north. Big plans had already been made for a sidetrack to the queen city and a railroad bed was already under construction outside of town headed that way.

They made their way down to the town. Saloon girls were sitting in open second story windows ready to talk to any potential customer on the boardwalks or striding in the street.

"Hey cowboys, come see me. The daytime appointments are always sweeter than the nighttime ones and cheaper."

JD kept his head down. Jesus swept off his hat and smiled at the Latin ones who spoke his lingo. He thanked them and then in Spanish said, "Not now."

"Where should we land?" JD asked.

"I guess the stables are on the next street or back at that O.K. Corral we passed earlier," Chet said, busy taking in all the people. They crowded on the boardwalk going back and forth, crossing the street, dodging fresh cow pies plopped down by the last ox to go through.

"Have you ever seen the like?" Jesus asked.

"In Fort Worth at the stockyards," Chet said. "Same thing as this. But I never saw it out west. I see why it is called the biggest city between St. Louis and San Francisco."

"What will we do?"

"Stable our horses and make a plan. Come on." Chet swung his horse around and a delivery rig about ran him over.

"Watch the hell where you're going you damn backwoods hick," the red-faced man on the reins under a cow-pie hat shouted.

JD laughed at the man's words. "Guess he knew where we lived."

Back in traffic headed west, they moved through and around the throng of rigs, teams, and wagons to the O.K. Corral.

A man who leaned on the wall sign of the business, shoved off with his shoulder and came over to confront them. "Me name's O'Leary. I can book your animals in here for fifty cents a day." He looked at the five horses. "Yeah, I got tie stalls. Grain's twenty-five cents more."

"Isn't that kinda steep?" Chet asked the man.

"Steep it may be, but where else you going to park 'em?"

"Can I store my panniers here?"

"Yeah,"

"We'll take a few days."

"Good. We're the best in town." O'Leary stuck two fingers in his mouth and whistled loud enough a deaf man could have heard him. Three Mexican youths came on the run from the hallway and collected up the reins.

"We will unsaddle them and care for them, señor," said the oldest boy.

"Good, put our panniers up too," Chet instructed.

"*Sí, señor.*"

After stabling their horses, Chet and his men and walked from the O.K. Livery to the nearby street corner. He wanted a place their conversations might not be overheard.

"We can sleep in the hay at the livery tonight. Jenn said that her daughter worked last in the Lady

Rose Parlor. That's on the left in the next block and upstairs. You ready for another ride, JD?"

"Sure."

"Her friends were Ivory, Red Rose and Eclare. Find one of them today and ask her about Bonnie Allen. All you can find out. We'll even pay her for more information."

"What if none of them are working today?" JD asked.

"Ask for one of them anyway. Someone may know something." Chet gave him five dollars.

JD thanked him.

"We'll meet back at six o'clock and go to supper. Jesus, I bet they have some putas around here."

"Oh, sí. I can find them." He nodded his head and smiled.

"Have you ever used one before?"

"Yes, I have."

"Maybe one of them knows something about her disappearance—Bonnie Allen."

"I can find that out."

Chet handed him five silver dollars. "Be back here at six. We will go to supper together."

"Give me some quarters. A dollar is too much for one of them," Jesus said with a grin of mischief.

Amused, Chet took back two of the dollars and replaced them with four quarters.

"That is good. I will be here then."

Smiling to himself about his plan for the investigation, Chet headed for Big Nose Kate's Saloon halfway down the block for a drink at the bar, hoping he could find out more about Bonnie Allen. His wife and Susie may kill him if they ever learned he'd sent those boys off to use saloon girls for information. What they didn't know wouldn't kill them, anyway.

After a block of rubbing elbows and dodging drunks among the boardwalk pedestrians, he pushed in the swinging doors and went to an open spot at the bar. Some woman of the night with her skirt gathered up exposing her bare legs was riding a guy's lap in a chair at a side table. She was screaming so damn loud it hurt his ears.

"Damn. Is she always that loud?" he asked a man in a dust floured suit beside him who was watching her antics.

The suited man looked mildly back at Chet. "That's Ruby Jo. She sings and does several other things. Yeah, she's that loud most of the time."

"Hurts my ears." Chet turned away from the bar when he heard a ruckus break out over someone cheating at cards. Chairs scraped the floor. He saw one man pop up, reach over for another, jerk him facedown on the table, and slam him in the head with his knuckles. Once, twice—that was enough.

Upset that no one had moved to stop him, Chet moved in and jerked the two men aside and caught the beater's arm. "That's enough." Eye to eye, he read the man's defiance.

"Who says so?"

"Me." Chet gave him a haymaker to the chin with his right hand. His blow left the man sprawled on his back among the onlookers and he remained limp on the floor.

"Holy cow, mister. You knocked him plumb out." One mouthy guy wanted him to look at the downed gambler. Chet didn't give a damn about the guy. He watched the crowd for someone who wanted to take up his war. No one made a move.

A bartender brought over a bucket of water and without even a grin, poured it in the man's face. The liquid spread out underfoot on the floor. A ragtag bum came and began mopping it up. Two men carried the unconscious man out the front door and came back too fast to have delivered him anywhere else but the boardwalk.

When satisfied he had no threats for his actions, Chet turned and the bartender had a whiskey bottle in one hand and a glass in the other. "How much do you want of this?"

"I don't drink whiskey."

"This one is on the house."

"You want to buy me one, make it a beer."

The barkeep shrugged. "Whatever. I'll get you a beer."

Chet spoke to the man next to him. "Who was he—the man I knocked out?"

"Billy Bragg."

"Who's he work for?"

"Old man Newt Clanton."

Chet nodded. "Might as well break in my first day in Tombstone society with a guy like him."

"What's your name?"

"Chet Byrnes."

"I heard of you. You're the guy ran down some rustlers and hung them?"

"I never saw my name in the paper." With a sip of the beer, Chet studied himself in the mirror back of the bar. He'd knocked out one of the most powerful men in the territory. What a good start he'd made the first day.

"I heard of your name," the guy beside him said under his breath. "They say you're tough. In the next few hours, you're going to learn how tough you are. His men will gather up to go home and when they hear that you knocked out one of their own, they'll come looking for you with their teeth bared."

"How many?" Beer in his hand. he turned to study the crowd. "How many of them in here worked for Clanton?"

"A half dozen, maybe more," the guy said. "They consider if anyone hurts one of theirs, they have to even the score or better it."

"Anyone ever stopped them?"

The man tossed his head. "You come in here over Boot Hill?"

"Sure."

"It's full of folks picked a fight with old man Clanton."

Chet downed his beer and grimaced. It didn't taste that good. Next thing to do was to locate his men and get a plan working. Damn. He could get himself in the damndest deals. He set the empty mug on the bar and headed outside through the batwing doors. On the boardwalk, he had to side-step the crowd gathered near the downed man. Lying in the back of a wagon, he was surrounded by people trying to revive him.

In a few steps, he was lost in the masses and headed back toward the O.K. Livery, stopping at the saddle repair shop on the corner to wait. His two would show up sometime.

Jesus showed up first. "I didn't learn anything, but I made some friends among the Mexicans who live here. They say she might have been sold into slavery and taken to Mexico City. But they did not know who kidnapped her—most of them did not know her."

"But someone did know her?"

"One boy had seen her on the street several times and said she was real pretty."

Chet nodded. "There was a fight in Big Nose Kate's. This guy had another facedown on the table and was hitting him in the head with his fist. Made me mad and I tried to separate them. The puncher kept trying to break by me, so I cold conked him with a haymaker."

"Wow. What happened?"

"Last I saw him, they had him laid out on his back in a wagon bed, trying to revive him."

"You kill him?"

"I don't think so. But his name is Billy Bragg and he works for old man Clanton."

Jesus opened his brown eyes wide. "That is the big outlaw, huh?"

"Clanton is."

"What should we do?"

"When JD comes back we'll talk about it. I never asked, but does that six-gun of yours work?" Chet nodded toward the well-oiled looking side arm.

"Oh, sí. I can hit tin cans with it. I have practiced much with it."

"I hope you don't ever need it, but these people

we face will be mean and would kill you for ten cents."

"Oh, I know that, señor."

They lounged on the porch waiting for JD. Jesus saw him coming. "There he is."

JD shook his head when he reached them. "I found Eclare. She had some cock and bull story how Bonnie Allen ran off with a cowboy."

"You didn't believe her?" Chet asked.

"Aw, she was so sold on herself, I really found her a boring liar."

"Tell him about the fight," Jesus said.

Chet explained the incident in the saloon and JD agreed they'd have to be on their guard.

"Let's go find this famous diner and eat supper. You talk to anyone else in the parlor house besides Eclare?"

"No, they were all sleeping, except her. And I couldn't shut her up." JD shook his head in defeat.

Chet and Jesus laughed at his obvious disgust over the experience.

Nellie Cashman's restaurant was impressive. Chet would have expected to find such an establishment in a major city. The hostess put their hats on a wall rack and promised they would be there when they were through with their meal. They filed to their table behind her. Grizzly-faced, dust-floured prospectors and men and women in formal dress ignored their passage, all busy eating or reading the fancy menus.

Seated across from Chet, Jesus peered around from behind the menu. "I will have what you order."

Chet agreed amused, but he was somber when he realized that Jesus could not read.

"Says here, oysters when available," JD said. "How would they get them here?"

Chet shook his head. Obviously the most sought after delicacy in the west, he once saw where such seafood was twelve dollars a pound when they made it to Preskitt. "Better ask the waiter."

They ordered sliced roast beef, potatoes, and sweet corn. Chet offered a short prayer before they ate and Jesus crossed himself after "Amen." The rolls were made with yeast in the dough and they melted in their mouths. The coffee served in china cups was delicious and the cherry pie mouthwatering. The meal went smoothly.

"We better eat at a street vendor after this," JD said, after wiping his mouth on a linen napkin.

Chet laughed. "I was celebrating the three of us getting here."

Both of his men nodded that they approved of this place. Chet paid the bill for seven dollars and they went back to sleep in the livery their first night in Tombstone. A few gunshots woke him once and he decided that some drunk cowboy was taking target practice at the moon and went back to sleep in the sweet smelling alfalfa hay.

In the morning, they saddled up and went to look for a place to stay. They found a rancher out on the flats west of town. His windmill by the corrals creaking in the wind, he shook their hands.

"Ira Hampton's my name."

"My name's Chet Byrnes. These are my nephew JD and Jesus. Ira, we're down here looking for a young lady who disappeared and no one seems to know where she went. I wondered if we could board here, pay for our horses' feed, and sleep under a tree."

"You're ranch folks?"

"Yes, our ranch is outside of Camp Verde. Quarter Circle Z is the brand. This girl is a daughter of a lady who befriended me when I came to Arizona to find a ranch."

Ira nodded. "I wouldn't charge you three a damn thing."

"Oh, we'll do something for you."

"Come meet the boss. She's up at the house." He smiled at them and shook his head. "Someone has to be the boss on the place."

They agreed. A slender attractive woman in her thirties came out to meet them. Her hair tinged in gray was braided and piled on her head. She wore an apron over her dress.

"Bee, these cowboys need a place to stable their horses and spread their bedrolls."

"Why lands, Ira, what did you tell them?" The woman frowned at him. "Land's sakes, we can sure board them."

"Mrs. Hampton, we just need a place to drop," Chet argued.

"My name's Bee, and you make yourself at home."

"Thank you, ma'am. My name's Chet, that's Jesus and he's JD." Chet pointed at the two young men.

"Nice to meet you all." To Chet, she added, You have a ranch?"

"Yes, up north of Preskitt, ma'am."

"Cooler up there, isn't it?"

"Yes, it is usually cooler. We won't be any trouble to you."

"Put that pack gear in the shop. It rains here every year or so." Bee Hampton grinned.

They laughed then set out to unload the panniers and put up the packhorses. When the job was complete, they rode back to Tombstone, stabled their horses at the O.K. and split up again.

Chet went to find Marshal White who was in the jail office with his boots parked on the desk. He put them down when Chet walked in the open door.

"Marshal, I'm Chet Byrnes of Preskitt. I want to talk to you about a young lady who disappeared down here."

The marshal sat up, straightened his vest and bushy mustache then he nodded. "Bonnie Allen."

"That's who. Anything you know would help me."

"I wrote her mother I had nothing on her disappearance."

"Jenn showed me your letter. She thanks you."

"Take a chair. No need to thank me. I couldn't find out a thing about the girl's disappearance. Sorry I won't be any help Byrnes. Most those girls don't leave forwarding addresses."

"People say there is big trade in white slavery with Mexico."

White did spider push-ups with his hands and nodded. "That's a tough business, but no one reports it when it happens. There is only whispering. Few people know where any of the girls are, and no one really cares about them when they're gone except their mothers."

"Any idea who would know?"

"Not really. But friend, if you found anyone, they would be tough to get to talk. You could probably burn their soles off torturing them and never learn a damn thing. 'Cause they have associates back home who would shoot them if they said a damn word."

"Sworn to secrecy?"

"Worse than that." White shook his head to show his stern impression of such men.

"Who heads it?"

"I don't know. That is how secret they are."

"Old man Clanton?"

The marshal shook his head again. "He ain't no angel, but I don't think he trades in white slavery."

"If you learn anything, I'm staying out at Ira Hampton's ranch."

White stood up. "Nice to meet you, Byrnes. I wish you good luck, but be careful. There's cut-throats on this border that are meaner than sidewinder rattlers."

"I will, thanks. You ever get to Preskitt go by Jenn's Café. She'll feed you good."

"I'd do that if I ever get up there. Tell her I'm sorry I found out nothing about her daughter's disappearance."

"Sure, thanks." Chet offered his hand.

Marshal White shook it. "Watch your back is all I can say."

"I will."

Chet left the marshal's office and stopped in a

narrow café that produced a fine aroma of the sign's contents STEW 30 CENTS A BOWL. He found a place to sit on a stool in the long bar that went way back in the café full of customers.

"What'll you have?" The short blonde in her mid-twenties wore a tough look as she waited for his answer.

"Stew, I guess. Coffee."

She wiped the counter in front of him. "You're new here, ain't 'cha?"

"Yes, I live up in Preskitt. Name's Chet."

"Glad to have you here, Chet. You don't like our stew, don't pay us."

"That's quite a deal."

"It's a real deal that we do here."

"Thanks. A friend of mine," he lowered his voice, "lost her daughter, Bonnie Allen. Can you help me?"

She looked around as if checking if they could speak, then she whispered sharply, "I get off at seven. Back alley. Talk to you then. Too many ears in here."

He nodded. Settled back on the stool, he waited for his mug of steaming coffee and the bowl of stew that filled his nose with its rich aroma. In a few minutes, she was back and left him a ticket for thirty cents.

"Pay before you leave."

He stood up and dug out two quarters from his pocket. "Here. Keep it."

She looked at the money in her hand and nodded. "Thanks."

He sat down and lifted the spoon.

"You must be rich," the guy beside him said.

"No, just figured she could use it."

"I could have used it to buy two beers."

Chet nodded, took his first sip of coffee, grimaced, and agreed with the man's comment. But the stew tasted wonderful. "For two beers, what could you tell me?"

"What do you need to know?"

The man beside him had not shaved nor changed clothes in several days. He appeared to be a derelict. But street trash knew more than cleaned-up people about things.

Chet said, "I am looking for a young woman who disappeared awhile ago."

The man slurped another spoonful of stew and looked at him. "What's she look like?"

Chet put her picture in the case on the counter.

The man picked it up and studied it in the shady light of the café's interior. "Her hair red?"

"Yes. You know where she is?"

He put it down and shoved it toward Chet. "What would you give me to know where she's at?"

"You really know where she is?" This guy could be lying to simply get money out of him.

"I might."

"What do you want?"

"I could use some money."

"If I tear two twenty dollar bills in half and you take me to her I'll give you the other halves."

"That might be hard. To take you there, I mean. I might know where she's at, but hell, there might not be any way to get her out."

"If I can find her on your directions, I'll pay you a hundred dollars."

The man whistled. "Where you staying?"

"At the Hampton Ranch west of town."

"I can find you."

"How long will it take you to get me the exact location of her?"

The man shrugged his shoulders. "Maybe a week, ten days."

"What name do you use?"

"Don."

"I'll be waiting for it, Don."

"You may have to move fast if I find out."

Chet gave the man a ten dollar gold piece.

He looked hard at the coin the size of a dime then pocketed it. "See yah." The man stood and lumbered out the door of the café.

Chet finished his stew and drank a second cup of coffee the waitress had brought him. The place had thinned.

She looked at him hard. "You serious about meeting me tonight?"

"Serious. I'll be there."

She nodded that she heard him.

He left the café and went on to the Palace Saloon. When he took a place at the sparsely populated bar, he wondered what his cohorts were busy doing. He ordered a beer and sat on a stool to take things in. He'd made two connections, Don, the lost soul and the blond waitress. Could they connect him with Bonnie Allen? Maybe. Or was it simply a plan to squeeze him for more money. Still,

someone had to know something about her disappearance.

He talked to an old man who had a rich mine
that needed funds to develop. The whiskered guy
showed him chunks of raw silver from the mine.

"I guess mine development is expensive," Chet
said to the man who called himself Sam Yooter.

"But you could make millions on this one."

Chet agreed, but had no wish to get into the
mining business.

Yooter soon moved on to another prospect. The
bartender came by and told Chet about a lovely girl
he knew was available at that time of day for a special price.

Chet shook his head, thanked him. He finished
his beer and crossed to the Occidental Saloon. A
patent medicine salesman there told him he had
the latest invention to make him live to be a hundred. Chet frowned. If things went on like his life
had lately, he wasn't certain that he wanted to stay
around that long.

A finely dressed tubercular victim coughing in a
bloodstained linen handkerchief and washing it all
down with straight whiskey introduced himself in a
deep Southern accent. "I'm a dentist. My name, sir,
is Doc Holliday. You look new here."

"I am. My name's Byrnes. I live in Preskitt."

"Do you like rooster fights?"

"Not really."

"Well, we will have a big, ass-kicking cockfight
right here next Sunday afternoon. Yes sir, we have
some man-eating roosters coming from Mexico to

supplement the local birds. Hellfire man, the feathers will fly."

"You must be a breeder of them."

"I am sir. I have some of the best."

"Good luck."

Holliday laughed. "You sir, need a diversion."

"Thanks, I'm fine."

"What do you do?"

"I have cattle and a ranch up on the Verde River," Chet answered.

"Well now, that is interesting."

"It's hard work."

"Riding and roping, huh?"

"Lots of that."

"I guess I'll pull teeth. Some of them come out real hard. I also play cards. You play cards?"

"No."

"Shame. There's some real good poker games going on around town. I'm going down to the Bird Cage Theater and play some right—" Coughing broke him up.

"Good luck," Chet said after him.

Holliday made the batwing doors before his coughing made him lean against the doorframe with his shoulder for support until he recovered.

"Good luck," Chet called after him. Turning back to his beer, he shook his head at the notion the man didn't have long to live.

"He's a strange guy, huh?" the bartender asked.

"Different. That is for certain."

"You know him and Wyatt Earp are big friends?"

"No, but I met Earp once when he was in Wichita before he went to marshal in Dodge City."

"Wyatt's here in town. You know that?"

"No. I'd like to speak to him about something."

"Come around tonight. He'll be here."

"I'll try to. If not, I'll catch him later. He may not remember me, but my name is Chet Byrnes."

"Harry's mine. Nice to meet you, Byrnes."

Chet left the saloon and walked the streets in the hot afternoon. The front door of the *Epitaph* newspaper office was open when he came under the cottonwood tree. He stepped inside and nodded to a man in an apron stained in ink.

"The boss is out today. Went to see about a guy who was shot by his wife."

"Oh."

"Yeah, they're back together."

"That might make a good new story."

"Not for me. My wife shot me, I'd be gone. She wouldn't get a second chance to do that again."

Chet waved to him and laughed. "Not a bad idea."

He later stepped off into the barrio neighborhood where there were no boardwalks, and goats on ropes greeted him outside the jacals beside the ungraded street. Near-naked brown children drew back at his appearance and a woman standing in a doorway beckoned to him. She looked to be in her twenties and wore a short wash-worn dress.

"You are looking for company?" she asked.

"No, I was just walking around to see how the town was laid out."

"I can show you the barrio."

"What does your guidance cost?"

"Huh?"

"*Dinero.* How much?"

"Oh, you can pay me for what I am worth to you."

"I can afford that. Show me."

She put on some sandals on the go as she hurried to join him in the dirt street.

The girl pointed across the street. "Over there lives Señora Gomez. She is an old lady. Maybe a hundred. She is so old that she remembers when there were no gringos here."

She walked beside him, naming various residents. "That is a cantina. We have three of them. That one is for old men."

Chet saw some burros in a pen. "That a freight company?"

"Yes. He hauls supplies to some isolated villages in Sonora."

"That's the church?" he asked about the small chapel nearby.

"Oh, yes. Our Mother of Jesus is there."

Abruptly changing the subject, Chet asked, "Who would kidnap a girl and take her to Mexico City?"

"Carlos Ramaras."

"Where is he?"

"Probably at his ranch down in Sonora," the girl replied.

"Does he do that often?"

She looked stone faced and nodded. "He does it all the time."

"Do you know of any girls he sent down there lately?"

She shook her head. "But two of my best friends, he kidnapped and sold them to a brothel in the capitol. One escaped. Maria came back and told me she would kill herself if he caught her again. After that day I never saw her again."

Chet stopped walking. "I have seen enough. You're a fine guide."

They turned and walked back up the street. A thirty-pound, long-haired, black shoat cut across the street in front of them, grunting as he hurried.

When they reached her house, the girl turned to Chet. "Come back again, señor."

He paid her two quarters and she beamed. "You are very generous."

"No, you are very gracious."

She about blushed. "I am just a simple puta."

"I know that. I am looking for another girl. Her name was Bonnie Allen."

The puta shook her head very quickly at him. "I don't know her."

"I am at the Hampton ranch. You can reach me there if you hear of her."

"I will. I will. I hope you find her."

Chet left the barrio and wandered back through the town, eventually making his way to the saddle shop.

His men came in late afternoon and met him there.

JD laughed. "Today, I talked to Ivory."

"Well, what's she like?" Chet asked, sharing a grin with Jesus.

"Whew. She is—"

Chet waved off JD's explanation about her charms. "What did she know about Bonnie Allen?"

"She's scared to death. But she told me Bonnie was going to meet a man the night she vanished. And they would kill her if they knew she said anything."

"Would she give you his name?"

"Aw, hell. She was so damn scared, she was shaking, but she told me his name. It's Bernard Whittle."

"Does he live here?"

"She didn't seem to know that."

"Does he work for old man Clanton?"

"Never said."

Chet held up his hand. "I can check him out with Marshal White. We have a name. That's something. What did you learn, Jesus?"

"Carlos Ramaras."

Chet nodded. "I heard about him today, as well. What do you know about him?"

"He is a white slaver who lives in Sonora, but they doubt he would take a white woman from up here."

"Why not?" JD asked.

Jesus shook his head and turned up his hands. "He is not afraid of Mexican authorities, but he fears a gringo backlash. He could buy off any official below the border, but couldn't hold off against an attack by angry gringos before the *federales* could stop them."

"You guys can hang around. I'm meeting a waitress who says she can answer our questions tonight about Bonnie Allen."

"Oh?" JD laughed.

"It isn't funny. We've learned lots already that even the law couldn't find out. If she has some information we can use, we'll even be more informed."

"I just thought it funny, you meeting a saloon girl."

"I know. We've been walking around like blind sheep trying to get some answers. But we're finding out some things and if she knows something we may need it." Chet sure didn't need to get angry at the two young men helping him. They were doing their part under less than perfect circumstances. They'd lost a lot of time already, so speeding things up was essential.

He left the two young men and was waiting when she stepped into the cat-infested alley from the lighted back door. He noticed her looking around—ready to spring back inside if threatened by anyone.

"Over here." He waved to her. From where he stood, he had a good view of the alley in both directions. No need to take any chances no matter how sure he felt about her.

"My name is Valerie."

"Mine's Chet."

"Come on. We can't talk here. I live a few blocks away."

He fell in a little behind and followed her. "Did you know her? Bonnie Allen, I mean."

She nodded.

Chet explained, "Her mother helped me when I came to Arizona two years ago. She's a very nice lady. That's why I'm here. I told her I'd look for her."

Valerie shook her head warily. "Bonnie Allen and I worked together in another café when she first came to Tombstone. She told me she wanted to work in a parlor house. We both went to see about a job up there, but I didn't want to do that. When it got down to it, I chickened out. She always teased me about that, but I didn't care."

She opened the door to her small house. "Actually, I tried it, but I guess my conscience got to eating at me. I quit and went to a Protestant church. They took me in. I went back to work as a waitress. I was threatened if I didn't come back that I might be raped and beaten up. I borrowed a loaded pistol and let them know I had it."

Inside, Valerie lit a coal-oil light then closed the door and barred it. "Sit down. Bonnie told me about this guy who said he could get her work for some big money. I was suspicious. I am not an angel, but night after night I hated having them smothering me, and as I said, I quit." She clearly shook with her revulsion.

"Can you tell me where this guy is if he took her?"

"No one has heard from him." She shook her head and sat down across from Chet.

"There is a white slaver in Mexico named Ramaras. He in this deal?"

"I don't know. But I have heard of him."

"Was it Bernard Whittle?"

She stood up and hugged herself. "Damn Chet, how did you learn that?"

"I've been learning things these past few days to try and solve this. Is the sumbitch upstairs in one of the whorehouses?"

"No. He has a house over by the Methodist church."

"Sit down. It's okay. So he deals in this slavery business too?"

"I'm not sure of that." Valerie chewed on her lip before she continued. "She said he could get her a better job through him."

She sat down and gripped the sides of her seat. "I am not a scared person. But these guys involved in this business can really hurt you."

"I can too. I mean, hurt him."

"I want you to find her—alive. I can't tell you anything else." She chewed on her lip again. "You're a married man, aren't you? I can tell. You have a *don't touch me* look about you. Your wife and Jenn are both damn lucky to have you."

"No, I'm the lucky one. My wife isn't in the place you are. But if I give you stage fare to go to Preskitt, you can work for Jenn, and I guarantee you won't be under any pressure up there."

Valerie closed her eyes. "She won't hire me."

"I know her. You want the stage ticket?"

She shrunk in the chair. "If you don't find Bonnie, she will blame me."

"No. A ticket is twenty dollars. My men will carry your luggage down to the depot and put you on the stage. I will wire Jenn and she will meet you tomorrow or whenever the stage gets there."

Valerie wrung her hands then nodded. "I accept."

Chet went over, unlocked the door, opened it, and looked across the street where those two slim boys of his were leaning their butts on the hitch rail. They'd followed him. Their pants were tucked in their boot tops, high crown hats were cocked on the back of their heads, and silk kerchiefs were around their necks. They stood, waiting.

Shaking his head, he waved for them to come over. With smug smiles, they came loose from their braces on the rack and walked over.

"Valerie needs some help getting her things to the stage depot. We're buying her a ticket to Preskitt."

"Who will tell my boss?" she asked.

"We will," Chet said.

"Tell him I'm sorry." She began to cry.

"Don't cry, Valerie." JD hugged her shoulder. "Men can't take crying,"

"I'm sorry. I left Texas to come out here to become a woman of the night. I found I hated it. Then I was trapped here. Now I'm going to leave here and make a new start." She sniffed. "I hope it will work."

"We'll be certain it is a good start," JD said, and they helped her pack.

Chet agreed. "I'll wire Jenn and she'll meet the stage."

"How do I thank you guys?"

"Smile for us," JD said.

"That's good," Jesus added when she forced one.

The three waited with her at the stage depot and at ten o'clock they loaded her things on the stage. Chet told the driver to be sure she got on the Black Canyon Stage at Hayden Mills. He'd already wired Jenn that she was coming. She stood on her toes and kissed all three. "Thanks."

Then she smiled and climbed in the coach. The driver climbed on top, took the reins, and shouted at the ready horses. The stage rocked out of Tombstone.

"Where are we going?" JD asked as they left the station.

"To tell her boss that she quit," Chet answered.

"Do you think we can ever find Bonnie Allen?" JD asked.

Chet nodded. "I haven't given up."

"I just asked."

CHAPTER 3

The café was closed when Chet and his crew got there and it was too late to return to the Hamptons so they slept at the livery. At dawn, they went down the block and he told her boss she'd left.

He scowled at them. "Why?"

"She got a better job in Preskitt," Chet said.

"Hell, I'd gave her a raise."

Chet shook his head. "It's not your fault. She needed to leave here. Too many bad experiences."

"You all three want breakfast?"

"Yes and coffee," Chet said to him.

They took seats at the bar and coffee was poured right away. Chet felt sorry for the owner. Customers would soon file in for their breakfast. They'd miss Valerie. She had lots of get up and go to get things done.

They got their meals and watched all the mix-ups made by the new help the owner had called in. Jenn would love that girl.

"This guy who told Bonnie Allen he had a better job for her, he lives in town?" JD asked.

"Yes. We're going to watch him around the clock until we figure out his business. We'll find Marshall White and get him to tell me where this Bernard Whittle lives."

They finished their breakfast quickly and headed to the marshal's office first.

"Don't you hate walking around all over this damn town?" JD asked, making a disgusted face over their situation.

Chet laughed. "Yes, I'd like a helluva lot more to ride."

"Me too," Jesus agreed.

"Sorry, cowboys, but this one's a leg job."

They found Marshal White in his office, yawning after his all-night shift.

"Oh, morning," White said recognizing Chet.

"Morning, Marshal. This is my nephew JD and Jesus. What can you tell us about Bernard Whittle?"

The marshal acknowledged the young men with a nod. "Barney is what they call him. He has some mining interest around here. Must make money at it. He lives pretty high."

Chet flat told him, "That good old boy sells women into slavery."

"Oh, hell. I had no damn idea. You sure?"

"I think we have three good witnesses that would swear to it. He a friend of yours?"

White shook his head. Scrubbing his beard stubble with his palm, he asked, "What can I do for you?"

"I want to confront him."

"If you have word on it, I don't blame you, but I can't do much unless we have solid proof."

"You've been square with Jenn, so I decided to tell you our purpose. We'll try not to break the law."

White warily shook his head. "I walk a tightrope in this damn town with old man Clanton on the left and the mine owners on the right. Throw in the merchants trying to make a living and it's real crazy."

"You have no idea who Whittle's contacts are?" Chet asked.

"No. No idea. People do shifty things and conceal them. If he's involved in this trade, he is a master of that business."

"Any use to talk to the sheriff?" Chet asked.

White blinked at him. "John Behan? No, he's not worth a damn either."

His words amused the three standing around him.

Frustrated, Chet asked, "Can you at least give us Whittle's address?"

The marshal nodded and gave directions to the slaver's house.

"You need some sleep. Thanks for the information." Chet shook the marshal's hand. So did the others.

"I just hope you find her."

"Oh, we're trying."

They set out with JD grumbling about being on foot again. Past the Masonic Hall, they went down the hill and found Whittle's wooden framed house. They climbed the porch and heard a back door slam.

"JD go see who that was and hold him if you need to." Chet nodded to Jesus to go along and back him.

They left on the fly.

Chet knocked on the door.

A gray-haired woman answered from behind a half open door. "Yes?"

"I need to talk to Mr. Whittle."

She shook her head. "He's not here."

"Oh, yeah he is," JD said, herding a gray-haired man around the side of the house.

"What is this about?" Whittle asked angrily.

Chet folded his arms over his chest. "My name is Byrnes." He turned to the woman at the door. "Ma'am, you are excused."

She frowned, but finally closed the door.

Chet went on talking to the man. "I want to know what you did with Bonnie Allen."

"Who's she?"

Chet stared hard at the man. "Have you ever had a cactus needle shoved under your fingernail?"

"No."

"I'm ready to do that to you to help your memory." Chet held his hard stare.

Looking very uncomfortable, Whittle searched their faces. "I don't know—"

Weary of his stalling, Chet grabbed his hand and forced it open. "See that center nail. I am going jab a thick cactus needle under it if you don't tell me all about Bonnie Allen."

Whittle's face turned white. "I—I don't know. I swear I don't know where she is now."

He didn't say he didn't know where she went or with

whom. "You listening to me?" Chet demanded. "You told her you had a get rich deal for her and coaxed her away."

Whittle swallowed hard and nodded. "Some of Ramaras's men took her that night. I swear I don't know where she is now."

"He's the one who lives in Sonora?"

Whittle nodded.

Chet grew anxious standing on the porch making too loud talk. They'd soon have an open forum. Several housewives were out gossiping at a distance about what was going on.

"Let's go in the backyard. We're drawing a crowd here." No need getting any more attention.

JD and Jesus herded Whittle around behind the house where a board fence shielded them from prying eyes. Chet strode forcefully behind them.

"May I sit down?" Whittle asked, looking around.

Chet nodded. "Yes, on the steps." He stood in front of Whittle. "I want you to send Ramaras a message to come up here and meet you."

Whittle looked aghast. "Why he would kill me if it was a trap."

"I didn't get you in this mess. How will you send it?"

Whittle put his index finger on his lip. "By a boy, I guess."

"Listen, you contacted him before. You better do it right or I'll do you in."

Whittle said, "I understand. He contacted me and said he needed a certain kind of female for a certain man. Bonnie Allen fit that. This man is not mistreating her. She's living in a palace."

"No, she's being held against her will." *Thank God, she might still be alive.*

"Who has her?" JD demanded.

"Oh, I can't say."

"By God, if you don't tell us, I may put that damn cactus needle in your eye," JD said. "I'm out of patience right now."

"His name is—Manuel Baca."

Chet looked at Jesus. "Is he real?"

"Baca is a powerful man and owns much land. He has a *grande* hacienda in Sonora."

"That sounds great. How much money did they pay you for her?"

Whittle shrugged.

Chet nudged his leg with his boot toe. "Answer me."

"Five hundred dollars." Whittle sat with his face in his hands.

"Don't act like it bothered you to sell her. You're a damn slaver like the rest. You're a scummy, sorry sumbitch. Guilty of the worst crime I can think of—selling a human being. I'm about ready to hang you. You get word to Ramaras to come in here and meet you now."

"What if he won't come?"

"I may hang you. JD is going to be your houseguest and stay here. You try to escape him, warn someone, or run off, and you'll be dead. Do you understand?"

"Yes."

"Let's go. Leave word for me at the O.K. Corral, JD."

JD nodded, not happy about the situation, but

he understood they were moving on the possible recovery of the girl.

That fact made Chet a little happier about the whole business of trying to find her. Still, getting her out of this Baca guy's hands might be tougher than any part of it so far.

When he and Jesus reached the top of the hill and the main road, a wagon passed them. At the sight of Chet, a man in back with his head all bandaged jumped up and pointed at them. Next, he was trying to get the driver to give him his pistol and making loud noises as the wagon went on.

"Who the hell is he?" Jesus asked.

"A man with a busted jaw, I guess," Chet said and chuckled.

"Good thing that driver didn't let him have his pistol."

"Good thing." Chet and his man went on to downtown and lunched at the stew palace. He'd write Marge a letter to share with Jenn about some of the information he learned from all their work. There was some hope. That was the best news. While walking all over town bothered JD, not having his wife to hug and kiss was a much larger longing for Chet.

He missed her and not just a small part, either.

CHAPTER 4

Mid-afternoon, Chet sat on a stool in the stationary and print shop with a quill pen and paper to write on. He dipped the pen in the inkwell.

Dear Marge,

I hope you and the one inside are doing well.

The boys and I have been busy. Today, we learned where Bonnie Allen may be held. This all sounds real. But there are still many things that need to be resolved.

I imagine Valerie is with Jenn by this time.

I miss you more than this pen could ever tell you. I think about everything—you and the ranches' operations, you and the cattle sales, you and the wind in the pines. I miss them all.

I will be home as soon as I can solve this mystery. JD and Jesus are a big help to me.

I love you.

Your husband Chet

He put the pen behind the small strip at the top of the desk. That was enough, he hoped, to hold her until he could get home. He handed the addressed envelope to the young man who worked the shop and paid for the stamp. The letter would get mailed from there.

He met Jesus at the stables about five and they went to eat Mexican food in the barrio. A street vendor lady made them large flour tortilla burritos filed with spicy chili, meat, and beans. They sat on a bench made from a split log and enjoyed her food.

"Did you know that crazy man we saw today in the wagon?" Jesus asked between bites.

"Yes, my first day, I was in Big Nose Kate's saloon and he was smashing a man in the head with his fist. I told him to quit. He threatened me and I gave him a haymaker and knocked him out cold. Must have busted his jaw."

"I heard the start of that deal. That was him? What was his name?"

"An old-timer said it was Billy Bragg. He works for Old Man Clanton, which put me on his death list."

"I'll watch for him. He must be loco. Will they try to kill you?"

Chet shrugged. "I am more worried how to get the girl back than about them."

Jesus nodded.

After supper, Chet sent Jesus to check on JD and see if he needed any help. If JD didn't need him, Jesus was to ride to the ranch and spend the night out there. Chet went back to the Occidental Saloon, hoping to meet Wyatt Earp. Maybe the ex-lawman had some idea what to do with this bunch of slavers.

Wyatt wasn't there, but Chet talked to his brother Virgil. They stood at the end of the bar and spoke softly. The tall Earp wore a thick mustache and the black clothing that was a statement from his cow town days.

"It's hard to prosecute them. Harder to find victims to testify against them. What evidence do you have?"

Chet shook his head, indicating not much. "I'm not a lawman. But they need to be stopped."

"I agree, but these bandits will only be replaced by more of them."

Chet nodded. "I know what you mean, but about six months back, there was a big story in the *Globe Dispatch* about two horse thieves and murderers that someone hung in a dry wash at Rye."

Virgil frowned, then he nodded. "Yes, at the time my brother Morgan and I were up in Globe and we wondered about that deal in the paper."

"It cured a problem. They'd stolen horses, murdered two good men, raped a woman, and beat up a man in front of his young children. They aren't here anymore to do it again."

"You answered your own question. These law-breakers only understand one thing—"

"What do you know about this slaver, Ramaras, down in Sonora?" Chet interrupted, anxious to get the information he needed.

"He's tough. They say he's protected by a private army."

That was what Chet needed to know. He emptied

his glass and set it on the bar. "Nice talking to you. I appreciate your information." He shook Virgil's hand and left the saloon.

No message had come from JD at the livery so Chet rode out to the Hampton ranch. When he was unsaddling, Ira came out from the house and spoke to him.

"You doing any good on your quest?"

"Some, Ira. We've found some good leads."

"That's a miracle."

"I know, and there is a chance she's alive, but getting her back could be a tough deal."

"You have a hard job."

"I have been running the family ranch for near two decades. Comanche kidnapped my siblings. Three of them. My father invested his life to find them and came home broken down mentally and physically. My mother lost her mind over that very thing. I have been running down loose ends since I was sixteen or so."

"Then you came to Arizona?" Ira looked amused at him.

"No, a family feud drove me here. They murdered my brother in Kansas while he was driving a herd to the stockyards. I had to move out. I couldn't cover every one of us."

"Well, I hope you find her."

Chet nodded. He did too. In the shed, he dropped into his bedroll. It was not a good sleep but a troubled one. In his dreams, they had found her, but she disappeared from them into the fog. He woke in the hot night, his hair wet with sweat—he couldn't let that happen. *Wouldn't* let that happen. He shook his head and tried to sleep some more, but found himself awake and got up. He went behind the shed, took a cold shower, dried and put on his pants and came back around the shed.

"You can't sleep?" The voice came from the shadows when he walked back to the bedrolls.

"Bee?"

"Oh, when I can't sleep, I get up, study the stars, and listen to the crickets." Wrapped in a belted robe, she stepped off the porch and motioned to one of the buggy seats on the ground for him to take a seat next to her. "Folks who can't sleep must share some of the same haints."

"I was dreaming. Shocked me awake." He buttoned his shirt, then sat down and rubbed his face in his hands. He still needed to shave when it got to be daylight.

"Tell me about your wife. I figure she's a special person."

"She is. Marge's first husband was killed in the war. He must have been Union. An officer. She was very young. Her family moved to Arizona from Kansas and she met her number two. He was off riding by himself, got thrown and broke his neck. Then she met me. I had a woman in Texas at the time. Not my wife, but we were close. In the end, she had to remain in Texas and care for her parents. I had to come here."

"Sad?"

"Yes, but there was no way I could stay in Texas. I had committed all of us to come to Arizona."

"So you married this women."

"Marge. Yes, a great lady who puts up with me."

"You wouldn't be hard to put up with. She married a white knight. When challenged, you rise to the occasion. She knew you well enough to expect that from you."

He nodded his agreement. "I sent her a note today at the stationary store and the man there mailed it for me. Told her I hoped she and our unborn were all right."

"First one?"

"Yes. She's never carried one full term. We have our fingers crossed."

"Kids are wonderful. Ira and I lost our two children to disease after we came here."

"They tell you what it was?"

"They guessed, I suppose. It didn't help."

He agreed. "I better go and try to get some more sleep. Tomorrow may be a big day."

She rose and nodded. "I will sleep knowing you are here."

"That isn't much." He chuckled and they parted.

Back in his bedroll, he drifted in and out of sleep. At Bee's triangle ringing in the first pink of dawn, he got up and nodded to Jesus who was in the shadows, rubbing the sleep out of his eyes. "We'll get some home-cooked food this morning."

"That would be good."

They ate a generous breakfast at the house and thanked her. When they went to saddle their horses, he noticed the two grave markers on the rise north of the house. Poor woman. He thought about Marge. *Lord let that child join us.*

They rode into Tombstone and JD was at the livery waiting for them. In the street, they dismounted and Chet asked him what he knew.

"Whittle committed suicide last night."

"Damn. That cuts off us from contacting Ramaras through him, right?"

"I guess. She said we drove him to it," JD said.

"No, he committed suicide because he was caught red-handed and expected to go to prison. Of course, we had no final evidence to prove it, but he didn't know that. We're going to ride to the Baca Hacienda and make Ramaras an offer for Bonnie's return."

"He'll want lots of money, I bet," JD said, looking troubled.

Chet shook his head. "We have one chance. I think I have a key to open the door down there."

"What is that?" JD asked.

"Some of the Barbarossa blood stock we have."

JD looked aghast. "Wow. He might exchange her for some of them."

"He can't buy any of those blood lines anywhere. I have the only stallion and his colt that is outside that hacienda."

"It damn sure might just work."

"That is the golden stud I saw at the Verde Ranch?" Jesus asked. "Oh, he is a fleet one."

"If Baca won't do it, I doubt we can storm his place and survive to get her out."

"What do we do right now?" JD asked.

"We send him a letter and ask if he would trade her for a Barbarous stud colt and maybe a filly or two. There is no sense in us storming a castle."

"How in the hell will we find out his address?"

"I think that could be done. Jesus, you will have to dictate the letter in Spanish."

"Tell me what you want me to tell him and I will simply go down there and tell him for you."

Chet shook his head. "No, I need to do that in a letter first and then go down there."

"And by damn, we need to go with you," JD said. "Surely to God, he won't kill us if we have something he really wants every bit as bad as he wants her."

"Tomorrow we will head south—" Chet saw Marshal White coming toward the livery. "Morning, Marshal."

"I guess you know it. Whittle committed suicide last night."

"He don't have any cactus needles under his nail from us."

"His wife says you three caused it. You can't prosecute anyone for causing a suicide. But she's got folks up in arms."

"He admitted to us yesterday that he lured Bonnie Allen to Ramaras, who sold her in Mexico."

"There will be lots of folks at his funeral."

"That no-good son of a bitch was not a nice little man. Bonnie wasn't Whittle's first one, either. He threatened another girl who quit the trade. He was a white slaver. He expected to be prosecuted and took the short way out."

"I understand. I appreciate you coming to me yesterday. He simply had many of us fooled."

"We're going to Mexico in the morning."

White looked taken aback. "If you three are going to Mexico, I'll pray for your souls."

"Good," Chet said. "We'll need lots of prayers. Plenty of them and candles burning at the altar."

CHAPTER 5

Mexico wasn't all blaring trumpets. Two days later, they were eighty miles of desert south of the U.S. border in a small village called Costa Something. All they could see was more Mexican thorny desert. There were lots of hip-shaking women in the cantina. Castanets were cracking and guitars were strumming like bumble bees in the background, then some would-be trumpet player would raise up and play the song Santa Anna had played for the Alamo defenders—"No Quarter Given."

Chet, JD, and Jesus drank red wine and watched the cantina activity as they ate fire-roasted chicken off the bones set in a big dish in the center of their table. The tortillas were hot and freshly made.

"How much farther to Baca's Hacienda?" Chet asked the bartender after they'd finished eating.

"Another hot day's long ride, señor."

"Good, we can finally get there." Chet thanked him, paid his bill, and he and Jesus left. JD was in the doorway, kissing a lovely brown-skinned girl good-bye and promising her he'd be back for her one day.

Halfway down the street, Chet and Jesus were laughing about him. They turned in the saddle when he shouted, "Wait, I'm coming."

In a small village named St. James, they found a small cantina and a bartender who told them how to find the Baca Hacienda. Sitting on homemade benches at tables, JD and Jesus drank a local-made, thick beer and Chet had a glass of red wine. From behind the one long board on top of barrels for a bar, the man talked to them about the three whores who were sleeping and how much beer cost him.

"I can wake them up if you want to use one."

"No, not today." Chet waved his offer away.

"But they are beautiful, señor."

Chet shook his head. They needed to eat supper and find a place to camp for the night. In the morning, they'd make the ride out to Baca's ranchero.

They left the cantina and found a place to camp along the small running river and bought a burro load of firewood for a quarter. About sunset, three riders stopped by their camp. They weren't ordinary vaqueros and Chet noted they were well armed.

The one who appeared in charge, said, "Good evening señor. I hear you wish to speak to my patron, Don Baca."

"Yes, if it's no trouble. I wish to talk to him about a colt I have. I'd like to bargain with him."

The man shook his head. "Señor Baca does not

need any gringo horses. He has some great stallions already of his own."

"My colt is a Barbarossa bred horse."

"You have such a horse?" The man with the thick mustache ran his finger under his nose and looked hard at him.

"Yes. I have a great stallion from that ranch."

The vaquero shook his heavy sombrero in disbelief. "No one has one of those outside that ranch. They geld all of them they sell."

"A boy on a mare once outran their best horse in a race, winning the horse for service to his mare. He sold me this horse, the only one outside of the hacienda. Will the señor talk to me?"

Very serious-like the man nodded. "I will tell him you are coming. Your name, señor?"

"Chet Byrnes, Quarter Circle Z Ranch at Camp Verde, Arizona Territory."

The man swept off his sombrero and bowed. "Welcome to our hacienda, Señor Byrnes. I am sure the patron will talk to you in the morning at the main casa. My name is Sanchez."

"Give my regards to your patron, Sanchez. We will be glad to meet him at last."

"You are a long way from home, no?"

"A very long way."

"*Adiós, señor.* We have to get back now." Sanchez nodded to Chet's men, remounted, and the three riders left.

"Why in the hell did he come here?" JD asked.

"He's the ranch security force. Three strangers from another land come to see his rich boss. His job is to check us out." Chet sloughed it off as pure business.

"I guess. Do you think Baca will trade for her?"

"We've got a shot at getting her if she's there. It's the only thing I could figure out, save we charge in, firing both pistols at the same time."

JD laughed. "None of us have another pistol. That would be wild."

Chet shrugged. "We have to try something."

"No, no. Chet it's a good idea. You always seem to come up with good ideas. I never thought you'd sell those colts to the guy who bought the Texas ranch, but that money saved us a long trek by riding the rails to west Texas before we had to drive the rest of the way to Arizona."

Chet agreed. "Tomorrow we learn Bonnie's fate, guys. Let's get some sleep."

Next morning, the three drew some stares as they rode by the hacienda's ag projects—orchards, vineyards, vegetables, and crops of alfalfa and corn.

"Be calm," Chet reminded them. "We are guests of these people. Don't do anything rash. We didn't come to fight them, no matter how this comes out."

JD and Jesus nodded, looking serious. After a moment, JD shook his head. "We're badly out numbered by the damn field workers alone."

"Indeed, we are," Chet said.

Sanchez was waiting for them when they reached the large sprawling house. He removed his sombrero and greeted them. "Good morning, amigos.

My men will put up your horses. The women have food fixed for you in the kitchen."

Chet nodded in the lead. "That is very generous."

"Oh, you are a guest of my patron."

"I look forward to meeting him."

Sanchez escorted them to the rich-smelling kitchen. They were seated at a long table by the woman in change. The young women who worked there were excited about their guests, pouring coffee into mugs and serving them. Plates piled high with food soon were set before them by the young workers, drawing Spanish from both of Chet's men to talk with their waitresses.

Chet thanked the lady in charge and dug in. No utensils were necessary as they ate flour tortillas rich with strips of tender beef, cheese, salsa, and black beans. The three had a good meal.

When they finished, Sanchez came and invited Chet to meet the patron.

Leaving JD and Jesus in the kitchen, Chet followed Sanchez to a small parlor.

Don Baca was a silver-headed man in a fine Mexican suit. He sat at a high back chair behind a desk with hand-carved features. He rose to greet Chet, extending his hand for a shake, and then motioned for him to take a chair. "Nice to meet you, señor."

"Don, my name is Chet."

"My segundo was very impressed by your story. He's says you own a stallion from the Barbarossa Hacienda."

"Yes. He's a wonderful golden horse. I know of no other that is not on that ranch."

Baca agreed. "But why ride so far to talk to me about him?"

"Because I have a question to ask you. I was told you have a young woman here named Bonnie Allen. Her mother sent me to bring her home."

"Why would I have her?"

"I am not making judgment. If you have her or you can get her for me, I will continue the discussion about the colt."

"Can you describe her?"

"Better yet, I have a picture of her." Chet half rose and took it from his vest.

Baca looked hard at the locket framed picture. His stone face never showed any emotion or recognition as he handed it back. "What if I do not have such a woman?"

"Then I will continue my quest."

"You are a very determined man."

"I am." Chet's stomach did a flip-flop. Was Baca playing games or wasn't she there? Up to that moment Chet had been convinced Bonnie Allen was there. Was the man lying? Hard to tell.

"I am told you have some large ranch holdings in Arizona."

"We're busy. How do you know about me?"

"I make it my business to know the men I want to do business with."

Chet nodded at his words. Baca damn sure was thorough. "That is fine. I am here for one thing, the return of the woman. I came to offer you a trade for her safe recovery. I have a fine Barbarossa colt. I would not sell him for a million dollars cash, but I would trade him for her."

"Has anyone offered you that much for the colt?"

Ready to tell him his real feelings, Chet shook his head. "He and my stallion are the only intact males off that ranch."

Baca tapped the desk with a fingernail. "I am amazed you rode down here with two boys. Mexico is a dangerous land."

"Those boys are men. If we had been challenged, I would not have worried. They're serious."

"What if you have lied to me about this horse's blood lines?"

"I don't have to lie about that. You will be proud of him."

Baca looked at Chet for a moment as if piecing something together. "Where will you look next for her?"

"I'll trace down more leads."

"What if she isn't alive?"

"I'd need to find out who buried her and get thorough proof she's dead."

Baca shifted slightly in his chair. "So you thought I had her and needed your colt. I am amazed at your skills. You must be a success at ranching."

"I work hard at that too. We are furnishing cattle now to the Navajo Agency."

Baca shook his head. "Start for home, mi amigo. In the morning, if I can find her, she will join you. My segundo will come for the colt in the fall when it is cooler."

"What if you can't find her?"

Baca shrugged. "Then, as you say, you will go on looking for her."

"That, I plan to do, sir."

"Yes, I believe you. You are a determined man, Byrnes."

"Thanks for your talking to me today. You have a beautiful hacienda." Chet left the man at his desk and went back to the kitchen, wondering, did Baca have her? Would he trade? Chet felt he had stuck a pin in the man, but he'd make a great poker player.

"Get the horses," he said to his men busy flirting casually with the kitchen girls gathered around them. "We're going home."

JD gave him a questioning look.

Chet dismissed the inquiry and tossed his head. "Let's go."

They kissed the girls on the cheek and fell in behind him. Their horses were hitched at the rack. Sanchez was not in sight. Ready to mount the roan, Chet decided to tell them part of the story. "We can talk on the road. The issue is not resolved—yet."

Satisfied, both nodded. The three rode away from the great house. On the dusty road going north, Chet began. "The matter isn't settled. Baca said if he could find her, he'd deliver her to us in camp in the morning and for us to head for home now."

"What about the colt trade?" JD asked.

"If he finds her, he says Sanchez will come in the fall for the colt."

"He must trust you."

Chet nodded. "He must. But he never admitted he had her."

"We could never find her if they had her hidden

on the ranch." Jesus shook his head. "Such a huge place."

"Aw, hell, Jesus give us a break. We want her and if she's there, we'd find her," JD said.

They laughed, but Chet felt it was an uneasy one. He looked back at the red tile roof behind him. He still didn't know this Don Baca and probably would never know him well enough. Behind that poker player façade, Baca was a complicated man. Chet couldn't congratulate himself for his idea of making a trade. It would only work if they received Bonnie Allen in their camp.

His thoughts turned to his wife. How was she? They'd be well over a week getting home—maybe ten days. He shuddered. Just so that it all wasn't in vain. . . .

Chapter 6

Chet sat on his bedroll, musing. The mesquite smoke from the campfire filled his nose as the fire ate at the dry wood he'd bought from a wood peddler, the red-yellow flames licking the air. He listened to night insects, an occasional coyote, and the hoot of an owl or two. There was a vast world beyond that fire. He, the boys, and their horses were but a grain of sand in all of it.

JD and Jesus had turned in earlier, and Chet felt quite alone in the world.

Suddenly, he heard horses. They drummed the ground. In an instant, he rushed around to wake the boys. "Riders coming."

They came awake and sat up with their pistols in their hands.

The lead horse stopped at the edge of the fire's light. Sanchez's familiar sombrero outlined him on his horse.

"Hold it. It is Sanchez," Chet ordered. Among the riders, he saw a woman's face under a sombrero.

"Here is your woman, señor. I will be at your ranch this fall to get that colt."

The words stung Chet for a moment, then he saw her dismount and rush to him in a dress and slip. A man rode forth and gave JD her reins, then heeled his horse to go back to Sanchez.

"Yes. Sanchez. We will show you our best hospitality." Chet walked forward and shook his hand. "Tell Don Baca thank you. Her mother will be grateful."

"*Sí.*" In Spanish, the segundo told his men, "We must ride." In a thunder of hooves, they were gone in the night.

Chet turned to the sobbing girl being attended to by his two young men.

"Oh, you must be Chet Byrnes. Mother wrote me about the man in her life."

The reflection of the fire shone on her wet face. He pulled loose his kerchief and dabbed her cheeks.

She finally took it from him and scrubbed her face. "I am sorry but when they told me they were taking me to a man who had bought me—I feared the worst. Sanchez finally told me your name and I knew I was saved." On impulse, she hugged him before giving back his kerchief.

Chet stuffed it into his pocket. "We better get some sleep. It's long ride home."

"I'll put up her horse," Jesus said, and undid the bedroll tied on her saddle.

Chet nodded. Some day he'd learn her story. It wasn't important at the moment. They needed to get back home and to the ranching operation. He gave a sigh. *Jenn, we have her and she is coming home in one piece . . . I hope.*

They settled in their own bedrolls. Bonnie and JD were still talking.

That was all Chet needed. He frowned at the direction of his thoughts. That was being cruel. He had his own life to live, not JD's. He rolled over and tried to sleep, but it escaped him as his mind continued to wander. Busy trying to settle all his operations problems, he'd be in the saddle a lot when he returned. But the trip to get back first across the desert country would be another challenge. Bonnie's homecoming would be a celebration. It would be good to sleep in his own bed . . . with Marge. He finally fell into troubled sleep.

He awoke before dawn to the smell of coffee. JD, Jesus, and the girl were busy with breakfast preparations.

Chet noted in the fire's light her slender, willowy form and how she naturally flirted with the two of them. Busy rolling up his bedroll on his knees, she came over and sat down beside him.

"Your men have told me that you ransomed me with a very valuable horse."

He nodded. "That is no worry. There are more horses."

"I'm very grateful that you came for me and did that. I know your friendship to my mother sent you here. When she first wrote about you, I thought she might marry you."

"No." He hoisted the bedroll on his shoulder to put on the packhorse. "But we were and still are great friends."

"When the four of us make it to the border, you and I will take a stage home. I hate to ride them, but I need to get home. JD and Jesus can bring the horses. Did they tell you I sent your friend Valerie to Preskitt?"

"Is she all right?" Bonnie asked.

"She's fine. She wanted out of Tombstone."

His bedroll loaded, they joined the others at the fire, sat down on the ground cross-legged, ate the boiled oatmeal, and drank coffee. Their fire dusted out, all four mounted up and headed north in the growing day's heat.

Without an incident, they reached Nogales in four days. Chet told the boys to take a day's rest and then head north with the horses. He gave each of them ten dollars and paid the livery bill for the horses and the grain bill. Then he bought two tickets for the Tucson stage and in an hour He and Bonnie were rocking in coach seats going up the Santa Cruz River valley. They arrived in the walled city at night and learned their next stage to Papago Wells was leaving in an hour. Chet hurried to the telegraph office and sent news to Jen and his wife that they were on their way home.

A quarter moon hung in the sky behind them as the stagecoach headed for Picacho Pass station. At the stage stop, they disembarked with the others. Two salesmen who had snored all the way were still acting sleepy. Light came from the stage office that left a path where the stage had stopped.

Out of habit, Chet shifted the gun belt on his

waist. Under his breath, he spoke to Bonnie. "The facilities are out back. Be careful, there isn't much light."

She nodded. Most of the trip she had slept, never complaining and no doubt worn out from the hard push they made to get out of Mexico. When they rounded the building two masked men armed with six guns told them to raise their hands.

One of two salesmen stuttered. "W-who are y-you?"

"Shut up." One of the robbers spun them around to face the other direction.

"Don't faint," Chet said to her.

She took the clue and crumbled to the ground.

Both robbers backed up in shock. When they looked up, they faced Chet's drawn six-gun.

"Drop your guns. Who wants to die?"

The two reconsidered and dropped their pistols.

Holding his gun steady, Chet glared at the robbers. "You two get facedown." When they were on the ground, he nodded to the salesmen. "Help her up, then hold their guns on them. Someone is holding the driver and stage bunch inside."

He nodded to her, busy dusting herself off and then rushed around the side of adobe building. He could hear someone ordering the people around inside and eased along the wall, counting on the man's back being to him. Fist closed on the cocked revolver, Chet said to the outlaw, "Drop that gun or die."

The robber whirled and before he could shoot, Chet put a bullet in his heart. The shot's percussion put out the lights and gun smoke filled the room.

The outlaw crumbled to the floor and everyone rushed outside. Chet backed out on the porch.

Bonnie rushed to hug him. "You all right?"

He holstered his gun when she backed off. "I'm fine. Better go tie those two up for the law."

Someone fetched a lamp. The two highwaymen were securely tied and the stage agent said they'd be turned over to the sheriff. The agent took his Chet's name and address. Bonnie's, too. "Oh, I thought you two were married."

Chet smiled and shook his head. "No, she's more like my daughter."

"The company will send you a reward, sir. Thanks again."

When all passengers had climbed back into the stage, it left the station. Wheels whirling, dust boiling, the thunder of the horses' hooves and creak of leather accompanied their ride. At the big well where many Indians and wagons drew water from the source, Bonnie and Chet switched to the next stage.

By themselves on the Hayden Mills stage, they made the various stops at stations along the way, drank bad water, and ate worse meals.

"We can get a room here and rest or go on."

She wrinkled her small nose at his offer. "Let's go on."

Grateful for her decision, Chet hurried inside the station and sent telegrams about their arrival time. He was anxious to get back to Marge.

That task finished, he and Bonnie climbed onto their ride north in the twilight, and he listened to her story.

"An older man told me I could live in luxury and only have to entertain a few men for the man who would pay me lots of money for my efforts. He told me that I'd be paid two hundred fifty dollars a month and have to service less than a dozen men a month. That is a good wage. He lied. I was held in jail-like quarters and there was no pay."

"Baca ran that place?"

"He may have owned it, but the man who ran it was named Conduras. There were drugs if you got too stir crazy and they whipped the girls who talked too much to their dates. No one stayed at that place for very long before they shipped those girls to Mexico City. I think they shipped them there when they were through with them."

He nodded. "We found that old man in Tombstone. Under house arrest, he committed suicide. There is another man named Ramaras, lives in Mexico."

"That bastard."

"I'm sorry. What did he do to you?"

"He gave me three days of rape and hell before he sent me to Conduras."

The lurch of the stage about threw them on the floor. He straightened her up and they both laughed.

"Shame I didn't get him, too."

"He's a real cruel one. How can I pay you back? I would do anything I can for you. JD said he thought you were very loyal to your wife."

Chet nodded. "I'm made a pledge to her when I married her. In my time past, I'd have been flattered by your sincere offer and accepted it. But those days are behind me."

"Did you ever consider my mother?"

"No. I love her, but not as lover." He slid down on the seat and folded his arms. "My sister Susie is, maybe, a little older than you and engaged now. She told me back in Texas to find a nice chunky German girl to marry who'd have my children."

Bonnie laughed and leaned over and kissed him. "Thanks anyway. Did you look for her?"

He shook his head. "I had an affair with a woman whose husband mistreated her. My enemies murdered her before she could leave him. I found her body and a note saying she wanted a divorce. She must have written it before the killers arrived. I tore it up."

"That must have been tough."

"Yes, it was. Another woman and I became very close. Her husband was dead." Chet skipped the fact he'd hung the man a few years before for stealing his horses. "She had parents to care for and had to stay in Texas. I had to move my family here to get out of a war."

"I knew Margaret before you met her. She was very rich and had a real fancy husband who— cheated on her."

"Oh?"

Bonnie elbowed him and smiled in the dim starlight. "He'd not said no to me."

"He got himself killed in a horse wreck?"

"Yes, and not a shady lady in Preskitt cried."

"Marge and I have a nice marriage. I don't question her past and she doesn't mine. We may have a baby next year. I really enjoy our lives together."

"Did she agree for you to go rescue a soiled dove?"

"Yes, she did."

Bonnie chewed on her lower lip. "I take back all the bad things I said about her in the past. Really, you are one of the most honest men I've ever met. When they took me to you I worried about you being my new master. You never asked me a question about my past or anything."

"My intention was to get you back to your mother. She's worried about you being in Tombstone ever since I met her."

Bonnie threw her hands in the air like she was feeding chickens. "You know, some of my times in this business were heaven. I thought I was a queen. But the black days were being beat up. Hurt by mean men for no reason and having to do things that made me sick. Do you think I could change and live a real life?"

"It would help to have some religion. Then, if you believe in God, you'd have someone to help you. I don't think leaving your profession will be easy. The thrills of that lifestyle will be hard to replace in ordinary day-to-day life."

She nodded and her chin slumped. "I'm glad I'll be home to think on it all. You are right. I went down there because I was bored to death in Preskitt. I wanted to dance on tables and seduce rich men. I thought I was good enough to seduce one in that crowd and he'd make me a rich mistress."

"I suppose you never found one?"

"Those bastards don't marry whores. They want to marry a rich family's so-called virgin and then go back to whoring around 'cause she never bucks in bed." Her laughter made him smile.

"Well, you are captain of your own ship today. I hope you find a way to live out your life."

"I will."

"Good."

She reached over and squeezed his hand. "I hope I have some of your strength."

"You will. You will."

CHAPTER 7

After Bonnie's disclosure of what had happened to her, Chet's mind drifted. How were his ranches doing? Sarge must be driving cattle to the Navajos. Who will meet the stage? Chet expected Marge and Jenn to meet them. He was ready to hug and kiss his wife. There were lots of unanswered questions for a man with a lovely wife and a life in Arizona.

A huge roar interrupted his thoughts. The crowd was there when the stage swung to a stop. The driver was laughing when he came down and undid the door. "What is this, Mr. Byrnes?"

"Bonnie Allen's coming home party." Chet stepped down, then took her hand and led her out of the coach.

Bonnie waved and called, "Hello everyone. It is so good to be back home."

Jenn raced to her, squeezing her in a fierce hug

and they went to shouting and dancing around in the midst of things.

"Good to have you home," his wife said in his ear, holding his arm.

"Better yet to be here." He turned and kissed her hard. Damn, he was glad to be back.

"Did you have any problems?" she whispered.

"Only at Picacho Pass. There were three holdup men. I had to shoot one of them." He leaned in close. "The baby all right?"

"He kicked me." She smiled big. "We're all going to drink champagne at Jenn's café. She said the bars were too rough to celebrate in."

"Good idea. Is Susie engaged?"

"Oh, yes. They will get married in three weeks."

He nodded that he heard her. "I can tell you more later." He looked around. "The whole troop is here. There's Hampt and May even."

"I sent them word."

Chet hugged and kissed his sister-in-law. "How are things?"

She about swooned in his arms. "Wonderful."

"Good."

"Great," she said, sounding as excited as he could recall she'd ever been since he knew her.

He shook Hampt's hand and then clapped him on the shoulder. "It's good to be home. How are things at your place?"

"The grass is coming back. If we get some more rain, I'll be back in the ranch business. We were lucky to have any regrowth. Those Hartleys let all them cows eat them out of house and home."

"It will work." Chet looked around again. "This is quite a party."

"I wish Hoot was here, but he was too far away tell him about it."

Chet nodded.

The wave of people moved up the hill toward Jenn's Café, singing and enjoying themselves. Jenn came in on the other side and hugged him with a bump of her hip. "Is she all right?"

"She's fine. Has lots to think about. She may find her way back."

Jenn nodded, matching his steps. "How much do I owe you?"

"Nothing. You helped me a lot and you're a friend."

"Oh, you must have spent lots of money going and coming."

"The most important thing is she's here right now. We have to convince her it is worth staying."

"She said you paid a fancy horse for her. How much was he worth?"

"A million dollars."

"Oh, land's. What was he?"

"A colt from my stallion."

"Why my lands, Chet Byrnes. You gave that expensive horse for her?"

"It was just a horse. Bonnie is here now. Don't worry. I can raise more horses. You can't raise another girl."

Marge squeezed his hand and nodded.

The lights were on and the café was open. Valerie rushed over and hugged him. "I do have a place in this world." She looked at Marge. "Oh, Margaret, I am so glad you let him go look for Bonnie Allen. I'd never be here otherwise."

"He's a real lifesaver," Marge said to her.

They went to a booth in the back and let Bonnie Allen meet her friends and well-wishers. The bubbly flowed, and several people came by and talked to Chet.

"Who was holding her?" one asked.

"I'm not sure. She can tell you, but I went to the biggest, richest man in that district and made him a swap. One of my horses for her. He got it done."

"Lucky that they didn't kill you," another offered.

"No one bothered us. The boys will be back in a week. Bonnie and I took the stage from the border."

"There was a robbery?" one asked.

"Some men tried to hold up the stage at Pacacho Peak station. Two went to jail and one to boot hill." He was chuckling. "I am getting a reward from Wells Fargo and or the stage line for doing that."

"Can we go to San Francisco on it?" Marge asked as the crowd around the table drifted off.

Chet frowned. "Who wants to go there?"

"I am teasing you."

"I need a lot of teasing and lots of you."

"So do I. Would it be impolite to simply go home?"

"No. Is your team and buggy here?"

"Outside and ready." Marge grinned.

"Let's tell them good-bye and go."

"I was afraid you'd never ask." They both laughed.

* * *

The drive home was dreamy.

When they got there, Marge found a nightshirt, soap, and a towel and they went down to the outdoor shower by starlight. To Chet, the water was cool and the night air even colder. He laughed and kissed his wife, then they ran to the house.

Monica was making coffee and heating a skillet on the stove. "I figured he needed to eat to have energy enough—" Embarrassed, she laughed.

"I'm going to shave him," Marge said, shaking her head, amused over Monica's comments.

"Well by damn, it is good to be home and have two wonderful women fussing over me again."

"You will think it's wonderful," Marge said, getting the shaving mug and a razor out of the cabinet.

"Hey. Any bad news from around here?"

"Not really. But you've been gone three weeks."

"We were on her trail or trying to find it all that time. Did you get my letter?"

Marge nodded. "Yes and I am saving that. Not many women have letters from their husbands."

"I just wanted you to know what I was doing."

"Oh, Reg sent you a letter. I opened it in case he had a problem."

"That's good. What did it say?"

She bent over him, razor in hand "You can read it after I get you shaved. All right?"

"Sure."

When the shaving was finished, Monica brought coffee and the letter. Chet turned the page to the light.

Dear Chet,

Lucy and I are busy as beavers chasing down mavericks. Our count is over two hundred branded and we figure there are a lot more. These cattle are wild. I don't think some ever saw a horse and rider before in their lives. Most are straight longhorns, but they are big meaty animals.

I am so glad I found her, and we are having so much fun. I can't tell you thanks enough for inviting me out here. How is JD? How is Mom? Tell Susie I said hi. She ever going to get married?

The house is coming along fine. Time you get up here, it will be built. Then they plan to build the cook shack and bunkhouse. Maybe we will get it up before it snows. My wife says it does that most years.

I don't know what I'll do if it does. I have only been in one snow in my life . . . where we lived in Texas.

> *Sincerely,*
> *Lucy and Reg*

Chet laughed. "He sure may see some real snow this winter."

Marge grinned. "Those two are having too much fun together. I can't believe it. Should you send him help?"

"No, I think they want to be by themselves up there. So they can get off their horses and make love whenever they want to."

"Oh, no."

"Yes, I think Reg found himself a real woman

who loves him and she don't give a damn where they are."

"But you said—"

"I said Juanita was lovely. Pretty girl—but all pretty girls aren't that loveable."

Marge shrugged and chuckled. "Well, a man would figure all that out."

The breakfast meal served, Monica went back to bed.

Marge sat on Chet's lap and they fussed around kissing and playing with each other. "Let's go to bed," she whispered.

"I thought you'd never ask me."

She began slapping him easily, like she was mad. "Dang you, anyway. Saying how Reg don't want anymore help."

"Aw, I'm ready to go to bed."

"Good thing." They went upstairs for another honeymoon.

In the morning, he and Marge rode to the Verde in the buckboard. She wanted to talk to Susie about her wedding plans.

Thinking of what needed to be done yet, Marge said, "My wedding dress is way too long for your sister. We've tried to alter it, but there's no way to make it work."

"We can afford a dress. Have her come into Preskitt and have one made. I'm getting a reward from the stage people that should pay for it."

"Oh, we don't have to wait for that, silly."

"I know. Just teasing."

"Now, how did you ever figure out that man would trade Bonnie Allen for a horse?"

"I have three quarters of an idea he never had her, but he must have known who did. Probably some Mexican pimp. So he sent Sanchez there and bought her, then sent her to me for the horse."

"When does he get the horse?"

"His man is coming for him, sometime in the fall. His name is Sanchez."

Chet reined the horse for the descent off Mingus Mountain and looked across the great valley spread out to the Mogollon Rim in the north. The sweaty horses acted impatient, but he stopped them to let them settle down some before going down the steep grade off the mountain. He turned and kissed Marge.

She hugged his neck afterwards. "I'm glad to have you back. Oh, your baby kicked me again."

"Wonderful." He shook his head, amazed.

Her smile beamed.

They reached the ranch at mid-morning and Susie came out on the porch. She and Marge hugged each other on the top of the stairs. Then his sister hugged him.

"You're back I see. Did you find her?" She looked up at him for her answer.

"You remember what Dad always said?"

"No, not really."

Chet grinned. "Don't send a boy when you need a man."

She drove her fist in his muscled gut. "Is JD all right?"

"I left him and Jesus in Nogales to bring the horses."

"Was she all right?"

"I think she was, but she's had a hard lesson. We'll see."

"Our man," Marge said proudly.

"Come in. I am going to talk to my brother about hiring a new employee."

"What do we need?"

"Sit down. I have hot water and want to make some coffee." Susie hustled around and added the coffee, telling them about a cowboy who broke his leg and that the doc had come out and set it. The cowhand was hobbling around up at the cook shack and couldn't wait till he could ride again.

She sat down and folded her hands on the table. "Leif needs a job. His dad doesn't have a very big ranch. Since I am a part owner, I can't cowboy, but can my husband work here? I would like to live in this big old house, even by ourselves."

Chet considered her request. "Let me think on it. I like him. No reason we can't find work for him. I don't want to anger Tom, but he doesn't have Hampt or Sarge any more. He could use Leif."

Susie clapped her hands. "Thank you. Sarge sent word they were on their way to New Mexico. He needs four hundred more head to add to the ones he has on hand for the November drive."

"I better line some up and send them up there, hadn't I?" Chet grinned.

"Yes," Marge said. "That means buy some cattle from ranchers around here."

He agreed, feeling good that his contract would start helping the other ranchers. He'd order a hundred head from four different men Saturday night to start his next month's sale.

"I think we have all our herds cleaned up here," he said to the girls.

Susie agreed. "That's what Tom told me, too. We compare notes a lot. He can hardly wait for those Herefords to start dropping calves on the Perkins Place."

"I am ready, too."

"Since my dress won't fit you, why don't you ride back with me tomorrow and we can get your dress order turned in?" Marge said.

Susie nodded. "Why am I so cold-footed about doing that?"

"You don't have much time left," Marge said.

"Maybe I'll wear one of my good dresses."

Chet couldn't take it any more. "Scaredy cat. Go with Marge, and get the dress fitted tomorrow. I'm going up to see Reg."

"That can wait until Sunday," Marge said. "You need to order cattle from the other ranchers at the dance on Saturday night."

"All right. Susie, you ride back to town with us tomorrow and I'll check on the lumber deal tomorrow and be back here Friday night."

Marge had a better suggestion. "Why not come back here Saturday and not ride yourself in the ground? I'll be here waiting and we'll have her dress ordered."

"Well, right now I want to check on the cook shack and tell Hoot about Bonnie Allen coming home. He knew her, too."

"Susie and I will cook supper. Come back and eat with us."

"Yes, ma'am." Chet gave her a mock salute.

Marge frowned at him. "Well, I know you, you get to talking and forget."

He kissed her. "Susie, I am so henpecked." He hurried out like they'd both get him for complaining.

He found Hoot and they sat down to talk. Things were going fine according to the cook. The crippled cowboy was peeling potatoes.

"You ever break your leg, Mr. Byrnes?" the puncher asked him.

"Chet's my name. No, I broke an arm as a youngster, but never my leg."

"I'll be so glad when it heals. I hate being the cook's helper. I'm a cowboy, not a cook."

"You could have broke your neck and been dead, too," Hoot offered.

They all laughed.

Late afternoon, Tom and the cowboys rode in from various points after checking cattle and watering holes—just regular ranch work.

Chet told Tom about his ordeal in Mexico.

His foreman nodded. "Poor girl was sure wild before she left. I hope she found herself."

"She may have."

"Where are you headed next?"

"The lumber camp. Then I may ride on to see Reg. I am going to order four hundred head of cattle from ranchers at the dance on Saturday. Should we keep them bunched or drive them up to Sarge?"

"We can do either."

"Each month, we will need six hundred head taken up there."

"Whew, that's over seven thousand cattle a year." Tom shook his head.

"I hope so. We can use that shot in the arm and so can the other ranchers."

Tom agreed. He turned to the men. "Any troubles out there?"

They all shook their heads.

He turned back to Chet. "Things are going fine, boss."

Chet nodded. "Let's go outside. I have one more matter to discuss."

Out under the pines, Chet told him that Leif Times was going to be his new sub foreman, since Hampt and Sarge were gone.

Tom laughed. "You have another family member, huh?"

"Might as well work for the best outfit, hadn't he?"

"What will JD think about it?"

"He's got another brother, I guess. He'll be getting back later this week."

"Boy, you had some adventure."

Chet agreed. He'd had a helluva time in Mexico. "Oh yes, a man named Sanchez will be here for the yearling yellow colt. I traded him for Bonnie Allen."

"We can handle that, too," Tom said and they shook hands.

The girls came out to the porch. They were ready to go.

Tom walked with Chet to the wagon. "Drive easy. Good to have you back."

Chet agreed. He helped the women into the wagon and climbed aboard.

CHAPTER 8

Marge wanted to go with Chet so badly she almost cried when he left the Verde ranch on Sunday morning after the dance. But after a long discussion between them about how fragile they considered her pregnancy, in the end she sent him off with a teary smile.

Past sundown, he reached the sawmill and the man in charge of his horse teams operation, Robert Brown. He had Chet's horse put up and found George the cook to fix him some food. They sat under a coal oil lamplight and drank fresh hot coffee.

"Things are going good up here," Robert said. "We're chopping logs and getting enough stacked up so they'll have timber to cut when the snow flies. The books show we are making money above our expenses each month. We have fifteen horse teams and eighteen employees counting George and me."

"What do we need?"

"Probably five more younger teams. Some of these horses are getting age on them."

"I will look for them. I guess these guys are selling their lumber?"

"We have hauled a lot to Hackberry. I went once up there. Your nephew Reg is sure a hardworking guy and his wife Lucy is really funny. I'd never thought there were as many mavericks up there as they've caught."

"I'm going up to see how they are doing."

"Well, they've driven lots of nails on those projects. It will sure be a great place when you get done."

"Robert, you've done a great job here. As long as we can make money, I intend to keep hauling logs."

"Good. I'll share that with the men. We are away from things up here and wonder sometimes what's happening."

"Hampt has the Hartley ranch we bought. He says it's coming back since we've have had some rains there. Sarge is handling the ranch we bought up on the high plains in the east. He's shipping six hundred head of cattle every month to the Navajos at five delivery points and they are satisfied with our deliveries. That's the best market we can reach until we get the railroad here."

"The mill people sure want the railroad here. It will open the lumber business with rails to ship it on."

"Oh yes, and more mills will move in and compete with them."

Robert agreed then changed the subject. "I met a lady the last time I was at the dance. I just want a nod that I can attend it more often. You won't miss anything. These men work hard."

"What is her name if I may ask?"

"Betty Jean Rhodes."

Chet nodded. He'd met her. The tall blonde reminded him of some of his sister's choices for him among the German girls in Texas.

"I wish you the best in that matter. Attend the dances with my best thoughts. I appreciate the way you are handling this sawmill operation."

The next morning, he met with the mill people. They were pleased with Robert and his men's efforts. McKnight, the superintendent, talked about Chet's needs and asked if he knew anything about the railroad.

"Nothing. But it is coming, depending on financial things back east."

After the meeting, they shook hands and Chet headed north on the good roan horse he'd chosen back at the Verde Ranch.

The San Francisco Peaks stuck out ahead as he followed the wagon tracks that joined the Marcy Road near their base. He smiled. His real estate man Bo Evans was supposed to be buying him land up there. He'd have to jar him loose again.

A wagon train was camped just west of the junction. He reined up to talk to a few men standing near the road. He dropped out of the saddle and introduced himself. "How are you folks?"

"Joe Andrews," a gray-headed man said, sticking out his hand. "We're pilgrims from Kansas, looking for new country. They say there is irrigated land available south of here. A place called Hayden Mills. You know about it?"

"I have been there. They grow barley, alfalfa, Mexican field corn, and grapes. Some places have citrus and date palm trees."

"What about water?"

"The Salt River and the Verde feed them with a year around supply."

"Is there room for more farmers?"

Chet nodded his head. "I am not a farmer, but the land under cultivation looks like it is a garden of Eden."

"Have you ever taken this road west?"

Chet shook his head. "No. I have only been part of the way to the Colorado River, crossing into California."

"They say it's hell to cross to the California coast."

"I have never been there."

"We don't know what to do. How far is Hayden's Mill from here?" Andrews asked.

"A week or so on horseback," Chet guessed.

The men discussed the matter among themselves.

A tall man in overalls asked him, "Where could we park the wagon train while a few of us go to Hayden's Mill?"

"I have a ranch at the bottom of the hill in the Verde Valley. You would be welcome to leave your families there while some of you went to see that land."

"We aren't beggars. Some of us can do blacksmith work, others are carpenters. If you let us park, we will respond in kind."

"Hey, I have a large ranch. I must warn you, the road downhill is steep and you will have to use logs to brake on the rear wheels of the wagons. We've hauled lumber for a while now. Stop at the log mill and see my man Robert Brown. He can tell you how to handle the grade.

"After that, take the first road right to the Quarter Circle Z ranch after crossing the river. Tom is my foreman and my sister Susie Byrnes will meet you and show you a place to camp. Tell her I said you could camp there while some of you look at the Salt River land."

"That is very generous of you."

"This is the West. We can afford to be generous. We need settlers to build our economy."

"You have several businesses?" Andrews asked.

"A couple cattle ranches, a log hauling business, and a contract to sell beef to the Navajo agencies."

"What do you have up here?"

"A large cattle operation we are building on deeded land."

"Deeded?"

"Yes. A man bought land that had been granted to a railroad company. He traded that land for several sections—sight unseen—of sagebrush and juniper-pine woods west of here. When he lost his backers and the government wouldn't take it back, my land agent found it, bought it, and my nephew Reg is developing it."

"We'll talk this over and talk to your man at the sawmill—"

"He's a good ride south. But he can tell you about the steep road down to Camp Verde."

"Good. We will do all this then we decide if we should go west. We thank you for your generous offer," Andrews said, and they shook hands.

Chet left them and rode on. The rolling open country held mule deer that bounded away at his approach and antelope that did the same, only faster. Big-eared jackrabbits bounded off, too. The pungent sage perfumed the air and fat clouds gathered for an afternoon shower somewhere on the high country he crossed.

By late afternoon, he began to doubt he could reach the high ranch before sundown and found a spring and made camp. A small pot of fire-boiled coffee and some jerky made his evening meal. He reflected on his time spent with his wife and her disappointment about not coming along. This was their honeymoon country, discovering the ranch with Lucy, Reg's new wife.

Before sunup, with the last coyote yapping at the setting moon, Chet had his horse saddled and the packhorse loaded. He squatted and drank the last cup of coffee before leaving. Satisfied the fire was dead, he climbed on the roan. For a long moment, he thought the horse was going to buck, but he talked him out of it. Leading the packhorse, he rode on. Taking a shortcut north, he caught sight of several cattle wearing a fresh Quarter Circle Z brand and two notches in the bottom left ear.

The ranch house stuck out on the next horizon.

A smile crossed his face as the sound of hammers and saws reached his ears. He had not looked at the ranch books in several weeks, but no doubt, it was a drain on the ranch reserves. But the high country was going to be great ranch land when it was developed, when tanks were dug, and windmills supplemented them.

He dropped out of the saddle and Lucy appeared at the door wearing a dress and waist jeans under it. "Wow! Wait till Reg learns you're here."

Chet removed his hat. "Is he around?"

She reached for a rope attached to a bell and rang it hard. "He don't hear that, we can try two rifle shots."

At the top of the new stairs, Chet hugged her ample rock-hard figure to him and kissed her cheek. "How did he get away from you?"

She blushed. "I had to do some house work or move out. We love this house. It's not finished, but Reg wants a bunkhouse for the hands before winter. He's up there where they're cutting hay around the trees and sagebrush."

"Is it working?"

"Oh, yes, but it looks strange to see the areas where they mowed the grass and areas where they didn't. Reg is set on having lots of stacked hay and he wants alfalfa planted, too."

With his arm on her shoulder, she showed him inside. "It needs lots of work to be a house. There is my fireplace." Lucy pointed across the room.

The large native-rock structure looked impressive. The hearth contained ashes.

"It must work?" Chet asked.

"Oh, yes. Works great. I can't wait until fall and I can fire it up."

She showed him a bench and went for the coffee on her wood range. "My sisters are so jealous of my range. They only have an old sheet-iron thing to cook on at home."

"Maybe they need to marry a Byrnes."

"Oh, Chet, I never thought I'd find such a great guy as Reg." She shook her head. "I am so happy. I think he's coming in. I hear a horse on the run."

They heard the sound of boots taking the stairs two at a time, and Reg burst through the open doorway. "Chet!" He tossed his hat aside, hugged and kissed his wife before crossing to shake his uncle's hand. They embraced.

Reg grinned. "How in the hell did you ever think to buy this ranch? Man, it is pure heaven up here."

They sat down facing each other.

"I'm sorry this was all I could find for the two of you" Chet teased.

Lucy and Reg laughed as she hugged Reg from behind. Those two were lovers. Maybe more than him and Marge, if that was possible.

"Any problems?"

Reg shook his head. "The days are too short."

"Wait until winter. Everyone is fine at the main ranch. Sarge is delivering cattle to the Navajos."

"Marge's letter said you were down on the border looking for someone's daughter?"

"Jenn, who has a café in Preskitt. She helped me find the crew and was so good to Heck and me when I was buying the ranch. Her daughter disappeared in Tombstone and JD, Jesus, who is Marge's horseman, and I rode down there, looking for her. Busy place, but we found a trail south to a hacienda and made a deal and got her back—no shots fired."

"Wow."

"I found an influential rich man who wanted a Barbarossa colt. We made a trade."

Reg drew his head back at Chet's words. "You must have wanted her back real bad. What would that colt bring in Texas?"

"I said a million dollars."

Reg nodded. "What is she like?"

"She knows she barely survived the experience, but what she will do next I don't know. Her mother could not deter her before from leaving. I only know she is back and Jenn is appreciative."

"How did JD do?"

"I worry about him. He's not the boy who rode with us after the horse thieves. Oh, he was good help, but he doesn't act like anything pleases him."

"Did that start when he helped that woman leave her husband?"

"Near as I can tell, yes. He left that deal bitter and fell into a bottle and a bed of doves."

"What can we do?" Lucy asked, frowning and concerned.

"Lucy, he needs to find himself. He's near twenty years old. He can do anything he wants on our ranch. But nothing seems to appeal to him. He'll have to find his own way. In the meantime, what's happening here?

"We're still cutting hay. I know the men need to go back and cut the alfalfa on the Verde, but we can wind up here in a few days and let them go back."

"Good."

"How is Marge?" Lucy asked.

"Did she hint she was expecting?"

"Oh, yes, but I expected her to come with you."

"We are being extra careful. She has never carried a full term pregnancy before so we decided it best for her to stay home. She cried about not being able to come along."

"Oh."

"The baby has kicked her. She was so excited. She's never had one do that before, either."

Reg stood up. "Let me show you the progress on the bunkhouse and then we'll show you the haystacks. The house can be finished inside when the snow flies."

"I can put up the packhorse," Lucy said.

"No, we will. You can ride along with us," Reg said to his wife.

"No, you and your uncle have things to say to each other that I don't need to hear."

"Lucy, we don't say much that doesn't include you. Come along."

"Chet, I just don't want to become a bossy woman. Reg puts up with me, but you don't have to, that's for sure."

"Lucy, I wish you were a little more honest when you talk to us," Chet said dryly.

Reg hugged and kissed her. They all three laughed then headed outdoors, Lucy to put up the packhorse and the men to inspect the haystacks.

Reg's haystacks looked like giant teepees. He had lots of hay ready for winter. He explained how he'd need tall fences to keep out the elk when winter drew closer. Chet figured Lucy was behind that notion. She'd lived in that country and knew what problems to expect. The mowed land did look like a checkerboard haircut, but it had solved his hay situation for the year.

The building projects were moving on. Reg showed where he wanted to plant alfalfa. He was going to rail fence it, then plow and clear the patches of sagebrush.

How he'd become such a farmer, Chet blamed on Lucy. He sounded like someone else he knew and chuckled to himself.

"Tomorrow we'll go chase mavericks," Lucy said when they were riding back. "We have some rank old range bulls that need to be cut and branded."

"Sounds like fun," Chet said.

"It will be," Reg said. "Right now, I am planning to have about a hundred good cows on this outfit by next spring. Will any of your Hereford bull calves be big enough?"

Chet laughed. "No, but we can buy some."

"I think we have a hundred fifty big steers, barren cows that we can sell this winter," Reg said.

"We're delivering for October now. I think we'll be all right for then. Tom and I bought some cattle at the dance."

"Things will get tight in the winter for buying cattle, won't they?"

"Not for a while. There's lots of cattle we can buy in north Arizona and folks will be glad to sell them. But in time, we may need to import some from other areas."

"There are a lot of Mormon ranchers in the

White Mountains. They may be able to supply some."

"I'll have to find them."

Reg agreed.

The next morning they set out to catch more cattle. As they rode, Reg told Chet how to catch them. "Rope the big guys around the horns—no small feat—and then ride past them, throw the rope over their back, and head south. That will flip them over. Lucy or I will use a pigging string to tie the legs up while the bull is stunned by the flip."

They located three older males in the brush and eased them into an open area. The bulls weren't moving fast, but Chet knew that didn't mean they couldn't run and charge. He watched as Lucy and Reg caught the first bull.

Lucy swung a large loop over her head and sent the blocky gray horse in for the kill. Her rope sailed from her hands and dropped dead center over horns on both sides. She jerked any slack then spurred the gray until he was running beside the bull. In place, she flipped the rope across the bull's butt and turned her horse aside, wrapping the rope on the saddle horn. She was riding south. *El toro* was going west. When the wreck came, the bull did a somersault and Reg rode up to do the tying. Lucy had swung her horse around and was reeling up her rope.

Chet rode up to them. "Nice job."

"It's easy to do on these big bulls. They're old

and not hard to catch. Them yearling mavericks can really run," Lucy said.

"Oh. I can see that. JD told me you two were great at this business."

"He's a good hand with a rope, too. He just hasn't done as much roping as Reg and I have."

Chet shook his head. "No, you two are an unbelievable team at this job."

"Reg broke this gray horse for me. Dad bought him a few years ago, but I never could ride him. He threw all of us girls, but after a week of Reg riding him and roping off him, I got him back. He's a great tough horse, but I'm still careful. I think sometimes he may try to buck me off again."

Reg stood and mounted his horse. "Go get the black one next," he told her and reined his horse around.

Chet stayed and built the fire they'd need to brand the cattle. The third bull was tougher and took up trying to hook them with his horns. A mature longhorn bull had long thick horns, unlike steers whose seldom got very long. The dark hided one obviously had a temper and when they rode up on him, he'd charge and cause them to quickly ride away.

Watching the pair ride in and out, Chet was ready to shoot the damn bull and let the buzzards have him. But Reg and Lucy were dedicated to subduing him. Lucy finally roped him. Reg made a pass to distract him and the bull charged him. She flipped the rope over his back, charged off to the side and threw the bull on his back—hard. The collision about unrooted the gray, but she rode it out.

Reg was off his horse immediately and three-footed him. By then, the bull was really mad, but all he could do was strain on the pigging string, a rope thick enough to hold a ship in dock. He flopped on his side like a helpless fish out of water and bellowed.

The irons were hot. Reg swiftly removed the first bull's seeds while Chet slapped the brand on him. Lucy ducked in and notched his ear.

"Leave him tied," Reg said to them. "We'll do the other two and they can lay here all day. We can come back and turn them loose later. It will teach them to be humble."

Everyone laughed. Branding completed, they put out the small fire carefully. Using canteen water they completed that job, then rode off looking for more mavericks. Chet enjoyed the company of the two. Lucy fed them some fried apple pies she had made the night before.

"How many more mavericks are up here?" Chet asked them.

"We don't know. Lots of them drifted up here over the years."

"There are lots of lazy ranchers, too," Lucy said. "They have had no easy markets so the incentive to work cattle wasn't there. My dad and a few others drove some cattle and sold them to the miners down on the Bill Williams River. We also drove some down to the Colorado River and sold them. The Havasupai Agency has also bought our cattle. It wasn't much, but that's how we survived living up here. "We also butchered cattle and sold the meat to wagon trains on the trail west."

"When we're ready to ship cattle from up here, I'll be sure to buy some cattle from your dad and the others who have worked so hard," Chet said.

She slapped the saddle horn. "They'll, by damn, be glad to hear that news." Then she shook her head. "I guess a wife shouldn't cuss, sorry."

Reg rode in leaned over and kissed her on the cheek. "Lucy, we don't give a damn."

They laughed some more. Before the day was over they'd branded six more younger cattle. Swinging their ropes and laughing with Chet, they rode by and untied the former bulls who staggered to their feet with little fight left in them from being tied all day. It was near sundown when they reached the ranch. The cook, Harry, waved them over.

"I saved you three supper. Had to use a hard spoon on a few of them hands but we have it."

"You're the greatest," Lucy said as she dismounted.

A youth named Willy took their horses and Chet shook his hand. "Nice to meet you, Willy."

"Reg talks about you all the time. Him and his brother had a real life in Texas growing up with you."

"Yes, a tough time, but we made it. Thanks for taking care of the horses."

"Yes, sir."

"That's Lucy's cousin," Reg said. "He's making a hand."

Harry told them the hay crew was heading home in the morning. "They have it all stacked."

Chet was glad. His hay contractor at Camp Verde

needed them back. "I'll see them off and thank them."

They took places at the table and were joined by some of the workers. Chet stood to speak. "Next year, we'll need mowers, rakes, teams, and a beaver-board for this place. I guess we need a couple plows and teams for this winter."

"Mr. Byrnes, where is your next ranch going to be?" one of the men asked.

"I don't know. I have more now than I can oversee."

"Hey, some of us have been working for you for over a year. We sure like working for you. We hope you have more for us to do."

"Thanks. I appreciate all of you mechanics. This is a long way from your families, but you all have done a great job. Maybe we can form a company back in Preskitt to do construction and you can work near home. I'll look into it."

A cheer went up. "Some of you know Jenn from the café. Two of my men—one was Reg's brother JD—and I went to Mexico and brought her daughter Bonnie Allen back from the hands of some evil men."

"You need to be the damn sheriff," someone shouted.

Chet held up his hands and smiled. "I could not hire all of you as deputies."

Laughter rippled in the crew.

He sat down to eat and gently elbowed Lucy beside him. Under his breath, he asked, "Did you two save those three bulls for me?"

"Naw, we've been practicing our roping on

Chet put his hand out to stay Reg. He rose slow-like. His right hand itched, but he had to think, not shoot. Innocent people could die in any wild crossfire. "You got some invisible brands we ain't seen?"

"You can't come up here and brand every calf out there."

"You the law?"

"By Gawd, we aim to make the law. Those cattle belong to the local ranchers."

"My name's Byrnes. I own that brand and those unbranded cattle belong to the rancher who catches them unmarked."

"Steward's ours. We intend to stop you."

"No, you either intend to die in those clothes or do a term in Yuma County prison if you even try."

"You can't shoot all three of us—"

"I can," Lucy said, parting the batwing doors. She fired a rifle shot into the floor.

In the deafening blast and the choking gun smoke that boiled up, the three found themselves covered by Chet's and Reg's drawn pistols.

"Get your hands up and get out of here," Lucy ordered.

Her rifle barrel pointed at them, the three men walked outside, followed by Chet and Reg.

On the boardwalk, Chet disarmed them and shoved them to the wall of the saloon to check for more weapons The card players stumbled outside coughing on the smoke.

"Damn Lucy. Next time use a smaller caliber."

The man's words echoed with laughter from the crowd.

Chet was satisfied the gunmen were disarmed. He stepped back and looked at Reg. "You have a justice of the peace up here?"

"Sam Goody. What do you intend to do?" Reg asked.

"Someone go get Sam," one of the card players said and a boy set out saying he'd get him.

In twenty minutes, court was set up in the aired-out saloon and the word was out. People rushed to make the event. The saloon was filled with men and, on the porch to listen, were the womenfolk and kids.

In a rumbled suit, Sam sat on top of the bar with a wooden mallet and block of wood to control order and hear the case. He was a short, fat man with small eyes and a white beard with a loud voice rusted from shouting. "Order in the court." He slammed the hammer on the board. "By the laws of the territory of Arizona this court is now in session. Any one making an outbreak will be fined ten dollars. Am I clear?"

Heads nodded.

"Now, who are the defendants?"

A man with a deputy badge stood up. "The men being charged with disturbing the peace and terroristic threatening are Wade Steward, Jefford Steward, and Clyde Steward."

"How do you plead?"

"Not guilty," Wade said, jumping up and pointing at Chet and Reg. "These sons o' bitches are stealing our cattle. No one will stop them."

Sam hit the board. "That is a ten dollar fine for that outburst. You will have your time to testify. Pay the clerk right now."

Wade nodded and dug the money out for the bald-headed man who obviously was the clerk.

Sam directed the other two to plead their case.

"Not guilty," each said. They did so without any other word.

"Who is swearing out this warrant?"

Chet stood. "I am. Chet Byrnes."

"Step up here, take the oath, and sit in that chair, Mr. Byrnes."

"Yes, Your Honor."

"Now, how did this all take place?"

"Reg Byrnes and I came into the saloon, met the bartender, ordered two beers and took them to a table over there." Chet pointed across the room.

"Continue, sir."

"We'd been busy working mavericks all day. We wanted a few quiet minutes while his wife Lucy shopped. We were minding our business when these three brothers came in, ordered whiskey, and demanded to see the men branding the maverick cattle. All three gave statements what they'd do to anyone branding maverick cattle.

"Wade threatened us openly if we did not cease our operation."

Sam nodded. "He told you to stop branding mavericks?"

"Yes sir."

"What happened next?"

"Reg's wife Lucy saw the conditions in the saloon as threatening. She fired a rifle shot at their feet from those batwing doors and ordered them to get their hands in the air. That ended the matter. We disarmed them. Your Honor, if armed men can demand that ranchers stop legally branding range cattle, this territory will never become a state."

"Did you feel threatened by their actions?"

"I have been in such gunfights with unreasonable men before. These men were at the point of being unreasonable unless I agreed to stop branding maverick stock on my own deeded land."

"I want the men in the room now, who were in this room when it happened, to stand, come forward, and take an oath to tell the truth."

Several men rose and walked to the bar where Sam sat.

The clerk rose and took the Bible over to them. All touched it. "Do you swear to tell the truth?"

"Yes," rang out as a chorus.

"Did Mr. Byrnes tell the court the truth as it happened?"

"Yes, Your Honor." Several spoke, others nodded.

Sam looked at Chet. "They have verified your testimony about the altercation." To the witnesses, he said, "Go sit down."

He turned back to Chet. "Mr. Byrnes, I understand you are a rancher in the Verde Valley."

Chet stopped. "Yes, and I own nine sections of land up here where Reg and Lucy are building a ranch for us."

"Thank you, sir. You may return to your seat." Sam looked at the audience. "You, the short one. Stand and come up here and take the oath."

He did—looking stone-faced.

"Sit down," Sam ordered. "What was your business in that saloon?"

"My brothers and I were tired of these land grabbers gathering all the unbranded cattle up here that should be shared by all of us."

"Wait. Mr. Byrnes owns eight or nine sections of private land. How much land does your family own?"

"We have a homestead."

"A hundred sixty acres?"

Steward nodded.

"Then if you three were to get on your horses, by virtue of the land your family owns, you must be entitled to at least a dozen head. How many mavericks have you branded lately?"

There was titter of laughter that Sam frowned at.

"Oh, some." Steward shrugged.

"Well, I'd say rather than threatening these people, you need to get off your asses and catch your own mavericks. I am fining the three of you one hundred dollars apiece for disturbing the peace." Sam hammered the board. "Court adjourned."

Chet thanked him and the clerk, then went out to join Lucy and Reg in the street and to shake hands with the other friendly, supportive ranchers.

"What do you think, Chet?" Reg asked.

"I'm going to send four good men up here. Don't you two go mavericking alone any more. This incident is not different from how the Texas feud started. It could become wildfire serious in the event of one death. Any of those cocky Steward boys steps out of line and there will be a shoot-out that will kindle a big fire. Reg protect what is ours, but don't let them lead you into that form of action."

"I'm not taking any of their shit, Chet. Lucy says they're blowhards."

"No, they're jealous ignorant fools, but that's what starts range wars and feuds. They want what we have without working for it. In there, Sam the JP, called their bluff. 'How many mavericks have you branded?' 'None.' That won't stop them from causing more trouble."

Chet knew that mavericking had been fun for Lucy and Reg. He'd just stopped it to prevent a feud busting out. "They'll catch you roping, not paying any attention, and shoot both of you in the back."

He shook his head to try and clear the dread he felt in his skull and stomach. Way too damn close for anything.

"I think we can go home." He had to stop and shake hands with several more men who passed on the word that those lazy boys wouldn't brand many mavericks. That was work. They appreciated the three of them for stepping in to cut off the bullying folks. He thanked them for their support.

He turned to Lucy and Reg. "Let's get out of here."

They mounted up and headed to the ranch.

"Chet, are you really concerned about a feud sprouting up with them?" Lucy asked.

"Yes, I am. Back in Texas, I'd known those Reynolds boys all my life. They never were good cattlemen—I'd called them hog farmers. We had some fistfights after school. My brother held my books and I once fought two of them.

"But the older they got, the cockier they got and the better our ranch did, the more they bad-talked us. We lost some horses. I am sure one of those boys took them, but I couldn't prove it. Rumors were spread about us. How my father was going crazy and we'd lose the whole thing. Hell, I'd been running the ranch for a few years by that time.

"I told you about some of them raping and murdering a woman who intended to be my wife. Reg told you about them stealing our remuda and the three of us running them down damn near to the Indian Territory. Women in that family told people it was a joke and they'd brought the horses back.

"I'm sorry, Lucy. I saw the same thing happening today in that Hackberry Saloon."

She rode in and clapped him on the shoulder. "We'll be careful for you."

"No." He dropped his head. "Make it safe for those kids you two will have and Marge and our baby."

"It'll be a spoiled thing," Lucy said, shaking her head, amused.

They laughed and rode home.

At the ranch, Harry had food ready for them. Lucy hugged the old man and the effort made that bald-headed, old devil's day. Chet considered her a great treasure for his nephew and the family. Lucy was simply a big-hearted, happy person.

* * *

Reg and Chet spent the next morning talking about what needed to be done yet. The buildings projects were getting along fine, but Chet wanted them finished soon.

"I'll push them at the mill harder before the snow flies so you will have the material you need to finish up here. So, despite the snow we can get done. I am hiring two or even four good hands for you if I can find them. Keep your eyes on the Steward bunch and don't you and Lucy go off after mavericks and let them bushwhack you." He still felt like something bad would come out of the lot of them.

Midday, he left and rode for home. His plans were to stop at the sawmill, check with Tom on the Verde place, and then get back to his wife before he rode off to see about Sarge and his crew. Things went uneventfully, except he swore there was frost on his blankets after camping out near the base of the San Francisco Peaks. He about froze to death making a fire for coffee.

By the next day, after his mill visit, he used the steep military road to come off the rim and the sun coming off the mountain warmed his bones. He reached the Verde operation before sundown.

The "howdy, stranger" from the crew made him shake his head. Hoot had supper ready so he and his about-to-be-a bride sister ate together while Hoot excused himself.

"Those two all right up there?" she asked, taking a seat across from him.

"Those two are in love, my dear. I've never seen the likes of their magnet-like relationship. They are still out roping mavericks and they can do it sweet and smooth. Except . . . while I was up there we had a run in with the Steward brothers, some local ranchers who accused us of hogging all the mavericks. Does that ring a bell?"

"Sounds like the Reynolds to me."

"Amen. I froze in my tracks." He shook his head. "Lucy says they're a lazy lot and want all the others to do their work."

"That sounds like a bunch of no accounts."

Chet agreed. "I told Reg I'd send them four cowboys and not to go out roping with only each other."

"Did they cry?" Susie laughed and shook her head.

"I knew they didn't like it. I was not afraid of those goons. I was afraid for Reg and Lucy."

Susie agreed. "What else?"

"The workers have the house done outside. They're working on the cook shack and bunkhouse and plan to finish the inside of all that this winter. So I came home."

"Your wagon train is camped west of here. Nice people. The leaders are still at Hayden's Mill looking at the situation. Their blacksmith made Tom a big spit to roast a whole steer on for the wedding."

"That's good. I'm going to get a few hours sleep and get on home. What is JD doing?"

She chewed on her lower lip. "We have not seen him since he came back."

"Is he in Preskitt or at Marge's?"

"Someone said he went back to Texas."

"Did he rob a bank? Where did he get any money?"

"Honest, Chet, I have no idea."

"I'll check on him and let you know. Sorry. This is your wedding week?"

"Yes. Leif and I are going on our honeymoon in Oak Creek Canyon at the Bailey's cabin. My nephews and my niece showed me how to fish this week. They stayed three days with me this week while May and Hampt had a little time to themselves."

"She happy?"

"Oh, yes. She sings."

"Sings? I never heard her sing outside of church and then she had a tiny voice."

"That was the old May. This one can sing and she has the best time with Hampt. I am almost jealous."

"It's good she's happy, but don't be jealous." Chet stood. "Get me up in a few hours. Thanks for the meal." He turned back. "You get your wedding dress?"

Looking wet-eyed at him, Susie began to cry. "Yes, and it is too pretty to wear. Oh, I didn't intend to cry—honest. Your wife is such a sweet person. I always wondered why she paid your bills when you first came here. That's simply her way. I know that now."

He swallowed hard.

She stood up and he hugged her, patting her back. When she recovered, he went upstairs and slept four hours. Near sunup, she woke him and fed him a small breakfast and coffee. He left his weary horse in the corral, chose another roan, and rode on before the hands were up, leaving Tom to handle whatever came his way.

Mid-morning, he came up the drive and Marge ran out on the porch.

"Stay there I'm coming," he said, dismounting.

Jesus was there to take his horse. "Good to see you hombre. How are you?"

Chet clapped him on the shoulder. "Things going all right?"

"Oh, *sí*. Everything is fine here."

"Wonderful. I better go see the boss lady, huh?"

Jesus looked up toward the porch and smiled. "I think she always misses you when you are gone."

"Good thing," Chet said, anxious to kiss and hug her. He climbed the porch steps and wrapped her in his arms.

"At last you are home," she said, squeezing him. "How are you?"

She whispered to him, "Wonderfully pregnant."

"That's what we want. Let's go take a bath and I'll change clothes."

"How is everyone at the ranches?"

"Fine, except my sister is scared."

Marge nodded. "I know that. We can talk later. It is a little cool for the outdoor shower." It sounded like she was concerned for him.

He shook his head to dismiss her worries. With her leading the way, they went through the house and kitchen, where he told Monica hi, and straight on to the back porch. He quietly asked Marge, "Have you seen JD?"

Tight lipped, she nodded.

"You give him money?"

She nodded again. "Should I not have done that?"

"It's no problem. I never thought about it until I asked Susie. She said she'd not seen him and that she had not paid him."

Marge nodded, looking a little upset. "You didn't want him paid?"

Chet shook his head then hugged her to reassure her he wasn't mad about it. "I should have known you were the soft heart in the family. It isn't anything, except he's probably either drunk or on a binge."

Arms full of bath needs, they went to the sheepherder's shower. The cold water about stopped Chet's heart as it struck his skin when he pulled on the rope. Whew. In combination with the cooler air sweeping his bare skin, the bath was a very quick task for him. Marge laughed the whole time, drying him off.

Under the long-tail nightshirt, he shivered going back to the house with her.

"Oh, did JD tell you why he needed the money?"

She shook her head. "I guess I should have asked. He said you'd pay me back when you got home. I said for him not worry about that." She ruffled Chet's hair. "You need a haircut. Want me to do it?"

"Sure. Go get a bowl."

She broke out laughing. "I'll go get scissors and a sheet. Oh, your friend the deputy came by."

"Roamer. Was he looking for work?"

"He never said so. Said he was working up here now and just dropped by to say hello."

"I'll look him up this week. Do they have a new baby?"

"Oh, yes and I guess they're working on having another," she said quietly.

They laughed again.

Inside, she went after things to cut his hair. Monica brought a ladder-back chair for him to sit on and asked how his trip was.

"Fine. We have ranches all over, but things are moving along at a good pace. My sister Susie, as you know, is getting married Saturday night."

"She is such a sweet person. I really like her. We all three went to the shop and she was so pretty in the gown at that fitting. Leif's a lucky man to be getting her."

"She's been my right arm for years."

"And I think you did the right thing for her," Marge said, coming back with her things, "when you took her away from feeding the cowboys."

"I broke her heart, but maybe Leif can mend it."

Marge agreed. "Monica and I have talked about it. We think he's strong enough to do that."

"Good."

"Lunch can wait. Get shaped up here," Monica said and left them.

When Marge was well into the haircut, Chet asked her, "Where was JD going?"

"I am not certain. Said he met a woman somewhere and needed to go see her."

"That might be a shock, too."

They both laughed.

* * *

The next day they drove into Preskitt. They went by and saw Jenn at the café. Bonnie and Valerie were working as waitresses. Both girls greeted them heartily and each of them kissed him on the cheek.

It was after lunchtime, so the crowd was gone. Jenn took a break, leading them to a back booth and she bubbled on how good things were going. How hard the two girls worked and how having two nice-looking girls serving food had increased her business.

Chet asked if she had seen JD. Jenn hadn't. In turn, she stopped Bonnie when she passed by to refill their coffee cups. "Where did JD go?"

"I am not sure, Chet. He was in here, oh, a few days ago."

"Valerie where did JD say he was going?" Jenn asked.

"I'm like Bonnie. I'm not sure. He wasn't very talkative that day with me. Bonnie had his attention."

They all laughed and Bonnie blushed. "Not so."

Jenn told the two it was fine and Chet would find him.

"I need four top hands for the ranch at Hackberry. They better like to round up mavericks 'cause Lucy and Reg do that seven days a week," Chet said.

"I'll find them," Jenn responded.

"Thirty and found. But they have to know how to rope and wear a gun."

Jenn frowned. "Trouble up there?"

"No, but you never know when it will start in. A big ranch is always a good place to steal from. Are you coming to my sister's wedding Saturday night?"

"We drew straws. I get to go. Those two are watching the store."

"I need to see Bo about some land deals. We better get going," Chet said.

Jenn and Marge exchanged a quick hug.

"I'll find you some cowboys and send them out to Marge's place to find you," Jenn promised.

Chet nodded. "Thanks."

The two drove over to the real estate office. Bo was behind his desk. He even looked clear-eyed and rose to shake Chet's hand and say hello to Marge. "Have a seat. I have news."

"Good or bad?" Chet asked.

"I've found two sections west of the road junction at the base of the Peaks and I can buy them for twelve hundred dollars. The seller needs the money."

"Are they on the track survey where we can have a siding to load cattle?"

"Yes."

"I'd take them."

Bo grinned. "Good, 'cause I already bought them."

Chet laughed. "How is Jane?"

"Mean as ever. It's like being married—excuse me Marge—it's like being married to a hellcat."

"Good. She'll keep you lined up."

"I agree. I am busy selling property."

Chet nodded. "What a nice way to live."

"Oh, hell, I don't have hangovers to get over, anyway."

"Have you seen Roamer?"

"He may be up at the livery. I ain't sure he gets on that well with his boss these days."

"Sims better thank his stars he has him. The sheriff won't get off his ass to get out of that oiled chair."

"You running for that office?" Bo asked.

"Hell, no. Now show me on the map that land tract that you bought for me."

"Right over here on the wall."

Both Chet and Marge went to look at the location of the property. Bo pointed it out and Chet nodded. He'd had an idea where it was, west of where he found the wagon train camped.

"Good. We will see you later." He and Marge prepared to leave.

"What? No land title you need cleared up?"

"Not this trip. Tell Jane hi for us."

"I'll try, but she's ornery." Bo grinned.

"Just what you need," Chet called as he and Marge left the office.

He found his deputy friend at Luther Frey's Livery sitting on a milk stool in the alleyway and whittling.

Frey's wife talked to Marge in the office while Chet and Roamer had a short visit. Things were fine with his friend. Their new baby was doing good. Had a helluva pair of lungs on him according to his father. He'd only gone by Marge's place to visit. Things were quiet since the Apaches were calming down, except for horse stealing, and

Roamer said that was due to so many folks traipsing back and forth though the country.

Chet told him about the arrow in his saddle and finished with, "Those two won't kill anyone else's saddle."

They both laughed.

Marge came out of the office and they headed home. She reminded him about the liveryman's wife and how she had worked in a brothel to feed her kids. Frey got her out and married her and she was pregnant, too.

"I hope Bonnie and that other girl Valerie find themselves a place in life," she said.

"You never can tell. JD was the best young man and he's a real worry now." Chet drove down the hill toward the Preskitt Valley and home, *Where in hell has that damn near-grown boy gone off to?*

Marge kissed him, turning his thoughts in a different direction. Damn he was glad he had her.

CHAPTER 9

A big crowd was gathering at the schoolhouse for the wedding, including Robert Brown from the mill—no doubt to court his girl. Jesus and another boy from Marge's crew had set up a sidewall tent earlier on Marge's orders. It was to be the bride's quarters. A fat beef was barbequing on a large spit the wagon train blacksmith had built especially for the event. A hundred dishes of food covered the tables. Women and teenage girls became the security force to shoo flies away.

Marge walked up to Chet, watching all the activity from afar. "I'm going to get Susie from the ranch with the buckboard."

"You may have to drag her," Chet teased.

"No, in the end, she'll come." Then she checked around to be sure no one was close before she spoke again. "I don't think she's been kissed by anyone four times in her entire life. We talked about it. She'll be ready."

"Thanks. I'll be here. Drive easy. You have lots of time."

"No worry, Mr. Byrnes, I will be careful."

He joined the ranchers and their hands under the shade of the cottonwoods. They had a pint of whiskey or two they were passing around, but he declined any. The touch of fall was turning the hardwoods. Cottonwoods higher up on the rim were already golden yellow. He planned to go find a big elk before it snowed.

Casey Monahan from the Three Stars outfit said the elk bulls were screaming up on the high country. Chet hadn't heard any, but made some mental plans to look for them when he rode up to the east place. He saw Sarge and some of his men ride in. The poor man had secretly admired his sister, but had never moved an inch toward her. Chet would bet there were more men in the crowd who had put their boots under her table and felt the same way.

Sarge reined to a stop and dismounted. "The last trip went wonderful. No Indians. No stampedes. We may be getting better at driving cattle. Tom says he will have the next sale cattle ready so we can take them home Monday, if that's all right."

"Sure. You two are the mainstays I count on. This cattle deal may be the best one yet for the ranch until we get trains in here."

Sarge shook his head. "Not much news about the rails ever coming at Gallup."

"Waiting for a train to build tracks is strange," Chet said. "Then one day, they come at a mile a minute laying track."

"We like herding cattle when things go smooth. I know winter is going to be hell."

"We can handle it." Chet shook the man's hand.

Sarge told him Jenn had arrived and he wanted to talk to her. Chet had gotten Sarge from her, like so many others she'd found for him when he'd started out.

Hampt and May, the boys, and the girl arrived. The two boys beat the adults and their sister over to talk to Uncle Chet about teaching Susie how to fish. The two were wound up. May had made them matching shirts. In their felt cowboy hats, new jeans, and boots, they looked spiffy. *"We taught her. Where is she?"*

"She and Marge are coming," Chet told them.

"Good. We could teach her, too," Ray said. His brother echoed, "We taught Aunt Susie good. She caught some big carp, too."

Chet shook Hampt's hand and hugged May as they caught up to the boys.

"I'm going to have a baby," she whispered to him.

"Wonderful," he said. "So are we."

"Oh, I knew that. Is Marge behaving?"

"Oh, yes. It kicked her, and she about raised the roof over that."

May smiled. "She'll get tired of that soon enough. Hampt's happy about it, too."

Hampt quickly agreed. "Everything okay, boss man?"

"If you are," Chet teased.

"Oh, God. I'm fine and about to bust my buttons over the baby deal. That woman is so good to me—"

"I understand. We're damn lucky to have them."

"May's worried for a week. She's going to sing

'How Great Thou Art' today. My land, she can sing, but she's afraid she won't be able to do it."

"I'll encourage her."

"Her father paid for piano and singing lesson when she was a girl, but she said she was so insecure she never played or sang for your brother. I found an old piano at a sale and we had it tuned. You need to come over and hear her play. She's real good."

"Hampt, for an old, uncouth cowboy, you ain't half bad at this marriage game. May's been around us for several years and I never knew a thing about her skills. Marge told me all about it."

Hampt shook his head. "She sings all the time at home. It is so great. I can't believe no one ever got it out of her before. She has them boys singing, too."

Chet shook his hand again, and went on to see the newest arrivals—the Yeager family. He had recovered their horses stolen by outlaws in Bloody Basin. They'd come a long way. Shelia hugged him and he shook his hand. They visited and asked if it was all right for them to join the festivities.

"Lord yes. My sis is my favorite relative and I have a boatload. Good to have you. Speak to her today. She'd like to meet you and so would my wife Marge."

"We will," he promised.

The ranch woman Gail Cloud, who'd helped them down by Hassayampa City, came over to Chet and introduced her husband Clay. Pumping Chet's hand, the man thanked him for the return of his good horses and for taking care of his wife while he was gone.

Chet excused himself. Folks from all over were filing in, along with the bride and his wife returning from the lower place.

He escaped the effort of the sheriff committee to get him elected the next fall. He took a taste of some meat sliced off Tom's steer. Tom's crew had gone and gotten mesquite wood to cook it and it tasted so damn good.

"She looks beautiful in that dress." Marge had come up behind him.

Chet turned and said, "Glad I didn't miss it."

"Oh, you. Come on. I brought a brush for you to use. You look all right, otherwise."

He laughed. "We've been busy. You know I should have invited Reg and Lucy."

"They came."

"Oh, that will please Susie."

Marge agreed and brushed his hair, then kissed him. "Well, family head, let's go give your sister away."

He made that walk down the aisle with his beautiful sister, talking in low voices to each other.

"Too many folks are here to have it inside," he said to her.

"Oh my, Chet. I am so high and I had nothing to drink."

"I know that. But breathe once in a while so you don't faint."

"What is it? In me?"

"It is part of the process. I had it when I married Marge. Enjoy it. You will be happy. I promise you."

"I'll try. I'll try."

He squeezed her hand. "I love you, sis. Have fun."

She gave him a short nod.

May sang her hymn and the crowd grew so quiet, he wanted to run over and kiss her when she finished. Hampt was there. Good.

The couple was married by the pastor.

The food—a banquet and a large cake—was served and enjoyed by all. Chet had a chance to speak to Reg and also told May how powerful her song was.

On the crowded dance floor, Chet waltzed with his wife and she beamed. "This was some wedding."

"I'd say you and Tom need a big hug or kiss."

"His wife helped us a lot, too."

"Everyone worked."

At last, the two newlyweds were off to an undisclosed location. Marge put her arm through Chet's. "This night should set the stage for their life."

He agreed and said a small silent prayer for the newlyweds. Then he and Marge were off to the tent to sleep—some anyway. Closing the tent flap to shut out some of the cooler night air sweeping off the rim, he smiled to himself. They'd have a honeymoon, too.

Monday morning, Chet was at the Verde ranch to help get the cattle up that Sarge and his men, along with some of the headquarters' crew, were taking to the east place for the November allotment. Things went well, aside from a horse breaking his leg in a hole and having to be destroyed. The herd left by ten a.m. and would be up at the ranch on top by Tuesday evening.

The cattle move was well on the way, so Tom and Chet rode back to headquarters together and talked about all the projects they had going on. Tom had rented a place to wean the Hereford calves to have a good winter growing space. They wanted to use the Hereford bulls as yearlings and that required a growing ration over the winter. They also wanted to get a crop of calves from the heifers as two-year-olds rather than at three years. This project would take some care, but the profits forced them to do it.

Tom was cutting out the cows that didn't have calves that season and culling them. Those culls could go to the next Navajo drive. This made it a big project for his men to cut those cows out on the range from the others and to send them back to the main headquarters. They had the skills. It was no small deal, but a good one.

Chet reached his wife mid-afternoon and went inside out of the cold wind sweeping the porch. Monica brought him coffee and smiled. "Margaret said you were the absolute father of that family walking your sister to the altar."

Smiling at her words, he hugged her shoulder and laughed. "I impress her too easy."

"No. You are the father for many of us and we love you, big man."

"Good. Thanks for the coffee."

"You are most welcome."

"I hate to think summer is about over." He

shook his head, slipping into the Morris chair and smiling at his wife on the couch. "But it was cold this morning and getting colder. I hate to think about it. Being a Texan, I am certain it will be tougher up here than I knew down there."

Marge smiled. "Monica, go bring that jacket we had made for him." She turned to Chet. "Trust me, you won't freeze in it."

Monica left the room and he frowned at Marge.

"Don't worry. You won't freeze." She popped up and helped her housekeeper hold up the coat. "Here is your birthday present. Try it on."

The jacket was made of leather, the inside lined with sheep wool. He eased into the sleeves and smiled when it covered his shoulders. "Wow, I damn sure won't freeze in this. You two are schemers. I can tell you don't want me to sit by the fireplace all winter, shivering."

They laughed and nodded. He slipped it off and Monica took it back. Then he kissed his wife and softly thanked her. They stood in each other's arms for a long while. Damn he had a good life.

A week passed without an incident. Marge's ranch crew worked hard stock piling firewood at the house and bunkhouse. They had lots already cut, because the cuts were not fresh-made on the ends, but they busted and stacked it in what looked like a mountain. Chet hoped hands at his other places were doing the same.

He rode to the Quarter Circle Z and went over

the main books. Susie and Leif were still on their honeymoon and Chet spent time looking carefully at the incoming money from the cattle sales—paid in script that could be cash when the federal money reached the Indian Agency account. He had expected that, but it was not cash at the moment. The cattle sales, when they finally got paid, would sure straighten things out. The two sales amounted to over a hundred thousand dollars.

No wonder old man Clanton holds onto those contracts. Chet frowned. He needed to keep that financial information under his Stetson. That much business was well worth shooting him over.

His reserves still looked all right and that money for the cattle would eventually come from the federal government. With a pad of paper, he studied the mill operation and what it would cost to expand. Currently, it was paying out lumber for his projects. Could the mill pay him cash when he completed his building? That was something he'd have to know about before he expanded his operation. He gave it serious consideration and decided if and when the railroad reached the mill, it probably would have enough business to make it work, but until then the freight charges would keep them from competing. He'd look it at later.

He met with Tom and his foreman who said Sarge already had the cattle and was ready to deliver them for November.

"Maybe in the winter we may need to drive them over there whenever the way is open. Can we secure feed on that end of the drive?"

"Good idea. I will have Sarge find some feed and a place to hold them on his next trip."

Tom thanked him. "I have a long list of sellers that say they are ready to deliver stock to us."

"It will help lots of cattlemen in this end of the territory. I like taking a hundred from each operator. That will provide enough money for them to stay here."

"Good plan. I'll watch so it gets around to the small ones, too." Tom shook his hand and Chet headed for home.

A cool wind at his back, he headed up Mingus Mountain. So far, the weather was still too warm to wear his big new coat. The blanket lined jumper was warm enough, but a big storm was knocking on his back door—some time in the near future.

He was surprised that Susie and Leif hadn't been back, but considered any lengthening of time away meant they were getting along and enjoying each other's company. A tall cloudbank on the northern horizon against the stars showed when he climbed out of the valley and it was dark when he got home.

His wife and Monica had a fire in the living room fireplace and he hung up his own hat, coat, and gun belt on the wall pegs in the hall.

"Anyone home?"

"Surprise!"

There were Leif and Susie, Marge, Monica, Jenn, Bonnie Allen, Valerie, Bo and Jane. He could also see the liveryman Frey and his wife, along with the banker and three men who'd ridden with him after the Anderson killers.

"Come blow out your candles." Marge said. "Before they burn the house down."

He kissed Susie on the forehead and saw her big smile along with the grip on her man's arm. They were bonded. Marge had told her the way and it worked. He didn't bother to ask if she had caught any fish.

The cake candles were finally put out. Monica brought him a plate of food for his supper while the rest feasted on his cake and asked him where he had been all day.

"I was checking the books and let the day slip by. Guess I kind of misplaced the time. Tom and I talked. Guess he knew you all had plans for me. He tried to push me away, but not obviously. November sixth is my day."

"Well, I wasn't sure you'd even come back," Marge teased him. "Oh. A letter came, but I didn't open it." She handed him an envelope.

"From who?" He looked at the return address— JD Byrnes, General Delivery Socorro, New Mexico Territory. Chet tore open the envelope.

Dear Chet,

Sorry I left before you returned. I couldn't stand to be in that country any longer and knew I'd go crazy. I am still looking for a place I can stand to be. I met Billy the Kid again. You recall us meeting him in Tascosa. He's in some range war down here. I wanted no part of him and took a job with a rancher named Newel Banks who is out of the range war. He has a place west of here—TYZ

*is his brand. Tell Marge thanks. I'll get her repaid
in time. Give Mom my best and tell Susie I wish
her and Leif the best of luck. Write when you get
time.*

Your nephew JD

Chet handed the letter to his wife. "Here Marge.
You all read it. Maybe that boy has found himself a
place to perch."

"Where?" Susie asked.

"Socorro, New Mexico, is his address." Chet
smiled at her. "He wished you two the best of luck."

"How did he get clear over there?" Leif asked.

Chet shook his head. "I don't know. He said he
met Billy the Kid again. We met him at the end of
Fort Worth to Denver tracks when we landed there
and took the wagons on from there. He's a famous
scoundrel in New Mexico. He's into a range war. JD
said that he has no part in it—which means he has
gained some sense."

"John Chisum, the big rancher in those parts,
hired The Kid to run off homesteaders and stop
rustling," Leif said.

"No telling," Chet said, shaking his head.

"It was my fault for introducing him to Kay,"
Marge said.

"No, he'd have met her anyhow. We couldn't
help what they did."

"I heard she married Tom Hannagan in front of
the JP in Prescott," Susie said and turned to her
husband. "Where did we hear that?"

"Camp Verde yesterday, coming up here."

"Fine." Chet dropped his chin and rubbed his short whiskers. "I'm glad you two are together. Did you fish? Those nephews are going to ask you that first thing."

"Hey we did, and even caught some," Leif said. "They were good eating, too."

Chet laughed. "Poor May. Those boys will nag her to death to visit you when they hear about that."

"Why didn't we ever know she could sing?" Susie asked. "That was so beautiful at our wedding."

"Yes it was." Chet shook his head. "My brother, I will swear, married her to take care of his kids, God rest his soul. We all thought she was the quiet daughter of her family, but I guess we never gave her a chance. Hampt took her on and brought all that out of her."

"She's very happy with him," Marge said. "I think she even gave up wanting you."

Susie quickly agreed.

"May never appealed to me—nice girl—good mother—but not for me," Chet protested.

They all laughed at his words.

The evening passed quickly. His guests left save for Susie and Leif who Marge had offered the guest cabin to. Chet walked them outside and smiled. The two were holding on to each other going across in the starlit cool night.

When the lamplight went on inside the guest cabin, he went back inside the house and hugged his wife. "Thanks. Nice birthday, nice to be home, nice to be thinking about going to bed with you."

"Yes, it is. Are the books all right? You looked at them for a long time, you said."

"Books are fine. When we get paid for the two shipments of cattle to the Navajos we'll be over a hundred thousand better off. That is really going to work. When we buy more cattle to resell we won't be that rich, but the ranch is comfortable with a good backlog of money."

"Wonderful. Let's go to bed," Marge said.

"I could hardly wait for you to ask me."

Whew. Things were sure all right in his world.

CHAPTER 10

The next morning, Chet looked up from the kitchen table at the sound of a buggy in the yard. Marge was still asleep and so were the newlyweds. Monica had made him fresh coffee and was frying eggs, baking biscuits, and making gravy with chopped ham in it.

Who was driving in? He rose and looked out the window. The driver, by himself on the seat, had pulled around behind the house to use the back door. Chet answered his knock.

"Morning, Mr. Byrnes. My name is Hailey Rasmussen and I'd like a word with you." He was about five-eight with white whiskers and blue eyes and looked the part of a horseman as well as a stockman.

"Come inside. It's cold out there."

"Aw, I've got on my working clothes. I can't go in your nice house."

"Hailey, this is a working ranch, too. Monica is making breakfast and you can sure have some."

The man stepped inside. He took off his canvas

coat and hung it on the wall along with his red wool scarf and weather-beaten, once-gray Stetson.

"Have a seat, Hailey. This is Monica, my wonderful cook."

"Howdy Mrs. Byrnes," Hailey said, ready to take a seat.

"No. Monica is our housekeeper. My wife is still asleep," Chet explained.

"Oh, excuse me, ma'am."

Monica smiled. "I am very flattered, but you sit down. No harm done. How do you like your eggs, sir?" She poured him a cup of coffee and refilled Chet's mug.

"The way you cook them. I haven't been asked that since I was kid." Hailey laughed, settled in the chair, and drank the coffee.

"What can I do for you?" Chet asked him.

"Someone's been rustling my cattle and I'd like you to catch them."

"That's a tall order, Hailey. You talk to the sheriff?"

"Hell—excuse me, ma'am. I won't go ask that stiff dude for a damn thing. Sorry Miss Monica. I'm use to talking to unbroken horses and the like—understand?"

Monica smiled. "Perfectly. Don't worry. Go on."

"Yes, ma'am. Well, ain't no need in telling Sims anything. He won't send anyone out to look. They say you can track down ants."

Chet laughed. "I am not that good. When did they rustle the last ones?"

"Three days ago. They butchered a fat cow and calf up in the canyon and hauled them out, I guess, on packhorses. But they can blotch up a trail so I can't track them nowhere."

"Anyone see them getting away?"

"Not that I've talked to. I never asked many of the folks on the road, but the two I did ask never saw no packhorses."

"How often are they taking one or two?"

Monica brought them eggs. She set a plate before Hailey and said, "I scrambled them."

"Just how I wanted them, ma'am. My, those biscuits look wonderful."

Monica beamed at his praise. "I have butter and I made ham gravy."

"You eat like this all the time?" he asked Chet.

"Yes." Amused, Chet smiled.

"Ma'am, could I ask you a question?"

"Sure. What do you want to know, Mr. Rasmussen?"

"Are you married?"

"No, I am a widow."

"Now ain't that neat. I am one, too." Hailey smiled.

"Oh. I am sorry."

"So am I. My Sarah died four years ago. Rest her soul. Would you call me a damn, I mean, a fool to ask . . . if I cleaned up and came by one Sunday afternoon would you go on a picnic with me?"

"I would have to ask for the day off." Monica stood ready to pour more coffee.

"If you want to go—"

Her frown cut Chet off from saying that she could go.

"I will ask Mrs. Byrnes if I might have the afternoon off," Monica said.

"Good. I can fix the lunch and repay you for this meal." Hailey smiled again.

"Thank you." She poured more coffee and turned to put the coffeepot back on the stove.

"How many cattle have they stolen?" Chet asked him.

"Maybe twenty over the course of time."

"In a year?" Chet picked up his coffee cup.

"Yeah, that's about the right amount. They usually take them to some isolated spot, I figure, to kill and slaughter them. Then I see the buzzards gathering a day or so later. I never found a real fresh kill, but I'm searching harder these days. They're still slipping in and taking them."

"Where could they sell that much beef?"

"If I knew that, I'd have caught them already."

"Let's try that end. I'll meet you in town tomorrow and we can start asking folks who sells beef in the valley."

Hailey shook his head, looking amazed. "Now why didn't I think of that?"

"You know cattle and how to handle them. You hadn't thought about the end product. They represent food—meat in particular. Where can you sell it? To merchants and café owners and boarding-houses and anyone else feeding folks, for that matter. Did the rustlers take the hides?"

"Sure. Why?"

"They may have them in their possession or have sold the branded ones. What is your brand?"

"I see that now. Double K Bar." Hailey shook his

head. "I never thought about that, either. All they left behind were the heads and guts."

"Oh, we have company," Marge said, coming into the kitchen.

"This is my wife, Marge, Hailey." Chet introduced him as they both rose for her.

"Yes ma'am. Sure nice to meet you," Hailey said.

"He mistook Monica for you earlier," Chet explained.

"Oh, she is a wonderful cook, isn't she?" Marge took a chair.

"Golly, she's more than that," Hailey said. "She's a nice-looking lady, as well."

"She certainly is that." Marge turned to Monica. All I want is some oatmeal, Monica."

"I have that ready."

"That will be fine."

Chet explained, "Hailey's having some problems with cattle rustlers. He can't catch them. He asked for some help—"

"Why did he not ask the law?" Marge asked.

"He has little faith in their methods. We are working out some plans to entrap them."

Marge sat at the table. "Hailey, you have a good man on your side. He usually gets them."

"I sure appreciate you letting me have him for this job. And I asked Miss Monica if she'd go on a picnic with me Sunday. She said she'd have to ask for your permission."

"Certainly."

"Can she be off at ten? So I can bring dinner in my basket?"

"Sure."

"I better get back to the ranch. I'll meet you in town tomorrow, Chet. What time?" Hailey asked.

"Eight o'clock at Jenn's Café. We can start from there."

Hailey stood and said to Marge, "Ma'am, you sure serve good meals to an old wrangler and I appreciate your letting Miss Monica off, as well." He looked at Chet. "See you in the morning." To Monica, he said, "And I'll bring my buckboard for you Sunday morning if that is all right?"

"Yes," Monica said quietly. "Thank you for asking me."

"It is my privilege." He turned and thanked Chet and Marge again.

Chet nodded and started to rise, but he saw Monica already had Hailey's coat, hat, and scarf ready for him and they talked going out onto the back porch.

When the back door closed, Marge asked, "How long has he known Monica?"

"About fifteen more minutes than you."

Marge threw her head back and laughed. "Short courtship, huh?"

Monica stayed outside despite the cool wind and talked with Hailey.

The back door opened and closed, and Monica headed right to the range.

"He's a polite nice guy," Chet said.

She brought the coffee over and refilled the mugs. "He is very polite and a nice man with manners."

"Good. I thought so, too."

Marge shook her head. "If he takes you away from me, I'll—kiss him."

Her words embarrassed their housekeeper who was shaking her head. "It is only a picnic."

"That's how things happen," Chet said as she started to leave the kitchen. "Monica, we love you."

She stopped and smiled. "I know that. I was impressed by him and flattered he made such a nice invitation."

Chet agreed. "It was a nice one. Go on the picnic and learn all about him."

"I am voting for you," Marge said.

"Thanks."

Monica left them and Chet considered the slaughter of Hailey's beef. Jenn may know more about it. He might ride into town and talk to her. If he could find some suspects, he could check them out. He'd do that.

He said to Marge, "I'm going into town and poke around about the butchering deal. Jenn may know something. Peddlers come around all the time. It is cold outside today, but I'll take the buckboard if you want to go along."

"Tie on a horse in case you need one. I will go along. I'll dress warm. I'll tell Monica we will not eat lunch here."

"I am going to hitch up the team if Jesus will let me."

"I promise I won't hold you up."

"No worry." He laughed.

They left in a short while and ate lunch with

Jenn in the cafe. When the crowd left, she slipped into the booth and asked why they were there.

"We're looking for someone who sells beef to restaurants," Chet explained.

"Why?"

"Someone who didn't buy the cattle on the hoof is selling the meat."

"Rustled them." Jenn frowned.

"Who brings you the beef you buy?"

"Old Jules. He has a van and comes around. He'll bring a hind quarter into our kitchen, fills our needs, and keeps the rest."

"Anyone else ever offer you meat for sale?"

"Oh sure. Let me think. A guy named Olson comes around every couple weeks and tells me he has a bargain. I bought one quarter one time. It was tough as shoe leather."

"Where does he live?"

"I can find out." Jenn slipped out of the booth, went to the counter, and spoke to a man sitting on a stool. He nodded and she thanked him.

She slid back into the booth. "He lives in Boulder Canyon. That's off the Black Canyon Road and south. It is a kinda all alone place. A wrecked wagon on the right marks the way in. What will you do now?"

"I'll ride up there and take a peek," Chet said.

"What are you looking for?"

"Evidence to shove under their noses."

Jenn shook her head. "I bet someone came and asked you to help him find the bad guys."

Marge laughed and squeezed his arm. "Of course."

"Is this Olson very valuable to society?" Chet asked.

"No."

"You keep Marge company. I'll be back by for supper."

"Be careful."

He agreed, went outside, saddled his roan Jack and rode for the Black Canyon Road. The wind from the north was cooler and high level clouds were rolling in. He hunched some under his jumper and rode on.

The wrecked wagon parts were beside the main road like Jenn had said. Wagon tracks went in and out of the narrow road that wound back into the pines. The steep walled canyon was lined with sheer rock walls, tall skinny pines, and brushy junipers.

He turned the horse into the road and wondered how far he had to go to find the place. From where he was, he saw the canyon wind back into the mountains. From watermarks, he could tell there had been floods from violent rains, but little sign water ever ran much in other times. He shrugged. The crevice wouldn't have a flood that day.

Farther on, he caught sight of a cabin and stopped his horse. He concealed the roan in a deep side place in the canyon and tied him. Then he looked at scaling the wall and decided it was the best way to get by the cabin undetected and search beyond it.

The climb was not easy. Hand over hand he pulled himself up. Out of breath and crouched in some brush, he gratefully saw lots of cover farther up the mountainside. Ducking to keep concealed, he moved along swiftly, taking stops to be sure no one had seen him. Reaching the top, he ran along the edge until he heard pigs fighting in a pen. Back of the cabin, he saw a woman walk to the outhouse. On his haunches, he held his place until she went back inside.

Close enough, he heard someone cussing. When that quieted down, Chet started the climb down. It was tough, but he found ledges for toeholds. He checked his six-gun after he reached the soil under his soles.

Four horses were in the corral, and recently worn packsaddles were set on top of the top rail. They showed the sweat marks of the pads. He made the first shed and slipped inside. It stunk of raw hides. In the near-dark shed, he peeled back the top of two stinking piles and lit a match. It about burned his finger before he saw the KKs—the brand of the Double K Bar. He had the evidence, and sighed.

On his feet, he felt for the gun butt in his holster. Satisfied, he went to the door and cracked it until he saw a man in a red underwear top with suspenders holding up his dirty pants coming from the house.

Gun in hand, Chet swung back the door and ordered him to put his hands in the air.

Shock-faced, the man did raise his hand. Then he shouted, "Winny, shoot this sumbitch!"

The back door cracked and a barrel appeared. "Make one move and I'll shoot you," A voice called to Chet.

In response, he put a bullet in the door high enough to miss her.

She fired the gun into the ground and her man ducked as the bullet's impact spread hot sand all over him.

"Get out here unarmed or I'll shoot you, lady," Chet ordered.

Disgusted, she tossed the rifle out on the ground and came out shaking her head.

"I'm going to tie you up, Olson. Get on your belly," Chet commanded.

"What're you going to do with me?" Olson asked as he got down on the ground.

Chet holstered his gun. With a rope he'd found on the packsaddles, he tied Olson's hands behind his back, watching the woman closely where she stood outside the door. She didn't move.

He left Olson lying on the ground and picked up the rifle. Then he saddled a horse for him.

"What will we do without him?" she asked when Chet had him in the saddle and had led him to the shed.

"I have no idea." Chet jerked the fresh hide out of the stack, rolled it up, and tied it on the saddle behind Olson. "You should have thought about that before he stole the cattle."

"That's easy for you to say."

"Yes, I guess it is. Maybe when he gets out of jail he'll not steal any more cattle."

She ignored him.

Damn. She'd gotten under his skin. He knew there were some small kids in the house she'd have to feed. "I'll speak to the Methodist preacher. He may have food and things for you."

She barely nodded, looking doubtful as Chet led the horse and Olson away.

At the side canyon, he mounted the roan and rode back to town in a long trot, leading Olson's horse. He wasn't going to take him in. Roamer could do that.

Sundown was settling over Thumb Butte, the great landmark west of town when Roamer came out of the lighted doorway and frowned. "Who's he?"

"A rustler. Hailey Rasmussen came by and asked me to help him. He had rustlers stealing his cattle. I learned Olson sold meat from time to time and found this fresh hide with Rasmussen's Double K Bar brand on it in his shed. There are more of them out there."

Roamer grinned at him. "I guess you want me to take him in, huh?"

"Yes, if it doesn't make any trouble for you. Hailey will be in in the morning and swear out a warrant for his arrest."

"You don't want to make a deal out of it, right?"

"Right. My wife is at Jenn's Café wondering where the hell I am."

"Oh, I'll handle it. Thanks."

"Thank you." Chet tossed Roamer the lead rope, spun the roan around, and rode hard for Jenn's.

"Where have you been?" Marge asked when Chet entered the café, wrinkling her nose at the hide smell attached to him.

"I found the thief. Roamer is jailing him. Let's go home."

"It was Olson?" Jenn asked in mild disbelief.

"You bet. He had the fresh hide in his shed bearing the brand."

Closing up, Bonnie and Valerie came over to hear Chet's short story. They laughed about it.

Bonnie said, "We could have told Mr. Rasmussen you'd find his rustlers."

Valerie agreed. "Our citizen lawman rides again. We love you, big man."

"You have any supper?" Marge asked.

"I can eat at home. Get your coat on." Chet was anxious to return home.

"I'll make him a sandwich. You can drive," Jenn said to Marge, and the two girls rushed off to fill the order. He washed his hands in a bowl behind the counter, laughing and shaking his head. "You're making too big a fuss."

They were soon on the wagon seat, his horse tied on back, and Marge clucking to the horses, while he tried to hold the huge ham sandwich in both hands. They climbed the tall hill and turned to the east, heading for the valley under the stars.

As his hands clutched the cheese, ham, sourdough bread, and its sweet sourness filled his mouth he thought another matter settled and he was going home with his bride. He was so glad that have her in his arms and be warm under the covers in another hour. He took another bite. What a huge meal those girls had made for him.

CHAPTER 11

Chet met Rasmussen at the turnoff to town in the predawn light. He drew up his horse. "You need to go sign a warrant out at the sheriff's office. I turned your thief—a man named Olson who lived down this road—over to deputy Roamer. I found a hide with your brand on it in his shed."

"Damn. Folks said that I needed you. How did you do all that?"

"Asked a few questions, went out to his place, found the hide in a pile, and took him over for Roamer to put him in jail."

"Oh, thanks. Say, I wondered if I was too strong asking your cook out?"

"No, we love her. She said she thought you were a gentleman and we told her to meet you."

"Good. Now what do I owe you?"

Chet shook his head. "Not one thing. I hope no one else will steal another cow from you or me."

"You know you should be the sheriff here."

"No, I am a businessman with lots of irons in the fire."

"Glad you helped me." Rasmussen stuck out his hand.

Chet shook the offered hand. "Good. I'm going home and get some work done."

"You need anything call on me," Rasmussen said and they parted.

Chet rode up to the holding ranch on the high plains early the next morning. He was anxious to see how things went at Gallup and the various sale points and figured Sarge and his bunch should be back from the drive.

Mid-morning, he stopped at the Verde ranch and had coffee with his sister, the new *Mrs. Times*. Tom and the crew were after a mountain lion that had been eating calves. Some guy named Lowe brought his hounds out to tree the cat and the whole crew spread out to get the killer.

"Well, how are things going?" Chet asked Susie as they shared coffee and cake.

"Very good. Tell Marge thanks. She was like a mother and very frank about many things I wondered about. Leif's a great partner and we caught trout, thanks to the boys." She laughed freely.

"Good. I'm going on up to Sarge's and see how they did with the Navajos. They should be back."

"Ride safe. I'll tell Tom you came by. He seriously runs this ranch. Leif says he's really been impressed how good Tom is at it."

"I appreciate him," Chet agreed, kissed her cheek, and left.

The ride northeast grew cooler as the day went

on. He chewed on some jerky and pushed his bay horse all day. Past sundown, he finally arrived.

Sarge met him at the house when the dogs heralded his arrival. "I wondered who was coming to see us. How have you been?"

"Good. How did the trip go?"

"Fine." Sarge turned to the young man who had come from the barn. "Clarence, will you put the boss's horse up?"

The man took the reins from Chet and replied, "Yes." He waited while Chet undid the bedroll then led the horse to the barn.

Chet took the bedroll with him to the house. Sarge showed him inside. The crew was playing cards for toothpicks at the large round table.

"You missed a good drive boss," a bald man named Harp said. "We got no arrows in our saddles this time."

Another offered, "An Indian woman named Blue Bell sent you her best regards. Said you gave her a horse when hers died on the road."

Chet nodded, recalling her. "How was she?"

"Damn good-looking. I'd give her my horse, too." They all laughed.

Chet and Sarge went off into the kitchen to talk about the trip. Sarge lit a candle lamp and poured some coffee. "We can get you some food. Victor's turned in. He gets up at three."

"Let him sleep. I'm fine. Any problems?"

"No. Some guy named Chester for the agency told me we were doing great at this delivery business, but he worried about winter. I told him we were a big outfit and could use feed wagons to drive the cattle if we needed to."

"Good. We may need to get some of those rigs up here in case we do."

Sarge agreed. "I talked to two ranchers up near Gallup. They'll sell us hay at ten dollars a ton, but want us to buy it now. The hay is good and I'm certain the cattle would eat it. My horse did and he's fussy."

"Let's buy twenty tons, just in case. That would be a small expense. Make sure we get that hay you tried on your horse."

"I can do that. How do I pay for it?"

"I'll make out a draw on the bank in Preskitt and have the money sent to them."

Sarge agreed. "They'd also like to sell you some cattle."

"Do they know what we need?" Chet asked.

"I told them we take only fat cows or big steers."

"Let's try that. I understand markets are short all over. We will buy twenty-five head from them at sixteen cents a pound. That would get them over a hundred dollars if they weight around seven hundred pounds."

Sarge nodded. "Those two men I met, Arnold and Kibley, are anxious to do business with you."

"Maybe we could trade cattle sales for their hay."

Sarge frowned. "I was pretty straight with them. I thought we would buy the hay. The purchase of their cattle was up to you."

"Well, we can afford the hay. You're going to send the word to them?"

Sarge nodded he would. "I will ride over there

and make the deal this week. I think if we go early, we can bunch those cattle at the Egan Ranch for a week or more. He has the water and facilities to hold them."

"Good. I won't worry about your operations and we'll keep sending you cattle. You did good over there."

Sarge looked satisfied. "Buying those cattle will seal our deal and connection with them. We needed that. Thanks."

Chet nodded. "I never gave us a chance at doing this, but it seems to be working and will insure lots of jobs."

"How's Jenn doing in Preskitt?" Sage asked.

"Doing great. I saw her two days ago." Chet told about him going after her daughter in Mexico and the rustler deal.

When he finished, Sarge shook his head. "When I went to work at the Camp Verde ranch I could not believe you could ever straighten it up. You and Tom did that. Then those Hartley brothers flooded the country with their cattle. It's been a hard ride, but we're finally seeing some good things happening. I worried a lot when you put me in charge up here. I know you said I could handle it, but I stayed awake nights fretting about it. First trip and we did it. Damn Indian raids—whew. You really helped me and offering to buying hay and cattle from Arnold and Kibley will really take some worries off my shoulders."

Chet nodded. "Good. Whenever the government gets the money to pay our script, the entire operation will be on track."

Sarge laughed. "Oh, they will."

Chet agreed.

After breakfast, Chet made out a draw for the hay and gave it to Sarge in case the cattle trade didn't work. He thanked all the hands working with Sarge, had a good visit with Victor the Mexican cook, and headed back to Camp Verde.

The weather had warmed some. The cottonwoods along the water sources had begun to turn golden yellow from the overnight frost as he shortloped the bay horse. He passed the mail wagon heading west and waved at the contractor on the seat. The man had a great record of getting the mail though to Preskitt from Gallup.

Past sundown, which came early, he was at the Verde headquarters and a hand put up his horse. Tom came from his house and Susie did the same from her porch to greet him. They went in to her table and Leif joined them, all anxious for Chet's report.

"Well, Sarge had a good trip. He found us a hay supply near Gallup in case we get a big snow. We are also buying twenty-five head of cattle from the same two ranchers to help with each drive. Sarge made the deal and thinks we are really covered."

Tom and Leif nodded.

"He really did a great job on that," Tom said. "I worried how we'd handle a hard winter. Oh, we got three lions. We think that will stop the calf slaughter."

"One was a big tom. Must have weighted two-fifty," Leif said.

"That was a big one." Chet had shot lots of them in Texas, but two-fifty was real large.

"We paid Lowe fifty bucks for each cat he treed," Tom said "He and his dogs were worth it, and he will come back anytime we need him."

"Good. We will need to get more cattle ready since we are buying most of them and get them up to Sarge. Tom, use your list of sellers less the twenty-five from each rancher Sarge has set up."

"He will have feed up near Gallup if we send a two month's supply of cattle?" Tom asked.

"I think so. But check with him before you send them. They had no problems on the last trip." Chet turned to his sister. "Susie, do you recall the Indian woman whose horse gave out near here? We gave her a horse to finish her journey?"

"Blue Bell?"

"Yes. She thanked Sarge and his crew for the horse again."

"She was a very impressive lady."

Chet agreed. "So we will have feed over in New Mexico and two ranchers there would help us hold any cattle delivered early, too."

Susie fed him while they talked about ranch problems. The man Chet originally hired to cut the hay up at Hackberry wanted out of the contract as Chet had expanded the hay acreage in the valley by renting more irrigated land. Tom was taking over the hay contract and cutting it himself with ranch help. The change was agreeable to both sides, so no one was mad. But he was getting his own hay equipment and going to do his own and some custom work. The ranch would set up their own crew.

Tom also mentioned they needed a crew to cut hay up at Sarge's, as well.

Chet agreed. "We can find a farmer to run that. We will need equipment for the Hackberry operation and Sarge, too."

Leif added to the conversation. "There is a blacksmith down at the wagon camp. I'd like you to consider him for the job if he will stay. He can make about anything. He made that spit for the steer we cooked for the wedding."

"What do you think?" Chet asked his foreman.

"We could use him if we're going farming," Tom said. "He can repair about anything."

"He's a real inventive guy," Leif said.

"What will he cost?"

"Maybe fifty, sixty a month and he'd need a house."

"I've never met him."

"Johnny Carter. He's in his thirties and great at working iron and fixing things."

"Where will we put him up?" Chet asked.

"There's a house could be fixed down the road on the Laird farm you bought." Tom said.

"Can we talk to him tomorrow?"

"Oh, I bet we can," Leif said.

"Let's do that." Chet felt satisfied a blacksmith would be a good addition to the ranch staff.

They went over everything on their minds until he decided he better get some sleep and headed upstairs.

* * *

Chet was at the cowboy breakfast in the cook shack for oatmeal or pancakes and syrup. He met some new hands and talked to Hoot.

"This dang place gets busier and busier. It ain't the same place I hired on working for you," Hoot complained.

"You want to retire?" Chet asked.

"Hell no. But when will it stop?"

Chet shook his head. "I don't think it will." Personally, he hoped it didn't.

"Well, I'll tell you when all these cowboys overwhelm me."

"Thanks. I count on you."

Chet left Hoot and went to find Tom, then he and Tom went down to the wagon train camp and met Carter.

A powerfully built man, he listened to their offer while wearing a blanket jacket against the cool wind. His wife Andi served them fresh coffee in the shelter of the wagon that cut down the breeze.

"Thanks. That is a fair offer. I need to talk to Andi a minute. Excuse me."

Chet nodded for him to go ahead and Tom agreed.

Alone, Chet asked Tom. "What shape is that house in?"

"It needs some work, but we can get that done in a few weeks. Some plastering and roof repairs. It isn't a bad house. Lot's better than a wagon bed."

"He ever make a windmill?" Chet asked.

"I bet he can."

"Good, Windmills would help our range management."

Tom agreed.

John came back. "Andi likes this valley. She'd about do anything to move into a house. Hayden Mills might be paradise, but if that house is livable I'll take the job."

Chet shook John's hand. "You and Tom can go inspect it. We will make it very livable for you and your family." He nodded to Andi. "That house will work, I promise you. Nice to have you as a part of the ranch."

She looked relieved and smiled. "Thanks. I'm real road weary."

"You are home, Andi. This will be it," Chet said and left John and Tom to work out details. He went back to the house and saddled his horse to ride home.

He arrived home after lunch and Jesus put up his horse. Looking at the cloudbank in the north while he headed for his wife, he wondered how the honeymooners were making it up at Hackberry. His sister acted very settled as a wife.

"Those clouds you're watching might be a snowstorm," Marge said, hugging him as he stepped inside.

"Sooner or later we'll get some." He rocked her in his arms. "You feeling good?"

"A little more morning sickness than I want. But I am more confident about the baby's survival. Have you had lunch?"

"I am fine."

"I'll make you some lunch. I sent Monica to town to buy a new dress for Sunday. Mary at the dress store can find her one."

"Oh."

Marge gave him a friendly shove. "It will be a big occasion for her, no matter what happens."

"I agree. You did good. My sister really appreciated all your coaching. You can see it on her face. She and Leif can't hardly not be touching each other."

Marge smiled. "Hmm. Sounds like us."

Chet laughed.

"There is water heating."

"Great. We'd better empty the shower soon so it doesn't freeze and bust."

"Jesus plans to do that tomorrow. Four men held up the Black Canyon Stage. Roamer came by to see you earlier. He had three men with him. I know how you hate businessmen riding in posses, but these looked like real ranch hands."

"When did they come by?"

"Sunup today."

Chet considered the situation. "I better get a fresh horse and see where they went."

"I was afraid you would want to do that, but I understand. Take your big jacket," Marge said.

He agreed and ran to the barn. "Jesus, saddle a roan horse and a packhorse. I'm going to go find Roamer and his posse."

"*Sí*. I told her you would go find him. Can I go with you?"

"Do you have a warm jacket?"

"Oh, *sí*."

"I'll tell her you're riding along."

"Raphael can handle this job. I'll be ready."

No need to tell his wife how excited her man was about going along. She'd know that. Chet shook his head. *Where is JD? No telling.*

Chet and Jesus left within a half hour with a packhorse and supplies. Marge hustled up things they'd need if they were out in the wild somewhere. Pots, pans, flour, lard, sugar, coffee, bacon, baking powder, and pinto beans. Two loaves of Monica's fresh homemade bread and a few cans of peaches. He'd begun to worry he'd need two packhorses. At the last minute, she added some of Monica's cookies, too.

Raphael helped finish the loading process. "Where will you go, amigo?"

"Down the Black Canyon route until we find where the posse went. Those bandits either went up the Bradshaws on the west or Bloody Basin on the east. I've been on both paths. We'll catch up with the posse by dark tomorrow, maybe sooner. They may have even caught the gunmen by then," Chet answered.

"I bet they wait for you." Raphael smiled and clapped him on the shoulder. "I wish I was riding with you."

"Thanks. Jesus is a good man. I am pleased he wants to go with me."

"Oh, he's a good young man. *Vaya con dios, amigo.*"

"Thanks. I'll need His help, too."

Chet and Jesus left on the run, being so far behind. Chet was pleased the packhorse led easy and kept pace. On the road and headed south, they trotted their horses downhill and met a man in a buckboard on the next flat. Chet introduced himself and asked the man if he'd seen Roamer recently.

"Newt Horace. Glad to met you, Byrnes." They shook hands without either man dismounting. "Yes, I spoke to Deputy Roamer about two hours ago. He was close to the place where the stage was held up."

"You have any idea where the bandits went?"

"I started out from Bumble Bee about dawn and never saw any riders on the road. So they cut off somewhere above that, either east or west."

Chet nodded. Just like he thought. The question was which way? "Thanks. We'll find them."

"You bet. Good to meet 'cha."

Mid-afternoon, Chet and Jesus reached the road that went to Crown King. No sign of three horses going west in the tracks. They rode on. Unable to discover the site of the robbery as it was not marked, Chet told his man they'd ride on to Hassayampa City.

The November day was short and they reached the village after the sun went down behind the Bradshaw Mountains. They found the town law, John Ed Michaels, and he said that Roamer had gone back, heading for Bloody Basin based on information from a man who'd been held up by the bandits on the road. They'd stolen his horse from him.

"Did he describe the men?" Chet asked.

"He said that they were rough-looking, but didn't know them."

"Wonder what he meant? Rough looking?"

"Whiskers, long hair, and dirty clothes," the lawman said.

Chet smiled. "Anyone stealing a horse at gun point would look rough."

Michaels agreed.

Chet found the liveryman they'd used before and he welcomed them. The horses put up, Chet and Jesus walked down hill, ate in a small café, and returned to the livery to sleep in the hay.

Chet woke Jesus up before sun up. When the horses were saddled and ready, they led them back to the café and hitched them. The owner made eggs and pancakes, served with hot coffee.

"You two are after the stage robbers, huh?" the owner asked.

Chet nodded. "We hope to catch up with Deputy Roamer today."

The café owner laughed and wiped his palms on the fresh apron. "If I was them, I'd put my hands in the air, Mr. Byrnes. You sure got a powerful rep at catching their kind."

"Jesus and I are simply along to help Roamer."

"I bet he'll be glad to have ya."

"I hope so."

"Lots of luck to you all in getting those worthless trash. They're bound to do it again."

"Thanks." Chet stood over the chair, fished out money from his pocket, and paid him. "I appreciate you getting up to feed us."

"*Mucho gracias,*" Jesus added and they left.

Heading east from the Black Canyon route by the time the sun cracked the horizon, Chet recalled the road he and Raphael had taken to find the horse thieves. It was still a faint one lane winding through the steep hills. He pointed out to Jesus where the killer outlaw horse thieves had shot two men, loaded their bodies on their horses, and ridden on.

Tall saguaros sentinels marked the steep hills and large beds of prickly pear covered many places. Yucca and century plants grew everywhere, as well. The summer rains had produced lots of grama and other grasses. It would be fine range forage for the cattle to get through the winter.

The mountain they climbed was steep and Chet motioned to stop on the top. After resting the horse briefly, they continued on, reaching Annie Smart's house by midday.

Holding her hand up to shade her eyes, she smiled. "Good to see you Chet Byrnes. Your man Roamer came by about three hours ago. He's real nice guy. He said you weren't home when he went by your place. We agreed he could sure use you."

"Good to see you again, Annie. I got there later and Jesus and I are going to join him. Tell me about the bandits."

"They watered their broncs and rode on cussing like you know what." She shook her head in disgust. "When they arrived, the big tough guy ordered me to get back in the house or they'd shoot me. I did. You need to catch them and hang them. They ain't worth nothing."

"I imagine Roamer wants to take them back to stand trial."

"And they'll get out and do it again. Ain't no one got any sense?"

Chet shook his head and he and Jesus rode on. They saw lots of wildlife. A black bear headed off for cover after noticing them. Several mule deer bounded off down a draw at the sight of them. A number of the bucks had great racks—ten- and twelve-point antlers.

They reached the Yeager Ranch in the late afternoon and saw the extra horses hitched at the rack. The one with some white on him looked like Roamer's roan horse.

Busy chewing on some food, the deputy came out on the porch. He grinned. "You lost, Chet?"

"No, I came to find you."

They both laughed and when Chet dismounted, they hugged each other.

"When were the robbers through here last?" Chet waved to the rancher Yeager.

"They never stopped here, but about dark last night they rode by."

"We can catch them unless they know their way east."

"Come have some lunch. Yeager's wife fixed us lots of food. It's so good to see you."

"Yes. This is Jesus." Chet pointed to the man with him.

"Good to meet you," Roamer said and shook his hand. "Come on inside and meet my men."

Roamer introduced Lefty Wilson and a shorter man, Haze Burton. In their thirties, they were soft spoken, but simple, tough, working men. Chet could see they were ranch hands and would have been his choice as posse men.

The rancher's wife Shelia hugged Chet and kissed him on the cheek. "This must be outlaw highway. First killers, now stage robbers."

"We're sorry they came this way, ma'am," Roamer said.

"Oh, how else could I get all these nice guys to come by and see me? Eat. I can make more." She left to put the children to bed.

"You know these outlaws?" Chet asked Roamer, finishing up his coffee.

"No. Three masked men is all we have." The two men with Roamer nodded.

"They shave, get new clothes, and get past Rye and no one will know their identity. Will we?" Chet asked them.

"Did you think that when you were here last time? That those killers would slip away?" Roamer asked.

"You bet. I didn't know where those two were headed, but away. Their neighbor Annie Smart was raped. They took turns on her. They'd murdered two good men. Marge's foreman and his man. If they'd ever gotten passed the next place, they'd have been scot free."

Roamer nodded. "I never learned anything in Hassayampa City. Did you?"

"No, except that the stage robbers had held up someone on the road and stole his horse. The livery man who helped me when I was after those two that had shot you didn't know anything but the fact that you three were after them. How much money did they get?"

"Oh, a couple thousand dollars and some gold dust."

Chet frowned. "Why was that much money on the stage in the first place?"

"Damned if I know, Chet."

"They must have gotten information that the money was going to be on the stage. You could hold up those stages a dozen times and get no more than a few dollars, a ring from some woman passenger, and maybe a gold watch or two."

"The money belonged to John J. Wilson. Wells Fargo was taking it to deposit in a Denver bank for him. The gold dust was from the Green Frog Saloon."

"Who knew about the transfer?"

Roamer shook his head. "Got me, but you're right. Those worthless outlaws that held up the stage and murdered your nephew got less than a hundred dollars."

Sheila had returned and refilled their coffee cups. "Chet, do you think they knew the money would be there?"

"The way the law in the territory has tightened against things like stage holdups, yes I do. No one smart would hold up a stage to get forty dollars. My thinking is they knew the money was going to be on the stage."

"Chet," Roamer began, "you're the best thinker I know on these cases. I will tell all of you, Chet went after the killers of an old man and his wife. He caught them and then told me who had the money that the killers didn't find. The dead man's own brother."

"Aw, that was luck," Chet said to dismiss the bragging on him.

Roamer went on. "I have been riding hard after the stage robbers for two days and all I know was the stage was robbed. You figured out how four strangers hold up a stage, get twenty-five hundred dollars in cash plus gold dust, and that someone must have told them it was on that stage."

"How did they know to take this route?" Chet asked.

"It damn sure is not a wagon road beyond here, is it?"

Chet shook his head "I bet they've used it before."

"Yeager said he didn't recognize them, even at the distance."

Chet nodded "They had to know this track. Too much wild country out here to ride it like they'd never traveled it before."

"Maybe they live over there," Lefty said, pointing to the other side of the mountain.

"That's possible," Chet said. "In the morning, we'll track them down. But we have to be quiet. I heard those last two killers talking about going to Rye clear as if I could hear one of you. I almost rode in on them and had to drop back."

Everyone agreed to talk soft and ride easy in the morning.

Before dawn, the smiling Shelia had breakfast stacked up and ready for the men. They teased her until she blushed—how if John ever didn't treat her right, they'd come take her away.

"Not much chance of that," she said. And they all laughed.

The posse headed down the other side of the mountain in the early hours. Talking low among themselves, Jesus had the lead. Chet had showed him the tracks of the horse that probably packed the strong box. The youth could also pick out the various horse prints from the day before when he and Chet had followed both outfits. He'd also learned a lot about tracking from Chet and JD in Mexico.

Chet wondered why the thieves had not shot the lock off the box and emptied it. But that was their business and his to find out.

On the ride, Chet was thinking of his family. Like always, he missed his wife's company and wondered how the little one was doing. A child of their own— a miracle. Marge was sure all right. She'd given Susie enough motherly advice to survive the honeymoon and settle in with Leif. He hoped JD found himself. That boy worried him more than anything else. He didn't know any past family history that his ancestors were ever in trouble, but his grandpaw on his mother's side had told him lots of them were bad guys in Arkansas. Then he'd laughed and his mother had frowned at the old man.

JD knew right from wrong. He'd somehow fallen out of being himself after the Kay deal. Her place had needed so much done and she wouldn't let him borrow any money to do it. Maybe he'd find himself.

Chet shook his head. Only God knew. So he

prayed for JD and for Marge and the baby. He rode on in the line headed downhill for the Verde.

Fresh ashes were spotted on the banks of the river where the robbers had stayed the night before. Maybe three or four hours ahead of them, was how Chet figured it. After fording the river, knee-deep on their horses, they scrambled up the steep tall mountain wall.

Suddenly, an unsaddled horse with signs he had recently been under one came out of the junipers and whinnied to their animals. Guns were quickly drawn. Chet sent Jesus one way and he went the other while the others caught the loose horse. He found the saddle and the empty strong box with the lock beaten open by a hammer or a rock. "Over here."

Roamer pulled up next to him. "That horse fits the description of the one stolen from the man on the road."

"This is probably his saddle, too. Looks like they emptied the strong box." Chet dismounted and shook his head over the discovery. He knew things would become harder.

Roamer had pulled off his riding gloves to stand looking at the plain brown horse with a TW brand on its shoulder. He waved his pointed finger at Chet. "Nothing's out of place now, is there? They got rid of the stolen horse and the strong box. We don't know a thing. Annie said they were tough, bearded men. Bearded . . . but without all that hair, she might not be certain enough to identify them. Now we are looking for three men with gold dust and money."

"They're within ten miles of being arrested or gone like smoke on the wind," Chet said as he swung back on his horse. "I say we give them hell and try to catch them. Annie Smart might be our ace in the hole."

Roamer climbed on his horse. "Let's ride." They turned and joined the rest of the men.

An hour and a half later, they came up a wide, sandy, dry bed to a small town. The tracks had been near impossible to read in the loose floor and only two sets of tracks appeared by then. Chet's stomach turned sour. The robbers sure might get away. A growing worry was gripping him. *Damn we'd sure gotten close.*

CHAPTER 12

No strangers in town. That was the word they collected in the two stores and the saloon. They learned nothing different from the blacksmith, stage stop operator, and two drunk Indians. Ranchers coming into the settlement shook their heads and so did sun-bonneted women in town to shop. Jesus searched the main road north and south for a sign of a familiar horseshoe track and came back empty-handed. Their leads had petered out in the Rye Creek Wash.

Chet met Roamer near the unpainted church. It was midday. The weather had warmed up and both men had shed their coats.

"Damn, we worried about this happening and it has," Roamer said. "They slipped back into their lives around here."

"Jesus rode up and down both sides of town searching for tracks. Not one familiar horse track going either direction. The south way would mean they'd headed for Hayden Mills, north is to Payson Junction or at least some small settlement up there."

Roamer closed his eyes. "When we go back, I'll stop and ask Missus Smart if there was anything else she noticed about the man who ordered her back inside her house. As far as I know, no one else saw their faces. What do you think?"

Chet shook his head. "The earth didn't swallow them. They're around here—somewhere."

"They say a Gila County deputy lives about four miles from here."

Chet nodded. The man's name was Franklin. Someone had mentioned him, and then laughed how he was the law. "He doesn't do much from all I've heard."

"Maybe we should go introduce ourselves." Roamer slapped his saddle horn. "How did they do this?"

"Aw, Roamer, we knew they were slick. They avoided Yeager's. Must have looped around them and Annie's place on their way to rob the stage. The only reason they stopped on the way back was because their horses needed a drink. I bet they regret that stop at Annie's now, too."

Roamer frowned. "What can we do?"

"Ask where Franklin lives?"

Roamer nodded. "All right. Maybe we can learn something from him. I doubt, from what I've heard about him, that he's going to give us any help, but let's go see him. I'll have my men keep checking around here."

"Good. We may still stumble on those robbers yet. Jesus can join us."

"Sure."

Rob Franklin's ranch was south of town and up

on the Four Peaks side of the road. They reached there past noontime. His headquarters consisted of a squaw shade and some pole corrals. A man of medium build about five-eight came out of the shade barefooted and pulling up his suspenders with a silver badge on the right strap.

"Rob Franklin?" Roamer asked.

He eyed them suspiciously. "Yeah, what 'cha need?"

"I'm from Yavapai County. Sheriff Sims's office. Three men held up the Black Canyon Stage a few days ago. We tracked them from there over to here."

"What're their names?"

"I was hoping you could fill that in for us."

"Well, this ain't in your jurisdiction. So what the hell are you doing here?"

Roamer's face grew red under his freckles. "I'm here in pursuit of four felons that held up a stage and stole a man's horse. Don't question my authority."

"Hell, they could be anyone. How can you find them if you don't have any names?"

"Come on Chet. He ain't any damn help." Roamer reined his horse around in disgust.

"Franklin, thanks." Chet tipped his hat to the man and turned to leave. "The people of this county can count on your able services to protect them from such felons."

"Go to hell and get out of here!"

They headed through the head-high chaparral for the road.

As soon as they were out of the angry lawman's

hearing, Roamer said, "He probably knows damn good and well who they are."

"I saw a horseshoe print back there that, I think, is damn close to one of theirs."

Roamer jerked his horse to a halt. "You saw what, Jesus?"

Jesus reined his horse to a stop. "I don't know how the last guy shod that horse, but it is on crooked . . . or the horse's right front leg is crooked. That horse was at Franklin's recently."

Chet pulled up alongside them.

Roamer pounded his saddle horn. "Sumbitch. Why, he made me so damn mad I never looked in the dust for any sign of them."

Jesus nodded. "Not many saddle horses are like that. The animal has probably learned how to move smooth enough, but he still has that fault."

Chet nodded. "Someone really likes him or is proud of the rest of him to overlook his fault." He frowned. What did the robbers want with Franklin? Was he in cahoots with them or was it just a passing through hell? Chet motioned them forward then turned to Roamer. "Do you know the sheriff in Globe?"

"I met him once when the state legislature met in Preskitt at the sheriff's party for the legislatures. His name is Gordon Blankenship."

"Rather than us questioning Franklin about who came by, why don't you go down to Globe and tell Blankenship our plight. You can ask the sheriff to require Franklin to tell us why the robber's horse was at the deputy's place."

"What's he so mad about, anyway?"

"He may be in with them. Or he may realize I hung those two killers in his district."

Roamer nodded. "I wondered about that. But near as I heard those men were drifters and didn't live around here."

"I didn't give a damn. Those ruthless outlaws had killed two good men and hurt a nice lady as well as stolen some good horses."

"Hell." Roamer shook his head. "They had it coming. I was sorry I wasn't there. That deputy never sent you any help. That made me sick."

"He wouldn't even let Raphael go to help me."

"Sims defended his doing that, too. Made me so mad I about resigned."

Chet hurried the conversation along. "What do you say? Ready to ride to Globe?"

"I'll head there. It will take me a few days to go down there and come back. Wilson and Burton are costing the county a dollar a day. Sims will ask me if I went crazy keeping them on the payroll while I rode to Globe and back."

"I will pay for those days. So don't worry."

"Thanks."

Chet acknowledged his thanks with a nod. "Meanwhile, we'll look for the crooked-legged horse and his owner."

Thirty minutes later, Roamer said, "See you in three or four days," and was gone.

The rest met in their camp in a grove of cottonwoods at the edge of town, and Chet told them how Jesus had spotted the hoofprint at Franklin's place and what Roamer was going to do.

"We are close then?" Lefty asked, and then spit tobacco aside.

"It looks that way. We may be grasping at straws, but Jesus thinks it is the same animal," Chet answered.

"What do you think? That Franklin got mad 'cause you were looking for his friends or was he touchy that we got in his territory?"

"I have to believe that he doesn't know the guilty party. He's a lawman."

"That don't pay much. But thanks for hiring Haze and me."

"No problem, Lefty. I owe Roamer, anyway. You two have work?"

"Day work is all," Haze put in.

"I have a ranch up at Hackberry. My nephew Reg and his wife Lucy run it. He needs some help. I bought nine sections. It's good country."

Haze looked interested. "They have any headquarters?"

Chet nodded. "They have corrals and a house. cook shack and bunkhouse are being built. Everybody will be inside before the snow flies."

Lefty rubbed his sleeves. "It is warmer down here than at Preskitt, but those days aren't that far away. Me and Haze talked about asking you if you needed anyone."

"I do."

"We'll go up there and try to please your nephew."

Haze agreed and they all shook hands.

Chet turned their attention to the task at hand.

"Now, we need to find that horse in case Roamer fails to get the sheriff involved."

"We ain't deputies."

"Right, but we are citizens, and citizens can try to find and arrest criminals."

Jesus laughed. "So we will wait. But I can show you what his tracks look like. If they ride him into town maybe we can find him ourselves."

Chet agreed. "That is our only lead."

So their search continued. The two cowboys frequented the saloons and reported on anything that sounded like news. Chet visited both stores and sat around the unfired stove talking to ranchers and men who gathered there.

Jesus spoke to the Hispanic people in the settlement. He came back to camp the second night and spoke to Chet. "Today I spoke to Ramona Chavez who is a puta. She thinks the men we should watch are the Cagle brothers. They own the Box B brand. She has no proof, but says they seem to always have money and never work much. I paid her two dollars for her information."

"That was good. Any names?"

"Uele is the older."

Chet began to write their names down in his herd book. "He the head man?"

Jesus nodded. "He sounds like the man who ordered the lady back into her house."

"Yes. You have the others?"

"Tim is number two. Lyle has a bad left arm. I never heard anyone say anything about a one-armed man. Did you?"

"No. We don't know much about them, period."
Jesus continued. "Wallace is the younger one."

"Where do they live?"

Jesus pointed over his shoulder. "North of here."

"We never saw the tracks in that direction, but they may have scouted around. Maybe we need to watch Franklin more and see who comes to visit him." To Chet, it seemed strange no one had mentioned these brothers in the conversations he'd had with ranchers at the store. He turned to Lefty and Haze and asked them about the Cagle brothers.

"I think they must have put fear in the ordinary folks," Lefty said.

"It's something even the drunks won't tell us," Haze said.

"Haze and I got a few men drunk, but they cut us off when we asked who they thought had robbed the stage."

"You never heard these Cagles mentioned?" Chet asked.

"No, but I bet that puta knows them," Haze agreed and laughed.

"Hey. Jesus may have found them thanks to her. We are all doing our part to find these—"

Haze interrupted. "We're jealous. We meet and greet the drunks and he gets the sweet jobs."

They all laughed

Chet quickly made a plan. "I have a telescope. Two of you scout out this Box B deal. Then one of us can keep an eye on Franklin."

"We'll take the brothers," Lefty said.

"I can go watch Franklin," Jesus said.

"Good. We may break this case open before

Roamer gets back." Chet hoped so, anyway. This dogged business of trying to solve the outlaws' identification grew older and colder by the day.

"I sure hope so," Haze said. "I'm getting tired of listening to these no account drunks' stories."

Chet agreed. "Even herding cattle beats that, I agree. But we are getting closer, I think."

They turned in and Chet had trouble sleeping.

Before dawn, they rolled out, built a fire, and made breakfast. Cold air just short of a frost had them huddled under blankets while eating the hot sweetened oatmeal before they set out on their tasks.

Chet went to see a rancher he'd struck up a friendship with. He felt Charles Hansen had some notions about who might be involved in the robbery.

When Chet arrived at Hansen's place, his newfound friend had a horse already saddled.

His wife came out and spoke to Chet. "Charles told me your deputy friend went to Globe to see the sheriff. Hope he does better than folks up here got out of him two years ago when we had some cattle rustled. He came up here, promised us a few more deputies, then went back to Globe, and all we saw was Franklin, who is lazy as a fat hawg." She shook her head hard.

"Velma don't like the man," Charles said coming out of the house. He mounted up and was ready to ride.

"Thanks, ma'am." Chet tipped his hat. "I hope we do more than that."

She smiled and told them to have a good day.

They rode off. Charles showed him some of his water development. One was at the mouth of a cavern in a canyon with a large stone mortar tank out in front collecting water from a spring inside.

"That water used to disappear in the wash ten feet from here. It waters cattle and wildlife here year round."

"Who laid the rocks?" Chet asked.

"Some boys from Mexico. They cost half a dollar a day. They built it in two months." Charles skipped a flat rock across the surface three times. "Damn nice, isn't it?"

Chet agreed and decided to try him on some suspects. "Several people have told me the Cagle brothers may be suspects in the stage robbery."

"They're a tough bunch. I doubt any of them can read and are proud of it, too." Charles shook his head. "They have tough ways. But I never caught them lying or dealing underhandedly."

"The man who led them stopped at a ranch over in Bloody Basin. A woman I met on my last tour lives there. He gruffly ordered her inside or he'd kill her. Would the elder of that bunch do that?"

"Did he say, 'Woman get your ass inside'?"

"No, that lady is quite plain and open how he said for her to get inside."

Charles shook his head. "Then it wasn't him."

"Who would be the sort to take command of things like she reported?"

"I don't believe it was them. Uele swears all the time."

"Thanks. I'll listen closer. Who rides a bay horse with a crooked right leg?"

Charles squeezed his chin. "Bay horse?"

"Both that lady and the Yeagers saw all bay horses go by. But one has a crooked leg. I figure he's special. Jesus discovered it and saw one of those prints in the deputy's front yard the same day we went to see him."

"What did he have to say about that?"

"We never got to ask him. He ran us off. Roamer has gone to ask the sheriff in Globe if he can find out from Franklin who was at his house before we got there."

"Roamer is still on the road?"

"Yes, and I'd bet Franklin pleads he can't recall if we do get the sheriff's help." Uneasy about their progress, Chet felt at a stone wall about the outlaws. "So far, we can't find that horse, but if we do, we'll have the outlaws."

"What else do you have on them?" Charles frowned at him.

"Annie Smart will identify him."

"Wow. You have a hoofprint and you stayed to find the owner."

"Charles, if they get away with this robbery, who will they prey on next?"

He agreed with a slow nod. "Anyone, huh?"

"We chased them maybe a hundred miles and then they vanished when they got here. We checked the road north and south. They never left Rye. Next day, the hoofprint was in that deputy's yard."

"I've never been in law work, but I understand you guys work damn hard to follow such little details. Thanks."

They rode downhill to another water tank that

had been built with horses and slips. Charles pointed out the rock spillway. "This is all fill dirt and holds good. My first one had no spillway and it wasn't rocked and washed away in a flash flood. We used a level on a tripod and a stick with marks to make that spillway."

"How long did it take to build it?"

"Maybe three months. I had two men and teams working on it."

"They moved lots of dirt." Chet knew such an operation would work in some places on the Hackberry ranch.

"I choose this spot because I knew it had filled in with dirt over the years. I would not have tried this way with lots of rock under it. I was lucky."

Chet agreed and they rode on.

Finally satisfied he'd learned enough from his new friend about water holding tanks, he went back to their camp. He found Roamer there and stepped off his horse to shake his hand. He didn't look pleased and Chet expected the worst. "How did it go?"

"I got a letter from him and I went by to see Franklin when I rode in. His reply was 'How the hell am I supposed to know who it was?'"

Chet nodded. "I feared that."

Jesus came into camp on the fly and everyone jumped up to see what was wrong.

"The crooked legged horse was hitched at the saloon when I left Rye. I don't know who rode him in, but he must be inside." Jesus's voice hitched as he took in gulps of air.

"Saddle up, we have the lead we need boys," Chet said.

The men scrambled to their horses. They charged for the settlement and reined up short on the main road. Roamer put Haze and Lefty to cover the back door. They swung off. Armed with their rifles, no one would get out the rear exit alive.

When the rest came in view of saloon, Jesus pointed out the second horse at the hitch rail. "That's him. I was crossing the street and saw the track. I have no idea if any more of them are in there."

Chet nodded. "You stay out here. Roamer, are you taking the lead?"

"I can do that." He tried his six-gun and dropped it back in the holster then nodded at them.

"I'm right behind you." Both men gave Jesus their reins and he headed to hitch all three horses on the opposite side of the wide street.

Chet's vision centered on the faded-green, bat-wing doors. He slipped between the famous horse and noted the 74T brand on the left shoulder. He saw the crooked leg, but it was a powerful horse and that's why the outlaw rode him.

"Ready?" Roamer asked in a low voice from the boardwalk.

"I am."

They went through the batwing door, Roamer stepping immediately to left, ready to draw. Chet followed, hoping his eyes were ready for the dim-lighted saloon interior. His hand rested on his walnut gun butt.

"Who owns the Seventy-four T branded horse?" Chet demanded.

"I do." A man with a trimmed beard rose at a table of card players. "What's wrong with him?"

"He was involved in a stage robbery. You're under arrest. Make one move and you're dead," Roamer said.

"You sonsabitches can't arrest me. You don't have any authority in Gila County."

"I'm a deputy U.S. marshal and that robbery was involved with a U.S. mail carrier," Roamer said. "Put your hands in the air."

"What's your name?" Chet asked the arrested one, impressed by Roamer's authority speech.

"None of your damn business."

"We'll learn it soon enough. What's his name?" Roamer asked the quiet crowd of customers.

"John Marconi."

Roamer disarmed him and asked the crowd, "Any others in here come in with him?"

"He came in alone," called out a customer.

"But he's got two brothers. Jimbo and Riley," called out another.

"That's three. Who else rides with them?" The cuffs on Marconi's wrist, Roamer shoved him toward the bar.

"Ole Man Marconi. His name is Olaf," provided a man at the bar.

"Thanks. I got it." Gun in his holster, Chet leaned against the bar and penciled in the names of the four men in his herd book.

"Set up the beer," Chet said to the barkeep. "I'm buying one round for every man in here."

A cheer went up. One man went over to Chet. "They have a place down on Tonto Creek. They've been suspects in several crimes and no one ever proved it. How did you catch him?"

"His horse. But we have witnesses that will identify them."

"His old man gets word you've got him, they may try to get him back."

Chet agreed. "They better wear their best suits or they'll be buried in the dusty clothes like he has on."

"I can tell you they're sure enough tough."

Chet shook his head to dismiss any concern. He watched Roamer searching the prisoner's pockets. He put those items on the bar and the three one-hundred-dollar bills looked very suggestive.

The deputy looked at Chet. "Can you write down the serial numbers? Wells Fargo has a record of them in Preskitt."

Chet laughed. "That will be damn good evidence."

"Damn right."

"What in the hell is going on in here?" Franklin busted though the batwing doors and stood, openly challenging them.

"Hold on, Franklin." Roamer put his hand up to stop him. "I am a deputy U.S marshal and this man is my prisoner."

"You ain't got any—"

"Señor, take your hand off that pistol. The marshal has told you who he is." Jesus said from behind Franklin and backed up his words with a Winchester on his hip.

"All right. All right. He's a marshal. He never told me that before."

"Do you know where this guy's family lives, Franklin?" Chet asked.

"Over on Tonto Creek."

"Could you show us the place?"

"I ain't got time." He turned to go out the doors.

"Maybe your boss would like to hear that comment," Roamer said.

"Tell him." Franklin went outside like a mad bulldog.

Roamer nodded in the direction of the prisoner, said to Chet, "Watch him," and went to the door. Holding it open, he shouted, "That's the man who was at your house the day we came to see you . . . the one you didn't remember."

"Go fuck yourself."

Roamer came back into the bar. "Thanks, Jesus. I don't think he'd have shot us, but you'd never know."

Jesus nodded and went back outside.

Haze came in the back door and caused everyone to whirl around and look at him.

"He's my deputy," Roamer said quickly.

"Any problems in here?" Haze asked.

Roamer shook his head. "Tell Lefty to come on in. This is John Marconi, and he has three hundred dollar bills that should trace to the robbery."

"Let me see one," Haze said. "I've never seen one in my life."

Roamer laughed and so did Chet, who handed him one of the bills. He felt much better now that they had solid evidence and knew the names of the other outlaws. Rye, at least, wasn't a dead end for their search. The criminals would not get away into nowhere. They had been found and identified, although he had never heard their names in the time he'd spent in the settlement. Strange— except the bandit's family lived east of Four Peaks range. They lived at a good distance from Rye by the mountain barrier.

"What had he been doing in Franklin's yard that morning?" Haze asked, looking at them for an answer.

"Testing the water about what Franklin knew about us, I'd bet," Chet said, deciding there was a link to Franklin.

Lefty joined them and Chet offered him and Haze a beer.

They accepted.

The bartender said, "There's food on the counter. Better eat."

"Thanks," came the chorus.

Roamer took Chet aside. "How soon will his bunch learn about his arrest?"

"Tomorrow. I figure someone has already left to tell the rest of the Marconis, and will ride a horse into the ground to get there. They will scatter like quail. Exposure will make them panic. They thought they had gotten away free. They never would have realized a young man would memorize a horse's hoofprint and one of them would ride that horse into Rye and be discovered."

"Hey," Roamer said. "We have had it tough on this case and I knew when I left Marge's I needed you. Thanks for catching up."

"Two heads are always better than one." Chet was proud of his friend. He felt they made a good team and the Marconi family would soon be behind bars.

"So before dawn we ride to their ranch?"

Chet nodded. "I'm game. They may meet us on the road coming to get him back."

"I thought about that. He can ride in the middle of us so they'll not chance shooting him."

They feasted on the lunch and several of the curious soon filled the barroom.

Charles came by and spoke to Chet. "The Marconis never entered my mind. A tough bunch. They've been in some scrapes before. I bet there are some individuals under the ground that were robbed and then killed. Riley McCain disappeared coming back from Globe with money from selling a ranch down near Mexico. They never found his body or any sign of the money."

Interested, Chet asked, "What about his horse?"

"They never found him, either."

"Shoot the man and the horse?"

"No sign of them was ever found." Charles shook his head.

"You ever been to their place?" Roamer asked.

"Once or twice. It's a stinking hog farm. Whew. Almost turned me off from eating bacon."

"Interesting," Chet said. "I was in Abilene with a large of our cattle the second year of its operating. Culls, like limpers, calves and cows were sold for a few bucks to local farmers who'd shoot them and leave 'em for the hogs to feed on."

"Oh, that's sickening."

Chet knew the rest of the story. "Veterans who

fought in the civil war always said they asked their buddies not to let the hogs have their dead bodies if they got shot in a battle."

"No way to prove that happened," Roamer reminded them.

"No, those hams won't talk."

"I don't know how many friends they have here, but we should move him to our camp," Chet said, concerned dark would catch them riding back.

"Get ready to ride," Roamer said and went to get his prisoner who had been chained to a chair on the side of the room.

Lefty and Haze went out to help Jesus get the horses. Without an incident, they mounted the prisoner, Lefty having the lead on his horse. "Jesus was right. That's a great horse and his front leg is crooked, but he don't show it. Where did you steal him, Marconi?"

"Go to hell. You ain't got anything on me."

Roamer overheard. "You got a smart lip for a man going to jail in Yuma for ten years. I may soften it. Where did you get that horse?"

"I bought him."

"Where?"

"Globe."

"Who sold him?"

"I don't recall."

"I'll write the sheriff and ask," Roamer said. "I figure that horse was stolen and we can sentence you to three more years."

"No need to do that. I remember his name. It was Holland who owned him. Jesse Holland."

Chet shook his head at Roamer. The man on the horse before him was lying.

Unspoken, Roamer agreed.

The posse mounted and headed toward Tonto Creek. As he rode, Chet's mind went in one direction then another. It would be weeks before they knew about the source of that horse. He was becoming uneasy about the days away. They sure needed to close this operation. What if the others already had been warned and fled. Never mind, the posse faced two days getting to the place and five days getting back to Preskitt.

His thoughts turned to family. *Marge, I am coming.* Setting up the cattle sales to the Navajo were going on as he rode farther away. Reg still needed more help than the two posse men who were currently riding with Roamer.

It was a long day's ride. Short of reaching Tonto Creek at sundown, they camped at a watering hole for the night. Shifts were drawn for guarding Marconi. Supper was jerky and water from their canteens. Bedrolls were spread out and they went to sleep.

Predawn they were up and saddling horses. After hot oatmeal and coffee for breakfast, they rode out, reaching the creek and the road north in midmorning.

Chet noted the prisoner was silent. He looked like a man planning to kill all of his guards. Marconi's sullen, superior attitude made Chet uneasy about the rest of his family. These people must be damn hard with no respect for the law or others.

Chet smelled the strong odor of the hog ranch before they even saw the buildings and pens. As they rode up, a woman armed with a scoop stood in a wagon bed, shoveling ear corn to a mass of muddy, squealing hogs behind a strong log fence. Two or three loose big ones went shagging off when they discovered the posse had arrived. Chet noted two more young women in wash-worn dresses came out onto the porch.

"I'm U.S. Deputy Marshall Roamer and I am looking for Olaf, Riley, and Jumbo Marconi. Are they here?"

She wiped her sweaty forehead on her sleeve. "Get the hell off our ranch and turn that boy loose. You ain't got nothing on him."

"Men, go search the house and outbuildings and see what you can find. Pardon me, ma'am, but put down that shovel or I'll have to shoot you. Count on it," Roamer said.

She held it a second or two too long. Chet rode in and jerked it away from her. "Lady, he will kill you." That said, he tossed it aside and reined his horse back.

"Johnny. Johnny, you all right?" She dropped her butt to the wagon bed and jumped off it, then ran around to where Johnny Marconi sat shackled to the horn.

"Oh son, they won't convict you of nothing," she cried.

"Get your hands off him," Roamer ordered. "And back up three feet. He's a federal prisoner."

"Go to hell. See that girl on the porch on the

left? That's his wife Julie and she's pregnant. Turn him loose. This whole thing could mark her baby."

"He will stand trial and serve time in prison for his part of the stage robbery."

"How do you know he was even there?"

"Mrs. Marconi, trust me. He will do a long prison term for his part in that robbery."

"No. Johnny, don't tell him a thing. You will be found innocent. You will have some good people say you ain't ever been wherever that robbery happened."

On horseback, Chet circled the buildings, leaving the gabby woman to argue with Roamer. He didn't trust her, but she looked less likely to do anything than she had earlier. Had her sons left any of the stage money with the women? Those young women were frozen on the porch and close to tears. He wondered if they knew where the loot was. Maybe hidden under the dress of the woman chewing out Roamer.

Jesus came out of the house. "I couldn't find any money or gold."

"Go back in and feel under the mantle inside the fireplace for a jar or can." Chet dismounted and hitched his horse. Looking around before he entered the kitchen with the ring of his spurs trailing him, he started looking in kitchen containers. Taking the lids off things like sugar, he stirred them with a kitchen knife looking for any hidden money.

Jesus came back with a jar, smiling. "There is gold in here. Pouches say Wells Fargo Gold. This is the stolen gold dust, isn't it?"

Chet nodded. "That's damn sure part of it." He

looked around a bit more and then dragged a chair over to stand on. He removed the top of a red, candy can and nodded, taking five fresh hundred-dollar bills out. "Here, write down the serial numbers of those bills in my log book." He tossed the book to Jesus.

"Put that back!" The woman stormed in the room. "You gawddamn thieves ain't takin' my money."

"Mrs. Marconi, step back. I bet those serial numbers are close to the money we found on your son. If they are not part of the Wells Fargo shipment, the money will be refunded to you."

"Where did you get that damn jar from?" She pointed to the one Jesus had found in the fireplace.

"Stay away from that evidence," Chet moved to block her and captured both her arms. In the struggle, he avoided her handy knee. She was tough as any man he'd ever struggled with. He knew she'd bite him if she got the chance. Jesus finally caught her around the waist and they forced her into a chair and tied her hands and feet with her cussing them out.

"Now lady, I am going to stick a sock in your mouth if you don't shut up," Chet threatened.

She closed her mouth.

Chet knew from the struggle that she wore a money belt and decided to liberate her of it. "I am going to take that money belt you're wearing off of you. You can stand up or we'll put you on the floor and remove it."

"That is none of your business."

"I'm tired of your mouth. Jesus find a gag."

"No. I will stand up, but I am going to charge you with rape."

Chet laughed. "I damn sure won't do that to you, lady."

She rose and Jesus held her bound arms. Chet unbuttoned her dress and found the canvas belt. It had three buckles, which he undid as she stuttered in anger. Then he pulled the canvas belt free. She swore under her breath.

"Set her down again Jesus."

"That is my money," she snapped.

"I don't want *your* money. Only the *Wells Fargo* money." Chet found two hundred-dollar bills in a compartment. They were fresh enough to be part of the loot. He recorded the serial numbers in his book and shook his head. "You are now an accessory to this crime."

"Prove it."

"What is your first name?"

"Shirley. Shirley Lynn Marconi."

"A warrant will be sworn out for your appearance in Preskitt. If you don't appear in thirty days, another warrant will be sworn out for you and two federal deputy marshals will come over here and arrest you and take you back to Preskitt in irons."

Roamer came in the room as he was finishing. "Chet told you the truth. You will need to go to Preskitt and file a bond or you will be on the wanted list and any bounty hunter can come get you and haul you belly down to Preskitt."

"I'm not scared of you or your law."

"You aren't dealing with a local sheriff, now.

You're in the federal system. Marshals will find you and your family members. Avoiding them will mean more charges and a longer sentence."

"She had two hundred dollars from the robber on her person. Jesus and I will initial them as hers. That jar has part or all of the gold dust in it."

"Lefty and Haze can't find anything. Shirley, will you tell us where the other three went to hide?"

She stomped both bound legs with her brogan shoes. "Hell no. You bastards will eat dirt when my husband gets through with you."

"Those men aren't around this place and we need to get back home. Make those girls fix some food," Chet said to Roamer. "Jesus you watch them."

"Make some beans," Roamer directed the two younger women. "There are some soaking on the stove. And make some corn bread."

Chet agreed. Everyone needed some real food in their bellies.

"What about her?" Roamer asked.

"If she promises she won't start shouting at us again, we can release her."

"Go to hell," Shirley spat out.

"Leave her tied." Roamer turned his back on her and signaled for the two young wives to get cutting on the meal.

The boiled beans, even with lots of pepper sauce, tasted flat to Chet. The corn bread was scorched, but good enough with the burned part sliced off. He'd not forget this poor meal for a long time.

When each man had eaten his fill, they loaded up their grumbling prisoner and then mounted their own horses.

The old woman was screaming again. The two young women had turned her loose. All three should have been taken in except no one in the posse would have wanted to stay and take care of the hogs.

On their way at last, going over the hill, Chet looked back at the stinking hog ranch. He'd not miss any of it. Roamer, too, acted glad to be away from there, but the strong smell of hogs would be stay in Chet's nose for several days. He could only imagine how far the three women would run.

They camped at a ranch that night. Leaving their prisoner chained to a wagon wheel, they ate at the house. The woman served well-cooked beans and bacon with some wonderful Dutch oven biscuits and real butter. The man, Howard Temple, visited with them about the Marconis.

"I never trusted them. Sneaky. I caught them hauling a cow carcass off. They said they found her dead, but they'd already skinned her out and she bore my brand. I recalled her being fine a few days before. But what could I do? I went to watching them and they must have noticed 'cause they didn't ride my range again."

"Where did they go?" Chet asked.

"Up on the rim I guess. There's lots of wild country up there. They must know you have evidence on them. You may never see them again."

Roamer shook his head. "Guess we will see about that, huh?"

Chet hated them getting away, but with federal and Wells Fargo rewards, the three may get run down by bounty hunters.

* * *

When they reached Rye the next day, Chet bought food supplies and loaded the packhorses. They headed west on the trail for the Verde. Nightfall came and they camped. The temperature dropped after sundown and everyone took a turn at watching the sullen prisoner sleep.

The next day they crossed the Verde river and reached Yeager's ranch by mid-afternoon.

His wife Sheila made them sit and eat a real meal. The saddle-weary crew never argued. They left the prisoner chained and under a blanket. The warmth of her house and fireplace drove the cold out of them. Her rich food spoiled them and they all smiled at her generous ways.

"Sheila," Lefty said. "Ma'am, if you ever need anything, let us know. For something as little as a polecat killing your chickens, we'll ride over here and get rid of him."

"Yes," Roamer said. "As long as you feed us."

They all laughed

Yeager shook his head. "We appreciate all of you coming by. We don't get many folks. Come by here any time. Sheila will always feed you."

On the way to Annie Smart's, Chet shot a fat deer and everyone helped him load it aboard the spare horse they were leading back to the man who'd had it stolen.

The short woman came out of her house shaking

her head and laughing. "Chet Byrnes never forgets me. Take the buck in back and we can skin him."

Turning toward the prisoner and then back to Annie, Chet asked, "We didn't get his father and two brothers, but do you recognize this one?"

"All I saw was that old man threatening me. Guess I am lucky to be alive. Hey guys, thanks for that fat deer."

They strung it up and three of them sharpened their knives. In a few minutes, the carcass was skinned and gutted. They hauled it up and washed it with buckets of water. Returning to the front of the house, they each hugged her then left.

Hassayampa City came next and they arrived there after dark, ate at the café, threw the prisoner in the small jail, and slept in the hay at the livery. At dawn, they ate again at the café, got the prisoner, and then rode north. On the way, Roamer pointed out where the stage had been held up.

By late afternoon, they came where the road forked east of Preskitt and pulled over to say their good-byes.

Chet said to Lefty and Haze, "I'll see you two when you fill out your papers for your money. You can't miss Marge's. I'll pay you my part there and we can get you ready to go up on the rim."

Haze shook his head, amused. "We're both going to stop and buy us some real underwear while we're here."

"Do that. If you haven't got the money put it on my bill."

Lefty reined up his anxious horse. "You really mean that, don't you?"

"I do. Cattle drovers say 'you'd do to ride the river with' about men they like and trust. Both of you would do."

"We've got the money, but thanks," Lefty said. "You too, Jesus."

"I am glad to have ridden with you. And you took Roamer." Jesus waved good-bye and he and Chet galloped down the Preskitt Valley for home under dull and cloudy skies in the late afternoon.

His wife came out onto the porch. "My men are home."

Chet gave Jesus the reins, dismounted, and met her halfway. He swung her around, then wondered if he was supposed to do that with her pregnant.

"I hurt you."

"Lands no. I loved it."

He kissed her. He couldn't get enough of her. She looked secure and happy, and the baby was still safe in her belly. He silently thanked God and counted his blessings. That was enough and he was home. Home at last.

CHAPTER 13

It snowed that night while they renewed their marriage in the bedroom. In the morning, a blanket of soft snow covered the land with three or four inches of the white stuff. Sipping coffee at a front window to study the early morning snow, he mused about his first winter in the high country.

"It will melt today," his wife said, joining him.

"Good. I can go to the lower place tomorrow."

"What took you so long going after them?" she asked squeezing his arm.

"Like I said, they almost fooled us over at Rye. No one there even suspected them of robbing a stage. It was real slow getting a lead. Jesus finally found a crooked-legged horse's print in the street. We matched the owner up with the stage robbery. Jesus did a real good job."

"I didn't hear of anything wrong, anywhere in the ranch system. Your sister came by on her way to get supplies. She acted very pleased with her husband, so the marriage must be going well."

"I thought so. No mail from JD?"

"No." She shook her head. "Do you fear he's in trouble?"

"I hope not, but who knows. He's a different JD from the boy growing up. Even when he rode to Mexico with Jesus and me, his attitude worried me."

"What else?" she asked.

"How he went off by himself all the time. I don't know if it was shady lady business or what. But he hasn't been the same since he broke up with Kay."

"She never talks about it to me and now that she is Mrs. Hannagan I don't suppose she will."

"How did Monica's Sunday go?" he asked in a low voice after making certain she wasn't within hearing distance.

"I think she found him interesting. She said she was surprised." Marge smiled.

"Nice. He was polite?"

"Oh, yes. What do you want to do today?"

"I guess get used to snow and stay here."

"We can go to town in a few hours. It will be melted enough."

"Good. I'll go see Bo and find if there is any deeded land we can buy that's attached to the Verde ranch. I can see if the bank was able to cash any of the script we got for the cattle drives, too."

"That is a large sum of money."

He agreed. "But they will pay it some day."

"There's always something to fret about."

He agreed with her and went in the living room

to look at the newspapers he missed reading. "Is your father all right?"

"I think he will marry her."

"And?"

"He wrote me a letter and said he planned to transfer this ranch to me. I wrote back and told him to make the deed out to Mr. and Mrs. Byrnes. Anything mine is yours."

"Whatever you think. I don't plan to die, but we need to make a will that gives this place to our children."

"Thank you."

"Hey, we are partners and need to think about such things and face them responsibly."

"Yes." She rose and mussed his hair. "I wish we'd been together all our life, but I really do enjoy our union. I'm glad I paid your bills so you could stay."

They laughed, hugged, and kissed. He so appreciated her drawing his attention to her.

Mid-morning, they drove to town in the buggy. The snow had melted fast and even in the shade the ground was mushy under the horses' hooves and iron wheels of the buggy as they cut through it.

Their plans included lunch at Jenn's. Both of the girls were still working as waitresses. They hugged him and Marge. The place buzzed with business. No doubt, the two attractive women made it *the* place to eat. Jenn was so busy Chet and Marge had little chance to talk with her except a few words, learning that things were going well.

Chet found Bo in his office. His new assistant Donald Jernigan shook Chet's hand.

"Don is a lawyer," Bo began. "He's passed the bar and was looking for work so I decided I could use him. He's already sold some property. Where's Marge?

"Oh, shopping. What's new?" Chet asked.

"I bought two forty-acre plots of land in the valley adjacent to the ranch property." Bo led Chet to the map on the wall and pointed out the property. "How is that?"

"Fine."

"A ranch next to the Hartley Ranch going to come up for sale soon. The Randle Ranch."

"What are you talking about?" Chet asked.

"Six sections. It is in an estate case now. The cattle operation isn't that great, but the property does go to the river. Thirty-eight hundred and forty acres. I feel ten dollars an acre could buy it when the courts settle who owns it. Plus some cost for the cattle. I understand it has not been managed very well."

"Where are the heirs?"

"New York and Texas," Bo answered.

"We can probably handle it. But Washington is holding up funds for cattle we have delivered to the Navajos. And that grows with every month. We could probably swing it, but check with me before you buy it."

"The trial is six months away, so I will have my ear to the deal."

"Sounds good. Tell Jane I said hi."

"You aren't the only one looking for a baby," Bo said as he walked Chet to the door.

"Good. We can both learn how to change diapers."

"Aw, I don't know about that."

"You will. Trust me." Chet waved to Bo's assistant. "It's nice to meet you, Don."

Chet left the real estate office and headed to the bank. He met with the banker Tanner in his office. The tall man in a tailored suit seated across from him was impressed with his cattle selling operation. He told him the bank could handle any ranch purchase he wanted to make.

"I suspect the state will start paying those warrants in the next few months," Tanner said. "I heard you helped Deputy Roamer capture one of the stage robbers."

"That isn't for public information. Sheriff Sims doesn't like my helping."

Tanner frowned. "His dislikes may cost him that job next election."

"I won't run. I have too many distractions of my own."

"I understand, but the people won't."

Chet held up his hands. "I can't be sheriff and run all the businesses I have going on."

"I said I understand. The people of this county don't."

Chet shook Tanner's hand. "Let me know if you hear anything on them paying those bills."

"I will. But don't be concerned. They will be paid and anything you need we can help you."

"Good. That takes lots of worry off my shoulders."

Chet left the bank and picked up Marge at the dress store.

The snow was almost gone and on the way home she broached a subject that had been on her mind for a while. "Now that my father has deeded the place to us, I think we need to sell off some cattle. He had drives before, but it has been two years"—she took a deep breath—"so . . . work us in. Since the place is now ours, we need to start operating it. Raphael can handle anything you need."

"Hey, no problem. Why don't we ship two hundred head each delivery until we get caught up? Sorry I never asked."

"I never thought my dad would find another woman, but he did." Marge clung to Chet's shoulder and kissed him on the cheek as the wagon rims threw mud up on both sides of them. "I hope you're happy with me."

"Marge, you are on my mind all the time."

"Good, because if anything happens to this baby inside me I think it will break my heart."

He switched the reins to his other hand and squeezed her leg. "No. We will have each other and I am proud of that."

"I may cry."

Chet slowed the buggy.

"Don't stop. Guess I am so involved in worrying, I even worry what you would do."

"I will be there for you. Understand?"

She dabbed her eyes with a handkerchief. "Thanks. I love you."

"Me too. Don't cry. We will always have each other."

He hugged her. She had nothing to worry about. He'd have to convince her of that when they got home.

That evening, he told her about the Randle Ranch and had Jesus ride to the Hartley Ranch and tell Hampt to come over when he had time. They needed to talk about some things.

Jesus came back late and said that Hampt would come in the morning. May wished to go into Preskitt and Marge could go with her if she felt up to it. Marge agreed she would go. So the next day was set.

Marge had a bad case of morning sickness. It finally settled down and she was better when Hampt and May arrived about nine. The two women went to town shortly thereafter.

"What do you know about the Randle place?" Chet asked Hampt seated at the table.

"You know Slim Randle?"

"No."

"Well," Hampt began. "He must be eighty years old. He has boys for ranch hands, 'cause he only pays them twelve dollars a month. As soon as they learn anything, they quit and get a real job. He doesn't have any British bulls, maybe a few crosses. We had it out already. I told him if any of his cull longhorn bulls got over on my property and bred my cows, I'd cut them."

"That family owns almost four thousand acres."

"I never knew that. Man, that is lots of deeded land."

"Six sections."

"They do put up some hay on land down near the Verde. I just rode by it."

"Bo says after they get the estate settled we can buy it."

Hampt shook his head. "That and the Hartley place would make a great ranch."

"Start looking at more of it. Maybe get Tom to look it over with you. Three heads are much better than one."

"This is all secret right?" Hampt asked.

"Oh, yes, it needs to be."

"I can keep it quiet. That place would give us lots of ranching. Reg, up there at Hackberry. Sarge up at the Windmill ranch, Tom and all the Verde operation, and then my two places put together."

"Does the place have some big steers?"

"Land yes. I don't know when they sold any cattle last."

"Selling off some cattle could pay for the ranch," Chet said thoughtfully.

"I believe it could. Wow. Wouldn't that be something? Buy a ranch and let the cattle you can round up pay for it?"

"I think Reg's place will do it, too. Haze and Lefty went up to help those two."

"Boy, things have sure moved fast."

"We got in on the frontier here. No railroads to ship on. No markets. When this country opens up, it will boom, and we will be well situated by then."

Hampt nodded. "Damn right. I never took selling cattle to be that serious. Never thought it would be that important. But you sure need money to operate on. I look at my books with May every week. I've been thinking about something called barbed wire. The blacksmith in town has started making it. It will turn back cattle. I need to fence those hay fields I have down on the Verde. Cattle keep getting in there. I can cut posts this winter and by spring plant them."

"How much is it?"

"Fifteen bucks a roll. A five-wire fence costs seventy-five dollars plus posts and staples for every quarter mile. It would cost a thousand dollars to build enough to close in the hay fields. May helped me on that math."

"Good girl. I think some day we will need miles of it to survive in this business. Order the wire and go look at some tight wire fences. I have seen all kinds. We used smooth wire and stick fences in Texas. You really need well-set corners so they hold the wire tight. Posts just support it."

"Before we stretch any, I'll know all I can about fence building," Hampt promised. "Thanks."

"We better order it now. They can't make those rolls that fast."

"Good idea."

The two men had a good day talking about cattle, land, and water resources. Chet told him about the water development he'd seen down at

Rye. Hampt talked about places where he had such springs that could use developing.

"We need to go to work on that, too," Chet agreed.

"All I do is cost you money," Hampt said, smiling.

"Hey, we are going to build ranches we can live and work on. I'll need to get our new blacksmith John to make us some clam type posthole diggers. I saw some in Texas that had two handles and you closed them to lift the dirt out of a narrow hole."

"I think I can find some Mexican boys to make and split posts. We better get to cutting on this deal. It will be spring before we know it."

"Marge's foreman Raphael can find them and they'll be good ones."

"Can I close in sixty more acres down on the Verde bottoms for more alfalfa?" Hampt asked suddenly.

Chet began laughing.

Hampt frowned. "I meant for later on."

"Sure. You are an expansionist as bad as Reg."

Hampt shook his head. "What the hell does that mean?"

"Means you want more than you've got."

"I guess so boss man, but I am loving it. May's the best thing I ever found and this ranch business—well I never believed I'd ever get a shot at running one."

"I think those women just drove up."

"We'll need to get home. Those two boys and that little girl will have that cowhand watching them treed. Curly said he could watch them, but I bet he's plumb wore out. The boys have outgrown those two old horses. We better find them some peppier ones."

"I'll have my livery man find them."

"Good. They could ride a billy goat and would try him, but May can't stand the smell on them when they do."

"We'll find them some horses to ride."

"There's enough kids over there now so they will hold school. They are going to have a four-month session."

"Good."

They shook hands and Hampt went to join his wife in their buckboard.

Marge had already climbed down and grinned at him. "Take care of her."

"Oh, I will ma'am. If she'll just mind me." He climbed on the spring seat and turned the rig in a circle to leave. May was waving and shaking her head at him.

Chet kissed his wife. "Have fun?"

"Yes. May is a changed person and she talks to me now."

"I guess she was under so much pressure being my brother's wife and a family member her lips were sealed."

"I think Hampt brought her out of her quiet silence. I think he made a happy woman out of her."

"Good. He's found more work for me. I need to talk to Raphael about some Mexican boys to cut fence posts."

"He'll find them for you. He knows the ones that will work, too. Where are you building fence?"

"Around some land on the Hartley place that has alfalfa on the Verde."

"When I have the baby I want to go down there and see that lower place. What did he think about the ranch next door?"

"He about cried. Never thought he'd ever get a chance to run a real big ranch. Let alone the size of those two combined."

"What else?"

"My nephews need faster horses." They both laughed.

"May told me they were going to get to go to school again. You know she's been home schooling them all this time?"

"I knew she and Susie were concerned about the short sessions and no school setup over there."

Marge hung on his arm. "Lots to do, isn't there?"

"I'm almost as busy as I was in Texas."

"Oh pooh. You have more irons in the fire than any man I know including my own father when he was building this ranch."

"All right. I am busy. We aren't getting it all done as fast as I'd like, but we are making strides."

"Big ones." They went inside the house, kissed, and she went to tell Monica about her day with May.

He read the Miner newspaper until supper.

The next morning Chet struck out for The Quarter Circle Z, arriving at the Verde Ranch mid-morning. He entered the kitchen where Susie was busy making cinnamon rolls for the crew as a treat. "Morning Mrs. Times," he teased, kissing her cheek.

She grinned. "Morning, Mr. Byrnes." She poured him a cup of coffee and told him the wagon train people were seriously talking about going down to Hayden's Mill and farm.

He found his blacksmith John in the shop Tom had thrown up for him. The man in his big leather apron was working on his anvil and forge. He took off his gloves and shook Chet's hand.

"Is it all going all right?" Chet asked.

"Fine. We're repairing the mowing equipment. It needs lots of work and some reinforcing. Those implements were made for cutting smooth orchard grass and timothy hay fields in Iowa. Not sagebrush in Arizona."

Chet laughed. "Have you ever seen those clam-like posthole diggers?"

"I think I have. Why?"

"Could we make some?"

"Sure. Why?"

"We are going to fence the lower hay fields on the Hartley place next year and we'll need several of them."

"I'll draw one up," John promised. "My wife said to be sure to thank you. The house is solid, dry, and warm with a fire in it. My kids are in school and we're settling down. Tom has gotten me everything I needed. We've fixed single and double trees, made parts for that boy up at the sawmill for his wagons, and kept busy. How are you going to fence it?"

"They make a twisted wire at the blacksmith shop in Preskitt with sharp barbs on it."

"I have seen that. We could make that here. Maybe when things settle down for the cowboys this winter we can use them to help."

"Let me talk to Tom about that," Chet said.

"Fine, but I bet we can beat the price in Preskitt."

"John, you have the right idea."

They parted and Chet went by the cook shack to see how Hoot was.

The old man was sitting down at the long table, drinking coffee.

"You all right?" Chet asked, concerned, stepping over the bench to sit down beside him.

"I been having some sorry days lately. Guess I'm just tired today."

"You need to go see a doctor."

"He got any pep pills? I'll come out of it. That last boy Tom hired—Clarence—can feed the hands. Susie's making rolls special for them today. She wanted to. I'll go lay down. Don't worry. I'll get over this."

"You should see a doctor," Chet advised.

"If I don't get better, I will."

"Do that."

Hoot shuffled off to the bunkhouse, leaving Chet concerned. He'd never seen the old man that low.

Back at the house, he talked to Susie about him.

She wiped her hands on her apron. "He's been failing lately. I've been baking pies, bread pudding, 'cause that boy, while he's good, can't get it all done, otherwise."

"Hire him a helper."

"I'll tell Tom. Hoot will listen to him. Me, it would be crowding in."

"He's not well. Hampt and May came over the other day. Singing May is really doing good as a wife."

"Why didn't we ever know she could do that?"

"Damned if I know. But she truly is happy and so is he." Then Chet told her about what the new ranch deal might be like.

"Man, you are hoeing and going."

He also told her about his wife receiving the home place as her own.

Susie shook her head. "You always liked being busy."

Since Tom wouldn't be back until late, he decided to ride on up to the Windmill Ranch and come back the next day. Sarge would be there and he wanted to see what his plans were.

It was past sundown when he arrived, but thanks to the mild day, the ride across country had been pleasant.

Victor cooked him some food as Sarge told him how things were going at Gallup. "Hay partners are set up. They didn't get the snow you got at Preskitt. We're doing fine here. Tom sent me a letter that the next shipment would be up here in a week. It will be early, but we'll head out right away to be at the Navajos for the December delivery. That okay with you?"

"You're the boss. This winter will be a booger to get cattle there on time but the agency knows that. They still happy?"

"Oh, they say they are. I hear all the time that some Texans are underbidding us, but so far they ain't won that contest."

"Rumors can be just that. The agency needs orderly deliveries. The last bunch couldn't do that, so they'll be wary."

"We got a bed. You are staying for the night. Boys grained and put your horse up already."

"Hey, I'm ready for bed." Chet turned to the cook. "Thanks, Victor, for caring for the men. This is a critical operation for our ranch."

"Ah, *sí.* You tell your wife to come see me."

"I will."

Satisfied, he slept in the bunkhouse and woke to eat Victor's breakfast with the crew and talk to the men, then he rode back to the Verde ranch without incident. Despite the sunshine, he kept his jumper buttoned against the north wind that kept him hunched up in the saddle. Next time he'd wear his sheep-lined jacket.

Tom was at the ranch when Chet returned in late afternoon. They visited at Susie's house. Leif was out with two others making sure cattle hadn't drifted too far north of their range.

A fire crackled in the fireplace and the radiant heat felt good on Chet's face. The two sipped fresh coffee.

"Any word on the three that got away from you and Roamer?" Tom asked.

"No. I imagine we won't ever hear about them again. We were lucky to get back the loot we did and that one brother."

"You hear anything from JD?"

"He's working for someone west of Socorro, New Mexico. He says it's out of that range war."

"I hope so. Some tough stories coming out of there."

"I'd say. We'll have to wait and see."

"No telling about him," Tom said. "He really went under after the breakup with that woman. She didn't appreciate all he had done for her."

"JD's father was a strange guy. The government said he was killed in the last battles in Mississippi during the war, but records weren't good in those last days. A lot of us thought he'd probably show up one day. He never did.

"He was a gambler and wanted no part of the ranch work. That was why I ended up running it. My mother always said he was like other relatives in the Byrnes family who ran sideshows and other flimflam deals."

"He never showed up again?"

Chet shook his head. "And I have not missed him."

Tom changed the subject. "All was well with Sarge?"

"He's fine. Expecting cattle is all."

"I sent him a letter. We will have those cattle up there next Wednesday."

"He's ready."

"Good. What else is news?"

Chet told him about the pending ranch deal, then Tom went to his house for supper.

Chet ate with Susie. Leif wasn't back and it was dark. She acted edgy at the meal over his tardiness.

"You finally have someone?" Chet asked her.

"Oh yes, and I enjoy every day. I dreaded marriage, but I love it and him so much."

"Good. I am going to turn in. I'll have breakfast with the boys in the morning."

"No, please don't. Leif will be up regardless and I'll have it here."

"Fine. Wake me."

"I will."

Susie woke him in the middle of the night. "Leif is back, but someone shot one of the cowboys. They brought him over here and sent for the doc. Tom is coming."

Chet woke quickly. "Who? What's his name?"

"Utah. He's a new hand Tom hired two weeks ago."

"I'll be right down." Chet dressed hurriedly and took the stairs two at a time.

Leif looked exhausted. He and two others had the victim on a cot in front of the fireplace. Tom arrived and so did two other hands. Susie was running around getting things.

"How bad off is he?" Tom asked, entering the room. His wife Millie was right behind him.

"He was shot in the shoulder and then thrown off his bucking horse. He was out most of the time coming back. I shot at the men who shot him, but they were riding hell for leather to get away. I'd have gone after them, but he looked in such bad shape I decided we'd be lucky to get him back here. We made a bed between two horses with poles and a blanket. Cole there rode double with me to get him back."

"All we had to cut them poles down with were some dull hand axes," Cole said, shaking his head.

Susie was putting wet compresses on the boy's head, trying to ease him some.

"Did you know any of those men who shot him?"

Leif shook his head. "We stumbled on three men—I counted—driving a half dozen head of yearlings up the mountain going north. They started shooting and got Utah. His horse went crazy, threw him down the mountainside, and we went to see what we could do for him. Cole told you we had to chop two poles and make a sling to haul him back."

"Randy left to get doc," Tom said.

"Cattle thieves up in that country. What next?"

Leif shook his head. "What were they going to do with them anyway?"

"I have no damn idea." Chet shook his head in disappointment. "What did you notice about them?"

Cole jumped in. "One guy had a gray horse, another had a red roan like your good horses, and the third had a bay. He had some silver on his saddle. It shined in the sunlight, didn't it Leif?"

"Oh, we could have found them from what we saw and their horses. But we couldn't quit Utah."

"No problem. You all did good getting him back here considering where you came from. Tom, send someone to my place and tell Marge what's happened and get Jesus. Tell him this will be a long ride and to dress warm. That boy can really track.

"Susie, we need food and supplies for two weeks.

Tom, we'll need two stout packhorses. I want my other roan—"

"Cole and I want to go along," Leif broke in. "We want a chance to even the score for Utah."

Tom nodded his approval.

Chet said, "Get ready. It will be damn cold up there and may get worse."

Things were moving. Lamps were lit to saddle horses and the whole crew was up. Chet sized the situation. "Everyone take a minute and get on your knees. We're going to pray for Utah here. He's in the Lord's hands now."

Quickly, everyone was hatless and he began. "Dear Lord Heavenly Father, we are just some cowboys living out here on the frontier. Tonight, we ask you to take one of our fallen men ambushed by the devil's workers and protect him and make him well. Utah is a member of our crew of hard workers. He may never have been in a place of worship, but he lives under the greater cathedral—your sky."

They made soft amens and he continued. "Lord, he's been our true partner and went to stop the outlaws stealing our cattle. Be with him this night and help him return to the job he loves. Amen."

The crew rising up didn't have a dry eye and quietly thanked Chet, then they went about doing the things needed for him and the others to leave.

"Leif, you and Cole go sleep. I can get it all ready. We can't leave till Jesus gets here. Go upstairs and fall on any bed. We'll wake you in plenty of time."

Tom, standing by, closed his eyes and shook his head. "Trouble never will end, will it?"

"Big as we are growing, I doubt it. Can't steal

much from some homesteader with a dirt floor,"
Chet pointed out.

"That's true. Some day I'll tell you how much
Millie and I appreciate working here. I thought my
stubbornness, reacting to Ryan, and getting fired
had cut my chances of ever having anything for the
rest of my life. But despite problems like this, we are
living as comfortable as any rich people."

Chet clapped him on the shoulder. "We all are
the luckiest people in the world."

Kneeling beside Utah, trying to comfort him,
Millie looked up. "Thanks for the prayer, Chet. It
helped us all."

"Good."

Tom left to check on the men. There was nothing he could do for the unconscious cowboy. Chet
felt the same and went in the kitchen to get some
coffee. Poor Marge, she had to do without him
again. At least she understood or always seemed to.

"Can you think who those rustlers might be?"
Susie held the coffeepot.

He shook his head and nodded for her to fill
him a cup. "But we'll find them."

"Just be careful." She poured it and then took a
cup in for Millie.

He sat at the kitchen table and mulled over how
he'd done things differently since coming to Arizona. But it hadn't made any difference. He'd just
traded feudists in Texas for outlaws in the territory.

CHAPTER 14

Chet and his three-man posse woke more than twenty-four hours later in their camp up on the rim and crowded the roaring fire. Jesus made coffee and the lanky cowboy Cole was heating water to stir in the oatmeal. He had no idea how cold it was, but his steaming breath marked a point way down the mercury tube.

The rustlers were still ahead of them, but they had tracks to follow, a description of their horses, and the deep determination of their leader to capture them. Doc had told them before they left the ranch that Utah had a chance to live. Chet hoped he was right.

"Does it ever get this cold in Texas where you lived?" Leif asked.

Chet shook his head. "Maybe once or twice, but not over two days."

Leif shook his head in mild amazement. "We'll see some warm days, but altitude and all, we will have winter up here. Where will these men go, do you figure?"

"I know little about this country. I have been to Hackberry which is north. Never farther west to what they say is desert on the way to California. I've seen the Grand Canyon. That is about all."

"They can go to California, but it's a helluva trip across that desert. They can go around the Grand Canyon and there is a ferry around there that's run by some old Mormon named Lee. It is the only place you can cross the Colorado River and go north into Utah. You came from the east so you know there are only a few stations on that Marcy Road."

"Rustlers stole some of our cattle and took them down on the Bill Williams River and sold them to some miners there. I sent Hampt to check on them, but they were gone. These rustlers wouldn't have gone up that damn mountain we rode up yesterday unless they had a market for them."

Leif laughed and then sipped his fresh-made coffee. "You're right Chet, you'd need a damn good reason to herd cattle over that goat trail."

Cole had the oatmeal, raisins, and sugar mix ready so he filled bowls around the circle and they ate breakfast with the fire's sharp smoke twisting around them from the wind. The hot cereal warmed them up. They washed the bowls afterward in boiling water, then saddled the horses.

In no time, they were on the trail headed north. The sun was slow to warm the air, but everyone was dressed well and they soon were on the flat rolling country on top of the Mogollon Rim. The open grassland spread out before them with islands of small hills covered in black looking pines called Ponderosa.

Chet liked this country better than the valley, but that area had less winter and produced lots of strong forage for livestock. Still, up on top it looked like a land untouched by man spread north, east, and west where a cowboy could ride all day and not see a farmer or a town.

At the Marcy Road they found the riders' tracks went east. Jesus said they weren't more than half a day ahead of the posse. Everyone was to keep their eyes open.

Chet was trying to figure if they were past Hackberry or still west of there. When he'd found his way up on top to capture Ryan and his henchmen, he knew he'd been farther west. Satisfied he'd figured it out, he said, "We are past our ranch up here."

"Where can they be going?" Cole asked, twisting around in the saddle.

"None of us know where they were going or why they were driving them up here," Chet said, feeling itchy that they were so exposed on the wagon track. "Let's ride."

They stopped a freight train scout mid-morning on the road. The buckskin clad man with a gray-flecked beard carried a .50 caliber rifle over his lap.

"We're tracking three men who shot a ranch hand and went this way, sir," Chet said. "You seen them?"

"I suppose. I spoke to a man I know as Karnes a

ways back. He wondered how far it was to Shakes Ranch."

"What did you tell him?"

"Take the road north to the ferry. It was on the edge of the Navajo Reservation, this side of the little Colorado and that Cameron trading post."

"He say where he was going?" Chet asked.

"Not directly."

"What kind of horse was he riding?"

"A gray, I think."

"You catch any other names?"

"No sir. The other two were real closemouthed."

"Thanks. You said you know him?"

"Oh yes. He sells butchered beef to freighters like us on this road. He never mentioned having any this time."

Chet closed his eyes. They butcher beef and sell it to freighters on the road. "Aw hell."

The crew laughed and the scout frowned at all of them.

"It's a private joke. Thank you, sir," Chet said.

"You are welcome, sir." He nodded and rode off on his thin dun horse.

When he was gone, Leif booted his horse in close to Chet. "This guy's been stealing cattle to sell to freighters on this road."

"Exactly. They need meat, never ask many questions, and pay cash."

"Sounds like the rustlers have been stealing from others and selling along here for a while."

"Oh, I imagine so. But a leak like this was damn hard to find."

"They could have sold them elk meat," Leif said.

"No, that would be too hard. They'd have to hunt and dress the animals a long way off. They can bunch the stolen cattle, slaughter somewhere close, and not have to hunt them down."

"I guess you're right. Damn. I'd never thought about that."

"Neither would I." Chet pushed them in a long trot to gain ground on the road.

When they met a long oxen wagon train hauling west, he halted to speak to the man in charge.

He wore a Scottish tam and kilts with high, loud, plaid socks. "Aye, Mr. Byrnes. That man yea mentioned, Karnes, talked to us a few hours ago. He's a butcher and has sold me beef many times from a tent he had set up."

"I have not seen his tent. He shot a ranch hand while stealing cattle from my ranch a few days ago. I don't even know if my man Utah lived, but I want Karnes to answer for shooting him."

"Aye and he should, but I don't know where he went."

"Thanks. If he's that close, we'll find him."

"God be with you, sir."

The posse trotted on. Jesus found the fresh tracks and they rode farther. A few miles past the military road they came to a hand-painted sign. It said WADES BAR AND STORE with an arrow pointing through the pines.

Chet could see a gray horse hitched in front of a log building. "Jesus ride around and cover the back with your rifle. If they're armed and shooting, shoot them."

"*Sí.*" He took off on his horse, making a wide circle to the back of the building.

"Take the left and don't shoot us," Chet said to Cole.

The man was gone in that direction. Chet and Leif charged toward the log building, jerking out their rifles on the run.

In the confusion, someone ran out of the building from the front door, looked shocked, and drew his pistol. That was a mistake. Cole reined up his horse and fired his rifle. The bullet struck the man in the chest and he staggered backward, firing his gun into his own foot, and fell down, screaming in pain.

"Get off your horse," Chet shouted at Leif. Sliding his horse to a halt, Chet took aim at a shooter blasting with a Winchester from the doorway. Leif's horse fell and Chet drove a bullet into the rifleman at the door. He fell face forward.

He rushed to see about Leif. The young man was unconscious. Chet's heart stopped as he sat on his knees holding Leif up. "Talk to me, Leif."

Leif's head was strangely loose. Chet let him down and heard more shooting out back.

A whiskered man in a stained apron came out hands high. Two Indian whores joined him. "We ain't got no hand in this mister."

Chet covered them all. "Good. I have a man hurt. Come see what you can do for him." The knot in his throat was choking him and his stomach was in a knot. Susie's new husband had to be just unconscious. Anything else was too hard to think.

"They're all dead," Jesus shouted, coming around the building. "Where is Leif?"

When Chet didn't answer, he ran to join him. Cole came, too, on the double. The bearded man put his ear to Leif's chest and rose, shaking his head. "This man is dead."

Dead? Chet closed his eyes. His mind went back to the wounded highwayman telling him outlaws had cut his nephew Heck's throat. Chet had emptied his six-gun into the highwayman's body at close range.

He collapsed on his butt, his hands braced behind him. *What in the hell will I ever tell my sister?*

CHAPTER 15

The toughest two-day ride of his life was leading his dead brother-in-law's mount, laden with his body wrapped in a blanket, back to Camp Verde. Leif must have broken his neck when his horse went down head over tail from the bullet intended for him. No one but Chet saw it happen.

Solemn-faced, they reached the sawmill and Robert Brown rushed out to see what was wrong. "Who is it?"

"Leif Times," Chet said. "We were after some rustlers." He swallowed hard. "They shot his horse and he broke his neck in the fall."

"When did it happen?"

"Yesterday. Up at a place called Wade's on the Marcy Road."

"What can I do?"

Chet dropped heavily from the saddle. "I don't know, Robert. I might have planned our raid on those rustlers better. Leif is dead. Nothing we can do for him, now."

"Oh, hell. Your poor sister."

"It will break her heart and it's all my fault."

"I want to ride down with you and give everyone some support. I wouldn't have this job, if it wasn't for you. I came to you from Jenn and if you had not given me the chance, I'd be starving back in Preskitt. I'm going back to support you and Susie. She's a great lady."

Chet nodded. He was short on words, bearing the weight of Leif's death heavy on his heart.

Cole and Jesus had tried to tell him it wasn't his fault. No tears ran down his cheeks. Only his heart pained him. But he had no answers, no way to speak about it more than a few sentences. *Leif dead.*

Chet didn't sleep—just lay in the bunkhouse bed with heavy eyelids that hardly stayed closed. He recalled burying his own brother on the prairie and going after his killers. How dark his days had been, how hard to keep centered on his mission to settle that matter. The three rustlers were dead, but he had to go back to the family and Susie and explain that an accident killed her newfound mate. Damn. At periods of this mad experience, he wanted to fade away.

The only woman in the world he held as high as his wife was his sister Susie. And in the next twenty hours he had to face her. God—he hated to do that. It would be worse than picking up Leif's limp body and getting no response.

Morning came. At breakfast the mill men offered their condolences to him. He thanked them quietly, mostly with nods of his head.

Chet, Cole, and Jesus saddled up in the cold air and rode for Camp Verde with the body tied over a good horse. Late afternoon, they rode up to the headquarters and the crew came hurrying to see who was dead.

Chet dismounted quickly and got around the men to head off his distraught sister. He caught her.

"It's Leif?" she cried out and then fainted.

He swept her up in his arms, calling to Cole. "Go tell the rest of the ranch Leif Times is dead."

Chet carried her toward the house. "Tom, will you go tell my wife? Don't let her panic. I am staying with Susie."

"We'll tell Hampt and May, also."

"Go tell Sarge as well."

"What about Reg?"

"I'll go tell him in time. Put Leif's body some place safe, first. We will decide the place to bury him. His father needs to know, too."

"Damn shame," Tom said. "He was making a real leader of men."

"Put me down." Susie struggled to her feet. "I want to see what they are going to do with his body."

"Easy. You fainted," Chet said.

She straightened her dress. "I want him in the living room. Not in some shed."

Tom's wife Millie came on the run and took her arm. "What can I do?"

"I am having his body taken into the house."

Millie looked up at the open front door. "I will fix a place for it." She bolted for the entrance to set things up.

His arm around her, Chet headed Susie up the steps and inside. He didn't want to hurry her, but felt the sooner Leif's body was in the grave, the sooner he'd recover from the horrible burden of bringing him home.

Millie had a sheet to spread on the main table. A cowboy helped her and then stepped back.

With care the four men carried Leif's body inside and laid it out on the table. Millie began to herd everyone outside. She stopped Chet. "Stay. Susie needs you. Tom has gone for Marge. He's sent the rest to tell others. Leif needs to buried today. That is not much notice, but we must do it that way."

"Thanks." Chet let Susie go back into the kitchen, sobbing.

Cole stood at the door. "Tom put me in charge. Should we start a grave next to that boy's?"

"Yes. If she wants him elsewhere we can change. Thanks, Cole."

"We have a fat steer hanging in the cooler, so we will start a fire and barbecue him. We are cutting the carcass up now so we can have him done by afternoon. The men are working hard to have lots of food ready 'cause when the word gets out we will have plenty of folks coming in. They are even baking bread. What else do I need to do?"

"Set up some rough tables. Rewash all the tin dishes we have so they're clean. How is Hoot?"

"He's sitting down and directing things. He says he's fine, but he's weak. I'll watch him. John is making a casket for the body."

"Good. We will need a row of chairs for the family to sit. Oh, a minister, we need one."

"I am not sure about that. The men want you to do it."

"Are you serious? Why?"

"They know that you and him were close. He rode with you on posses and you've prayed with us. If our request is too hard, we can get the minister who married Susie and Leif."

"Stay here. I need to ask her."

"Sure."

Chet went back into the kitchen. Susie looked up and met his gaze.

"What?" she asked.

"The cowboys have asked me to give the graveside services at the funeral."

Numb, she nodded. "You were his hero. Yes, he would have liked that. I know that is a burden to put on your shoulders after all you have been through, but I would be pleased, too."

"I will do it. We have many things taking place. The whole crew is cooking food for the guests they expect today. They are really pitching in to get things done and they will be ready. I will ask May to sing a hymn if she can do it."

"Good. Millie and I will dress him in his best clothes."

"Fine. I am going to try to sleep a few hours."

"Its near midnight now. Get some rest."

"If I can sleep."

"Chet. Thanks. You always get things done. We all appreciate you. Good night, brother."

He went back and told Cole he would handle the services.

A soft smile crossed his mouth and then a nod. "Good. I will tell the men."

"Aren't you shorthanded?" Chet asked, concerned.

"The women and men from the wagon train came, as soon as they heard, to help us."

"Good. I am going to try to sleep a few hours."

"Yes, you will need it. Things are moving. We will be ready. We'll dig the grave after daylight."

"Good. We can talk in the morning."

"Yes sir."

"Thanks." Chet clapped Cole on the shoulder. Tom had picked a good man to put in charge. Upstairs, Chet fell into bed and was soon asleep. Some time in the night his wife quietly joined him.

When he awoke and sat up, she caught and hugged him from behind. "I am so sorry I wasn't there. I know you have had two hard days."

"Nothing anyone could do. I feel more sorry for Susie. I didn't take him along to get him killed."

"It will be hard, but I survived it. Hurts like someone kicked you in the guts, but you survive. We talked last night. She's a strong person. Married only a few months and he's already been taken away from her."

"First Heck, now Leif. What am I?" Chet took in a deep breath, letting it out in a sigh.

"A strong family man. What now? I brought some good clothes. Tom and his wife are so nice and this cowboy Cole Emerson, he's a good one. Things look in place to me."

"I need to write a script."

"You want a bath and shave?"

"Yes, I better have that."

"I'll arrange for it. Anything else?" Marge asked.

"Coffee and some breakfast when someone gets time."

"They will. You can write up here. I'll arrange the rest."

Chet kissed her. Then she got up and dressed.

At the desk, he began scribbling ideas on paper. He'd need a prayer to start. Then he must write about the young man who'd come and asked to ride with him. Leif wanted to help and rode with the posse who went after the killers of the old couple. He went along to find Roamer's shooters and holdup men. He'd proved himself and became part of the Quarter Circle Z crew. He courted Susie and they married a short while before this tragic accident occurred, running down three worthless rustlers.

Hampt came upstairs and stood in the doorway holding his hat.

"Come in, Hampt, and sit down," Chet said, looking up for moment.

"I didn't come to trouble you."

"You aren't."

"May will sing 'How Great Thou Art.' She cried some coming over, but when she heard you were doing the services, she straightened up and said, 'Oh, I have to do it.'"

"She's a lovely lady and you have done more good for her than any of us."

"Aw, hell, boss, I'm so lucky to have her. She's such a bright light in my life. I won't know what to do without her."

"Great. Hug and kiss her for me. We did get those three thieves that caused Leif's death. They were rustling cattle, butchering them, and selling the meat to freighters on the road."

"I didn't know there was a way up the mountain to March Road. Cole said it was steep going in lots of places."

"Hard. How are things?"

"John and I talked some about making our own barbed wire this winter."

"He says he knows how, but getting the stuff from the end of the tracks to here would be a helluva big job."

"Hell, boss we can do that."

Chet chuckled. "Oh, well go on. You say we can, then we can do it."

"Good. We're going to find out how and how much."

"Do it. I need to take a bath and shave. How cold is it outside today?"

"Warm enough. It will be fine by the time you have services."

"Thanks and thank May for me."

Hampt looked around. "I never knew before, but Sarge has a big crush on your sister. He knows it is way too early, but he told me he was not going miss getting her this time."

Chet agreed. "He's a solid man."

"Yeah, hardworking, too. I thought I'd share his intentions with you."

Chet heard steps on the stairs. "I think my wife is coming up to tell me she has bathwater ready."

"Hampt, how are you?" Marge asked, stepping into the room.

"Sad that we lost him, but I'll be fine."

"Good." She looked at Chet. "The water's hot."

"Hampt and I were just talking. May will sing this afternoon."

She nodded that she knew. "She will be the icing on the cake."

"See you, Chet. Ma'am." Hampt said and started out.

"You call me Marge. We're all family. I'm not someone special."

"Yes, Marge. I will do that."

She reached over, caught him, and planted a kiss on his cheek. "Marge is who I am."

Hampt was embarrassed, but he was laughing. "I won't forget."

Equally amused, Chet knew Hampt would not forget it.

They went downstairs—he to be bathed, shaved, and to eat an early lunch, Marge to welcome the people who were coming from everywhere, and Hampt to find his wife. The south wind swept the dust of churning wheels across the open land between the house and the road.

Dressed at last, Chet passed the coffin, noticing that the women had cleaned up the body and dressed it in a suit. Leif's father was in the kitchen and they shook hands, shared a few words, hugged, and patted each other on the back.

Chet's Aunt Louise and her man came to the house. Dressed in black, she looked straight-backed, but Chet could feel she was very devoted to the man. He could hardly believe how much she'd changed since they'd left Texas.

He made his way over to them. "Aunt Louise, I'm so glad you're here."

"Chet, I know how this has stabbed you, but you are so important to this family. Keep your head high. You lead these people. I only wish JD would come back and be a part of us again. He sent me one sparse letter, but I guess I should be grateful for that. Reg's woman Lucy sends me short ones, but quite often. I do enjoy them. Lean down. I want to kiss you for all you've done for us and poor Susie."

He did and her kiss burned a hole in his cheek. "Thanks," he managed.

Two o'clock, six cowboys including Tom carried the coffin from the house to place it on the saw-horses at the gravesite beside Heck's monument. The family was seated in the front row chairs. Chet took his place before the crowd he estimated at over a hundred and fifty folks.

May sang the hymn. Her voice sounded so strong and he was moved as he thanked her.

"Ladies and gentlemen, we come before you today to lay to rest a fine husband, a fellow worker, Leif Times. His time here was cut short by a horse wreck as he bravely fought outlaws who had shot a cowboy while they were rustling cattle. This young man came to me wanting to help bring the lawless ones to justice. He never asked for any special treatment other than what the rest of us had on those days spent in the saddle. He never complained.

"His marriage to Susan Byrnes was a great union for both of them and his loss leaves a great space in her life and heart. But we never know when we will depart this world. I can only suppose God needed Leif's work in heaven. We do know He choose a great man to help Him. All of us who rode with Leif loved him . . . or at least liked him." Chet smiled and the crowd gave a soft laugh.

"So on this day we say farewell to a good friend. We must support his father who has lost a son he loved and who was proud about his accomplishments, as were all of us.

"Please stand. Let us pray.

"Dear Lord, we are gathered here to intern a friend, a son, a husband, and a great human being, Leif Times. Receive him into your hands and make him welcome in his new home. We will remain here and ask you to heal our loss of him. Be strong in our hearts. Give us the wisdom and ease our way forward. Amen."

He stepped over to Susie and hugged her then hugged Marge sitting next to her. They nodded their approval and the men lowered the coffin into the grave using ropes.

His hands held high, Chet turned to the crowd. "The service is over, but please stay. We have lots of food fixed and I am certain Leif would want you to be friendly and have a good time. Thanks for coming."

May joined them and he mused to himself how

forward she had become; not brazen, but proud and part of the three-woman team. Her face shone and he swelled with pride at her new appearance.

"Should we help serve them?" she asked her co-hosts.

Marge shook her head. "Those ranch hands are serving it well enough. It is their way of helping."

"Thanks, brother," Susie said. "You were long enough. He would not have wanted a longer one."

"Good. I always get tired most times. That may be why the boys wanted me to do it."

"No," Marge said. "They respect you and knew you'd say the right things."

"Oh well. Now, I'm hungry."

"Feed him," Susie said. "I told Sarge he and I could eat together. He has been so nice to me through all this. I am impressed."

"He's a good man."

"I don't need a man, thank you, but he has been very thoughtful."

"Sure." Chet had better hush up and take his wife to the food line. Walking beside her, he wondered how she felt. Obvious she was growing bigger, but it looked all right to him—that would be their son or daughter some day. "You feeling all right?"

"Fine. Morning sickness is part of this deal. It isn't more than an inconvenience here and there, but greater things will come from it. I am happy about being with child."

They filled the plates she had brought along and found their fold-up chairs, no doubt set up for her by a ranch hand. The weather was warm from the radiant sun on the front side and cold on the backside. He put a shawl from the back of the chair over her shoulders, then took his plate back. With his fork, he picked at the fine, tasty meat.

"You ever hear any more about those stage robbers? The Marconis?" a rancher stopped and asked him.

"No, but we will. Rewards are posted for up to a hundred dollars for them now. When Wells Fargo raises it to two hundred, that's when they'll turn up. Bounty hunters will find them for that kind of money."

"It's one more deal Sheriff Sims owes you for."

Chet shook his head to dismiss the matter, but he knew Sims had no plans to do anything about it.

By late afternoon, most everyone had gone home. Chet and Marge decided to stay at the big house with Susie, rather than go home so late and the days so short. Of course, she was with Sarge who'd been escorting her around all afternoon. Eventually, he brought her back to the house.

Marge had made coffee and the four sat around the living room with the big fireplace heating the house. Plenty of wood had been stacked inside.

"Thanks, brother," Susie said with a cup in her hand. "You did well. Everyone said that. I am always glad to hear your voice when you speak. Did anyone invite Leif's father to stay?"

Marge shook her head. "I spoke to him about it and he said he needed to get home."

"I can understand. This would be too big a reminder for him, anyway. He is a sweet man. And Sarge, thanks for looking out for me."

Straight-faced he shook his head. "You have done so much for everyone Miss Susie, anything I can do to help you—send word. Unless I am on the road with cattle, I'll be right here."

"Good to know. Thanks."

"Yes, ma'am. I better go to up to the bunkhouse and find a bed."

"There are plenty of rooms here and I'll make breakfast early if you need to ride back," Susie offered.

"How would that look?" Sarge's voice sounded concerned.

"It looks like you don't have to sleep in the bunkhouse tonight," Chet said.

"Why don't we play rummy awhile," Marge said. "That could occupy our minds."

So they agreed. Chet wasn't a great card lover, but he knew it would settle them all down and lower the tension in the room. The fire crackled and burned. He rose and backed up to it as the girls set things up.

Sarge joined him and spoke softly. "I know she's hurt deep, but she's taking it better than I thought. And thanks. This has been the best day of my entire life. Up close, she is so real."

"Good. I know you've helped her through the tough part and I appreciate that."

"Me staying don't bother you?"

"No, and it will beat the razzing you'd take from the crew in the bunkhouse."

"We're ready. Come on card sharks," Marge called to them from the dining room.

Susie, in her style, had fixed a large piece of

Dusty Richards

apple pie for everyone and set it out by their place. Plus, she'd refilled the coffee cups, being sure everyone around the table was fixed up. Sarge moved her chair in when she sat down.

He damn sure, in Chet's estimation, was working the whole deal and might win her broken heart before it was over. Chet pulled out his chair and sat down. Of course, he and Marge would beat the pants off them playing rummy.

In bed upstairs, Marge whispered to Chet, "Sarge does have his heart set on her. Doesn't he?"

"I think he's trying and it is working. I'm pleased."

They kissed and fell sleep. The north wind whistling in the eaves was the last thing he recalled.

CHAPTER 16

The temperature dropped overnight.

Breakfast was scrambled eggs. Susie must have hoarded them. Most laying hens molded in the short days and eggs were hard to find on a free-range situation. There was also fried ham, wonderful brown-top biscuits and thick flour gravy, German fried potatoes and onions, and some figs she'd purchased from Hayden Mills in the summer and preserved. And of course, coffee—good strong coffee.

Replacing his cup in a saucer, Sarge said, "Boss man, do you have a job over here I can do? If I got an occasional chance to eat at your sister's table once in a while I'd be happy working for twenty a month."

Shaking his head and laughing, Chet said, "Hell no. I need you at the Windmill Ranch." He could have sworn his sister blushed, but they were all laughing. "Besides Sarge, you have my second best cook—Victor."

"Oh, yes, and he goes the extra mile, but Susie outdid them all this morning. Thanks, Susie."

"I'm glad you know my name," she said amused. "All day yesterday I wanted to tell you I was not Mrs. Times."

"I'm sorry. I was just being polite."

She reached over and clapped his hand on the table. "I know, and it was a trying day, but no one knows what tomorrow or the next day will bring any of us. I know you're a busy man, and serve in an important position for the ranch, but anytime you come over, you can stay here, and I'll fix you breakfast, lunch or supper."

"Can I take you to the dance?"

"In time. I don't want to look too indifferent to Leif's death, but I know two things. He would have wanted me to go on with my life and I do not intend to be the widow dressed in black, forever." She shrugged her shoulders. "Is that too outspoken for you?"

"No ma'am. That's fine. I appreciate you being so open with me. I understand you need time. I'm not—"

"You are a polite, elegant man. But tell me—you worked here for maybe a year and never spoke to me that I can recall. Why?"

"I didn't think I was in your class. I'm a farmer's son who enlisted in the army and ate beans until I was sick and tired of them and resigned. Jenn introduced me to Chet and he took me on. I am not a roper, though I have learned how, but you were like the boss's daughter. I was like a peasant in Europe, not allowed to talk to the princess."

Susie began to laugh. "I am a tomboy. How did you ever get a princess out of me?"

"I told your brother I regretted not meeting you personal-like before it was too late."

"Is that why you never danced with me before I was married?"

"Yes."

"Sarge, I am so glad you got over your fright of me." Then she began to cry.

Marge rose and handed her a napkin.

"I am sorry—" *Sniff.* Susie dabbed at her eyes. "Of all the people to think I was a princess—I am so sorry. I simply had to know."

"Stand up," he said softly as he rose. "I want to hug you."

She did and he gently held her in his arms. "Susie, I won't crowd you, but if in the end you still consider me a good man, I will be here for you."

"Thanks so much. What did your mother call you?"

"Raoule Pollaski."

"What's that?"

"He was a Prussian general. She read about him in a book. She was so glad when I enlisted. She said, 'See you are going to be a military man.'"

"Where is she now?"

"She died a few years before I came here."

Susie kissed him on the cheek. "I am sorry. Is your father alive?"

"Yes."

"Would he like to join you here in Arizona Territory?"

"I could write him. He's in Iowa."

"What do you say Chet?" she asked over her tears, but still in Sarge's arms.

"Yes. He is welcome to come. We can find a place for him. I'm sorry you two are having to put up with Marge and me in the middle of your private life."

"No," Susie said. "We're family. I don't want the world to think I am some impulsive fool and in disrespect of my late husband. You two are my strength and my loved ones. Let's all hold hands."

Sarge looked ready to bust, but he held it well.

"Chet, pray for all of us, please?" Susie asked.

"Of course. Heavenly Father, we are trying to find our part in the future of the ranch and the family. Thank you for letting us make this move to Arizona and for all our blessings here. Be with JD wherever he is and give him the guidance and let the things he learned as a youth be his guide. And Lord bring him back to us.

"Protect all the ranch people, especially Reg and his wife Lucy, Hampt and May and the children, Robert and the crew at the mill, Louise and her man, and Marge's father and his woman. Lord lead and guide these two, Susie and Sarge. They are good people and need your hand to help them travel the route to their future. In Jesus' name. Amen."

"Amen."

"I am not sure if you'd make a better preacher or a sheriff." Marge elbowed him.

"Neither one. I am going to harness up the team and we are going home. Sarge, you be careful. This next drive could be a booger."

"I will. This has been the greatest morning in my

life." He hugged Susie and she smiled. "If you change your mind, I will know I tried. This was a dream I never thought could come true. We have a long way to go to really understand one another, but I will be patient. Thanks for making me a part of the Byrnes clan."

Chet nodded. "Write your father. Invite him out here. We can pay his way. He might freeze to death coming now, but he's welcome here any time."

"With him snowbound in Iowa, he may want to come here right away."

"I'll be hooked up in fifteen minutes," Chet said to Marge as he put on his heavy coat, scarf, and hat.

"I will be ready then."

He kissed her and ran outside. The cowboys saw him coming and set in to hitch up the buckboard before he could.

Cole stepped in and stopped him. "We'll get you fixed up. Your last deal was a tough one, but if you need a hand, remember me. Other than losing Leif—it was a helluva good deal to be rid of those rustlers."

"I'll have you in mind, Cole. I get into more things without even trying, but I guess that is life out here."

"You've solved lots of them. I am still shocked they rustled cattle and butchered them to sell to the freighters. Oh well, anything to get out of work."

"That was their work," Chet said as one of the younger boys drove his team up.

"You are right. I'll see you, Chet, and thanks."

"Anytime, Cole."

Chet drove to the house, the sharp wind in his face, tied off the reins, and jumped down to load his wife. She was smiling, despite the wind. "What a morning."

"A whopper of one."

"I met the second son of a German family once, before I remarried. He always said 'Bully, bully' about such days."

"Was he a rich remittance man? Some of those get large allowances?"

"Large or small, I did not want him." She wrapped up in the extra blanket she'd brought along. "He was so fussy and such a baby."

"You could have been rich." Chet slapped the reins and they were on their way.

"I am rich. I have you. My, my, I never expected what happened back there. But your sister is like you—a spade is a spade. I couldn't believe Sarge ever considered himself a peasant."

"A farm boy from Iowa joined the army. Worked up to Sergeant in maybe ten years. They don't usually give that rank in less than twenty years even if you were a hero in the Civil War."

"There is no telling what he has seen, is there?"

"No, ma'am. But thanks to you, Susie found marriage was a good place to reside. And I think we know the story for those two."

"Yes. Now, if you had JD back and in the fold, you'd be more settled."

"I would. But I have the places and jobs will be assigned. I must go tell Reg and Lucy what happened to Leif."

"They probably know already. But do what you

must. I will curl up at the fire and sleep. I think
being with child is the most work I've ever done. I
could curl up and sleep on our way home, right
now."

"You all right?"

"I am fine. Tom's wife Millie agreed that being
with child is exhausting. Whew. She never lied
about that. Maybe I am a baby. I have seen farm
women working in the fields, stop, and deliver right
there in the field."

"My heavens. We don't have to do that." Chet
shook his head, driving the team up the steep
grade.

She began laughing. "I am only complaining
about myself. Oh, Chet Byrnes, there is never a day
without excitement in my life since I married you
and I do love it. The brothers and sisters I never
had, I have now. The excitement of you chasing
down killers and the like. Range wars. Oh my
heavens, what a world we live in. And our baby is
going to see it all, next spring."

"It ain't easy," he said, making the team take the
center of the road rather than the edge so he could
see the whole road for a good distance before it
ducked to the left again. Easier to see if someone
was coming down. He didn't want to meet them
head-on. The air was not warming, but the front
side of his body was heated by the sun. Grateful for
the coat to shield his back, he clucked to the horses
to move them along.

They reached the ranch and Jesus, who had ridden
home after the services the day before, met them.

"A man is waiting to see you at the house. He is a

lawman. He wants to see Chet on business. Monica said she would make him comfortable."

"You did good as usual," Marge said to Jesus as Chet herded her inside.

"Come back. We'll talk later," he said to Jesus.

"Ah, *sí*. Thanks."

"He's going to be a good hand someday."

"He is now."

Monica met them and whispered. "A U.S. marshal—Paul Sipes—is here to talk to Chet." She shook her head like she knew nothing more.

"He can handle it. Help me get out of this blanket and coat, Monica." Marge turned to Chet. "She can help me. You go see what the marshal wants."

Chet nodded and went through the kitchen and dining room to see a sharp-eyed man standing by the Morris Chair. Five-eight, frosted black hair, bright blue eyes, he looked like a man who had sat in the saddle for a good part of his life.

"Marshal, I'm Chet Byrnes. What can I do for you?" They shook hands and Chet told him to sit in the chair.

"Oh, I've been hearing about you for months. I decided I needed to look you up today, so I swung over here with a map drawn by your friend Roamer."

"He's a fine man. He and I are good friends."

"He tells me you should have a deputy marshal badge, and from the reports I've heard, you do need one. The job has no pay unless you arrest a criminal. We pay ten cents a mile, four dollars for the arrest, and a dollar a day to feed anyone you arrest. The captured must be alive when you deliver him to collect any of this. You may hire deputies to assist you if you feel you need them. We pay them a dollar a day as posse members."

Chet held up his hand. "Marshal, I don't need another job."

"I know that well, but with this badge you can demand things of people an ordinary citizen can't. Local law is to aid you when you need help. If they deny it, they face charges of contempt with the Arizona judges. Sheriffs and deputies have to jail your prisoner or prisoners. You can look at their records and files without a warrant. These are all things you needed in the previous case you worked on."

"I don't have time for this work."

"But you have been doing it in the past. Say a fugitive goes over a state or territory line, you can run him down wherever he goes."

"Marshal, I'm a busy man."

"I know. I didn't come here to put you to work. I want you to have authority when you do go. Put the badge in your pocket and when you need it, tell them who you are. Roamer told me he had to do that at Rye."

"Yes, and it damn sure worked." Chet dropped his head and nodded. "I can't always come when you need me, but thanks for dropping by and asking me."

U.S. Marshal Sipes quickly said, "Thank you. Raise your right hand."

Chet did.

"Repeat after me. I swear to uphold the laws of the United States of America, to be honest and fair in my judgment, protect the public from their enemies, and be respectful of all laws. So help me God."

Chet repeated the oath and Sipes handed him the star badge. Chet looked at it in his palm. It was a big honor. He hoped he had the time to serve his country.

"Pin it on."

Chet did. "Once again, I appreciate your coming out here and accepting me as part of your team. I will do my best to get the job done."

"That's why I came."

Marge stepped into the doorway. "Gentlemen. Monica has supper ready. Nice to have you here, sir." She nodded at the marshal.

"Paul is fine. So nice to meet you, Mrs. Byrnes."

"My name is Marge." She took him by the arm to the dining room.

All three laughed and sat down.

"I haven't heard a word about the Marconi trio, have you?" Paul asked.

"No. We've been to the funeral of my brother-in-law," Chet told him.

"I understood that from your lady Monica. I am so sorry."

Chet nodded. "A very simple accident. He landed wrong. We tracked down and had a shoot-out with three men who had shot one of my cowboys while they were rustling our cattle."

"Why in the world did they rustle cattle up here?" the marshal asked.

"They butchered them and sold the meat to freighters on the Marcy Road."

"I guess that was a good business."

"Free beef. It should have been."

"Untaxed liquor is a big problem. If whiskey and spirits don't have a federal seal, they are illegal. I spend more time running down illegal stills than any other part of my job."

"I never paid any mind to that."

"Well, there are lots out there as you will discover. Kindly arrest them, bring evidence for the trial, and bust their still. If you like, I can leave handcuffs and a set of keys."

"I don't know how many I'll find, but if I do I will bring them in. The handcuffs will come in handy. Thanks."

"Is untaxed liquor a profitable business?" Marge asked with a frown.

"Makes it easier to sell without the two dollar stamp to collect as well."

Marge shook her head, amused. "Where do you live?"

"My home is in Tucson, but while the courts are in session here, I live in a boardinghouse."

"Offer him the cabin," Marge said without hesitation.

"Paul, we have a nice, small cabin out back. Snug. Jesus would keep the fire up when you're gone and you can stay—for free. Monica likes company and she'll feed you."

"I couldn't do that."

"Oh yes you can. It's a short ride out here. The crew will care for your horse. You need another, we have plenty."

"My wife Rita comes up sometimes for a few days and we use a hotel then."

"No need. We have plenty of buckboards to use when she is here. You need to move out here and stay when you are in Preskitt."

Paul smiled and looked at Marge. "Since he took the badge, I better do that, huh?"

"Yes. I am glad that is settled."

Paul changed the subject. "I understand you two have a ranch up at Hackberry, as well."

"The ranches belong to the family. No problem. I am just the ramrod. But yes, we do."

"Do you go up there often?"

"Not often enough. But yes, I go. Marge is looking to have a new one next spring so she stays home right now."

"Whenever you plan to go up there, I would like to accompany you," Paul said.

"Sure. I'll do it in the next few weeks."

"If I am not busy in court, let me tag along, since I have invaded your privacy and all."

"You are part of us. Don't fret," Marge said.

"Any reason?" Chet asked.

"No, but I have never been up there and would like to see the lay of the land and meet the people."

"Summertime I love it on top. Being a south Texan, winter I don't care for."

They all laughed.

After the meal, they showed Paul the cabin and he made plans to move into it, then left. The two were alone again in the house.

"He is a nice man," Marge said.

Chet unpinned the badge and slipped it into his vest pocket. "Yes, he is. I don't know if I will ever need this"—he patted the pocket—"but it won't hurt to have it."

She hugged him, standing before the fireplace. "Oh, it sure won't hurt you to have it."

"When I was a boy, I wanted to be a Texas Ranger. But before I could be accepted, I had to become the manager of our ranch. I always had something that kept me home when others could ride off and see the world. I couldn't. I was the boss."

"Well, you've seen a heck of lot out here, and you drove cattle to Kansas, too."

"Boy, that was headache. Swimming flooded rivers, horse wrecks, stampedes in the night, and gunfights with drunks in Abilene. Indians threatening us for cattle to eat. I must have been seventeen that first year. Flossies all over the place. I wanted to go home. But I sold the herd for a fair price and had thirty turn-back cattle. That made me mad. I sold them for five bucks a head to some pig famers and was lucky to get that for them.

"I had over a hundred thousand dollars from the sale. That was at seventy bucks a head. Some of it belonged to our neighbors who'd sent their cattle along with me."

"Did you pack it back?"

"Heavens no. I had Wells Fargo take it to San Antonio and put it in the bank there. When we got back, I paid the neighbors off right away and they all about died considering the amount of money they got for their part. I paid off the bank loan and still had lots of money. That was the start of building the ranch. I made three more drives, then sent my brother to Abilene and the Reynolds killed him. Heck rode night and day back to Texas to get me. That boy was tough for his age."

She agreed. "I never heard all of the story before. How did you find your way up here? You'd never been here."

"Joe McCoy—he's the one who set up Abilene and the yards—said to go to the Red River crossing north of Fort Worth and follow the wagon tracks to Jessie Chisholm's trading post on the Canadian River, then follow his tracks to the Salt Fork. He'd had men plow a furrow to Abilene and stack sod as markers. That was the second year of the trail, so there were lots of marks. We always pointed our wagon tongue at the north star each night in case it was foggy or cloudy."

"Were you ever scared?"

"Mostly about the river crossings. Some of them boys could swim like beavers, but a few, despite what they told me, couldn't swim a lick. I lost two of them and that was a kick in the gut. Boys I knew all my life swept away in muddy water. I rescued two at different crossings, but the next year I made them swim rivers in Texas before I hired them. And still lost another one in a swirl of cattle halfway across the Red River."

"What about the other drivers? Did they take you serious?"

"I could hit a tin can four out of five times in rapid fire with my old Army .45. Everyone knew that the Kid from Mason County, Texas, was serious."

"I can imagine you were. Let's go to bed. I love your stories, Marshal Byrnes." Marge grinned.

Laughing, with his arm over her shoulder, they headed for the stairs.

His story had brought back memories. Back then, those days were tough. He had it made in Arizona with all his family except JD in attendance. Chet said a silent prayer for him, climbing the steps behind his wife.

CHAPTER 17

Mid-November, Chet and Jesus took four pack-horses and went up on the rim and made camp with skiff of snow on the ground. They could hear the bull elks bugling when they finished their tent set up and supper project.

"They are calling to us," Jesus said.

"Have you ever shot one?"

"Oh no. I only saw some running off when we were up here to get those rustlers."

"Neither have I. I hope we get two big ones. I have seen lots of elk antlers around Preskitt."

In the morning they rode out, rifles across their laps. They heard bugling and followed the noise about two miles until they found a great open meadow. Quiet as they could, they dismounted, hitched their horses, and crept up on the meadow where a large buck was chasing a cow elk.

Chet used a pine tree for a gun stand, cocked the hammer back softly, and took aim.

The bull turned sideways, testing the air.

The wind was coming in from the north so Chet knew he couldn't smell them. He waited.

The bull turned broadside and attempted to mount the cow. Chet aimed for his heart and the echo of the shot rung out. The bull staggered to his knees and his love interest ran off.

Chet shot him again and he spilled onto his side. He and Jesus clapped each other on the shoulder.

"We got him."

"*Sí* and he is *mucho* big."

They walked across the grassy meadow and looked at the buck. Chet cut his throat so he would bleed out. When he rose, Jesus had counted the tines.

"He is a ten point."

Chet nodded, dreading their job ahead. The animal must weigh 1,200 pounds. They would be hours dressing and skinning him.

Jesus walked back across the meadow to get the horses. When he returned, they worked hard at the job of slaughtering the big elk. The blood dried on their fingers until they were stiff and had to be rinsed in precious water, only to go back to the task over and over. At last it was finished—skinned and gutted. With his nose full of the copper smell and sourness, Chet straightened. "Next time, we'll bring more help."

"You bet we will."

"I think one bull is enough, right now."

"Me, too."

They hauled the carcass back to camp and hung up the quarters so no bears that might come by could get to the parts. They ate supper and fell into bed early.

In the night, the horse acted up and Chet, in his underwear, got up and took a few shots at some re-treating bears.

"Any grizzlies in them?" Jesus asked.

"I couldn't tell. Just bears, is all I could see in the starlight."

"What now?"

"The horses will warn us. let's sleep." Chet shoved more cartridges in his chamber. "I doubt they come back."

But two hours later, the horses woke him again. This time, he stayed in the tent hoping mister bear was close enough to shoot. The stars and moon were out and the open country was silver coated. The bear rose on all fours and sniffed the air. That was his mistake. Chet put a .44/40 in his chest and he fell backward. By then, Chet was standing outside and shot him twice more until he quit growling and clawing on the ground.

His breath coming out in a fog, Jesus said, "He don't look as big as that buck."

"I don't think so, partner."

Late that evening, they reached the Verde Ranch. Sleepy cowboys soon met them and helped unload the packhorses and hung the bear and elk meat.

"That's a big rack," one of the hands said about the elk antlers.

"He was a big one to skin and slaughter, too," Jesus told them.

They laughed.

"The bear was not any easier," Chet said as Susie joined them in the candle lamp light.

"He was a big bull."

"Jesus and I learned to take more help next time." He hugged her.

"Come to the house when you finish. I will have supper for both of you."

"We won't be long," he promised her and turned to speak to Tom about things on the ranch.

"Nothing is wrong. I think Sarge will leave tomorrow for Gallup and the December delivery. Hampt came by and got his posthole diggers that John made. He wants to see where they need to be made tougher."

"Hampt is serious about this fencing business."

Tom smiled. "And most cowboys hate them."

"He wants a cow-proof meadow to put hay in."

"Our post and rail system works well enough, but that would be a sure enough way to turn them back."

"Jesus and I are going to eat some food."

"Go ahead. We'll handle this. You going to mount the elk head?" Tom asked.

"I hope to. Thanks. Come on, Jesus." They headed for the house.

Susie had supper almost ready. The biscuits were still in the oven. "You two look bushed."

"We had enough work. That bull was huge and the bear no small one," Chet pointed out.

She grinned. "Do I get the bear rug?"

Chet smiled. "Sure. How are you?"

"I am fine. Sarge is going to New Mexico tomorrow. He sent me a note."

"Tom said Sarge was leaving then for the December delivery and that another herd will up to the Windmill by the time he gets back for the New Year drive."

"Time goes fast in that business, but the income will make the ranch work, too."

"Oh, I know. Sarge takes it very serious."

"What are you going to do next?" she asked.

"I probably need to go see Reg and Lucy. I found two more cowboys who need work. I may ride up there with them next week."

Susie pulled the biscuits from the oven. "I might like to go see them."

"Think it over. It is a lot colder up there than down here."

She rubbed her sleeves. "I know."

"No word from JD?"

"I haven't got a letter. My sister-in-law got one, didn't she?"

"I suppose he sent it to her to inform all of us of his well-being."

"Oh, I don't mean to sound mean about it. I love her. I was just put out he didn't write me. I have been his aunt since he was little."

Chet sipped the coffee. "I can see that. But he didn't write me, either."

She swept her hair back from her face. "I don't think anything will satisfy me any more."

"I can tell." He smiled at her.

They laughed and Jesus smiled.

After her midnight breakfast, they dropped into beds upstairs and slept with no interruptions.

Jesus and Chet woke early to eat more and ride back home. Susie was on the porch to say good-bye. "We've been having some bucking out here"

"Those new horses that Tom bought?" Chet asked.

"Yes, they were supposed to be green broke. I don't think those head slinging broncs were even taught anything, but they are now. Wow. I have been watching. There are some real riders in that crew."

"Good entertainment, huh?"

"Oh, yes. It has been a long time since you and Reg rode out some green ones back in Texas. I thought they'd kill both of you before it was over."

"He was about sixteen then and he got good at riding them."

Chet and Jesus mounted their horses.

"Oh, be careful both of you. You two make a nice team. Take care of him, Jesus."

"I will, señora."

They left the ranch for home with one elk hind quarter for Monica, one large elk skin, the head, cape, and antlers, and Susie's bearskin rug to have tanned.

When they arrived, Marge ran out to greet them, dressed warmly against the cold.

"You sure didn't take long to get him." She hugged Chet's arm as Jesus directed the others how to unload the elk.

"Oh, we got a black bear. too," Chet said.

"Did you bring any of him home?"

He pointed to the bearskin. "Only his hide and Susie wants it tanned for her house."

"Good. I am not a fan of bear meat." Marge shuddered.

"Hey, neither am I, but the cowboys will eat him and lick their lips."

They walked into the house.

Marge hugged him again. "I am glad you are home. Water is heating."

"Wonderful." He scrubbed his whisker stubble with his palm. "And a shave."

"I can do that," She guided him into the backroom. "Anything else happen?"

"No. Sarge left for New Mexico today. Tom has the next herd ready to drive up there to the Windmill when they get back."

"That is going smoothly, isn't it?"

"Yes, very smooth."

"How is Susie?" Marge asked.

"She acts like an ant. Can't be still."

"Maybe I should invite her to come here."

Chet shrugged. "Whatever. She is as restless as I ever saw her."

"Monica says it will snow again. She gets stiffer when the storms start for here."

"It might. I have some business in Preskitt tomorrow. You want to come along?"

"Sure, if there isn't a blizzard."

He laughed and hugged her. "I bet it won't snow tomorrow."

"I won't bet. The water may be warm enough now for you to take a bath."

"Good. Let's get that over with." He followed her

out, already thinking of what business he'd find out the next day. Bo even might have the ranch deal pending.

Marge rode with Chet in the buckboard, wrapped under blankets to stay warm. The team moved out sharply and in no time they were in town. He left her at the dress shop and she said if he was over an hour she'd be at the mercantile.

He went on to Bo's office and found the two men busy working on papers.

"Any news?"

Bo looked up. "No. It's still in court to see who gets the ranch. I suggested in a letter to both parties that they should put you in charge of the ranch until it was settled. I have not heard back from them."

"Good."

"I heard from a man who has a gold claim at Horse Thief basin in the Crown King region. He says he has the mother lode and needs a partner with money to develop it."

Chet frowned. "I know nothing about mining."

"What if I get opinions from two experts? You know, he might actually have a mine worth developing."

"I want to meet face-to-face with each expert, before I advance a penny. All I heard about are failures in that business."

"Yes, but there are some good ones, too."

"Get the experts to look at it first."

Bo nodded. "Yes sir. We have two more homestead deeds we are authenticating in the area of the Hereford herd."

"Perkins?"

"Yes, both one-sixty. And on the river according to the owners."

"High priced?"

"No, ten an acre will buy one and the other we can get for seven."

"Buy them. We will need that private land some day."

That business taken care of, Bo asked, "How is the cattle sale business?"

"Fine, if the government ever makes good on their paper."

"I know other federal employees are waiting. Some are discounting it to survive."

"I am not ready to do that—yet. The money will be available at the bank. You make the time and notify me."

"Great. We are looking all the time for the opportunity to get some of your money."

Chet shook his hand and left.

At the bank, he told Tanner about the land purchase and asked about any payment from the government.

Tanner shook his head. No word. He thought it would be after the New Year.

Discouraged, Chet left and went to find his wife. Enough was enough. He wanted to do something— but was not sure what that was. Oh, well, things were secure for the moment. In the store that smelled of spices, sweet grain, and yard goods, he found his wife in a crowd of women.

Something was wrong.

A tall, nicely-dressed woman was crying in their midst.

Marge pulled him close and introduced him. "Betty Lou Scales, this is my husband Chet Byrnes."

The woman sniffled. "Nice to meet you, sir. I have heard about you. You are quite the helper around here. Many folks speak highly of you."

"Just another guy." He tried to dismiss her compliments.

"On, no. More than that. I told your wife and these others that my husband went to Utah two months ago to close a deal on his deceased parent's place. He sent me a letter that he was coming back, but never came home. Leroy was never like that. Then I got this letter in the mail two days ago. Here you may read it." She handed him the letter.

Dear Mrs. Scales,

We are holding your husband Leroy Scales for ransom. Listen, if you ever want to see him again you must send two thousand dollars in small bills concealed in a well-wrapped package to Sam Gordon, General delivery, Honey Grove, Utah.

If you go to the law and report this letter, we will cut his throat and kill him. You have only thirty days to do this or he will die. Any attempt to rescue him and all they will get is his corpse. Here is a locket of his hair. You have thirty days to do this or he will die.

WE MEAN BUSINESS

Underneath, in a different handwriting, was written:

> *Please, Betty Lou, do as he says. These men are killers.*
> > *Leroy*

Chet looked up at her and Marge, then shook his head. "Where is Honey Grove?"

"Just across the Arizona line," Betty Lou said.

Marge squeezed Chet's arm. "She is so worried and stopped me to ask if you could help her. I didn't know what to say."

Chet nodded. "Let's go to Jenn's. We can sit down and figure this out and eat lunch."

"Come along, Betty Lou. He's a good figurer."

"I know you are so busy, Mr. Byrnes. I hated to bother you."

He herded them out and into the buckboard saying she was no problem. With both women loaded on the seat, he drove the team to the café, kneeling on his knees from behind the seat.

Inside, the girls welcomed them to the establishment and Bonnie seated them at a table in the back, took their orders, and delivered coffee.

In a low voice, Betty Lou asked Chet, "You rescued those two?"

He nodded. "What did the sheriff say about this letter?"

"That it was probably a hoax and they'd send him on when they didn't get any money. Besides, it's in Utah and he has no authority over the line to do anything. I tried not to cry, but I didn't know what to do. Several at the store said the only answer was you. I'd never met you before. Then Margaret, I mean Marge, came in. I knew her from the fair. So I imposed on her to ask you."

"Where is this place, Honey Grove?"

"A road the Mormons called the Honeymoon Trail comes down through Utah and Honey Grove. It crosses the Arizona line south of where you go over the Kaibab Mountain and down into House Rock Valley on to Lee's Ferry.

"There, you cross the Grand Canyon and use the ferry to cross the Colorado River. You travel with the red bluffs on one side and the Grand Canyon on your right coming down to the San Francisco Peaks. The military road leads to Camp Verde."

Chet nodded. "I know that about the Peaks. You come around the east side."

"Yes. Ten years ago when Leroy and I married and the Church sent us down here to populate this land, others went to the east side of the territory when they got to the peaks. I can draw you a map."

Their food arrived. Valerie set the plates down and left quickly.

"That would be good. I can find the road. Finding these kidnappers will be a trick."

"What should I do? I don't want him killed. I wouldn't know what to do without him."

"Eat. We can figure this out—somehow."

"You all just in town today?" Jenn asked, dropping by their table.

Chet spoke up, but not loud. "Betty Lou has a problem, but we need to keep it quiet. Her husband is being held as hostage up in Utah—for ransom. She's been to Sims, but he can't do anything 'cause they're in Utah.'" Chet made quotation marks with his fingers.

"He can't do much, anyhow," Jenn said.

Chet raised his hand. "Never mind that. We're making plans to find the kidnappers."

"Betty Lou, you are in good hands. If you need my help, I'll do anything you need done. He's such a dandy man." Jenn turned and left them to talk with another customer.

"You two are friends?" Betty Lou asked.

"Yes. Jenn really helped me when I first came here looking for a ranch."

"I see."

"She really did. She found him help and all that," Marge said.

Betty Lou gave a slight nod. "Back to my problem. I don't have that much money."

Chet had given the situation some thought. "I think you must write him letters every few days. And in each letter send him twenty or fifty dollars, like you are really scratching for money and are trying to get the banker to make you a loan. Include a plea to the kidnappers each time. Something like . . . but please don't kill my husband."

"I don't—"

"Marge will have the money for you. Send it in wrinkled, small bills . . . maybe even a few coins."

Betty Lou was confused. "What will that do?"

"It will bait this Sam guy to go to the post office."

"How?"

Chet looked around the café and saw it was near empty. "He'll be anxious to get the letters, hoping for the big money. I am a U.S. deputy marshal. The post office has to work with me. When he comes and gets the bait, I can trail him to his hideout."

She put her hands to her mouth. "How did you figure that out?"

"Betty Lou, my husband can think his way out of about anything he wants to." Marge chuckled.

"Sounds easy, but we haven't found him yet. He'll get the first letter about the time I arrive, I figure. After we eat, we will go to the bank and quietly get some old money from Mr. Tanner's office. Eat up ladies." Chet took a hearty bite of his sandwich.

"What else can I do?" Betty Lou asked.

"Don't mention me. The kidnapper may have lookouts here. Some crooks are smart. Be sure to tell them you begged or borrowed the money you send and that you will try to get more this week."

"I understand. Oh, I was so sick when I left the sheriff's office. I thought and prayed there was an answer.

"I know there is a chance they may kill him, but at least you're doing something. I will pay you back, I promise."

Chet waved a hand. "Don't worry about that. Your husband's life is what we want to save."

"How should she space the letters?" Marge asked.

"One now, then one two days later, small amounts in them. Then three to five days later, send like fifty dollars. We should have them by then."

"Oh, Mr. Byres I am so—"

"No, you need to be the woman who is crying

and quietly desperate to find enough money. So if they have a lookout here, he won't know anything but that you're trying to raise the money."

Betty Lou sighed. "I never thought of that. I will be."

"You walk to the bank. We will already be there and you ask to see Mr. Tanner. He is good man. He won't let anyone know any different."

She leaned back in the chair and breathed deeply. "Thank you, my most Heavenly Father, for all your help. Please protect my husband from the kidnappers. Amen." She stood and said, "Thank you for the meal, Mr. Byrnes. Marge, it was nice seeing you again." Nodding at them, she left the café and walked in the direction away from the bank . . . just in case someone was watching.

Chet paid for their meals and escorted Marge to the bank. He gave her some instructions. "You will need to ask Roamer to keep an eye out for Betty Lou and see if the kidnappers have someone watching her."

"I can handle that. This is a bad time to go all the way to Utah. Don't get caught in a blizzard."

"I'll be all right. I am going to ask Cole Emerson at the ranch if he wants to go. He's the Indian shooter. I'll go on up to the ranch today, after I get you home. Jesus will have to come along. He's good help and can bring the horses up tomorrow morning and we can leave from there."

She warily shook her head under the coat's hood. "I bet it is three hundred miles to where the kidnappers are."

"I have no idea. We'll just go till we get there."

"It could take over a week."

"I can't fly like a bird, so we will simply ride and then find him."

"It is just like always. You leaving worries me. Just be careful."

"I will." From what Betty Lou said, it was a damn sight farther than he had imagined. Since he knew of no stage line to Utah, he and the boys would have to tough it out, perhaps in the real cold. He'd see some new country, anyway.

Marge sighed. "Oh, mercy. I will walk the floors."

Chet hugged her to him. "No, I will be fine. You and the baby will also be fine."

"All right. I'll keep my chin up and pray."

"Much better."

Having completed the arrangements at the bank with Betty Lou and Banker Tanner, Chet drove them home.

When they pulled into the drive, Jesus came out to meet them. Chet sent Marge on in out of the cold then asked Jesus, "Do you have some wool underwear and socks?"

"*Sí.* Where are we going?"

Chet shook his head. "We are going to Utah. It will be a long ride and probably cold. You will have to have some real warm clothes. A woman's husband has been kidnapped up there and the outlaws want a large ransom for his release."

"*Sí.* When do we go there?"

"I am going to the Quarter Circle Z today and get Cole Emerson to help us. You bring everything we will need on packhorses tomorrow morning. I'll ride one roan; you can ride the other one. Bring some horse feed, too.

Jesus thought a moment. "It may take four pack-horses."

"It doesn't matter. Just so we have a tent, bedrolls. Cole will have his own. Make sure we have plenty of food and cooking utensils."

"I will be there early."

"Be careful in the dark. Bring a rifle, too."

Jesus nodded. "Extra cartridges, too?"

"Yes. Have you ever been to Utah?"

"No, but I guess I will see what it is like." He laughed and so did Chet.

"We're off on another adventure. No one but Raphael needs to know our business."

"I won't tell anyone," Jesus said determinedly.

"I'll—"

Jesus interrupted. "No, you go to the house. I will saddle the roan horse. He will be ready when you are."

"Gracias amigo." Chet knew it would be hard to leave Marge again, but they needed to find the men holding Scales.

"Raphael will be back soon and he will help me load."

"Good." Chet turned and headed to the house.

In the kitchen, his wife sat at the table talking to Monica. She looked up when Chet entered. "I told her what happened and that it is a secret."

"Good. I am set with Jesus. We will need some good ponies to make this trip so we're each riding a roan. He'll have the packhorses ready to load in the early morning. Raphael is gone right now, but he is coming back and he'll help him."

Chet kissed his wife then he pecked Monica on the cheek. "Take care of her. I will be coming back."

They walked him outside and he left with them waving on the porch. The temperature had risen to respectable and the roan was spirited going out under the cross-over bar. No chance he'd buck, but he danced some on his toes like he might as they headed for the road.

Halfway down the mountain, he unbuttoned his coat and relaxed. The pony was easy to ride and they made good time getting to Susie's ranch.

Tom met him when he spotted him coming. Susie came out to the porch wearing a coat, waiting while Chet explained he wanted Cole to ride with him. "Be sure he has enough warm clothes and socks. It could be tough riding all the way to Utah. Marge says it's three hundred miles or more."

"I bet she's right. I'll be sure he has them. Want me to send him to the house for you to explain it all?"

"Fine." Turning to Susie he called, "I'm coming. Go inside."

She made a face and he laughed, but she obeyed him and closed the door.

Tom shook his head. "She's real antsy. I think she'd have ridden to New Mexico with Sarge if it wouldn't have looked so bad."

"She will have to wait."

Tom said with an Irish accent, "That impatient Byrnes blood is in that lassie."

"You are right. It flows down. Both my grandfathers came from Ireland. The only one I can recall is dad's father. He sounded just like that."

They parted. Tom went to get Cole Emerson and Chet went on into the house.

His sister hugged him as soon as he came inside the door. "What is wrong?"

He hung up his hat, gun belt, and coat. "It is a long story. No word needs to get out. For all anyone knows, I'm going to see Reg. But Jesus—Cole, if he wants to go—and I are going to Utah to find a woman's husband who was kidnapped. Now here is the whole story. Sit down."

When he finished, she was about ready to cry. "Oh, that is a long way."

"Very long. But we have to do what we have to do."

"Oh, Chet. I really want to go to the Windmill Ranch and meet Sarge when he comes back."

"Impossible. He lives in a two-room house and has eight hands living with him."

She closed her eyes and shook her head. "All I want is to be around him."

"Send him a letter and tell him when he can to come here."

"That sounds too bold."

"Living among nine men might be bolder." Chet grinned.

"I think he wants me but—"

"He wants you. But you didn't hear that from me."

"Good. I will write him and walk the floor till he gets here."

"It will take him almost three weeks to make the turn around with the cattle and get home."

"Fine."

"We will be gone for several weeks I figure. Check on Marge. You two can share being alone."

"That's not funny. Chet Byrnes."

"No, I know, but you aren't pregnant—"

"That may be another thing. I may not be, but that's not settled either." Susie shook her head.

"You're a widow. There is no shame in that."

"I know. I know. I am too impatient, but I don't want to get married and be big as a bear at the wedding."

"That's between you and Sarge."

"What if he's not ready for a family?"

"If he wants you, he'll understand these things happen."

"When you get used merchandise?" Susie whispered.

Chet shook his head. "It didn't bother me a bit."

She reached over and squeezed his arm. "I didn't mean anything but my own case. You and Marge have a match made in heaven."

"You will find one, too."

Susie hugged her arms. "Oh dear God, I hope so. Now I'll fix you supper so you can get some rest tonight and I promise I will go see Marge. My land, I underestimated her so bad." She rose and set to fixing supper.

Cole arrived, knocking on the door. Chet invited him in, took his hat and coat, and led him to the living room. "Have a chair and I'll explain the entire deal."

After he explained the whole story, the young man smiled and said, "I'd love to ride with you and Jesus to Utah. I'm honored you'd ask me to go along."

"Make sure you have plenty of warm clothes because there is no place to stock any on the way. We can get some here, but we won't see many faces between here and there."

"I do have some. I spent a winter in Nebraska with a cow outfit and learned about cold."

"Good. We'll head north in the morning when Jesus gets here. I imagine it will be before daylight."

"Come eat you two," Susie called from the doorway.

"Yes, thank you ma'am." Cole about blushed at her words.

Chet grinned. "He's been telling me that he cowboyed in Nebraska."

"One winter is all." Cole held up one finger to show her. "That was all."

Susie shuddered. "I imagine that was real cold."

"Yes, ma'am. Stark cold and forever."

"I bet it was an experience, though." Susie turned back to the kitchen as the men walked in.

"Mighty one for me. Thanks for having me for supper." Cole stood behind a chair at the table.

Susie waved him to sit down. "No problem. I used to cook for the whole ranch."

"I took her job away, Cole," Chet explained.

"Yes, he really did. Made me so mad I almost shot him." Susie grinned.

Cole smiled. "I'm glad you didn't. I might not

have a job here and this is the greatest ranch I ever worked on."

"Thanks," Chet said.

They ate her chicken fried steak, mashed potatoes, biscuits and gravy. Then her apple raisin pie as well.

Cole thanked her again, told Chet he'd be ready whenever, and left.

Susie watched him go. "He's nice young man."

"Yes. A good man, too. Tom and I talked about his shooting those two Indians. Tom said he took it in stride and said he was glad to be with us like he told you. His dad died young and he went north on his first cattle drive at fourteen to help his mom out. So he's ridden the rivers and that is a real test for a young man. On that drive, he went from cook's helper to a full cowboy job when they lost some hands. His boss paid him full wages as a hand when they got to Abilene."

"Did he go home?"

"Yes. He told Tom, when he got back to Texas he practiced swimming all summer long."

"Is his mom still alive?"

"Yes. She remarried and he decided she didn't need him so he moved on."

"She raised him right. He's very polite."

Chet changed the subject. "Will you look in on Marge? How is May?"

"Ready for a baby and still happy as can be with Hampt. I swear she is not the same person."

"No, she bloomed."

"Bloomed again and again." Susie nodded. "I will

go see Marge. She will be upset, I know. This is no small job you're taking on."

"Right. I'm going to sleep better knowing you are checking on her. I am going to bed now. Get me up about five."

"No problem. I will set an alarm."

He hugged her. "Maybe we can find a replacement for Sarge's next trip. Would you like that?"

"Yes."

"Tom might be able to handle it."

"Thanks." She put her face against his shirt. "Be careful for me, too."

"Always." He headed up the stairs.

Chet slept deep.

Susie's words from the doorway woke him.

He opened one eye. "Is Jesus here already?"

"Yes. He is downstairs with Cole, eating breakfast."

"I'm coming. Be right down."

"I'll save some for you." She laughed and left him.

In a few minutes, he dressed, went downstairs and smiled at his men. "Well, the posse is here, anyway. Good morning. It is something to be sleeping while my crew is ready to go."

"We aren't that ready," Cole said.

Jesus looked up. "We are not in that big a hurry."

Chet grinned. "Cold outside?"

"Cold enough not to hurry," Jesus said, busy eating pancakes in syrup.

Chet considered his answer and nodded. "We'll

get plenty of cold, I guess, going up to Utah and coming back."

"*Si.*"

"They get the roan horse for you?"

Jesus nodded. "He's saddled to go. I made sure of that. I am proud you let me ride him."

"You deserve a good horse on this trip." Chet ate his scrambled eggs before starting on his pancakes. Food is great. Thanks, sis."

Susie grinned at the compliment. "You three are too easy to please."

Chet finished and left the young men eating more that she offered. He found Tom in the cook shack and they talked privately about getting Sarge out of the next drive so he could *maybe* marry Susie."

Tom smiled. "Can I send Hampt? He's been up to Windmill Ranch. Those cowboys know all the details, but he could handle a wreck."

"On the quiet, all right?"

"You bet. Where will they live if they do get married?"

Chet shrugged. "Maybe in a wagon."

"I simply wondered."

"Take care of things while I'm gone. We need to bring Scales back. Sims wrote it off as it was in Utah."

"He sure won't run for reelection on what he's done here."

"I can't help it. I have to do it. Leroy Scales is a husband and a father."

"Be careful."

* * *

They rode out before the sun came up in the east, crossed the shallow Verde and headed north for the military road. Four packhorses trailed them, but moved smartly. Jesus knew the animals and had chosen them well. On the rim, they stopped at the sawmill. Chet spoke to Robert for only a few minutes and they pushed on.

They camped near the forks of the Marcy Road. No tent was set up. They ate a hot meal and went to sleep.

Before dawn, they had the fire going, boiling coffee and oatmeal. Breakfast was eaten, pans and dishes washed, and they rode east on the Marcy Road to circle the snowcapped San Francisco Peaks.

The weather was bright and warm enough to ride with their jackets open. They passed many Navajos herding sheep and goats. Most were women wrapped in blankets using small dogs to control the animals. It was a wide space of land painted in many colors.

They reached the Cameron Trading Post on the Little Colorado River at an early sundown. They ate Indian fried tacos filled with chili beef. The Navajo girl inside the trading post who waited on them took good care and treated them like they were special.

After the meal, she brought them each a large taco with sweet apple filling inside.

Under his breath, Cole said he might marry her.

"Don't ask her till we come back," Chet said and they laughed.

They turned in right after supper and slept in their bedrolls.

Up early the next morning, Chet saw the young Navajo girl standing back in the shadows. He nudged Cole and told him he'd finish the pack-horse.

"Oh—thanks." Cole swept off his hat and went to speak to her . . . so softly Chet and Jesus couldn't hear him. Cole and the girl exchanged some things. She gave him something. He gave her something.

Chet slapped down his saddle stirrup to warn him and Cole came on the run. They mounted up and took the cable ferry across the Little Colorado, the dark waters slapping the sides. The ride was short, but they were grateful not to have to ford it.

"By the way," Jesus asked, "what is her name?"

"Nana—I can't say the rest of it."

"Nana will do," Chet said and winked at Jesus.

It was a hundred miles north to Lee's Ferry. Chet knew they'd not reach it in one day, but they pushed hard with the Vermillion Cliffs on their right and the Grand Canyon on the left. For sure, it was not great grazing country and he had no desire to own any of the rocks that fell off the tow-ering cliffs.

"Those Navajos didn't get the best land," Cole said, standing in the stirrups.

"They wanted it bad," Jesus said. "They were being held down in New Mexico in a place worse than this. Many were dying. Then the government said they could go home. Many more died on the way back here. I know some of them that live around Preskitt."

Chet continued the story. "When we came out here just out of Rio Grande Valley with our ranch wagon train, we met a woman whose horse had died in harness. We hooked her to us and in the end gave her a horse to get home with. Her name was Blue Bird. She told us some of the history of her people."

"Oh. Okay. Well, how far will we get today?" Cole asked.

"Part of the way to the Ferry. I think we will be there by tomorrow night. Two days later, we'll be in Honey Grove."

"Sounds like it is long way. I rode back from Nebraska to Texas and swore I'd never get home. Took me months." Cole shook his head at the memory.

They laughed at him.

Standing in the stirrups, Cole held his slim hips and stretched. "Boy. Crossing this country in a saddle gets old."

Jesus spoke next. "I walked from my home down in Mexico to Nogales. I found a loose burro and rode him to Hayden Mills. Then I rode on a freight wagon to Preskitt. That was long ride, and I had to eat off the land. I didn't get much."

"You win that contest," Cole said. "That must have been bad."

"Real bad."

"But this trip, we've got good horses and we should make it, so simply ride," Chet said.

"We weren't complaining about the job," Cole said.

Jesus agreed. "We like this job. I would be shoveling horse shit at home."

Chet nodded. "Good."

They rode on through the sterile-looking land. They camped, made a meal, and turned in early. Chet slept well and dreamed of his wife at home. He always missed her.

They slept till daylight and, making breakfast, found they had invaders.

"Hello, buzzards," Cole whooped at the low flying birds, waving his hat at them.

"Something is dead around here," Chet said, whirling around and seeing nothing.

"Keep your gun handy," he said to Jesus, who was working over the cooking.

He and Cole spread out and found the body of a man lying behind a rock. He'd been moved there by three men according to the tracks.

"What killed him?" Jesus asked.

"I'd say a bullet in the back of his head," Cole said.

Jesus shook his head. "Damn."

Chet gave orders. "Search his pockets for any ID. We need to bury him."

"Take several hours," Cole said.

"If you were dead, would you like the ones behind you to bury your earthly remains or let buzzards eat you?"

"No case, boss man. I'll get a shovel."

"Here is a letter." Jesus handed it to Chet. It was flat from being in the man's hind pocket and sat on when he rode.

Chet unfolded the note. Water stained, the script was difficult to read.

Dear Joseph Smith,
   We hope this find you. We hope you can come
home by Christmas. The kids are fine. The cow
still gives milt. Everyone mixes you. I hope you got
money for the estate we have nOne but we kin get
by till yous get hume. Louise youz wife St David
Az terr

Chet looked at his young posse. "His name is
Joseph Smith, same as the Mormon prophet. His
wife lives in St. David down by Tombstone. He was
settling an estate, I guess in Utah, and she hopes
he's bringing money. He must have settled the
estate and was riding south toward home."

"How much did he have?" Cole asked.

"It doesn't say, but he was killed in Arizona and
in Sims's county."

Jesus stood. "He doesn't have any money on him.
Whoever killed him even took his boots."

"Had we not come along, no one would have
known who or where he was," Cole said.

Chet nodded. "Right and his killers are a day or
so ahead of us. The ferry people will know. They
can tell us who the killers are."

They shoveled out a grave, buried him, and put
a big rock on top to save wolves from digging him
up. Then they trotted half the night to reach the
ferry before sun up.

Impatient to cross, Chet fired his pistol in the air
to wake Lee, the ferry man. A light soon came on
from the other side of the river.

A man in his late forties brought the vessel
across. "I was coming. It will take two trips to get

all your horses across. The last guy complained about it, but he had too many horses."

"What was his name?" Chet asked, riding his horse onto the ferry barge.

"Olaf something. And Jimbo."

"And Riley?"

"Yeah. You know them?"

Jesus rode onto the ferry, leading two of the packhorses as Chet continued asking questions. "Did they have Joseph Smith's horses?"

"Yes. Olaf said the man got a wagon ride and sold him the horses so he could get home faster."

"How long ago were they here?"

"Mid-afternoon. They rode west to Joseph's Lake."

"We can find them."

"What did they do?" asked Lee.

"Murdered Joseph Smith. We buried him about ten hours ago. I have a letter from his wife in St. David that we found on him."

"Those bastards. They said he sold them his horse and gear because he caught a ride with an Indian in a wagon."

"Lee, those men are wanted for robbing a stage in Arizona." Chet was upset by the man's obvious lack of concern for their lawlessness.

"I don't enforce the law. I ferry people across the river. At least, those that have the money. The rest can swim."

"How much money do you think Smith had on him?"

"Maybe a thousand dollars."

"Really?"

"He said he would pay off what he owed and have money to live on for several years."

Chet did some mental figuring. "Maybe even more than that. How far is it to the base of the mountains?"

"Fifty-sixty miles across House Rock Valley."

"Thanks Lee. They won't cross it before dark." Chet turned to Jesus. "When we get all the horses across, will you take the packhorses and follow us? I want me and Cole to try to catch them before they get into those mountains. Take your time. We may ruin two good horses, but I want those killers."

Jesus nodded and smiled in the predawn light. "I understand. I'll come with the pack animals."

When Cole and the rest of the animals came across, Chet explained his plan to capture the Marconis before they got away. Cole agreed in the faint light of sunup pinking the mountaintops in Navajo country. They refilled their canteens before setting out.

"Take your time," Chet reminded Jesus, and he agreed.

Chet and Cole left in a hard run uphill from the river to the flat valley with the tall red cliffs running east and west on their right-hand side. Bunch grass and sagebrush covered the open, rolling country and dim wagon tracks formed a road westward.

"Not bad range country," Cole said when they reined the horses down to a walk to cool some.

"I noticed that, too. But it would be hell to find a market for cattle up here."

"I never thought about it when I came to Preskitt, but most ranchers who needed help could only hire day help. The fact that they had no sales was the reason, wasn't it?"

"Lots of cattle and no place to sell them is right. Railroads will change things, but that may be too late. That's why we are so proud of the Navajo beef deal. They could change their minds and get a new supplier. All we have now is script for our troubles."

"Tell me more about these killers we're after," Cole said.

"Pig farmers from over on Tonto Creek. Real rough people, I understand. Their place stinks bad."

"They held up the stage. You went to help that Deputy Roamer?"

"I caught up to his posse over in Bloody Basin. The robbers—the Marconis—were headed for Rye." Chet told Cole the story of Jesus recognizing the hoofprint of the crooked legged horse. "Jesus found the horse hitched at a saloon. We captured John Marconi there and he had hundred-dollar bills with serial numbers that showed they came from the robbery. Someone tipped the others off before we got to the hog farm and the other three fled."

"I see why you bring Jesus along. He's a sharp guy."

"He'll do his share to find things out, I promise."

"Can we catch them today?" Cole asked.

"Let's get going again. I want them arrested before they get away this time."

They left in a gallop. The sun soon warmed up the land and they pushed on. Creosote smell in his nose, wind in his face, Chet made the roan run hard. They only had one chance to catch the Marconis.

Midday, he wondered if they'd made any distance. They dismounted, and as they walked their horses for half a mile, Chet asked Cole where he had lived in Texas.

"Oh, before my dad died, we had a good farm east of Dallas. He must have been a good farmer. I recall crops of tall corn, watermelons, and beans— green and pinto. He could plow more land in a day with his mules than any of our neighbors. That might have killed him. Mom couldn't plow. She was a small woman and I was a boy of maybe ten.

"We sold the farm and went south of Waco to buy an angora goat deal and some sheep. I hated that, but we had to eat. When I was fourteen, Mr. Ackens came by and offered me the cook's helper job to go to Kansas. Twelve dollars a month. Why, I'd make about seventy dollars he said. Maw told me, 'You can go, but don't spend your money. We will need it this winter to buy food.'

"I agreed. Pa had a good saddle and bridle. From the undertaker, Ma bought a pair of used boots that fit me for fifty cents and he threw in a weathered old cowboy hat I wore. She gave me her blue silk scarf for a kerchief and I was proud of it. Mr. Ackens armed me with an old .44 cap and ball pistol that sprayed hot lead out the side at anyone standing beside me. Between the cylinder and barrel was lots of daylight from wear. I learned how to clean and to shoot it when we had time. Mathieu the cook showed me how to do that before the herd arrived and we had time to practice shooting tin cans.

"In a few weeks, I could bust bottles and tin cans. One big baby got homesick and struck out one night. I knew he was a quitter. Then Bruce Taylor's horse fell in hole and Bruce broke his leg in the spill. He had to ride in the chuck wagon and then a black boy, Ethen, who was a real good cowboy, got snake bit and died. So I got promoted to cowhand. I could ride and figured, 'how hard could this be.' It was little sleep, stampedes, and lots of riding, but you know. You took cattle to Abilene, too."

Chet and Cole mounted up and ran their dried horses hard again for miles, chewed on dry jerky, and watered their horses at water holes. Hours later, the weak sun had made a long swing across House Rock Valley. In the distance, they saw a fire and some stick figures standing among some horses.

Chet signaled to stop. "That may be them. Get your Winchester out. Ride more to the side so we aren't easy targets."

"You bet, boss."

Smoke from a pistol rose in the air. They were way out of the range, but Chet felt certain only criminals would shoot at men who weren't Indians approaching them.

He wheeled up on a rise and so did Cole. "Try a long shot at them. Elevate your rifle and give it a try." From his saddlebags, he slipped the brass telescope out and looked through it at the three bearded men dressed in black clothes floured in dust.

Cole made the shot and Chet watched one of them go down.

"Did I get him?"

"Yes. In the leg. I think that will cool their desire to fight." Chet continued his observation through the telescope. "All right! They are waving at us that they surrender. But it could be a trick."

"I'll be ready for them. I'd never thought about elevating my gun. Thanks for that tip."

Chet chuckled. "Beats the hell out of me how we found them this far north. I guess it's because it is the only way across the Grand Canyon except way south and west down by Nevada. Watch them close. They could be sneaky, especially with a murder sentence on them, too."

Reined up, he stood in the stirrups and ordered, "Lay flat on the ground, arms way out. One move and you won't live to see the light of day again."

When they rode up close, Cole waited for them to dismount, holding his six-gun on them.

"Jimbo's shot," the older, bearded man said.

Chet had no sympathy. "Olaf, so was Joseph Smith. In the back of his head and left for the buzzards over in Navajo country."

"We don't know any Joseph Smith."

"I wouldn't either if I'd shot him." Chet removed a gun and big knife from the silent youngest one. "You must be Riley."

"I don't have to tell you shit."

Chet hauled off and kicked him hard in the guts. Riley screamed, holding his stomach and rolled off the small pistol concealed by his body on the ground.

"One wrong move and we'll shoot all of you. Hear me?" Chet growled.

"Yes," Olaf confirmed.

"Oh, you killed me," Riley moaned. He began coughing and rolling on the ground.

Chet jerked him up by his collar, tore it half off, and had to get another hold. "Your life is paid for. I don't have to take you in and I may still string you up, chop your head off, put it in a gunny sack, and get the Wells Fargo reward."

"Y-you can't do that."

"You just try me, boy. Just try me." Still steaming mad, Chet put the cuffs on him behind his back and began to search him. He found five dollars. Then he shoved him to the ground, roughly pulled off his boots and tipped them upside down. Bills rained out of them. "Is that Joseph Smith's money?"

"I don't know him."

"You should. You three killed him. What else did you find on him?" When there was no answer, Chet handed Cole a set of cuffs for the old man.

Once cuffed, Cole searched him. "More money and a deal addressed to Joseph Smith." He flipped it out to read it. "A receipt from a bank for three thousand dollars. No wonder they killed him."

Chet nodded. "Handcuff this wounded guy and split his pants. We'll look at that wound."

"Oh Gods, it hurts. Don't touch it," screamed the third outlaw.

"You should have asked that before you robbed the stage, pistol whipped that guy for his horse, and murdered Joseph Smith."

* * *

By sundown, Jesus arrived with the packhorses. Chet had collected over six thousand dollars, none which looked like the Wells Fargo loot. So they must have been murdering and robbing others on the way so that the law could never prove anything. At least Smith's wife in St. David would get her share.

Jesus built a fire and cooked them a good supper of stew. He'd bought a beef roast earlier from Lee's wife. Then the question arose, *what to do with their prisoners?*

The Marconis had ten head of good horses, no doubt some were Joseph Smith's, plus two pack-horses, and four saddled and probably stolen somewhere along their back trail. Wagging all the horses and the prisoners into Honey Grove might scare off the kidnappers in Utah. They didn't need to know Chet was an U.S. deputy marshal.

In the firelight, he began to examine the contents of the saddlebags. One belonged to a cowboy named Chuck Shaw according to the mail in it. He had a saddle made in San Antonio. A damn well-made saddle. The letter was from his sister in Texas.

Dear Chuck,
    The cotton is going to make this year. We could sure use you to help gather it, but I know how you hate cotton. Lisa Moore finally got married before she had your baby. Some old man over at Wickett married her and took her over there. It was a boy. She named him Allan for her paw. Gracy Hammer asked about you. She says she ain't pg. Maybe

*you'd know? I better get to bed. I got your chores
and mine to do.*

Rachael

A second letter, one he'd started to Rachael, was
unfinished.

Dear Rachael,
      *Thanks for the letter. I never touched that
Hammer girl. I'm sorry about leavin' and Lisa
marrying some old man. I won this money, well
part of it, in a poker game in some sleepy town in
New Mexico. The two hundred dollars is for you to
spend on what you like. Don't give any to anybody
else. You are the only one cares for me anyway.
Don't worry or tell anyone. I got plenty more and
you can mail me a letter to the general delivery to
St. Johns A. T.*

"Where did you kill Chuck Shaw?" Chet asked
the three.

"We never killed no one," Riley said.

"I ought to kick all three of you to death. Right
here is the evidence. He had money. You killed and
robbed him."

"Get one thing straight," Olaf said. "None of us
can read."

Washing dishes, Jesus shook his head. "You
mean none of you can read?"

"Hell, no."

Jesus shook his head again. "Even a dumb Mexican like me can read—some."

Drying the dishes, Cole shook his head. "I heard Chet say it, but you three are really dumb."

"Go to hell," Riley said.

"I may, but at least I can read." Cole put the dish he was drying back in a packsaddle.

They took turns guarding the prisoners who were cuffed together. While Chet watched them with a rifle over his lap, coyotes cut the night. He watched for the big dipper and waited for his time to wake Cole to relieve him. His mind wandered as he waited. The night wasn't too cold. He kept going over what to do with the Marconis while he, Jesus, and Cole chased down the kidnappers. He had no idea. No prison wagon was going to come along to take them back to Preskitt for trial. They'd lived like kings in Utah or wherever they settled. He had two more saddlebags to check. More victims, no doubt. Damn, damn he wished he was home in his own bed with his wife, instead of sharing coyote country with the bloody Marconis.

He was relieved when his shift was over.

In the morning, they had sweet raisin oatmeal and coffee, then began the steep road that went on to Joseph's Lake on top of the Kaibab plateau, according to the crude map Lee had made. A store and ranch was all Chet knew about it. They reached it in late afternoon.

A man in a suit came out on the porch of the log building to meet them when they reined up. "Good day. Welcome to Joseph's Lake, gentlemen. My name is Kimes. How can I help you?"

"Do you have a prison here?" Chet asked.

"Sort of one. It is made of thick logs and has an iron door."

"Cole, go look at it."

Kimes dispatched a towheaded boy to show him. "Why do you need a jail? I see those three in irons. You must be the law."

Chet dismounted. "We need to talk privately."

"Come inside. We can talk better in there."

He followed the shorter man inside. The store smelled of usual things. Half of the items he recognized.

Chet quickly explained his plight of being a marshal and what he needed to do up north. Could he hire Kimes and his crew to watch the prisoners while they tried to save the kidnapped Mormon Leroy Scales?

Kimes nodded. "I can hire two men to guard them, but I'd have to feed them."

"I can pay you five dollars a day. They're killers and you need to always watch them."

"For how long?"

"Not over ten days. I need to get back home. We are also leaving some horses, too."

"Fifty cents a day per horse. I have to have all the hay hauled in here, but we will take care of them."

"I understand. For the sake of the kidnapped man none of this must get out. Those men outside killed a man named Joseph Smith on the Navajo Trail. We found his body three days ago, maybe less, then we ran those three down."

"Oh. Smith stopped by here a few days ago to rest. Nice man and they murdered him?"

"Yes, they're killers."

"They won't get out of the building. I will also chain their legs so they can't run."

"Good."

Cole came in. "They won't get out and chained will be better. One of them was scratched by a bullet in our shoot-out. But that won't kill him."

"My wife will have supper in a short while. Let's put them up. We can get some chains and locks here in the store."

Prisoners in the *jail house*, legs chained, Kimes locked the door.

"Thanks. We appreciate your help. We'll leave in the first light for Honey Grove. How big is it?"

"Small town. Maybe a dozen businesses is all. What are you doing up there?"

"Some guy has a Mormon husband held hostage for two thousand dollars or they will kill him. I gave his wife money to send them in bits and pieces so they don't kill him and when they pick it up we can follow them. It is a general delivery pickup."

"You may catch them that way. Who'd thought of that?"

"Me. These men are my workers on my ranch down at Camp Verde. We came to save Leroy and on the way we found these killers."

"You must have a large ranch to afford to do all this."

"I have several. One ranch is at Hackberry. My nephew runs it. We are starting it up. I have nine sections of those railroad plots in deeded land there. Another ranch sits between Camp Verde and just south of the Marcy Road. Then at Camp Verde the ranch stretches up the river. My wife has a place in Preskitt Valley." Chet didn't even mention Hampt's part.

"You've been busy. Nice of you to help folks out like that man's wife. I bet she ain't got the money."

"No, she doesn't, but she is a nice lady in trouble."

"There ain't much law here. The federal government squared Arizona to cut back Utah, but no one told them this triangle is out of touch with the rest of the territory, save for the ferry."

"I'm learning. But they won't ever learn that. You know your county headquarters is in Preskitt, yes?"

"Right. Hundreds of miles away. We have no law up here."

"I understand."

"My wife has the food ready and my boys can help you unload and unsaddle after we eat." Kimes ushered the men into the house.

"Mrs. Kimes, it was so nice of you to have all this lovely food and to share it with me and my men," Chet said.

"No problem, Mr. Byrnes. Be seated, and your men, too."

"Mrs. Kimes, if you ever come to Camp Verde, come out to my ranch or to my house in Preskitt Valley. We will treat you like a queen."

"I would hardly know about that kind of treatment, but thanks, I will." She appeared amused by the attention laid on her. "You young men eat like you were at home."

They nodded.

Her food was tasty and after the bean and oat-meal diet, Chet could see the pleasure on his two men's faces, chowing down on a real meal.

He thanked God and went back to eating. After the meal, their horses all put up, they went to a guest cabin and put down their bedrolls. Chet fell asleep quickly. No doubt his concerns over his prisoners were set aside. They'd make it to Honey Grove the next day, and begin their intended business to find the kidnappers.

A teen boy woke them before dawn like he had requested and informed them their food was ready.

Dressed, they went to the house with steamy breaths in the night's cold air. Of course, no coffee, Chet noted, but breakfast was hot, fresh, and there were plenty of choices. The guys bragged on her berry jelly and choke cherry syrup. In a short time, with help, their packhorses were loaded and saddle horses made ready.

With a loud thanks to the Kimes, they went out the gate and headed north with Chet in the lead. He was back to the smooth team of him and his men riding after kidnappers just a day's travel from this spot on the mountain to the Utah border in the north.

They rode off the plateau and back to the sage-brush-bunch grass desert. All day long the route crossed the rangeland on another nongraded road—more dusty sections without a soul living on the land. They found Honey Grove on a small river under some leafless cottonwoods and split up.

The young men made camp outside the village

and Chet went for a meal and a bed in town. This separation was to cover their plans to find the kidnappers' headquarters. Jesus was to be available when someone picked up Betty Lou's letter.

Chet left the roan at Atkins livery to be rubbed down and grained. After finding a room in the hotel, he ate in a café and the waitress quietly told him which house the Postmaster Harold Clark lived in. He paid her a fifty-cent tip for her discretion, then casually walked along the boardwalk until he reached the house. His knock on the door was in the closing darkness.

A woman half opened the door. "May I help you?"

"I need to speak to your husband."

"Harold, a man needs to talk to you," she called over her shoulder.

He came to replace her. "What do you want?"

"I am a U.S. deputy marshal and I need to speak to you." He held out the badge issued him. "My name is Chet Byrnes."

"Come in, Marshal. Carmen, this is a federal officer."

Chet held up his hands. "Please don't tell anyone. I am here to capture some kidnappers."

"Oh. Have a seat on the couch."

"May I get you something?" she asked.

"No, ma'am. I just finished supper. I am here to find the kidnappers who wrote Mrs. Scales demanding she send two thousand dollars or her husband would be killed. They get their mail sent here to a Sam Gordon, General Delivery, Honey Grove, Utah."

"I don't know who he is. His wife—at least she

says she is—comes and gets that mail. She's been by twice this week to get it."

"Where does she live?"

"I don't know. She comes in, gets the mail, and I don't see her again."

"Does she sign for it?" Chet asked.

The postmaster nodded. "Delia Gordon. She's not illiterate."

"I want to save Leroy if he is still alive."

"She usually comes before lunch. You can stay in the post office in back, and I can signal you when she comes in."

"Don't scare her. My men can track her to their base."

"Sure. I understand your plan and it should lead you to them."

"What time do you open?"

"Eight in the morning and stay open till six."

"Thank you. I will be there."

Clark put his hands on his knees to get up. "I hope this works. How long have they held her husband?"

"Over a month."

He shook his head in dismay. "I'll look for you in the morning."

"Yes and thanks. Thanks to you too, ma'am."

Breakfast came early in a café. After his meal, Chet stood in the shadows talking to Jesus who'd come into town alone.

"The postman said a woman came in and got Sam's mail. He doesn't know anything about her, but thinks she may come today. Stay close. He makes her sign for each one since she isn't the addressee on the letter. I'll be right out to point her out when she leaves. Jesus, you be careful. They'll kill you if they think you're the law."

"I will. I'll be loafing around close by. Cole is still taking care of our horses this morning. We didn't learn anything last night when we came in and wandered about the town. But she must be coming in for the bait."

"I figured that she would."

"See you later." Jesus turned and walked away.

Chet headed to the post office. The winter cold was deep enough for him despite his jacket. He'd have to get used to it living in this climate.

Clark was unlocking the back door in the darkness when Chet joined him.

Once inside, Clark lit a lamp. Split wood for the small cast iron stove was stacked along the wall.

"I'll start the fire. There is a desk and chair. No one can see anything back here. I will show you the peephole to look at anyone at the counter. When I have a coughing fit you will know she is here for the mail."

Chet nodded. "Good. I can feed the stove with this wood stacked here. Go do what you have to do."

"Thanks. I feel creepy about this deal. Do you think this man is alive?"

"I think they have him alive in case Mrs. Scales demands to see him before she pays them the total amount."

"That makes sense. I never thought of that."

"That is why they're in Utah. So Arizona law can't get to them. Of course, Arizona does so little up here anyway. The sheriff had no time for her."

"I know of only one case investigated by the Utah side of the U.S. marshal's office. A man had sold land to someone by mail and instead of being an irrigated farm, it was all boulders."

"What did the marshal do?"

"When the seller got the money, he left here with no forwarding address. I had dead mail for him, and the lawman opened it and read it. He told me the buyers were lucky. The man was supposed to sell them more rocks."

Clark lit a second coal oil lamp for Chet and took the other one up front to hang for light while he sorted mail and put it in the boxes. In the back, Chet read wanted posters. There must have been a stack of a hundred on the desk.

Clark came back and put a coffeepot on to boil on the top of the stove. "You Mormon?"

Clark shook his head.

"I'm one because my wife was when we married. But I still need coffee in the morning and get none at home. I don't drink spirits, quit cigars, but I still need coffee in the morning. She knows it, but doesn't say anything. My sin for the day." He looked at the ceiling. "Father forgive me." Then he went back up front to continue sorting mail.

Amused, Chet returned to looking at the wanted posters. When the water boiled, Clark came back and added roasted coffee grounds.

"We'll have some shortly; I have two cups."

"Thanks. Sounds and smells good."

"If you are going to sin, sin with the best kind you can find, right?"

Chet laughed and nodded. "Best you can afford, I always said."

"Are you married?"

"Yes I am. I was married last June to a great lady."

"What do you do in Arizona beside marshal?"

"I have some large cattle ranches and some very good foremen running them."

"I was the postmaster down in Chandler."

"How did you get up here?"

"My wife wanted to come back to Utah. She told me to put in for a transfer. I think she expected I'd get Salt Lake. We didn't, but we are in Utah. She can't complain."

"My ranches are at Camp Verde, Preskitt, and over by Hackberry."

"What is Hackberry like? They offered me a post office there. I saw the map and knew it was not near anything else."

"You are right. Small town, less stores than here. Cattle and sheep country."

"I knew it would be bad. They offered me thirty dollars more a month to go there. Let's drink our coffee. One cup is my greatest sin, but you can drink more. Anyone asks me, I'll tell them it is a postal inspector back here drinking it."

"Right."

Clark opened at eight and the bell rang on the door when someone came or left. Chet had his peephole and watched several folks come in and ask for mail. It was ten o'clock when he heard Clark coughing. He stood up on the wooden crate and could see a rather attractive brunette lady in her twenties remove her sunbonnet and sign the release.

"You must have some money in this one, ma'am," Clark said.

"My sister in Prescott, Arizona, is very rich and helps us out."

"Oh, how nice to have a generous family member to be able to help you along."

"She's quite generous. Good day, Mr. Clark." The doorbell rang as she went out.

Chet went out the back door and waved to Jesus. "Blue sunbonnet, a nice looking brunette. She went left on the boardwalk."

"I will find her." Jesus left in a run for the front.

Chet went back inside. At the front window, Jesus gave him a quick nod as he went past the post office. He had her in his sights.

Plan A was working, Chet thought. If his man could follow her they'd soon have her location. Before sundown, he'd know something about the deal. Whew. Would he be glad to get home. This job went on and on—forever. He could imagine sleeping in his own bed with his own wife. That would be nice.

The day passed slowly. He stayed out of sight in the back of the post office. Clark's wife brought them lunch, and they ate on the desk in back. She had lots of questions to ask about his wife and if he had any family. He gave her an overview of his moving from Texas and meeting Marge.

"Children?"

"One on the way. We only married last June."

Carmen shook her head, disappointed. "We've never had any of our own."

Chet mused how Clark had brought her back to Utah, but they had no kids. His impression was having many children was a church tradition. He had no comment, except to thank her for the lunch of rye bread, mustard, cheese, and sliced beef roast, pickles, and oatmeal cookies.

She smiled and took her wicker basket back home.

Four o'clock, Jesus came back in the front door. Clark called to Chet, "Your man is here."

"What did you find?" Chet asked as he came into the front.

"They are at a ranch by a small lake."

"That's Lovely Lake," Clark said, like he knew all about the place. "It is the only lake around there. Charlie Stokes owns it, but he doesn't live on it."

"Where does he live?" Jesus asked.

"Salt Lake. Did you see any men up there?"

Jesus nodded. "Three. Two young cowboys and a big guy in buckskin clothes. Fringe hanging down."

"I don't know him. You think he is this Sam?" asked Clark.

Jesus shook his head. "I don't know."

Able to get in a word at last, Chet asked his man, "Any sign of the hostage?"

Jesus shook his head. "I couldn't get close in the daytime."

"How far is it by horseback?"

"An hour, maybe more."

"That will get you there," Clark said.

Chet shook his hand and thanked him. "If

anyone asks me, I will say you should be the post-master in Salt Lake."

"Oh, please don't. My wife would spend all the money I could make."

Going out the door, Chet said, "I won't tell her or them."

"Good."

They met Cole in camp. Ready to move on, they loaded up everything and headed out on the main road that went west. Cole said he'd learned nothing. He was excited that they had the location of Sam Gordon.

It was already sundown when they reached sight of the place. They turned back and camped on the far side of the lake. Chet's plans were to make a ranger-style arrest. They would ride over in the night and just before dawn while everyone was asleep, they'd ride in and arrest them. Around the small fire they'd used to cook, they slept that night with their rifles.

In the predawn, Cole stood with Chet as he fired a rifle in the air and shouted at the house, "Hands in the air. Any action against us, we will shoot to kill."

Jesus was already searching the outbuildings.

Two young men staggered out. The woman came out in a housecoat and then a man six foot six ducked his head and, holding his hands high, came out grumbling about what the hell did they want.

"He's alive," Jesus shouted from out back. "He's alive."

"Good," Chet answered while Cole searched the kidnappers for guns.

"Who in the hell are you?" the big man asked.

"U.S. Deputy Marshal Chet Byrnes. I am here to arrest you for kidnapping Leroy Scales."

"How are you going to prove that?"

"Are you Sam Gordon?"

"Hell, no."

"Then this woman is going to prison for impersonating him. She has been signing federal postal forms that she is his wife. What is your name?"

"You find out."

"What are your names?" he asked the boys. Still mounted he held his rifle on them.

The taller boy swallowed his Adam's apple. "Newton McCoy and he's Harrison Duval."

"What's your name, ma'am?"

"Kathrin Arnold."

The big man growled at her. "Don't tell him nothing."

"Sam Whatever, shut up," Chet ordered. "You had your chance to talk."

"My name's Evan Evans. When my lawyers get done with you, you won't have a damn badge."

In the first golden light of dawn, Jesus came from around the house with a bedraggled man. "Leroy, that is my boss who found you."

Chet smiled at him. "Betty Lou sends her best."

Leroy's legs collapsed and he sat on the ground. "Thank you Lord for answering my prayers. Thanks for these lovely men. Praise the Lord, my prayers have been answered. Amen."

"Tie their hands behind their backs," Chet said to Cole. "Kathrin, you make one move, you will be shot along with them. Leroy, are you all right?"

"I am glorious, sir. I never thought I'd be alive. Who sent you? Betty Lou?"

"Yes. She'll be glad to see you."

He began to cry. "God bless her. Is she all right?"

"Fine, if she hasn't worried herself to death about you. Where did they kidnap you?"

"What do you mean?"

Chet dismounted and put his rifle up in the scabbard. "I mean, where were you when they kidnapped you?"

"Oh, down in Arizona Territory . . . before you climb the Kaibab."

"That's good."

"Why?"

"'Cause the law will try them in Preskitt." Chet turned to the kidnappers. "You men sit down on the ground. My rules are short. My men will shoot anyone who tries to break away, start any trouble, or disobey an order. So if you want to die in agony on the ground, break my rules.

"Jesus, you and Kathrin make us some food. Load their food up. Cole, we will need saddle horses. Take Newton along and have him help you. If he tries anything, shoot him. We will need five saddle horses. Make it four and hitch the buggy horse that she drove to town. The rest we'll drive or lead behind us."

All left to follow Chet's orders.

"Who owns this ranch?"

Evans never answered him.

"You walk a couple days with a rope around your neck, you'll get lots politer. Hear me?"

"Yeah. You can't do that."

"You can walk to Honey Grove for that."

"Aw, hell. You sent that damn money to bait us, didn't you?"

"Like crow hunting, you toss out some corn and they come and you shoot them."

"She'll get the money, she said. But she was only stalling so you could find us."

"You will have plenty of time to think about a lot of things—walking to Honey Grove."

Evans began cursing him.

That was enough. Chet went in the house and found a rag, came back out and gagged him. "You will learn to speak when you are spoken to and shut up the rest of the time."

Evans's muffled protest suited Chet just fine. He took Leroy aside. "Are you strong enough to ride all day? I know you've been tied up for a long time."

"Oh, Marshal, I feel strong enough to do anything."

"Maybe you could ride in the buggy to Honey Grove."

"Whatever you think. I'd do anything for you I could. I never thought . . . well you heard that before."

Chet jerked his head toward the house. "Who is she? Do you know?"

Leroy shook his head and spoke in a low voice. "She fed me and tried to make me comfortable.

I don't think Evans would have even fed me if she had not been here or hadn't insisted. He slapped her around a lot, but me and them boys could only watch. I think she left her husband for him. He acts like a big shot, but we got lots better food when my wife's money started coming. I couldn't imagine how Betty Lou got any money. I left the money I got from the estate in the bank in Star City and they are going to ship it to me in Preskitt. I told them only if they got a letter postmarked Prescott, A-Z-T were they to send it to me. Lots of people are never heard from again going down this road. I listed Betty Lou as my heir if I died."

"Pretty thorough job. In ten days, you will be home, the good Lord willing."

"What will I owe you?"

"Nothing."

"I will see that you get some reward." Leroy shook his head as if still in a daze. "That smiling Mexican boy who found me said, 'You're free.' I hugged him. He must have thought I was crazy."

"Jesus knew. We've been coming for weeks. Glad you're all right."

"Food's ready," Jesus called.

Chet caught Evans by the collar and set him on his feet, then the other boy.

Cole came back with his prisoner who was untied. "We have all them loaded and saddled. We still need to hitch the buggy."

"I think Leroy will ride in it with her to Honey Grove," said Chet.

"Fine, but we are close to ready anyway."

"I want Evans tied in a chair. He tries anything, we shoot him."

"I can do that."

"You hear me?" Chet asked the gagged outlaw, who nodded.

The table was covered with plates of pancakes, a big kettle of oatmeal, and a stack of hot biscuits.

"All we had," Kathrin said, and held her palms up for them.

"We can eat it. Anyone who doesn't drink coffee, can have water," Chet pointed out.

After they ate, he told the two boys to wash the plates and cups, and Jesus to watch over them. Cole went to hitch the buggy.

"Kathrin, get your things." Chet retied Evans's hands behind his back and put him to sit on the porch. "Don't even think about running off. I'll take your decapitated head back to Preskitt in a gunny sack."

"You won't get away with this. I've got friends in Utah," the big man threatened.

"Keep on and I'll gag you again."

She brought out a tied-up blanket full of her things. Cole had the buggy there and stepped down.

"Kathrin, load your things. Leroy is going to ride into town with you," Chet ordered. He turned to Leroy. "You still doing all right?"

"Oh, I am fine, Chet. Just got some sea legs is all."

"I savvy." He turned to the young cowboys. "You two boys plan to run off?"

"No, sir."

"You can ride untied to town, but I won't stand any moves to run off. We will catch you or shoot you. You won't get away. Understand me?"

"We won't," Newton promised. The other boy nodded in agreement.

"Good. Cole, you lead Evans's horse. You boy, get some leads from Jesus. We've got enough horses to start a ranch." Chet shook his head thinking about the extra ones at Joseph's Lake. "Kathrin, you lead the way. Go ahead. I'll be behind you, then Cole next, leading the prisoner and then Jesus." He nodded as they started after the moving buggy. He'd still have to consider charging her. The law, at times, could sort of overlook women who weren't real participants in crimes. Obvious from his report, she had treated Leroy all right.

But why was she with Evans? Maybe he'd learn on this trip home. The warm weather would not last, but they were headed home. Ten days, maybe, on the road? Maybe more. *Marge, I'm coming home.*

CHAPTER 18

The whole damn town turned out to welcome them. The street was crammed full of rigs and horses—curious men, women, and children. They filled the boardwalks and barely made room in the street to let the posse through. A hundred questions were cast at Chet.

Finally a man wearing a star stepped in his path. "I'm Deputy Sheriff Stoney Lake."

"Good. I am U.S. Marshal Chet Byrnes. I have four prisoners here. Do you have jail space for tonight, sir?"

"I will have to see your papers on these prisoners."

"Lake, I just arrested them. That man in the buggy, Leroy Scales, was being held captive for ransom for over a month. Now, you either jail those three men or get the hell out of my way."

"I'm the law here."

"Lake, I have federal authority over you. Either

you back down or we're going to fist city to start."
He held up his hand. "Easy Cole. I'll handle this."

People began to shrink away. The postman Clark
came through the crowd. "I helped this man appre-
hend those outlaws. He is a marshal and these are
the kidnappers."

"That's right. That guy there kidnapped me
down in Arizona and brought me back up here,"
Leroy said.

"I'm the damn law. Why didn't you tell me?"

Leroy sat on the buggy seat shaking his head.
"How in the hell could I do that? He had me tied up."

The crowd laughed.

Chet booted his roan up closer. "Stand aside,
Lake. I have better things to do than listen to you
all day."

"We'll see about that." But despite his threat,
Lake did step aside.

The crowd applauded Chet and his posse in passing though.

"Jesus, go get those food things we need at the
store and keep a packhorse. You can catch up later.
Get ten locks and fifty feet of chain, too." Chet
stood in the stirrups to dig the money out for his
man. Under his breath, he said, "I am not asking
Lake for cuffs."

Jesus nodded. With a stern look at the deputy
who stood across the street with his arms folded on
his chest, he scowled in disgust at him.

"He won't bother you. You are a sworn posse
member for the U.S. marshal service," Chet said.

"Good."

"We will go to the edge of town and wait. You

take too long and I'll be back for you. Don't get in a gun fight with him."

"*Sí*." Jesus took the packhorse least loaded and went to the store, hitched both horses at the rack, and went inside.

Chet rode over and told Kathrin to drive her buggy on. She gave a serious nod and the mare stepped out. He turned up his collar on his new coat against the sharp wind. The effort covered his neck from the draft and he gave Cole a sign to ride on with the prisoners.

"I wasn't going to kill him," Cole said. "Just backing you."

"Thanks. I didn't want things to explode. Let's get back to Arizona." Chet looked from the brim of his hat to the azure blue skies for help. He still needed to make a decision about her and those two boys who were probably pressured by Evans into doing anything bad that they'd done.

Half mile from town, they waited for Jesus on a windy ridge. They sat around eating beef jerky and washing it down with stale water. To his relief, he saw his man coming on the run. "Kathrin, he's coming. We better get started."

"How far will we go today?" she asked, ready to get on the buggy seat.

"I'd like to be out of Utah. Deputy Lake has some stake in this deal." Chet rode in closer. "Do him and Evans have any relations?"

She climbed on the seat. "I'm not sure enough to say."

"That's fine. I just wondered."

On the seat, she reached for the reins and said,

"Evans must have had some help getting that ranch job."

"Thanks." Chet watched her drive off wondering why a deputy sheriff got so upset about a U.S. deputy marshal arresting anyone. Oh well, he might learn more before this whole thing was over.

The faded sign nailed on two posts said ARIZONA TERRITORY BORDER. The sun was getting low and he recalled a place ahead they could camp. No water, but in the cold air the horses would be all right until they made Joseph's Lake the next day. They'd watered them good before they'd gotten to town earlier.

The two boys helped Jesus unload. Cole tended the horses.

Chet set Evans on the ground off by himself with his hands tied behind his back where he could watch him, rifle cradled in his arm, and talk to Kathrin. "Tell me about those two boys."

She looked up to be sure no one else was in hearing distance. "They were scared to death of him the whole time. He hired them to be cowboys to run that ranch he told me he was going to manage for some guy." She shook her head. "My damn husband married a teenage girl 'cause I could not conceive, I guess. Then he said he was also going to marry her sister so he'd have two young wives. I'm sorry but I was not going to live with him and two other teenage girls. So I left him. He didn't care that I was gone. But it was tough. I had no money. I got a job as a waitress. When a single, twentysomething-year-old woman runs off, she's a whore. Evans came along and treated me nice. Oh, he's a really smooth liar. He brought me that buggy and mare, told me to take my things, and meet him at this ranch he was going run.

"It sounded so nice, I did what he said. Meanwhile, he went and hired those two boys, followed Leroy down here someplace, and kidnapped him. Them boys didn't know what they were in on either, but he told them he'd kill them and me, too, if we didn't do what he said to do.

"We had nothing to eat but rabbits and a deer the boys shot with a twenty-two. Then the money started to come in her letters. I bought food with it. I didn't know anyone I trusted in town and never got to talk much with the boys—but the food I made was better than before."

"I may send them home," Chet said.

"Ask Leroy. This was all Evans deal. What about me?"

"Leroy said you saved him from starving. My wife or a gal named Jenn in Preskitt could figure out a better life for you."

Busy on her knees, feeding the small fire to get it started, she looked up suspiciously at him. "Why do that for me?"

"Because I can. I am a rancher, but I'm also a human being. I'm a very happily married man and have no desire for you as a woman, but as a human being, my heart is sad for your predicament. Tomorrow, we will pick up some more killers at Joseph's Lake. The next week, going to Preskitt will not be pleasant, but you have your buggy and you will have privacy, I promise you."

She was blotting tears with a soiled rag. The fire started, she rose, "May God bless you, Chet Byrnes."

"He has, Kathrin. Many times. Your way will not be easy, but you will find a way out."

"Hug me. I am shaking. Oh, Chet, thank God."

He did and then she nodded. "I'll be fine now. The boys are back."

Chet took the boys aside after supper. Newt McCoy was the speaker. "Harrison and I thought we had real jobs as cowboys working for him. We didn't know about the kidnapping when we hired on, but I told Harrison late at night if he ever gets that money, Evans probably would kill all four of us. We didn't dare run away. He said he'd cut our ears off."

Chet listened carefully and made his decision. "In the morning, you boys completely avoid Honey Grove and ride on home."

"Really?"

"Hush. I can't guarantee you that those horses and saddles you have are not stolen, but I will write you a note and if you get in trouble over them going back, write me at Preskitt and I'll get you out."

"Oh, Marshal Byrnes, that is such good news."

"You boys live around Honey Grove?"

"No sir. We live eighty miles north at Skyler."

"As I said, avoid going through Honey Grove."

Both of them nodded their heads in the dark.

"For now, I want you two to help my boys guard. You hear anything let us know. Evans may have help around here, following us."

Solemn-faced in the starlight, they agreed and shook Chet's hand. Then they went back to the fire. He had a chain and lock put on Evans's foot, the other end locked around a juniper tree. Cole had the key. The crew built Kathrin a lean-to shelter against the north wind that reflected the fire's heat back on top of her.

When Chet went to sleep, he left orders to awaken him if anything happened, plus he got the last watch shift. Some time in the night, Newt woke him whispering, "We've got company."

Chet sat up, immediately awake. "How many?"

"Three or four. Cole spotted them coming on foot from the west and we're all up now. They ain't Injuns. They're wearing hats."

"Keep down."

About then, the invaders fired their guns in air. "We got you surrounded."

When one of the raiders fired his rifle in the air again, it gave the defenders a chance to see them. Three rifles poured fire into the intruders. The still night air was foggy with gunpowder smoke.

"What's happening?" Kathrin hissed.

"Tell her, Newt." Chet and his two men advanced through the shin-high sagebrush ready to shoot at anything that moved.

The groans of the wounded were loud. Making certain none had rifles, Cole caught one by the arm and dragged him away, screaming, so he couldn't get to one. Jesus listened to one of the quiet ones' heart.

"Don't bother. He is dead," he said.

"This one is, too," Cole said about another.

"Newt and Harrison, over here," Chet hollered. "Get their guns and horses. Come daylight, you boys will have to go back to Honey Grove and take them—the wounded and the dead—with you. The wounded ones would die before I could get them home with me."

Kathrin had a pitch torch when she came over. "One of the dead is Lake."

Chet frowned. "I better find some paper and write this out."

To whom it may concern.

　On this night, four men attacked our camp in Arizona Territory to rescue their friend, federal prisoner Evan Evans. My posse men and I resisted their attack. Two of the attackers are dead. The two wounded, I sent back to Honey Grove with Newton McCoy and Harrison Duval.

　If you have any other questions contact me in Prescott A.T.

> *Sincerely yours,*
> *Chet Byrnes*
> *U.S. Deputy Marshal*

Chet handed the note to Newton.

In the chilly morning, the two boys led the wounded back toward Honey Grove. Leaving the dead where they lay, Chet, his crew, Kathrin, Scales, and the prisoner Evans went south.

One evening later, they were at the Joseph's Lake trading post.

Kimes came out and greeted them. "You must have got your man." He tossed his head at Evans.

"We did and the man he held is all right." Chet pointed at Scales, then turned back to Kimes. "Do you know anyone who has a stout team of horses and a wagon they might sell?" Chet asked him.

"I know one. Big draft horses. The wagon is not spanking new, but it is solid."

"Where is it?"

"I'll send my son to get them. They can all be here in the morning."

"How much does the man want for all of it?"

"One hundred and fifty dollars. They are big black Shire horses. Six and seven years old. They are stout, but not fat. He works them hard in the log woods."

"Get them. I have chains and locks for the prisoners. It is still a long way to Preskitt."

"You're going to buy a team and wagon?" Cole asked Chet privately, dismounting and leading his horse.

"Yes. It will here in the morning. We have a helluva long way still to go. Chained in the wagon, they will be easier to keep an eye on."

"Good idea. Kimes have any trouble with them?"

"He never said, but they might not have tried him. He's tough," Chet pointed out.

Cole agreed. Jesus joined them.

"I have a big team and wagon coming to haul the prisoners in," Chet told him.

"Good. The other three here?"

"Yes. Tomorrow we will head off this mountain for the ferry. That's two days from here or longer."

Both of his men agreed.

Cole had one more thing to say. "Hey, Chet. Jesus and I have enjoyed being with you. It won't be any picnic going home, but we'd sure ride the river with you."

"Thanks."

"Hey, you three," Leroy called out from the buggy. "It's been a wild deal to get here, but any way I can help, I'll do it."

"Kimes is sending for a big team and wagon to haul the prisoners. You ever drive a Shire team?"

"They got hooves. I can drive them."

Chet smiled and looked at his men. "What about that?"

"Wonderful," Jesus said.

"Yeah, thanks." Cole shook his hand.

"My wife's got food cooked," Kimes announced.

"Chain Evans to that log wagon wheel and we'll go eat," Chet said.

That done, everybody but Evans headed for the store-house combination.

They filed in, washed and dried their hands, then sat down at a long rough-cut wood bench and table. The food was hot and good to the crew who'd had little variety in their meals over the past days. The venison was flavorful, the potatoes mashed. Gravy, mustard greens, and great biscuits that melted in their mouths completed the meal. Dried apple pie finished it off.

Chet could have used a good hot cup of coffee. He wasn't a Mormon. Oh, he could imagine a cup of rich coffee served by his wife or Monica. He missed both of them. Oh well, the road home got under way in the morning.

Before he left, he thanked Mrs. Kimes for the dinner.

Chet, Jesus, and Cole went to check on the Marconis in the shed. It stunk of piss and human waste. Their cold silent glares told Chet they were still mean killer dogs who, unleashed, would try for his throat.

Evans, chained again, was put in with them. He sprawled on the ground with a blanket, his leg iron locked to a thick pole. He and the Marconis had been fed beans and bread by the Kimes's help.

Chet and his men put out their bedrolls in the guest cabin. The horse herd had been fed grain, hayed, and watered. When Chet laid down at last in his bedroll, his back muscles complained. All he could think was they'd soon be trudging home—not near fast enough for him.

At dawn, he examined the big black horses who were breathing steam. They did look gaunt, but solid—ready to go.

Leroy agreed they'd be a handful, but even with the wagon loaded with the prisoners and some saddles, it would not be a problem for the big horses. "I can drive them. What do they call them?"

"Gill is the left one, Coby is on the right," said the youth who'd brought them.

Leroy thanked him.

The prisoners were marched out, chained, and locked at the ankles. Then they were loaded by a ramp and all sat down in the bed at the same time huddled under their own blankets.

Chet let Leroy drive out first. He was fearful the big team might run over Kathrin's buggy if they were spooked. He waved her in next, and his two men drove the horse band out of the corral. He paid Kimes all he owed him, and for the care of the prisoners. The U.S. marshal service would repay most of it, and he could certainly find a use at the ranch for the big horses. He mounted his horse and followed the others.

An edge of high clouds were moving in from the north when he found a place in the pines that gave him a good view of that direction. He considered them harbingers of snow. He shook his head then booted his horse to the right to bring a stray grazer back into the horse herd—one who had veered aside to snatch a mouthful of bunch grass.

So many things rode on his mind—his sister and Sarge, Hampt with the herd headed for New Mexico, the main ranch, and all his operations. Plus Reg and Lucy who must think he'd left them. Oh well. He booted the roan off the mountain.

Up ahead, Leroy was managing the big horses, holding the wagon back on the steepest grades handily. That pleased Chet. The man was a real driver. The way down and off the Kaibab was a tough mountain road and he'd be glad to be at the base by nightfall.

They stopped on a flat place to give the horses a rest. He dismounted and checked on Kathrin. "You doing all right?"

"Oh yes." She was on the ground stretching and bending. "I am a hundred percent better. Where did you meet your wife?"

"On a stage coach coming from Hayden's Mill to Preskitt."

"Oh."

"I was looking for a new ranch in Arizona. My family was involved in a family feud in Texas. We needed a new address."

"Do you like Arizona?" Kathrin asked.

"We're doing well here."

"Sounds like it. Cole and Jesus have told me lots about you. I consider myself fortunate to be in this train."

"If you hang on, we'll find you a new future."

"I look forward to that. And I mean what I say." She paused, ready to get back in her rig. "Thanks."

He gave her a high sign then turned his horse. Prisoners reloaded and seated in the wagon, he waved to Leroy to head out.

Standing in the wagon, Leroy spoke to the big horses and they began to start out in a movement very much like a dance that singled out their breeding.

Kathrin's mare and buggy went next and then the horses led by a dun gelding that was bossy and barred his teeth at any challengers who wanted to pass him. Leaders like that kept a band of horses together like a bell mare.

The grumbling prisoners were a pain in Chet's backside and he wished he had them all in jail. He tried to ignore them, but they were a constant complaining force. The cold air and increasing bank of clouds made him conscious that things could grow worse before the gray day was over.

They crossed House Rock Valley under the side of the red rim of the Vermillion Cliffs.

Mid-morning it began to snow—dry flakes, at first, on his cheek. He trotted the roan to the front of the train and on a high place, viewed the far away gap concealing the ferry. It would be another day reaching there, with or without snow. He nodded to Leroy and shook his head. "This is all we needed."

Over the clop of hooves, rattle of wheels, and jingle of harness, Leroy said. "Hey, I am free. That is better than the weather."

Chet gave him a thumbs-up sign and rode back for the others. It was a great third day for Leroy who had barely lived, tied up as a hostage for over a month. Chet nodded to Kathrin as he went by her and she made a face at the snow.

He shrugged. "I can't help it. We will make it. Have no fear."

She smiled.

In the back, he spoke with Cole and Jesus bringing on the horse herd.

"This snow looks like it's going get worse," Cole said.

"As a south Texan, I saw only one snow that covered the ground," Chet said. "It melted by noon the next day."

Cole shook his head. "I loved Nebraska in the summer, but my winter there it snowed early and never let up. Folks said it was the worst one in years, but I didn't want to be there for another record."

"My first snow was the first winter I came to work at Preskitt," Jesus said. "I had heard of it. But when

I slid down on my butt, I knew it was going to be crazy to work in."

They laughed.

Noontime, they stopped and ate a cold lunch—beef jerky and cold biscuits. Chet was saving the small amount of firewood stored in the wagon for the night's fire. The prisoners were allowed to empty their bladders and then they squatted under blankets, grumbling.

"We should be turned loose," Old man Marconi complained.

"Yeah." Evans added. "We will sure freeze to death."

"My alternative is to tie a rope around all your necks and then tie it to the wagon. You can run to keep up with those big horses. That would warm you up."

"That would get us drug," Evans said.

"You aren't as dumb as I thought you were. Now shut up or I will gag you." Chet pointed at the outlaws. "Load up. I will still shoot you if you try anything, snow or no snow."

They moved out again. The snow stopped, but it began again when they reached a watering hole in late afternoon. The weary business of unloading the prisoners went on again. Building a cooking fire was up to Jesus and Kathrin. The horses, after being watered, ate from nosebags. Snow really began to fall in large flakes. Chet shook his head at the turn in the weather while making certain the chain on the prisoners was locked on a wagon wheel.

"You going to let us freeze to death out here?" Evans demanded.

Chet shrugged. "I don't really care what happens to you."

"I know that. Maybe your men would turn us loose if you were dead."

"I imagine they'd vote to hang you on the first tree they found and not have to listen to your mouth."

"My lawyer—"

Chet kicked him in the leg. "Shut up."

"Don't upset him," Old man Marconi said.

"I don't give a damn. He's going to let us freeze to death out here."

"Better listen to him, Evans." Chet walked away. His concern was getting all of them out of this desolate land.

Chet talked to Leroy and the others at the campfire.

"This snow shouldn't hamper us getting to Lee's Ferry," Leroy said. "But we've got four days to get to the Marcy Road and about a half of one to get to that sawmill."

Chet agreed. "We can rest there."

"That Cameron trading post on the Little Colorado, we can rest there, too," Leroy said.

"You are talking about almost two weeks drive to get back."

Leroy nodded. "It will take us that long to get to Preskitt."

"I am not complaining, but I'd sure like to be there already." Chet shook his head. It would be step by step.

He rolled up in his bedroll thinking about his wife. She was in a warm bed, anyway. He'd sure like to be there with her. His guard duty was the last one. He better get some sleep while he could.

They reached the ferry midday and Lee met them in the melting, slushy snow. Their crossing would take lots of time and several trips. The horse herd would go on the last two. Lee also sold them a rick of wood and some hay that was loaded into the wagon. The grain Chet bought went on the pack animals.

The trips began and in no time the prisoners and wagon were across. Chet and Leroy guarded them. Kathrin and the buggy went next with the saddle horses, and Chet rode back to help get the loose horses loaded. They didn't like the hollow sounding barge but the first were soon over, and they were winched back for the last load. Mrs. Lee, a British lady, had generously fed them all, including the prisoners. Chet paid her ten dollars for her effort after he settled the fare, grain, and fire wood charges with Lee.

She was so excited and thanked him as he was going out the door. "Oh that is so generous of you, sir. Come again please."

He thanked her again and headed back to the ferry.

Jesus waited for him and the last of the ponies to arrive. The others had gone on ahead to get as much distance as they could before dark. Lee and his helper brought the rest of the herd onto the ferry.

"I am so glad we made it this far." Jesus crossed himself.

"Me too, *amigo*. I will be damn glad to be home and may not leave the house for a century."

Jesus laughed. "I bet you are gone in two weeks, helping someone."

Bundled against the sharp wind, Chet smiled. He hoped his man was wrong about that.

Three cold days later, they reached the large trading post at Cameron. Chet bought another rick of wood and loaded it in the wagon.

He sent Kathrin shopping for their food needs. Her concern was they'd be much higher priced than at Preskitt and she'd limit them to their real needs. He thanked her for her concern. It had been a costly trip, but more than worthwhile. The Wells Fargo rewards for the three stage robbers would please his two men, too. The three faced murder charges as well.

His back was sore from riding so far in the saddle and sleeping on the cold ground. Home would be a wonderful relief.

The next morning, they were moving south again—over fifty miles left to get to the fork in the road.

* * *

Bone weary, they stopped, camped and turned in early. He felt certain the next night they would sleep at the sawmill. The snow was crunchy under foot, only the ruts were icy.

In the bitter cold with a blanket over his shoulders, he served his guard time, seating cross-legged, breathing out large clouds of vapor, and keeping the fire going for the morning cooking needs.

Kathrin came awake early and began to make preparations. "You will be glad to home?"

"Amen to that. We will be at the sawmill tonight and sleep in beds, I hope."

"Then the next day at your ranch?"

"You bet."

"I hope I don't make your wife mad—I mean, being with you all this way."

"You won't. She doesn't worry about those kinds of things. We are together and that is all that is important."

"She's lucky."

"No. Her first husband died in the war. Number two was thrown off a horse and died. As a last resort, she ended up with me." He laughed.

Kathrin shook her head about the time Jesus came to join them. "Your boss says his wife is not lucky having him and he was the last resort."

"Oh, I am glad to be here, 'cause at home she would be walking the floors and asking me, 'You think he is all right?'"

They all laughed.

They soon had the prisoners and crew up. Her hot breakfast of pan-fried potatoes and bacon, along with Dutch-oven biscuits even made the prisoners shut up. In an hour, they were on the road again. The sun felt some warmer. The big horses jogged and they made great time reaching the junction and at last the sawmill in mid-afternoon.

Robert ran out to greet them. "Who did you arrest?"

"A kidnapper and three murderers." Chet pointed to the buggy, then the wagon. "This is Kathrin, and the hostage we rescued is Leroy Scales." He wheeled the roan around. "Take a couple men away from the sawmill work and relieve my men of guarding the prisoners. Find her a private, safe place. I am going to the Verde Ranch. They can all drive on down there tomorrow."

Chet shook hands with Cole and Jesus and told them they'd be relieved of guard duty till morning and to meet him at Susie's. He did the same to Kathrin and left.

It was long after dark when he reached Susie's house. She came on the run and hugged him. Tom had put on his coat and came over and so did half the crew.

"You all right?" Susie asked.

Chet nodded in the candle lamplight. "I am fine. Leroy Scales is well. We arrested his kidnapper and the three Marconi men who had robbed the stagecoach. They also murdered a man on the road going up there. Good to see all of you."

They cheered.

"We'll have more time to talk later. Cole and Jesus will bring the horses and prisoners here tomorrow.

They are sleeping at the sawmill tonight. Saddle me a fresh horse. The roan is worn out."

"You are going home tonight?" Susie asked.

"Yes."

"Sarge and I are going to be married tomorrow night. We hoped you'd be here to give me away again."

"I will. I wish you two the best."

"I know I can't stay up there at Windmill because the only house is the bunkhouse."

"We will build one for you two."

"I didn't know if we could. I worry about all the expenses we've had. In the spring, I'll use a tent. Until then, we will get along. He really likes the cattle driving business and wants to keep that job."

"Good." One less worry for Chet.

"Remember, the wedding is tomorrow," she said quietly.

"I'll be back for it."

The fresh horse came saddled. He spoke briefly to Tom. "All well here?"

"Tomorrow, some of us will go meet Cole and Jesus and help with the prisoners."

"I want them held here until Monday and then we will deliver them to the jail. Cole and Jesus have worked their butts off. They deserve lots of the credit. I will send Mrs. Scales down here to meet her husband tomorrow. He is a great guy as well. I want everyone to see these pitiful outlaws delivered to Sims on Monday."

"We can handle that."

"Susie, in your wedding preparations, I would

like Leroy and his wife Betty Lou to be your guests at the house tomorrow night."

"Fine, Chet. Right after the wedding, Sarge and I are going to Oak Creek for our honeymoon. Millie can entertain them."

"Swell." Chet stepped into the saddle, swung his leg over the cantle, and slid into place. "They will be so glad to be together they won't need much."

Susie laughed. "Ride careful."

"I will. Thanks guys and gals. I'm going home." He swept the fresh roan around and headed for the cross bar at a healthy run. On the Camp Verde road, through the starry night, and in the silver landscape, he let him out. The grade was steep. He let the gelding walk and halted on the top for him to get his breath.

Then he set out again in a lope.

At last, reaching the cross bar over the open gate, he charged up the drive to the house. Sliding to a stop, he began to undo the girth and gave a loud, "Yahooo."

A light came on in their bedroom and he dropped the saddle and hot pads on the ground. The roan wouldn't leave. He might graze some. There was little snow on the ground there.

The front door opened. "Chet! You're home!"

He took the steps two at a time and hugged Marge's warm form.

"Where are the others?" she asked as they went inside.

"Everyone is fine. We have the kidnapper. Leroy is all right. We also caught the Marconis. They killed a man on the road. A lady, Kathrin Arnold, got mixed up in it, but she had no hand in it. She's a Mormon and her husband had married one teenager and planned to marry another sister, so she left him. The kidnapper had picked her up and she had no choice but go with him. She and the two boys he hired as ranch hands looked out for Leroy."

"Where is she?"

"She's coming down with Jesus, Cole, and the prisoners. I promised her that you and Jenn would help her."

"Of course. You look a little bushy, but I don't care. You are safe and healthy." She hugged him again.

Monica stuck her head in the room. "I started the boiler. It was already warm. I have some cake and soon will have coffee."

"We're coming. You spoke to Susie?" Marge asked.

"Yes. That's why we are going to bring the prisoners into Preskitt on Monday. I promised her we'd be there tomorrow."

"I am sure some will think it is too quick, but both of them want each other. So who else has any word in it?"

"No one. Let their tongues wag. I want her happy . . . and him, too."

Monica's chocolate cake was wonderful.

But before she got away, he asked. "How is your friend?"

"Oh, he's fine. He's taking me to the wedding

tomorrow. Marge said we could sleep in separate bedrooms at the ranch. Is that all right?"

"Or use one." He laughed, but she was gone.

Marge snickered. "They might, anyway."

By the time he bathed and shaved and they went upstairs it was past three a.m. It would be a short night, but who cared? He'd have her in his arms and be in his own bed. Thank God.

CHAPTER 19

Up at eight, they hurried to get ready. Raphael sent a vaquero with a buckboard to get Leroy's wife Betty Lou and take her to the Verde ranch. He had a note and instructions on what she should do. She was to keep quiet about the whole thing and she needed to bring clothes for both of them to wear at the wedding.

Marge had his best clothes cleaned and pressed. They were packed in a small trunk with her best dress. The buggy hitched and a horse tied on behind, they left for the Verde ranch.

Monica was in a dither before they left, but her date wasn't in sight when they turned east for the main road and headed for the ranch. They had the fast team and he let them go. They slowed going downhill and in no time were on the flats. Marge was so excited about his return, she could hardly contain herself. Having him home and safe at last, he figured out, recalling Jesus's story about her worrying where he was when he was gone, was probably true. The baby inside her was not a problem.

They reached the ranch in early afternoon and Susie rushed out to hug her. "How is the momma doing?"

"Oh," Marge swept the hair back from her own face. "Wonderful, now that he's home and safe. Let's work on your hair and get you ready."

"There is food in the house," Susie said to him. "We decided to have less of a wedding than last time. There will be plenty of food, but we cut back some."

"You didn't need to."

"I know, but the government owes you lots of money."

"They will pay us."

Susie wrinkled her nose at him as they walked inside. "The men from the mill aren't here yet, either."

"They will be coming. They are no doubt taking their time. We sent a man to get Betty Lou Scales. His name is—"

"Orlando," Marge said. "A polite vaquero who will deliver her here with fresh clothes to wear. And Monica is bringing her rancher and they will sleep in separate bedrooms."

Susie laughed. "Our aunt is coming with her man. They will sleep in one."

Chet made a sliced beef sandwich with mustard. "Either of us get a letter from JD?"

"No. But Lucy and Reg were invited by mail in plenty of time."

"They'll come if they can."

"He may not want her to ride in her condition," Marge said.

"She'd be a damn sight harder to convince than you were," he said before taking another bite.

"Someone is coming now," Marge said, looking out the front windows.

"That is my husband to be and he is driving the buckboard he and Hampt rebuilt with John the blacksmith." Susie ran out, kissed him, and on the way in she told him that Chet was back.

A big smile on Sarge's face, they shook hands. "Glad you're back, boss man. This has been a whirlwind, but I couldn't be any prouder that she wants to be my wife."

"She said you want to stay at Windmill and herd cattle. I said we'd build you two a house to live in. Weather lets up, she wants a tent over there, but we will start on it as soon as they get done at Hackberry."

"You can't beat that. I am impressed and I'll do my damndest to make it work. We've got time for a short honeymoon and then she's coming back here and I'll need to head for New Mexico. The boys have them all bunched close so we can leave in a week."

"Sounds great. Robert from the sawmill will be here. We'll start cutting timber for your house over there."

"Boy, I recall riding out here the first time and saying, 'Well, I'll try this job and in six months I'll go on down the road.'"

"You ever want to?"

"No. I was so busy and having so much fun, I never thought about that again."

"You've made a good hand and you'll make a good brother-in-law partner in this outfit."

Sarge wet his lips. "Hampt and I both talked about the deal we've got here with Tom and we all three said it won't get no better."

"It will. We'll be real big ranchers one day," Chet predicted.

"You worried any about this paper they hand me for the cattle?"

"I'd like to have the cash, but that's how they do business in D.C. If they can't pay us, they can't pay lots of their suppliers. My banker isn't worried. He says it will come through. Meanwhile, we will supply them cattle."

"You feel safe. I won't worry."

Chet clapped Sarge on the shoulder. "We will survive."

"Good and thanks. I am very proud to get to marry your sister. I know people will talk about it being too soon, but life ain't that long. I don't want to miss a chance to have her for my wife. I was too dumb before so she escaped me, but not this time."

"I hope you two have a great life together. I won't trade mine for anyone else."

"We will. Susie said you will have some federal prisoners held here at the ranch?"

"Yes. I aim to deliver them to Sims on Monday. Know that we won't ever ranch on the north rim of the Grand Canyon." Chet shook his head.

"Tough country?"

"Very harsh. I liked the Kaibab Plateau and the Joseph's Lake region, but I'll leave it for others."

"How tough were the men you arrested?"

"Just thugs."

Sarge nodded he understood. "We haven't had any more Indian trouble. Guess they are in a wickiup till spring."

"Keep your eyes open. They have not called it quits yet."

"We will."

The train had arrived from the sawmill. Tom assigned guards. The prisoners were chained together and he locked them in a log barn. Marge took charge of Kathrin, escorting her up to the house. Chet assured Leroy they'd jail the prisoners on Monday and that his wife was on her way.

"Oh, that is so good of you. I sure have missed her. But if you and those two men had not come— I'd be dead. All I went to do was to settle an estate and come home. I didn't carry any money because that road is steeped in people getting robbed and killed."

"Naw, you'd have found a way out. Thank Betty Lou, too. She came and convinced my wife to send me looking for you. One of our men went to get her since we knew you wanted to hug her."

"Hug her? Oh, you are sure right."

"Stay and enjoy the wedding. You can take her home in the rig tomorrow. There are plenty of rooms at the big ranch house tonight."

"Thanks. We will have an enjoyable time." Leroy shook his head. "I am glad that I don't have to haul those outlaws another mile."

"We will deliver them, like I said, on Monday, but I'd like you to be there to talk to the prosecuting attorney about Evans's actions."

"Oh, I will be there."

"Thanks."

Marge showed up, wearing a light coat over her dress. "How are your men?"

"I guess fine. I have not spoken to them yet. Just Leroy here."

"Oh. I really like Kathrin Arnold. I think we can help her. She appreciates all you have done for her. I would, too."

"Fine. Everything is going well. We will be ready for it all."

"I imagine you are worn out, aren't you?"

"I'm fine. I am home at last with you. That's what counts."

She hugged him. "So am I."

Despite the weak sun, he felt warm to have her attached to him. Something about being with her simply made him feel good. Of all the great women in his life, Marge had power that they shared and it powered both of them.

Cole and Jesus found them.

"We're coming to the wedding. Tom has guards to watch the prisoners," Cole said as both of them took off their hats in respect to her.

"Chet tells me you have been busy," Marge said.

"We sure have, but I can tell you that isn't any place to take a vacation," Jesus said to her and they laughed.

"Chet did mention he thought it wasn't ranch

country," Marge said. "Thank you for looking out for him."

"He looked after all of us," Jesus assured her.

"I know," she said. "We all use him."

Chet shook his head at their banter. "You two guys have a good time tonight."

"We will," Cole said. And the young men left them.

Chet and Marge walked to the house to change clothes. Betty Lou arrived and she danced with Leroy in the yard. Chet saw them from the window and smiled. "They'll have fun tonight."

Marge joined him and watched the two dancing. "That is wonderful. Well, I'm just glad things are settling."

"A few months ago, I would never have gotten away with changing clothes at the same time with you," she said buttoning up her dress.

"I am not that numb, but it didn't seem proper with all we have to do."

She kissed his face. "I was only making a point."

He two-arm hugged her and kissed her. "Next week, I will be yours."

"No. You have prisoners to deliver. You will want to check on Reg and then Sarge's deal while he's on his honeymoon."

"I swear I will."

"I know and I love you. Don't change for a silly pregnant wife's whims."

"Good. It has been a tough near ten days on the trail."

She silenced him and they kissed hard.

* * *

The wedding was ready to start. The schoolhouse would bulge, but there was room for all. Standing room only. Chet led Susie down the narrow isle and they chatted under their breath.

"You two have fun up there," Chet whispered.

"We will. He's a wonderful guy."

"Yes, he is. All right, you are on your own."

"Thanks Chet, I love you, too."

After the ceremony, the married couple ran out to the buckboard, and folks threw rice at them before Sarge took charge and drove away.

Chet and Marge faced the crowd. "Let's all go eat. There is plenty of cake and we should have fun," Chet hollered. He was ready to go to the ranch house, but they stayed and danced.

All at once, someone shouted, "Reg and Lucy are here."

Soon the tall Reg came through a doorway crowded with well-wishers. Lucy, on the end of his arm, was coming along behind, talking to everyone.

Chet's nephew looked exhausted and his wife shook her head at Chet. "You've been out chasing outlaws again."

"Yes, we got them, too."

"Hey, we tried to be here on time," Reg said. "I guess we missed the newlyweds."

"They drove off minutes ago. How are the two of you?"

"Fine," Reg said. "And Lucy's doing great. House

is nearly completed and she says the baby will be a boy."

"This spring we'll have a new generation of kids in this family."

"We'll each have our own gang." Reg laughed. "Snow has slowed down our mavericking and we could've come faster on horseback, but I worried about her. She didn't think it would hurt her and the baby, but I wasn't taking any chances."

"Good idea. I'm sure you're getting lots done up there."

"We are sure trying."

"Good. Cattle delivery is going fine. We have not been paid for any, but my banker says it will come."

"God, I hope so." Reg looked taken aback by that news.

"Standard federal procedure. Before you go back, I want us to sit down with Tom and look at all the things you need."

"Good enough. Lucy and I made a list."

"Go get something to eat. We'll be here."

"They are the cutest pair on this earth," Marge said as they headed for the food line, talking to each other all the way. "I loved her when she showed us around that first trip, but those two together are simply cute along with sweet to one another."

"I agree. We better dance." So they waltzed and then danced to another tune. They had magic and she moved so smoothly with him, he really enjoyed dancing. Good to be back home. That damn country above the Grand Canyon was a real wasteland.

About midnight, they went back to the big

house. All parties came over about the same time. Without Susie to organize things, Marge made coffee and served them cinnamon rolls Susie had laid out for them. Chet's aunt and her man, Monica and her rancher, Betty Lou and Leroy, plus Reg and Lucy made a houseful. Hampt and May had gone home to their place earlier. Tom and Millie dropped by, but by then Chet and Marge were tired. They told them all good night and headed up the stairs.

From the stairs, he stopped and thanked them all for coming and said he was sure happy with the ranch, all the workers, and the wedding. "We are all one here."

They cheered.

In bed, Marge said he was so sweet to tell them that.

"I wasn't lying. This is growing into a large successful operation on the frontier."

She snuggled closer to him. "I know what you've done for the ranch and me."

They kissed and he wondered if the baby was going to survive their frolicking. So far so good.

In the morning, Monica and Marge made breakfast. Lucy and Betty Lou joined them and the meal was soon set out. Chet sipped coffee and watched them take their places. Susie would have been proud. He was surprised she hadn't stayed to make this meal herself.

Dishes done, he and Marge headed for their house. Tom was bringing the prisoners in a buckboard and then taking them into Preskitt in the morning. He'd have four armed, mounted men to guard them. That would cover it.

The trip uphill was without incident. The sun had warmed some when they turned toward Preskitt and headed home. It was a sparkling day and Chet was satisfied that things should iron out across his operations. JD was still on his mind, but that boy was big enough to take care of himself. Wherever he was.

CHAPTER 20

Word had spread all over about the prisoners and Preskitt was crowded with the curious despite the bit of cold. A known stage robber gang and the kidnapper of a local man drew their attention. Lots of folks knew Leroy and wanted his kidnapper in jail.

Chet rode his roan in, balancing a rifle on his leg. He and his men rode up to the courthouse. Tom stopped the wagon with the prisoners next to them.

An undersheriff, Ralston, came out. "Who are these men?"

"U.S. Deputy Marshal Chet Barnes. Three are Marconis wanted for stage robbery and the murder of Joseph Smith in this county near Lee's Ferry. The fourth man is a kidnapper, Evan Evans. He kidnapped Leroy Scales in this county and took him to Utah and held him for ransom. His wife was to send him money for his release."

"Marshal Byrnes, are you prepared to file these charges?"

"I am, sir."

"Are there any rewards on these men?"

"The Marconis have a Wells Fargo Reward on them. That goes to my men."

"Are these men wearing your irons?"

"They are."

"Where's the gawdamn Sheriff?" an angry on-looker shouted.

A yell went up from the crowd. "Sims! Sims!"

Chet shook his head, but they didn't stop. The prisoners were marched inside and the door closed on the jail entrance.

He spoke to his men in the crowd that he'd buy them a beer at the Palace and turned his horse to go across the street. He hitched the roan at the rail and went though the left side tall doors with the batwings tied back for winter entrances.

He found them all at the bar. "I'm buying two beers for this bunch."

The bartender counted noses and gave the count to him. "Be two dollars."

Satisfied, Chet put the money on the bar. *Must have a few noncrew members in the lot—oh well.* He waved away any change and turned on his heel. Outside the bar, he mounted his horse and rode over to Jenn's diner for lunch.

The girls welcomed him and had to hear his story. He made it brief and ordered a plate lunch and coffee. Jenn came out and slid in to talk to him. "Do you know the Nelson brothers? Lonnie and Delta?"

"No, why?"

"I got word they've been hired to gun you down."

Chet frowned at her. It couldn't be true. "Who hired them?"

"I'm not sure. But word is out that they're coming to kill you."

"I trust your information, but is there any description of them? I'd also like to know who hired them."

"I'll find out what I can. Meanwhile, you better get loaded for bear."

Chet nodded. He, Tom, Hampt, and Reg were meeting in the morning. Maybe one of them knew the pair. Damn. Where in the hell did they come from? He picked at his food. A shame Marge hadn't come along with him. He'd go back home and try to find out who they were. His problems never ended.

The meeting of ranch foremen was at his house. All except Sarge were there. Chet had paper and pencils set out for taking notes.

When they were all settled with coffee, Chet began. "Thanks for coming. I wanted us to go over the operations and get everyone's ideas on what we should do in the future. I mean, we all are in this together, so I want to hear about each aspect and what we need. But first, I want to ask have any of you ever heard of Lonnie or Delta Nelson?"

"Where are they from?" Reg asked.

"Damned if I know. Jenn said she had word they were hired guns coming to kill me."

"I never heard of them," Hampt said. "She know anything else?"

"Not any more than that. But Jenn doesn't carry idle threats around. She's looking for more information."

"You think they've been sent from Texas?" Reg asked.

"Wait. Let me look on the sawmill payroll. Several of those men have come and gone. Robert has fired some for drinking on the job. I figured most of them were on the run anyway and liked the isolation up there better than working on the ranch."

Chet nodded. "Check it and let me know. Last time I looked on those books the sawmill was making us money. Now we still have another house to build on the Windmill Ranch for Sarge and Susie. You all know we have not been paid yet for any delivered cattle, but Mr. Tanner at the bank says that is not unusual, and that we will eventually get our money. It will be a considerable amount, but we will keep it for a rainy day and try to buy the Rankin place. Now, how are we doing with other things?"

Hampt began first. "I have three hundred mother cows and I think the range, if we have rain, will improve. I have fifteen Hereford bulls and we cut any longhorn bulls on our range. I should have a half whiteface calf crop by next year and all part whiteface calves the next year. We are fencing some acreage down on the Verde with barbed wire this winter. John has ordered wire. We'll twist and put barbs on it here. It was the cheapest way to go. I have four Mexican boys cutting posts."

"Everyone knows those log fences don't keep cattle out of alfalfa."

"We used wire and stakes in Texas. This barbed wire takes less maintenance. I think our hay fields are under stake and wire."

"It takes two full-time men to keep it repaired, too," Tom said. "Of course, the previous management used the cheapest material to build it."

"Our hay contractor is going to return our equipment. He's buying his own. We need for John to look at it and have it ready. We need hay equipment for Sarge, and for you two, Hampt and Reg. Tom, what we have may not be worn out too bad for you to use for a year or so. To get anything new here, I need to order it soon." Chet wrote it down on his list.

"Tom, how are you doing?" he asked next.

"Four hundred fifty range cows and twenty-five bulls—either Hereford or Shorthorn range bulls. That doesn't count the purebreds. We have around a hundred of those and five bulls at the Perkins place. I weaned eighty-nine calves. Forty are good bull prospects, five were culls, and the rest are heifers. I have them on some fenced grass upriver that I rented."

Chet tapped his pencil on the table. "You have some big stuff from the past years we can sell to the Navajos?"

"Yeah. Ryan tried to sell all the cattle as calves. My estimate is about two fifty yearlings plus. We sold some. But I will have a better count at roundup next spring. I have about three eighty head calf crop from this season."

"How is our range?"

"Oh, I think it improved this season, but I'd like more forage on the stalk out there. The departure of the extra cattle sure helped. We can heal in time."

Chet looked at his nephew. "Reg, how's your deal?"

"We have eighty mother cows, sixty calves, and a bunch of old stags—seventy-five now. I have a few shorthorn cross bulls I left standing. I'll need some hay equipment and—"

"Wait." Chet held up his hand. "These are all maverick cattle you and your wife rounded up and branded this year?"

"Yeah. We're still finding them. The two cowboys you sent me can rope anything."

"You may stock that Windmill ranch yet."

Reg smiled. "We're trying hard."

Chet nodded. "You'll need water development this coming summer. Either windmills or tanks. I looked at some over at Rye that really work."

"I built some tanks at a few springs with my boys and they work," Hampt said.

"It is the only way we can get the stock spread out to eat the grass," Tom said.

They agreed.

Chet continued the meeting. "We have no word on the Rankin Ranch. We will add that to Hampt's place when it comes. Now on to horses. We will need horses to pull the mowers and the stacker, rake and sweep the hay. I may need to send back east for some of these things, but mustangs and knotty-tailed saddle stock won't do the job. Frey may know where we can get work horses. Keep your ears open."

"We all need about two dozen more saddle horses to run our operations," Tom said. "I know they cost more money."

"Sarge, for sure, will, too." Chet was writing it all down.

"I'm going to need some alfalfa seed to plant twenty more acres, probably need some barley for a nurse crop, too." Hampt shook his head. "Have we spent all your money, now?"

Reg shook his head. "I won't get any land cleared catching cattle this winter so I'll put planting off till next year."

"You sure?" Hampt asked, and then laughed.

It was time for lunch. Marge told them to put all their papers up. Monica, May, and Lucy had fixed them a big lunch.

"I bet you had a hand in it," Hampt said.

"Oh. A little bit." Marge smiled at him, dealing out the plates.

May brought silverware and Lucy had coffee cups. Monica brought the fresh coffee.

Plates of fire-cooked steaks, potatoes, green beans, and applesauce in bowls along with brown topped sourdough biscuits and flour gravy appeared on the big table.

"Raphael cooked the meat for us," Marge said. "The four of us did the rest. Who needs something else?"

The men applauded. Chet invited the women to join them.

Marge shook her head. "No, we have more interesting things to discuss in the kitchen, but we will check on you."

"Now ain't that like a woman," Hampt said. "More important things to talk about than ranching."

They all laughed. The women retreated to the kitchen and the men sat down at the table.

Chet spoke as the food was passed around. "Christmas is coming. I think we need to have a party for our hands maybe at the Quarter Circle Z. Most don't have families around here. I want each man to have a sack of hard candy, a couple oranges, maybe a kerchief, and ten dollars. The gals can fix them up for the party. Sarge's men will be on the road so I'll go up there when they get back and have one with them. Reg, you and Lucy can take things back for your people. Tom oversees the sawmill log haulers so he can have a party for them."

"Let's invite them to the ranch," Tom said. "They need to be part of us, too."

"Good idea. I bet Robert invites his girlfriend." Chet looked at the men at his table. He was so blessed to have them working for him. "Now all of you, I'm giving you an extra month's salary this year. We are doing good. And Robert gets a foreman bonus, too."

"You know Hoot ain't going to be here much longer," Tom said. "Can we buy him a large rocking chair?"

"We'll put ribbons on it," Hampt said.

"Sure. Marge will handle that."

"What am I to handle? Anyone need coffee?" She said as she and Monica entered the room to pour refills.

Chet smiled. "Get the old cook a big rocker and a wool blanket for Christmas."

"I can sure do that."

Things had gone fine enough to suit him during the meeting. Lucy and Reg were spending another day with them before they left to get the Christmas things to haul back to Hackberry.

Tom pulled Chet aside and talked to him in private. "I think Cole is a good man. I am sending him to ride with you until we know who those hired guns are. We don't want you shot. I'd say Jesus should ride with you, too."

Chet started to protest but Tom held up his hand. "I am serious. You are the one who holds this operation together. I want you to accept them as your guards."

"I'll think on it."

"Reg get over here," Tom said. "I want those two men who rode with him to Utah to be his bodyguards."

"Good idea. Do that Chet."

"I'm not afraid—"

Reg cut him off. "But you got a baby coming that will need you. You won't let your wife ride a horse. So I say yes, the two men go where you go."

"I'll see," was all Chet promised.

Reg stuck his head back into the kitchen. "Marge, come in here."

"No, don't get her involved."

Once Marge was in the room, they all turned to her. "Tom wants Cole and Jesus to ride with him all the time until we find out more about those hired guns," Reg said to her.

Marge nodded. "Good idea. You do that, Chet Byrnes. I don't want you hurt, either."

Chet looked at the tin squares on the ceiling for help. None came. "All right. Send for him. Jesus is here."

"Good," Tom said. "Marge, thank everyone. I need to get home and be sure all is all right."

Chet shook his hand. "Thanks. We had a good review. This ranch will work."

Tom left, then Hampt and May. She kissed Chet good-bye and thanked him for the day and said how much she enjoyed it. They should do it more often.

"I'll try to do that. Hampt tell those boys I am still looking for small horses."

May shook her head. "Those boys are getting to be something else. Last time I was gone, they shot a skunk with a twenty-two."

"Oh?"

"I was worried about them shooting anything without one of us there. But worse than that, they shot it on my front porch. I asked them why they shot it there. They said 'cause it was trying to get in our house." She waved her hand in front of her nose. "It has smelled bad for a week, both inside and out."

Chet kissed her cheek and hugged her shoulders. "They love you."

"I am not sure I love them at times."

They were off. Marge was laughing as she closed the front door. "Those boys will be boys."

"You will have your turn at that."

She hugged him. "Oh God, I hope so."

"You will. I promise you. Marge, you agree with what Tom proposed, don't you?" Chet asked.

"Oh, yes. I definitely agree that you should have your *companyeros* with you at all times."

"No one has a letter from JD?" Lucy asked, coming into the room.

They all shook their heads. "He didn't write you, either?" Chet asked Lucy.

"No, Chet. And Reg is concerned. At least he wrote to us for a while. Now nothing."

"Lord, I hope I don't have to go and try to find him."

Reg shook his head. "He knows we'd come if he needed us. But like Chet says, he's a damn long way away in New Mexico."

"I am going to find those two hired guns. I don't need bodyguards."

"Until they're gone to hell or jail, you do," Reg said.

No one is going to take his side—might as well give up. The four of them played cards and laughed a lot that afternoon. They ate leftovers for supper. Afterward, Reg read magazines. The girls sent Monica off and did her dishes. Chet looked at the things he needed to buy and figured he must order them shortly or they wouldn't get there until after hay session. *Bodyguards.* He never thought he'd be tied to them, but Marge would make him promise to use them.

When Cole came up a little later to stay at the upper ranch, Tom sent a note with him that said the Nelsons had never worked for the mill operation. No one by that name was on the ranch books. Also, without Susie there, he'd need to hire a bookkeeper to write checks, keep the accounts up and straight. No way could she run the ranch and keep the books from the Windmill Ranch.

He also wanted to know who would move into the ranch house. It was too good not to use. And a house not lived in soon fell apart, got roof leaks no one noticed and so on.

Chet would have to think on that one for a while. She'd be there until spring, anyway.

It snowed the next day, but it was light. Reg and Lucy rushed around to get everything they needed and the Christmas deal arranged as well. Chet knew his nephew was concerned about going home in the buckboard if the snow was deep up on the rim. No telling about that and no way to get word and find out.

Most of it melted around Preskitt and then it turned cold that night.

Reg and Lucy left the next morning with plans to stay at the sawmill if it looked bad. Chet, Jesus, and Cole rode to town. They met the new owner at the mercantile—Ben Ivors—and he invited Chet into his back office to discuss merchandise.

Chet said, "I am going to need some mowing machines, hay rakes, buck rakes, and stackers. I've seen some in the catalogs. I know if I don't get them ordered, they won't ever get here for next year."

Ivors nodded. "Exactly. They could get to the end of the tracks over by the east New Mexico line and then take forever to get here. What brand you want?"

"I have some Case mowers now. I want six to start. Plus three rakes, three buck rakes to gather the hay, and three stackers."

"Oh, man you need a lot of machinery. I can order some extras to sell when they get here and maybe save some money for both of us."

"Good." Chet could see his two men waiting out in the store for his return.

"I can send a telegraph today and see if Case has any closer than Iowa."

"Do that. I have the money to pay for them and you get us the best price."

"I will. It's sure nice to finally meet you, Chet."

"My pleasure. I'll drop back in a week and see how you are doing."

Ben rose to shake his hand. "Hey, anything I can help you with, let me know."

Chet stood. "Good luck. You must have had some experience at this business. I see new items and things I never saw in here before."

"My family was in business in Kansas for twenty years. I wanted to come west and found this store was for sale."

"Come down to Camp Verde schoolhouse. We have pot luck and dancing on Saturday night."

"My wife and I will do that."

"Folks don't let it get wild. So you can bring your family."

"That's swell. I only have my wife. Thanks for ordering all this from me."

"Good enough. Let me know you're coming. We have extra beds at the ranch house so you won't need to drive home over the mountain after the dance."

Chet returned to the front of the store, picked up his two men, and they went over to Bo's office. There were magazines to read and Chet invited them inside with him. After a thorough look around outside, they went in.

"Who are they?" Bo asked.

"Oh, Jenn heard word there were some killers coming to get me. My family said I needed them."

"Ha. Now I'm getting even."

"No, they don't tell me what to do like those two I hired to dry you out."

"I still miss getting drunk, but I know you did me a big favor."

"Anything on the Rankin place?" Chet asked.

"No, they are still in court. Might be six months or more. I won't lose it."

"Tell Jane hi."

"Her and the baby that's coming?" Bo grinned.

"Yeah. I'll have one by May, the good Lord willing."

"That will be something. Me a daddy. I'm swearing to do better than my old man."

"I hope so."

"See you."

The three left and Chet went by the bank and saw Tanner in his office. He handed Chet a telegram that said the U.S. Treasury was to pay the first six months' vouchers.

"What about the second? Will they pay those, too?"

"Yes. They say they will pay the second half of the year or at least part of it when they get back into congressional session."

"Thanks."

"I think your money for this year will be here by next March."

"Good." Chet nodded. "I ordered some hay machinery hoping to get it here by May or even June."

"I have a loan in arrears on some equipment. I may have to recall it. Two mowing machines and two rakes."

"Have they been kept up?"

"Never used. They're still in crates. However, the lady seems unable to pay on them."

"Is her first name Kay?" Chet asked.

"Yes. Her man shot himself, they tell me."

"I won't go get the equipment for you, but if you have to take it in, I will buy it."

"Thanks. You have some problems there?"

"My nephew JD moved her out when she wanted a divorce. He tried to help her. She remarried someone else when he left to do a job for me."

"I won't say a word."

"Thanks." Chet left the bank and told the two

young men waiting for him that they were going to Frey's and talk horses around his potbellied stove.

Frey's wife was home, so they had the warm office to themselves.

"Man, what 'cha three doing in town on a day like this?" Frey asked when they entered the livery.

"Draft horses. I need about sixteen teams," Chet answered.

Frey had a coughing spell and when he finished he apologized. "Damn winter cold. That is a big number for me to find. What they going to do?"

"Make hay with them."

Fret whistled. "You need stout ones. Some big stage horses can do that. You want them broke?"

"That would help. But we can break some of them this winter if we have to."

"All right. I have three teams I can sell right now. One is green broke, the other two are all right to hitch up. Cost you three apiece for the two broke ones. Two for the other team."

"When will you have them here?"

"Oh, Friday," Frey said.

"I want to see them and try them out before I buy them."

"That one team is only green broke."

"That means they will lead?" Chet asked the stableman.

"Well, sort of."

Chet's henchmen laughed.

"Aw, how soon are you farming?"

"Springtime. Haying mostly," Chet said.

"I can find them by then. Look at these Friday and I'll get some more that I know about."

"Good. Get busy."

Frey looked at Jesus and Cole. "What are you guys? His horse breakers?"

"Naw, we're just learning the business," Cole said.

"Well, Chet can teach you two a lot."

"He has already," Jesus said.

"You two help him get those outlaws out of Utah?" Frey asked.

"They were there," Chet said.

Leaving Frey's, they went on to lunch at Jenn's, choosing a booth near the back.

Jenn crowded in beside Chet to tell him something.

"You can talk," Chet said. "These are my guards. When everyone heard about the pair prowling for me, Marge and the others made them my helpers."

"Good for her. I learned more about those two Nelsons from a new woman in town—Kathrin Arnold."

"We brought her back from Utah with us," Chet said.

"Yes. she is staying with Leroy Scales and his wife Betty Lou. Kathrin thinks those two were hired by her ex or a former husband in Utah."

"Marge was going to help her get on her feet. We had the wedding for my sister and then a meeting. Kathrin must have left with the Scales. Didn't see her go, but wondered where she got to."

"They're all Mormons. I imagine she felt better with her own kind."

"I guess. She is a good person. I hope it all works out for her."

Jenn shook her head. "Divorces are not easy to attain nor are they done without being shunned by many people. But she thinks that Arnold hired the Nelsons."

Chet told Jesus and Cole, "We need to go by the marshal's office and find out what we can about those two."

That part of business taken care of, Jenn said, "Well, your sister is married to Sarge. I hate that I missed it. He is a special guy and what I saw of her, she is special, too."

"They will do well together."

Jenn stood and said to the young men, "You two watch out for him. Those Nelsons don't need to harm a hair on his head."

"We will," Cole promised her, and she left them to eat the heaping plates brought by her daughter.

Chet introduced her to them.

They were all smiles. When she swished away, they watched her retreat without a comment.

The next week Marge, Chet, and his two bodyguards had an early Christmas with Robert and his crew. They took his girlfriend up with them. Marge had promised her folks she'd chaperone. It was a fun evening and everyone was shocked when Robert gave the young woman a ring. She was shocked even more. They planned to get married in April. Robert had found a cabin he could buy near the sawmill. Several of the drivers cried after opening the silk neckerchiefs Marge had bought for them.

The fivesome went home the next day. Robert's girlfriend showed off the gold band and talked all day about the men and what all happened.

They did Tom's crew next. The rocking chair was made of hard maple and the wool blanket colorful enough to please a squaw. The old man had wet eyes over it and hugged Marge. A ten-buck bonus, oranges, candy, and a silk neckerchief was too much for several of the men as they sang Christmas carols. Chet hoped Reg's bunch had fun, too.

Susie and Sarge came in while it was going on and she cried. Susie, Sarge, Chet and his two helpers were going up the Windmill in two days to have a party there.

Hampt's outfit was next—five cowboys and the four Mexican boys cutting posts, along with May's boys and her daughter. She promised them they'd go to Aunt Marge's house for their Christmas. They were fine, but Chet could still smell traces of the skunk.

He still needed two small broke horses for those boys. May sang three Christmas carols and everyone wanted more. No one could believe the bonuses and neckerchiefs.

There was no end to Christmas. The Byrneses and the bodyguards arrived at the lower ranch early, fully loaded for the Windmill Ranch party. Susie drove the team to the Windmill with Marge beside her. She wouldn't stay home. She didn't want to miss a thing. They arrived in the night and told everyone to go back to sleep. They'd party all the next day.

All the men danced with Marge and Susie while

Victor played the music and another cowboy fiddled. Chet's head was full of names when he passed out their money in envelopes. Candy, oranges, and the silk neck rags made a sparkling morning.

Smiling faces saw them off the next day because Sarge had to go to New Mexico with cattle for the Navajos.

"We have to have Christmas with your hands as well," he reminded Susie, helping her into the buckboard all bundled against the cold.

"Oh yes. I know we need to. It spreads such good cheer to all of us."

Susie drove the team home. Except for the celebration of Christ's birthday and the good feeling that someone cared about them, the whole trip was uneventful.

It was after dark when they got back to the Verde Ranch. Chet knew his wife was worn out, but happy.

The Preskitt Valley bunch included several married men and their wives, so they and their children were in the big barn. The sun outside was warm enough to enjoy the outing. Raphael hired a band to play Mexican music and they shuffled on the dry dirt floor.

The food was cooked and lots of it. Many Mexican dishes and plenty of barbequed meats. Everyone's lips were greasy. Chet paid the workers ten dollars and they all got oranges, bags of candy, and a silk kerchief. Marge had shawls for the girls and straw hats for the boys and more shawls for the mothers.

Raphael could not believe his bonus. "There is a mistake here, no?"

"No. We will be going over your herd report and all when we get a break. I know it is accurate. You do a fine job for us." Chet clapped him on his shoulder. "Have fun."

"Gracious, amigo."

Chet said, "Feliz Navidad."

"Oh, *sí*, that too. This has been a wonderful event. My men will never forget it."

The employee Christmas business all finished, Chet and Marge retired to the house. It was close to bedtime and he had his boots off when the yard bell rang. It was the signal his men had set that something might be afoot on the place. Immediately, he blew out the lamp in the bedroom.

"Trouble?" she asked.

"There might be something." He buckled on his six-gun. "You get into bed and stay down. They try anything, the entre ranch crew will be up and moving."

Boots on, he hurried downstairs and looked out the windows to see if someone was moving around in the yard. There was plenty of starlight to make it all silver outside. But he saw nothing moving.

Then someone shattered a window by firing a few shots into the living room. He heard footsteps on the porch and saw a figure jump off it and get on a horse. He opened the front door and fired the Colt five times after him. But standing in the cold air, he was not sure he'd even scratched the invader because of the pines and other trees in the yard.

"You all right?" Jesus asked, coming on the run. "Something told Cole we needed to watch out tonight."

"There was one—"

"Are you all right?" Marge called from the top of the stairs.

"Yes. Stay up there. He's gone, whoever he was, thanks to my sharp men. We need to cover the window he shot out is all."

"When are you coming up?"

"When I get the window fixed."

Monica came in next wearing her robe. "Anyone shot?"

"No and they got away. They did break out a window. The boys have gone to get something to cover it with until we can get it repaired."

She waved her hand. "The gun smoke is bad in here."

"How did the bell work?" Cole asked.

"Asleep, I may have missed it, but now that I know the sound, I bet I wake up," Chet said.

"Should we go after him?" Jesus asked.

"In the morning. Not tonight."

"Yes sir. We can fix the window. Go to bed."

"Thanks. I will." Chet made no move to go upstairs.

"Go ahead. We have it," Cole promised.

"All right. I am off to bed again." Chet still didn't move.

The words sounded funny and Cole laughed. "Next time, I'll have a ba'r trap set for him."

Chet laughed and went on up to bed.

"Pretty bold of them to try to sneak up on you here," Marge said as she sat up when he entered the room.

He undressed in the dark. "They're setting bear traps for him next time."

"Oh my God, really?"

"No just kidding," He hugged her. "Try to sleep." *Who are these idiot killers anyway?* Snuggled up against her, he finally fell asleep.

CHAPTER 21

Raphael sent his riders in every direction to learn what they could about the invaders. Jesus found nothing outstanding about the hoofprints in the yard. No traces of blood, so no doubt Chet had missed him. Someone had gone to town to order a new window. Canvas was tacked over the empty space in the wall, in the meantime.

Marge was still shocked about an attack on her house. Monica offered to bash the shooter's head in with an iron skillet. And Chet figured the ranch crew might hang the whole gang for their insulting attempt to kill their patron.

"Will they come back?" Marge asked him at lunch.

"I don't know. If they're smart, they won't. This place is too tough for them."

"Well, I don't like it one bit, them breaking out my window and shooting at you."

"I bet that'd scare the bejesus out of them, if they knew that." Chet grinned.

"Oh, you are not being serious with me."

"Honey, they made one raid and failed. We will find them and either arrest them or hang them. Now, lets get on with our lives."

"Oh, Chet if I lost you—"

"You are not losing me. By dark-thirty tonight, Raphael's vaqueros will have them located. Those are tough men and they will get answers. There is no place on this mountain the gang can hide."

Someone rode up. It was Roamer. Chet put on his jacket and went to meet him.

"Holy cow, what's going on? Everyone in Preskitt is up in arms this morning saying some hired killer about killed you last night," Roamer exclaimed.

"My guards heard him coming and rang a bell for an alarm. He was on the porch, shot out the living room window, and then jumped on his horse and rode off."

Roamer took off his hat when Marge came out. "Howdy, ma'am."

"Hello. You two come inside and talk."

Chet nodded. "We will. I guarantee he's not around here to pick me off."

"Come in anyway. It's cold out here."

Roamer laughed. "If those men are in the country, I bet they're hiding. Everyone is out looking for them."

Marge stepped aside as the men came in the door. "That worries me. Someone will get hurt over that. My vaqueros can handle about anything that comes along, but ordinary folks won't shoot fast enough."

"I can tell you, men are scrounging the country

looking for them," Roamer assured her as she led them to the kitchen.

"I told her they'd probably tree them by dark," Chet said.

Roamer agreed and sat down to cake and coffee.

"Señor, señor!" came a cry from the yard.

Chet ran to the door and saw a rider on his sweaty horse holding a rifle on his knee. "We got them cornered on Apple Creek."

"There," Roamer said. "I told you so." He gobbled the cake and washed it down with coffee. "Go get a horse." On the way out, he said thanks and trailed Chet outside.

Raphael brought Chet a saddled horse.

"The vaqueros have them pinned down in a shack. They will still be there when you get there."

"Gracias." Chet nodded to the rider who'd come in with the news to take the lead.

He rode beside him. "How did you find them?"

"Someone saw them. They have only been here two days, asking lots of questions about you. Made people suspicious."

Chet, Roamer, and the vaquero covered lots of ground before they arrived at the head of a canyon where several more vaqueros stood armed with rifles.

"They are down there in a cabin," the man Chet knew as Romez said.

"How many?" Roamer asked.

"Two is all, but they are good shots. I told our men to stay back; that you were coming."

"That's good. You did right." Chet clapped him on the back.

"What are their names?" Roamer asked.

Romez shook his head. "We don't know."

"That's fine." Roamer dismounted. "What do you think, Chet?"

"They can't run out the front door and get away so let's set it on fire."

"Might be hard to burn."

"Naw. It's going to burn easy. I don't see any windows in back. I'll go set it on fire."

Roamer caught his arm. "One of the men can do that. I don't want Marge on my neck over you getting shot."

Chet didn't like it, but he agreed.

A torch was made and a ranch hand rushed downhill to set it beside the logs on the bottom. Then he hightailed it for the hillside and some cover.

"Come out with your hands up or you are going to cook," Roamer shouted.

They came out firing their pistols in all directions and running for the timber. Mounted men with rifles began shooting at them. Chet and Roamer were on their horses and heading after them, too. The smoke from the half dozen rifles and burning cabin soon filled the air. Chet saw they'd soon be in the trees so he spurred his roan hard. The mountain pony whipped through the low brush, jumped a log, and set him up to track the fleeing outlaws. They must have emptied their guns, 'cause they were running and no longer shooting.

He holstered his six-gun, grabbed the riata tied on his saddle, made a loop over his head, and threw it. When it settled over one of the fleeing assassin, he hand jerked the slack and made a dally on the horn. His roan slid to a stop that slammed the man down.

Roamer rode past him to catch the other. Close enough, he bailed off his horse and took the man smashing to the ground. After a bit of a scuffle, Roamer cuffed him and walked him back to where Chet had roped the first outlaw.

By then, the ranch posse had their rifles on both outlaws. Chet demanded, "Who the hell are you?"

"Lonnie Nelson."

"Why in the hell did you want me?"

"Delta and I figured if we killed a famous guy like you we'd get all kinds of jobs killing people all over."

"This is going to be your last job. All you'll be killing are rocks in the Yuma County Jail. Did a guy named Arnold pay you to kill me?"

"Yeah. He said you took his wife."

"Not me. She left him for an outlaw named Evans. I never met Arnold, but you'll have plenty of time to visit with him in prison."

"Got enough information?" Roamer asked.

"Dumb, stupid outlaws are what they are." Chet shook his head in disgust.

Roamer tossed his head toward the vaqueros. "Next time you need a posse, get these guys to work on it."

Chet agreed.

Then both Roamer and Chet went around and shook all their hands.

The men were pleased and thanked him, too.

Roamer loaded the two prisoners on horses the

ranchmen found and headed for town. Chet rode home with the vaqueros and Raphael met them. They rode in like conquerors and their families came to cheer them. Marge and Monica were on the porch dressed for the cool temps, beaming at the news that the would-be killers were in jail.

Weary, Chet came up the stairs. "That is over. Now we return to peace again."

"Don't send Cole home yet." Marge said. "You have enough enemies in this world. He and Jesus still need to ride with you."

Chet shook his head. The problem was solved and he still had to have bodyguards. He loved her so he didn't argue. When he got some rest, he'd think clearer and make a decision then.

Marge slid her arm through his. "I am glad you are unharmed."

"I know. I know."

"Do you want supper?"

"No, I am going to bed."

"I'm sorry. Are you mad at me?"

"No. I love you. I am just tired. I never saw such a force like your vaqueros. They tore up jack and found the shooters. Then, organized, they forced them out of hiding and would have shot them. But Roamer needed to arrest them, so I helped him."

"So why are you mad?"

"Marge, I am not mad . . . except at those stupid criminals."

He knew it wasn't enough. She was upset. But it would have to pass for an explanation. It would have to. He was worn out. Step-by-step, he trudged upstairs, undressed, and went to bed.

Sometime in the night, she woke him up, apologizing and crying. "I'm sorry, but I worry so much about someone killing you. I don't know what I'd do without you. Hold me."

He held her and kissed her. "I know this baby is a big concern and has you upset about everything. But you married me and you knew what I do, what I have done all my life. I am not going to stay inside and hide. I never have and won't start."

"Oh, I was sick about you going to Utah and then these killers coming here for you."

"Listen, listen. I am thirty-three years old and I have to be myself."

She kept her face away from him. "What would I do without you?"

"I have no plans not to be here."

She rolled over and faced him. "I mean, if you were killed."

"Get that out of your head. No one is going to kill me."

They were sitting up and holding each other in the dark bedroom.

"You have to get hold of yourself. You got on this ride because of who I was. You can't expect me to be your gardener and housekeeper around this house."

She was agreeing with him, wiping away her tears, and acting more settled. "What should I do?"

"Thank God that we have each other. Be grateful

for that baby we want so badly. It's coming on, isn't it?"

"Yes, I guess. I have never been pregnant this long before."

"Good. I need to find some small horses for those boys of May's."

"I smelled her skunk when we went up there. I never said anything. My, she was upset about that."

"They are real boys and have been since they were smaller."

"Where will you find the horses?"

"Maybe down at Hayden's Mill. There are more people down there. And maybe a greater choice of horses."

"When will you go?"

"Tomorrow."

"With your guards?"

"Yes."

She fluffed her pillow. "Thank you."

He hurried around the next morning. His men loaded a packhorse for a few days' trip to Hayden's Mill.

Chet, Jesus and Cole rode out in the sunshine that was weakly trying to heat the vast blue sky. He pushed hard to cut the trip to two days and by midday they were in the saguaro country where the sun was hotter on the front side. They spent the rest of the day carrying their jumpers and coats over their laps. Stages passed, leaving them in a swirl of dust.

That evening they had some meat and bread that

Monica had put up for them. They washed it down with boiled coffee, turned into their bedrolls, and listened to a coyote or two as early sundown shut out the sun.

Day two, they rode onto the Mill. The ferry crossing the Salt River was a main point in north-south trade. The stage from Preskitt ended there, connecting with the stage from Tucson—the same one he'd ridden when he'd met his wife.

Chet and his men checked the liveries for horses to buy. At one, they found a small dish-faced two-year-old. But something told Jesus he might be a loco weed victim and he was concerned.

"He don't show it, but he is priced cheap for such a good-looking colt," Chet said as they discussed him. "I may buy him and see."

"We better find a third one then," Jesus warned them.

Chet paid for the horse and they went on. Some small ponies, too small, were shown to them. A barefoot boy riding bareback brought a small spotted white horse. He was gentle acting and the boy could get him do anything he wanted him to do. The gelding was mouthed by Jesus, who called him a five-year-old.

"I have to have eighty dollars for him, mister," the boy said.

"Why?" Chet asked.

"I need to buy a real horse and saddle so I can become a cowboy on some ranch."

"Your mother know about that?"

"Oh yes, she does. She heard you wanted to buy a small horse and said this would be my chance."

"She'd let you go? Become a cowboy?"

The boy straightened his spine. "She said she would."

"What is your name?"

"Kyle Ryan."

"Can you buy a sound horse and saddle for eighty dollars?"

"I can, sir."

"I'll buy you one. You give the money for your horse to your mother and come to work on one of my ranches," Chet offered.

"Really?"

"Yes."

"I can sure do that. What's your brand?"

"Quarter Circle Z."

Kyle nodded. "When do we leave?"

"Two days. Now, pick out a horse and saddle."

"I can help him," Jesus offered.

"I really thank you, mister."

"My name is Chet Byrnes."

"I sure appreciate it, Mr. Byrnes."

"Just make hand is all I ask."

"I will do that."

The boy found a solid young horse and a good saddle. Chet paid the livery owner for Kyle's new horse and gave Kyle eighty dollars for his horse. It was decided he would meet Chet, Jesus, and Cole in the morning to ride over to Mesa to look for another small horse in that community. They watched him ride his new horse home to tell his mom and pack his things.

* * *

"What did your mom say when you told her you had a horse and a job?" Chet asked as Kyle rode up.

"Wow."

"You give her the money?"

"She cried. That was hard."

Chet shook his hand. "You did good, Kyle. You'll make a hand, I know."

Kyle looked ahead, nodded, and swallowed.

Chet knew he had hired a real hand. They could always use another one.

The ride to Mesa was uneventful, but the day went slow. One small horse was obviously wind broken. Another too old. The next one tried to bite them. Bad hooves, stove up. The list continued until someone arrived with a line back dun mare. Seven years old, broke to ride or drive. Chet bought her on the spot.

They rode back to the Mill. Kyle went home for his last night. Chet and his boys went into a bar that sold food the livery guy had recommended. All three ordered beer and the house special— barbeque and beans. The food looked super when it was delivered and the three were about to dig in when a big hairy guy waving a pistol came busting inside.

He didn't need to speak. He was obviously drunk. Everyone rose and started to back up to the walls.

"Hold it right there, pard," Chet said to him, knowing the bartender had a bat and was only five feet from the drunk behind the bar.

"Who dee hell are you?" The drunk floated backward into the bar.

"Why mister—"

The barkeep connected and the man's knees collapsed. Chet kicked his gun aside and told everyone to go back to their tables. Then he handcuffed the big man behind his back.

"Thanks. Are you the law?" the bartender asked.

"I'm just passing through. Thanks for the bat."

"Man, I'd not have tried him if you hadn't got his attention. You damn sure weren't afraid of him."

"That's for you to say."

"What's your name?"

"Byrnes. Chet Byrnes."

"Let's give him a cheer." The yeas went up. "Whatcha drink?"

"This glass is enough."

"Then I'll feed you for doing that."

"That'll be fine."

A lawman burst in.

"Marshal Paul, that man there did all your work." A patron pointed to Chet.

"Them your cuffs?"

"Yes. I'd like to have them back."

"Toss me your keys. I've got cuffs. Where you from?"

"Preskitt."

"You county law up there?"

"No. U.S."

"I'm glad you were here, sir." Paul looked at the crowd. "Couple of you big guys drag him down to my jail." He soon had two husky volunteers. "Oh, you get to keep this pistol. He won't need it." He handed it to Chet.

"Thanks."

The barbeque was good and they enjoyed it.

Cole finally said, "Next time, give us some warning. I thought he'd shoot you."

"You'd have shot him then, right?"

"Yeah, but I'd have to tell the Mrs. that I didn't shoot fast enough."

"Just so he didn't walk away." Chet finished his coffee.

The waiter came by. "Boss said you all eat free."

Chet flipped him a silver dollar. "We enjoyed it." Then he stuck the revolver in his waistband and they left the bar.

"How did you feel when that bartender cracked him on the head?" Jesus asked as they walked to their rooms.

"A helluva lot better than before. Back home in Texas, these two guys beat me up so bad I was laid up for weeks. Since then, I try to stay out of those situations. I didn't think he was mad drunk. Mad drunks will kill you. But he damn sure might have shot at someone. I just did what I thought I could do. He never saw the barkeep coming with his bat. I planned for him to do that."

"I hope I am that strong some day," Jesus said.

"Live long enough, you will be."

With their new cowboy, they rode north the next morning. Kyle wore brogan shoes and had enough clothes for the colder climate. Another north wind was blowing down off the rim. It would be cold up in the high country and they'd be home in plenty of time for Christmas. Chet had bought a few small sleigh bells and some red ribbon to put on the gift horses. But he'd had no idea what to get his wife. She had about everything a man could find to buy her.

He thought about what he'd purchased for his family. He had two new dresses for May and two shirts he'd had made for Hampt who was too big for store-bought sizes. Two shirts for Tom and two new Sunday dresses for Millie. Long tail, canvas coats for Susie and Lucy. He'd had one duster special-made for big Reg and one to fit Sarge. A doll for May's daughter and some nice dresses, too. Marge had told him to get those. There were dolls for Tom's girls and for his oldest boy, a felt hat.

It was all crazy—but nothing for his wife. Maybe Susie would go buy her something. All that and two good horses for the boys, plus a spare if he worked out.

On the sunny porch, Marge was dressed warm with Susie beside her when they returned home. They must have seen them coming, Chet decided.

The women admired the horses and approved. Jesus and Cole took the stock and led Kyle to the bunkhouse. With a gal under each arm, Chet walked them into the house. Monica came and hugged him, too.

"Who is the young man?"

"Marge, he's Kyle. He wants to be a cowboy."

"More who knows strays, Susie." Marge shook her head.

Susie agreed. "He's been bringing them home every chance he got all his life."

"I won't break him of it?" Marge asked.

Susie shook her head. "No chance."

Well, at least Marge's sense of humor was back.

Chet left the women in the living room and headed to the kitchen. Standing on a chair, Chet put the pistol up on a top shelf of the cabinets. It needed to be cleaned and oiled. It was a cap and ball and from his observations, had been abused. But unloaded and cleaned, it would be a good one, aside from the fact that there was a little space between the cylinder and barrel that meant it would spit hot lead at people.

He never mentioned the gun nor told anyone how he had acquired it. Simple enough, it was another revolver. He planned to replace his own sidearm with a new cartridge model. Several men he talked to said the new cartridges were more reliable. He kept his own clean and dry as he could and maybe only one in thirty shots proved to be a dud. His caliber choice would be a .44, then he could use the same ammo in his handgun and rifle.

Marge and Susie came into the kitchen and he sat and talked with them around the table until supper. He could tell his sister took pride in her new man and sounded very pleased with him.

"I swear, he's been bachelor so long, he's having to learn a lot."

"Like what?" Madge asked.

"That he can't simply undress. He has to learn to hang everything up like he was going to be inspected in the morning." Susie laughed freely. "But he's catching on pretty fast."

Chet noticed the mail his wife had opened carefully with a sharp knife and pulled it closer to read. One note was about an old man dying that his father knew in Arkansas when both were boys. As men, the two had fought in the Texas Revolution. The man's daughter, who Chet didn't recall, wrote it to his father and it had been forwarded to him.

He handed it to Susie to read.

The next was a letter from his banker Tanner that he was having a man pick up the mowers and rakes and would deliver them to him for two hundred dollars. What place, the man had wanted to know.

Chet looked up. "I better stop by and pay Tanner for the mowers and rakes."

"Does he have one?" Marge asked, busy darning a hole in a sock.

"He told me Kay had two she never paid him for. I said I would not go get them because of previous things, but I would buy them."

Marge shook her head. "I am so disappointed in her. We were friends. She treated JD so badly after she was free of her husband, I could not believe it. Oh, sorry. Gossip, of course. Have you met the new man at the mercantile? Ivors?"

"Yes. Ben. I ordered some farm machinery from him a week ago."

"People say his wife's so fussy no one can please her and she plans to leave her husband for moving here."

"I guess they won't come out to the dance then. I invited him to come."

"She must come from money somewhere back east. Preskitt is not a bad place to live compared to the rest of the West."

"Well, I like him. He's a nice guy."

Marge thought of something else. "Oh, I saw Kathrin in town. She's still at the Scales, doing fine and said to thank you again for helping her get here."

"She was a perfect lady and it wasn't an easy trip with those four outlaws."

"Did they make her uncomfortable?"

"No, she ignored them, but it wasn't easy."

"What are you doing next?" Susie asked.

"Oh, not much. I may go over to Hampt's and look at his fencing project. There is plain steel wire in El Paso like we used in Texas for stake fencing, but I bet it takes months to get here. Maybe a dealer down at Hayden Mill has some we can start with."

"We have some of that stake fencing at the Verde ranch, don't we?" Susie asked.

"Lots of repairs. Tom has two men always fixing it. Ryan used poles too small to save money. Now, I can't believe what we've done with that place. It is one helluva ranch."

"Who will live in the big house, when I'm gone?"

"Susie, I don't know. I am going to hire a couple to stay there and keep it open. We like to stay there after the dance. And a house setting empty soon collapses."

The women agreed.

"Monica can find us a couple when the time comes," Marge said.

Just then, someone rode up with several horses.

"Bet he wants to sell them to you," Susie said.

Chet put on his coat and stepped out in the chilly wind. "Howdy," he said to the red-faced man with his head wrapped in a scarf, riding a good horse.

"You Mr. Byrnes?"

"Yes."

"I'm Jim Rose. Mr. Frey said you wanted some stout horses. I bought these horses in California about three months ago. I have three big teams that came from the Orange County Stage line dispersal. They're hard to find—but maybe you know that or you wouldn't be looking for them."

"What are they worth?"

"Four hundred a team."

"Awful high."

"Let's pen them and let you look. Heading for Utah next. Won't be back, and I'll say it again. Good big team horses like these are hard to find."

Having heard the horses, Jesus was coming on the run. Chet hollered to him. "Open a corral, so we can cut out those teams and look at them."

Jesus took off, and the two riders with Rose moved the two dozen horses in that direction.

"You sick?" Chet asked the man coming out the yard gate.

"I got a tooth been killing me for days. Ain't had a place or time to stop long enough to get it pulled."

"If you're headed for Utah, there isn't a dentist for two hundred miles. One of my men can take you back into town and you can get it pulled. The horses are fine here. I won't charge you. Your men can eat with my crew. We've got bunkhouse space. Go get it fixed. That is a helluva trip and you won't make it like this.

"Cole hitch a team. Mr. Rose needs a ride back into town to get a tooth pulled."

"We can do that." He took off to get it done.

"Jesus, you and Rose's men catch three teams. I want to harness and have someone drive them."

"We can do that. Three teams?"

"Maybe more if you look them over. There are two others that will work as a team." Chet turned to Rose. "Come in the house. I have some whiskey for your ailment."

Rose held up his hand. "I can't barge in here."

"I don't know why not. Come on."

Finally inside, Chet introduced his two women and sat Rose down.

"He probably doesn't need coffee. Where is the whiskey? He has a bad tooth."

"What needs to be done?" Marge asked, getting up to go for some.

"Cole's taking him back to town to get it pulled."

"Good idea."

"I sure didn't aim to bother you ladies," Rose said.

She poured him about four fingers in a glass. "You sure aren't."

He took a big swallow. "My heavens, ma'am that's almost too good a whiskey to treat a tooth with."

"Hold some in your mouth. It may numb it."

"Sure. Whew, that is expensive stuff, I bet."

"We don't drink, so it was just wasting in the pantry," Marge offered.

"You Mormons?"

"No. We just don't drink."

He held the next swallow and then nodded. "That does help. I've been out of my head with the pain. Never thought of whiskey, though. I almost rode on instead of stopping here. I've been hurting so bad."

Cole came in. "I'm ready."

"Let him drink one more glass, then take him to the dentist." Chet smiled.

"You bet. The boys are cutting out the teams."

"Jesus can handle that. I'll go down later and see how they are doing."

The men started out of the house.

"Catch Cole for me and ask him to get the ranch mail if there is any," Marge called out to Chet.

"Sure. I'll get him." His sharp whistle caught his man's attention. He hurried to stop him. Rose was already on the seat.

"Cole, get the ranch mail for my wife while you're in there."

"Sure thing, no problem. I'll bring it back when they get him fixed up."

"Thanks. Be careful."

With Cole and Rose on the road to town, Chet watched the teams being driven around. They were a little high headed, but they had not been driven in quite a while so that didn't seem to be a problem.

Jesus was checking them for age and soundness. They found two more teams—not as big—but that would do fine on hay rakes.

The old boy—Happens—who'd come with Rose was spitting tobacco and thanking Chet in a long drawl. "I couldn't talk no sense in Rose about that durn tooth. I sure do appreciate you taking charge, Mr. Byrnes."

"What about the rest of these horses?"

"They're all young ranch horses. Aw, they might buck—a little. My paw said a horse won't buck wasn't worth—well you know that word rhymes with buck. Anyway, there's three nice mares in this lot. I understood they were Kentucky stock."

"They open?" Chet had been watching them. They might make good brood mares for his golden stud Barbarossa.

"Sure are and they've been pure hell to drive. And they come in heat all at different times."

Chet laughed. He could imagine some proud cut geldings and some mares could be a mess to drive. Everyone, *everyone* rode geldings on drives.

"Look at the mares, too," he told Jesus in passing. He heard him.

"You sure got a pretty spread up here," Happens mentioned.

"This was my wife's family ranch. My working outfit is down on the Verde north of here."

"You ain't no Arizona regular."

"No. We came from the hill country in Texas."

Happens frowned. "You like it here that well?"

"I like it better than the damn Texas feud I was in back there."

Happens straightened his suspenders and buttoned his coat against the cold. He spit aside before he spoke. "I damn sure would, too."

The men had the horses all haltered and tied so they took a break, waiting for Rose's return. There were five teams possible. Ten cowponies had been ridden and the three mares checked out.

"Why, hell"—Happens spit tobacco aside—"you buy all them then we ain't going to Utah. That makes me happy."

"I'm going to try. Good horses are hard to find, especially out here."

"Your man says you got a Barbarossa stud. I ain't never hear of one of them outside of that big hacienda."

"A boy had a mare and he put out a challenge. If his mare could outrun the patron's best horse could he get a stud fee? Lose the race, he'd loose the mare. He beat their best horse and the patron bred the mare. The colt was too valuable for him to own, I bought him as a yearling, and brought him to Arizona with my family. We came by wagon from west Texas."

"You must have a tough family." Happens shook his head. "Damn nice to meet 'cha."

"We are indeed tough. And I'm glad you all came by. Come to the house. Cole will be back soon. Where is your other man?"

"He went to the cook shack. I probably should go there, too. Being on the road it's hard to stay clean."

"Marge won't mind. She's married to a cowboy."

Happens cleaned his mouth of tobacco with a finger. Then he rinsed his mouth at the pump and spat it aside. He wiped his whiskered mouth on his old rag of a handkerchief. "I'll try to show my manners."

Chet laughed and clapped him on his jacket. "Don't worry. Women here are used to cowboys."

Chet hung his coat and hat in the back hall and Happens's too. They went inside and he introduced Monica and his wife to him.

"We have coffee ready," Marge said. "Do you drink coffee?"

"Oh sure, ma'am. I'd love some."

"Cream and sugar?"

"No, just coffee. You sure have a beautiful home here."

"Chet, Cole is back, but doesn't have Mr. Rose with him, Monica said, looking out the kitchen window.

"What happened to him, do you reckon?"

"He's coming to the house. He's got mail, too."

"Where's Mr. Rose?" Chet asked, taking the stack of letters from his man.

"The dentist made him stay overnight. He was bleeding a lot and wants to treat him. Said the ride might shake him up. I can go get him in the morning. He'll live, Doc said." He dropped his voice. "There's a letter in there from your nephew."

Chet's heart stopped. "Thanks. Plan on going back in the morning and get him. Rose and I have lots of trading to do."

"He really thanked you."

"Good."

Happens rose. "Ask him to wait. I need to see where to bunk down while he's going. Thanks ma'am. That's the best coffee I ever had in my whole life. Sure appreciate your hospitality."

"Come again." She crossed the room, pale faced and holding a small envelope in her hands. "Look at the address. Look—Socorro County Prison, Socorro, New Mexico."

"Let me open it." Chet used his jackknife to slit open the envelope and pulled out two thin sheets of paper. He unfolded them. It was JD's script.

He went to the table and sat down to read it aloud to the women.

Dear Chet,

This is my third letter to you. I hope it gets there. I bought three branded horses in the mountains from two guys I figured were honest. They gave me a bill of sale and their bill of sale, as well. I didn't know the brand, but figured I could sell them for a profit. When I came out of the mountains, I headed northeast on the road that goes to New Mexico. I wanted to see the country where we unloaded the wagons and look it over again.

Three deputies entered my camp at dawn with guns drawn. Told me I was under arrest for stealing horses. I said I have papers and I guess the head man could not read and stuffed them in his pocket. I told him it was proof that I needed to show that I was innocent. He scoffed it off and handcuffed me. I was taken to Socorro and thrown in jail for five days. I asked to telegram you. They said the lines were down. I knew better.

I was hauled before a judge and they all spoke in Spanish. I savvied most of it. They told the judge they caught me red-handed and I had stolen the horses. They never let me talk nor would they give me back those papers that showed I owned them. The judge asked if I was guilty. I said not guilty.

A young man Josh Raines was sent to me as my lawyer. I told him you would pay him. He was so jumpy it is a wonder he didn't shed his skin in my cell. He kept saying, "Plead Guilty. You will be out in ten months." I said, "Hell no. I didn't steal those horses. I bought them. Make the deputies produce those papers they took from me."

He said, "No. No. Plead guilty. You don't know how powerful they are." I told him they couldn't shoot me. I had not stolen those horses.

The trial was a farce. The judge, not a jury found me guilty and since I did not plead guilty I was sentenced to three years in the county jail. New Mexico has no state prison. As I said, this is the third letter I have written to you. I had them smuggled out to be mailed. I think they must have stopped the other two, but this one was to be posted in Belen.

I pray a lot, Chet, for strength. Do what you can when you can. I hope to God you can get this straight.

Your nephew JD.

Chet turned over the envelope. It was stamped Belen, New Mexico Territory

The three women were white-faced.

Susie was the first to speak. "What can we do?"

"The lawyer in Prescott?" Chet asked.

"His name is Sam Egan," Marge said.

"Yes, I recall him now. One of you copy this letter and we'll take it to Egan. He can contact the New Mexico attorney general tomorrow and I'll need a good lawyer to meet me in Socorro in four or five days. We will have Christmas here tomorrow afternoon and night."

"Good. You are not going to wait?" Marge said, sounding relieved.

"I'll wait till Christmas Day to catch the stage. I don't want him in there any longer, but the family needs me here. The young ones expect it. We will have Christmas Eve here."

"Oh Chet, how could they do that to him?" Susie was on the verge of crying.

"They haven't seen my wrath and fury yet. Everyone is entitled to a jury of their peers. I hear that every time there is a crime. This is not Mexico. I bet those sale bills he had for those horses are now conveniently gone."

"How can we find them?" she asked.

"Beats the hell out of me."

"What should we tell his mother?" Marge asked. "She will not be here tomorrow."

"Send her a letter and do the same for Reg and Lucy. I need to go tell my two men what we need to do on Christmas Day."

"Yes, you need to do that. You will sure need them along as mad as you are."

"I will calm down when I have things working."

Marge went over and hugged him. Susie joined them.

Chet stepped back. "Tom can come up and buy those horses from Rose when the poor man gets well. I'm going to see this Sam Egan this evening."

"Take it easy today," Marge said. "Susie and I can go see him the day after Christmas. We will have him get a good lawyer to meet you in Socorro. We can run things pretty good here."

Chet agreed. He put on his coat and hat to go to the bunkhouse and talk to his two men. Once outside, he noticed a snowflake or two in the air. The sky looked like a fluffed goose's belly. All he needed was a big snow. It would be a long trip there and back. Lots of things to tie in. Lawyers, the New Mexico law enforcement, and the territory's attorney general . . . at a place he'd never been.

His fingers closed on the U.S. deputy marshal badge in his coat pocket. That might come in handy, too. The sun was already setting. One of the shortest days in the year, he hunched under his heavy jacket against the cold.

Boy, he could get in some real fixes and if he didn't, his family members did.

Dear fans and readers,

I sure appreciate all the folks that have been following the Byrnes Family Saga. It's been fun to write and to research things going on in the Southwest in that era.

The Sharlot Hall Museum in Prescott houses the old *Daily Miner* newspapers. The people were very generous to Pat and I several years ago when we were doing research. Whenever you are in Preskitt (Prescott) Arizona stop by and look through their exhibits. Have a meal at the Palace Saloon and study that great bar. Cowboys saved that bar about the turn of the century when a fire raged through Whiskey Row and they literally, by hand, hauled it out to the street.

Several famous people have been there or lived there. Tom Horn rodeoed there. So did Tom Mix, who became a great western movie star. *Junior Bonner,* the movie starring Steve McQueen, was filmed there. The Earp brothers were raising hogs in Prescott before they went to Tombstone. There is a great statue of another Arizona hero, "Bucky O'Neal," who was a past sheriff and mayor and who died in action as a Rough Rider in Cuba with Teddy Roosevelt.

With one of the oldest professional rodeos in the

U.S., it is a busy time in Prescott around the Fourth of July. In August, there is a cowboy gathering and poet deal—check it out. We had a great time at those sessions. Another attraction is an early in the century movie theatre that has been restored to hold concerts.

Today, Prescott it is a modern city with a nice mix of weather and not too rough winters. Folks from Phoenix flood that country in the summer to escape the heat. There are still dude ranches in the region.

I am beating the computer to death pounding on the keys to get the Byrnes stories out. Thanks for buying them. I have a website, www.dustyrichards.com. I answer e-mail which takes more time than I have, but no problem. Send questions or comments to dustyrichards@cox.net. Sorry, I don't do Twitter and Facebook.

Thanks for all your support. We have one thing in common—we like to read westerns. God bless you and yours.

Dusty Richards

P.S. Don't miss Book Five in the Byrnes Family Saga. We're working on it right now.

GREAT BOOKS, GREAT SAVINGS!

When You Visit Our Website:
www.kensingtonbooks.com
You Can Save Money Off The Retail Price
Of Any Book You Purchase!

- **All Your Favorite Kensington Authors**
- **New Releases & Timeless Classics**
- **Overnight Shipping Available**
- **eBooks Available For Many Titles**
- **All Major Credit Cards Accepted**

Visit Us Today To Start Saving!
www.kensingtonbooks.com

All Orders Are Subject To Availability.
Shipping and Handling Charges Apply.
Offers and Prices Subject To Change Without Notice.

THE EAGLES SERIES BY
WILLIAM W. JOHNSTONE